A Terrified Teacher at Ghoul School! Vol. 6

Mai Tanaka

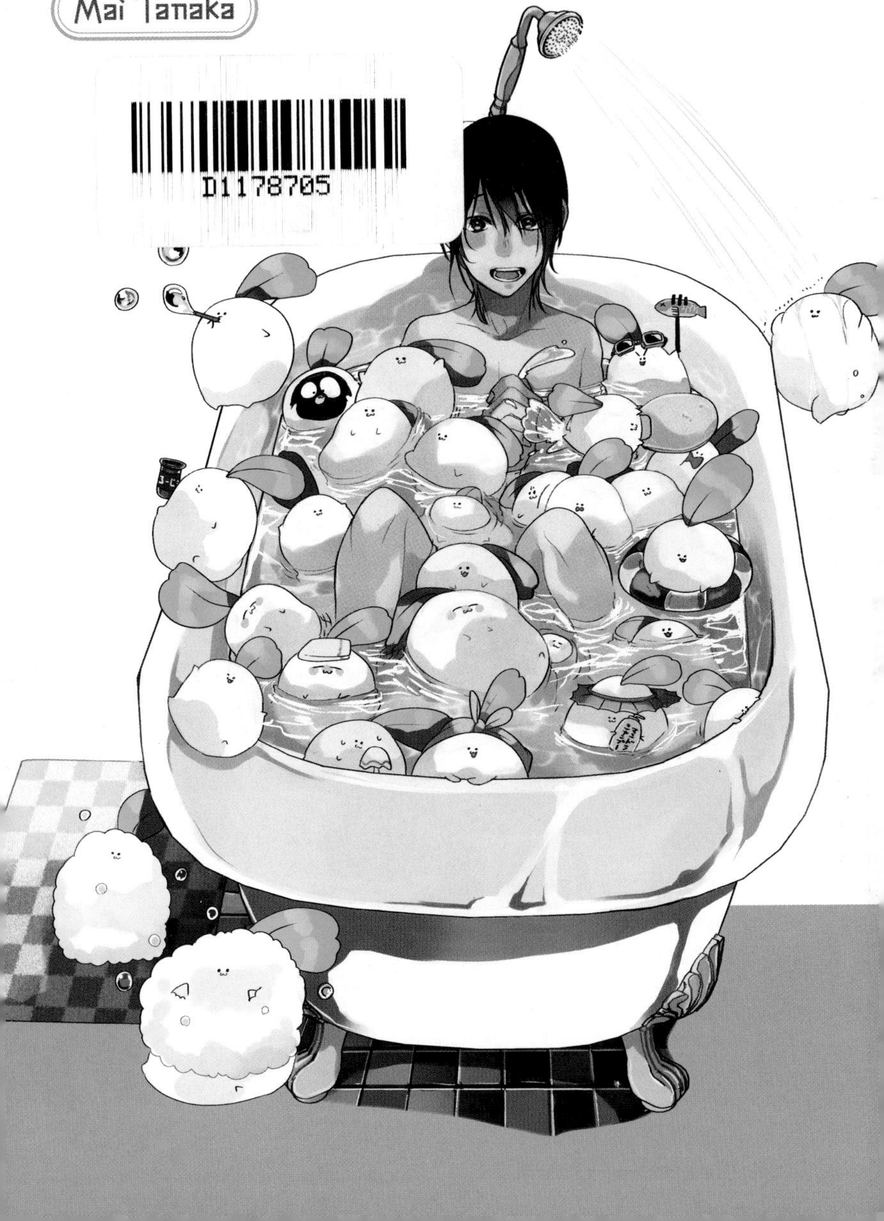

CONTENTS

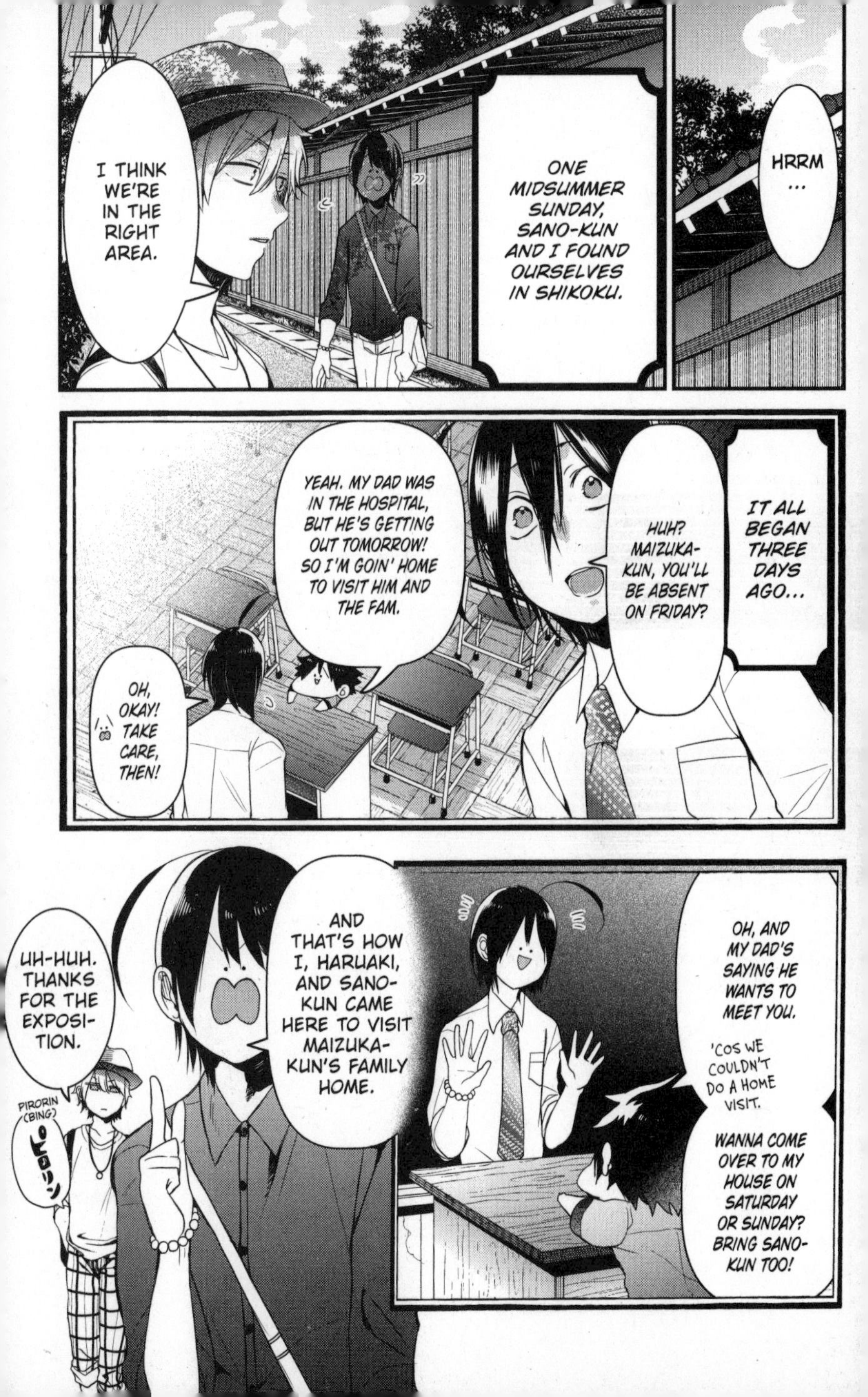
HRRM...
ONE MIDSUMMER SUNDAY, SANO-KUN AND I FOUND OURSELVES IN SHIKOKU.
I THINK WE'RE IN THE RIGHT AREA.
IT ALL BEGAN THREE DAYS AGO...
HUH? MAIZUKA-KUN, YOU'LL BE ABSENT ON FRIDAY?
YEAH. MY DAD WAS IN THE HOSPITAL, BUT HE'S GETTING OUT TOMORROW! SO I'M GOIN' HOME TO VISIT HIM AND THE FAM.
OH, OKAY! TAKE CARE, THEN!
OH, AND MY DAD'S SAYING HE WANTS TO MEET YOU.
'COS WE COULDN'T DO A HOME VISIT.
WANNA COME OVER TO MY HOUSE ON SATURDAY OR SUNDAY? BRING SANO-KUN TOO!
AND THAT'S HOW I, HARUAKI, AND SANO-KUN CAME HERE TO VISIT MAIZUKA-KUN'S FAMILY HOME.
UH-HUH. THANKS FOR THE EXPOSITION.
ピロリン
PIRORIN (BING)

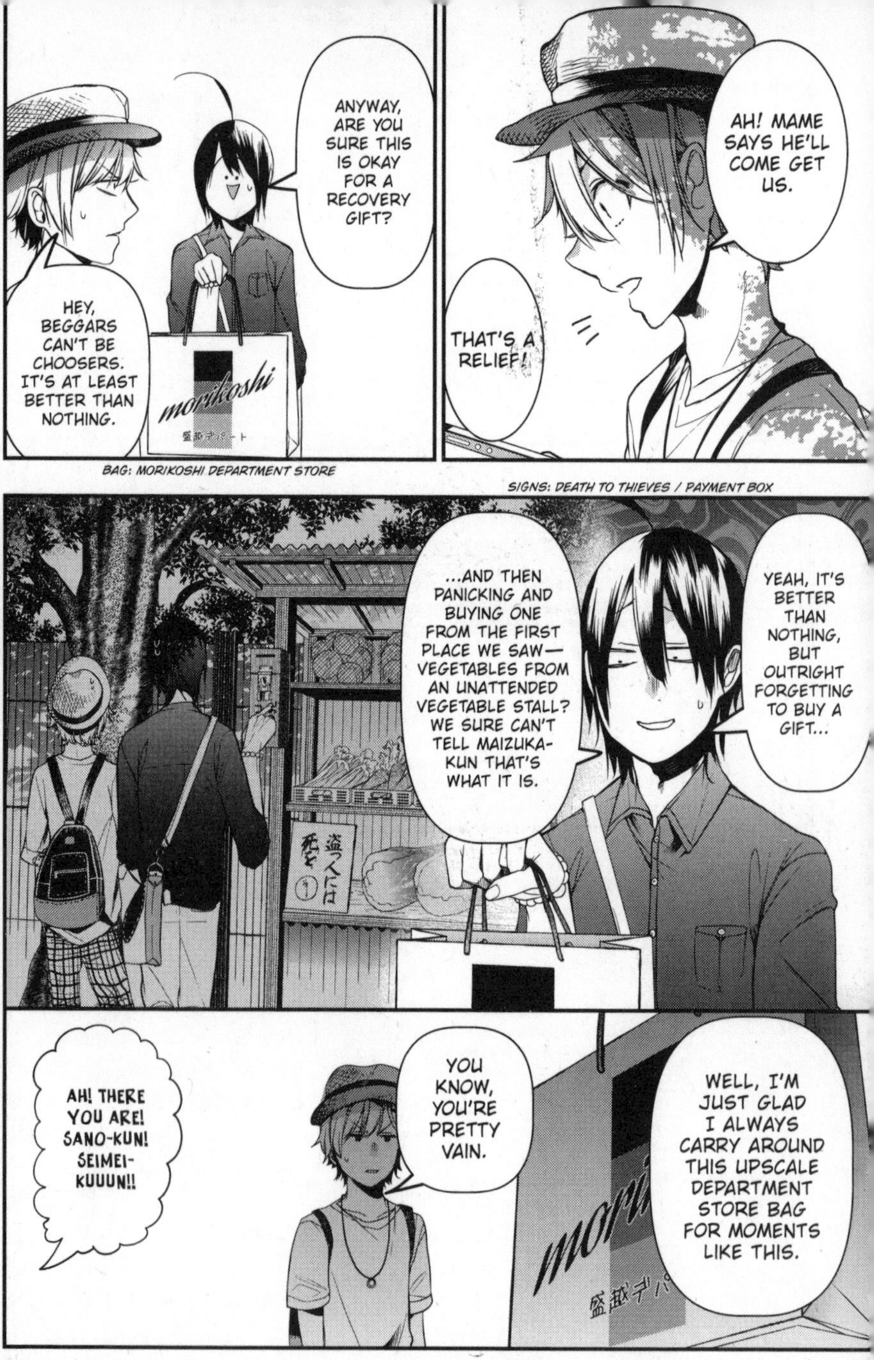
AH! MAME SAYS HE'LL COME GET US.
THAT'S A RELIEF!
ANYWAY, ARE YOU SURE THIS IS OKAY FOR A RECOVERY GIFT?
HEY, BEGGARS CAN'T BE CHOOSERS. IT'S AT LEAST BETTER THAN NOTHING.
morikoshi
盛越デパート
BAG: MORIKOSHI DEPARTMENT STORE
SIGNS: DEATH TO THIEVES / PAYMENT BOX
YEAH, IT'S BETTER THAN NOTHING, BUT OUTRIGHT FORGETTING TO BUY A GIFT...
...AND THEN PANICKING AND BUYING ONE FROM THE FIRST PLACE WE SAW—VEGETABLES FROM AN UNATTENDED VEGETABLE STALL? WE SURE CAN'T TELL MAIZUKA-KUN THAT'S WHAT IT IS.
盗っ人には死を
WELL, I'M JUST GLAD I ALWAYS CARRY AROUND THIS UPSCALE DEPARTMENT STORE BAG FOR MOMENTS LIKE THIS.
YOU KNOW, YOU'RE PRETTY VAIN.
AH! THERE YOU ARE! SANO-KUN! SEIMEI-KUUUN!!

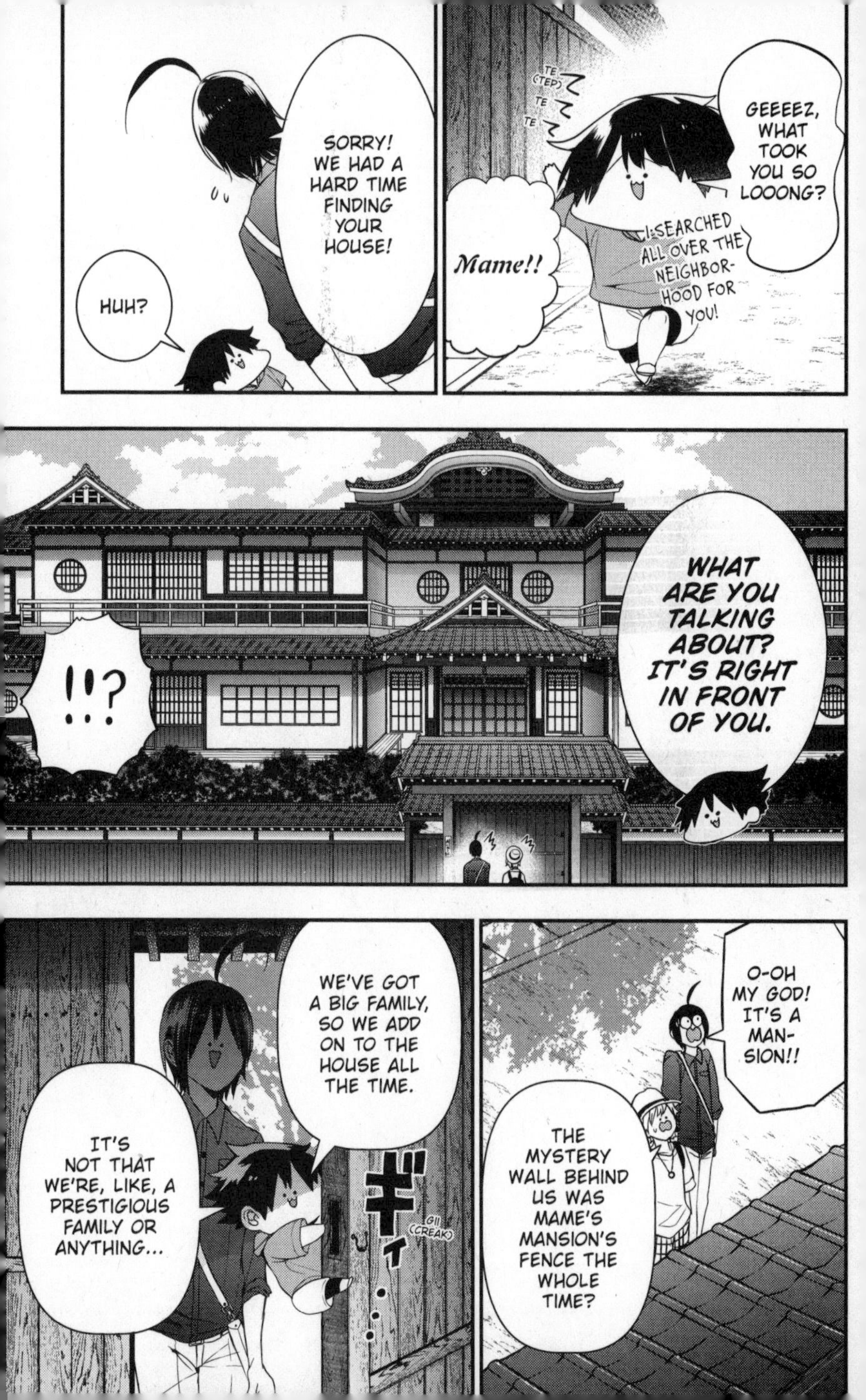
GEEEEZ, WHAT TOOK YOU SO LOOONG?
TE (TEP) TE TE
I SEARCHED ALL OVER THE NEIGHBOR-HOOD FOR YOU!
Mame!!
SORRY! WE HAD A HARD TIME FINDING YOUR HOUSE!
HUH?
WHAT ARE YOU TALKING ABOUT? IT'S RIGHT IN FRONT OF YOU.
!!?
O-OH MY GOD! IT'S A MAN-SION!!
THE MYSTERY WALL BEHIND US WAS MAME'S MANSION'S FENCE THE WHOLE TIME?
WE'VE GOT A BIG FAMILY, SO WE ADD ON TO THE HOUSE ALL THE TIME.
GII (CREAK)
IT'S NOT THAT WE'RE, LIKE, A PRESTIGIOUS FAMILY OR ANYTHING...

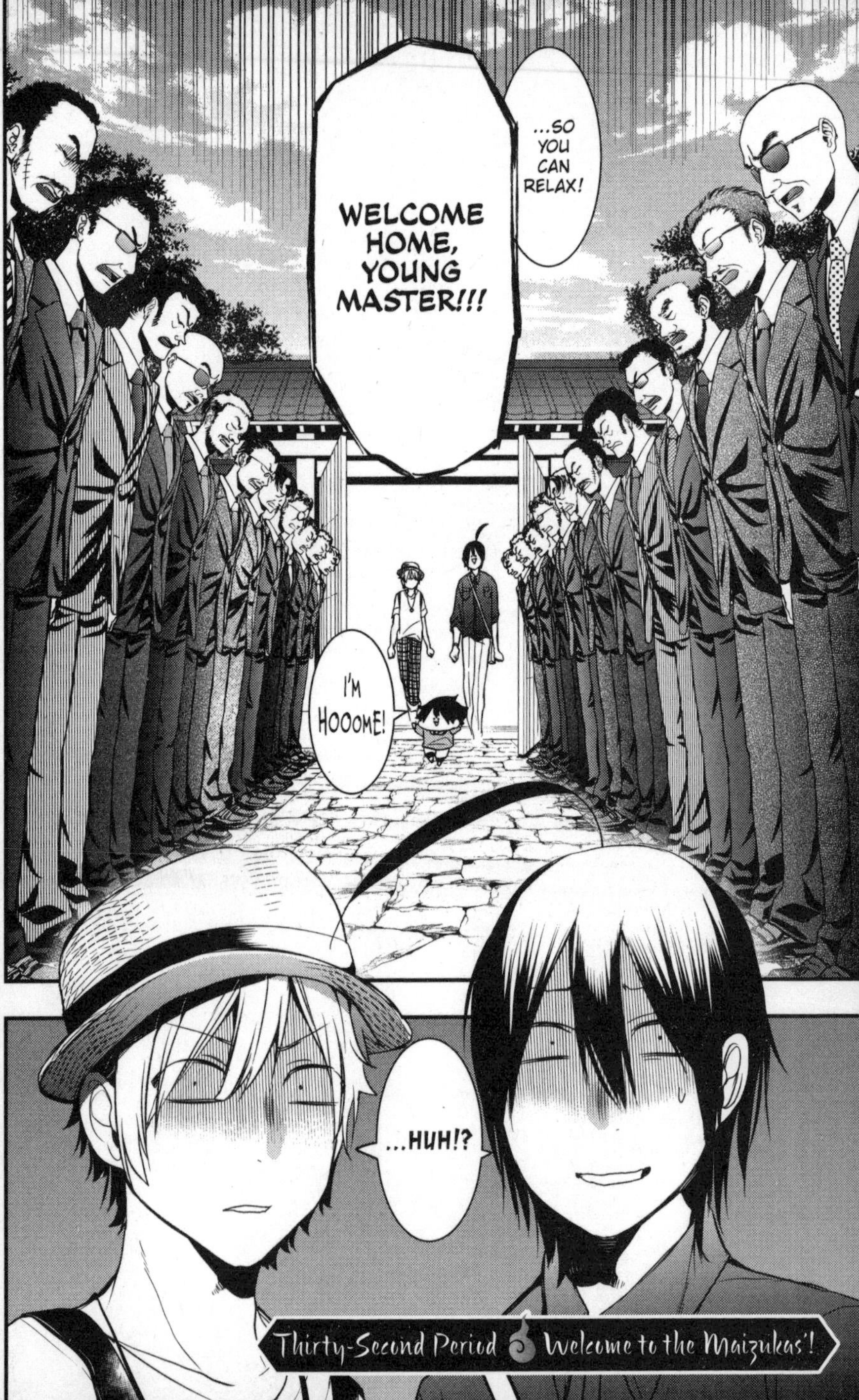
...SO YOU CAN RELAX!
WELCOME HOME, YOUNG MASTER!!!
I'M HOOOME!
...HUH!?
Thirty-Second Period Welcome to the Maizukas'!

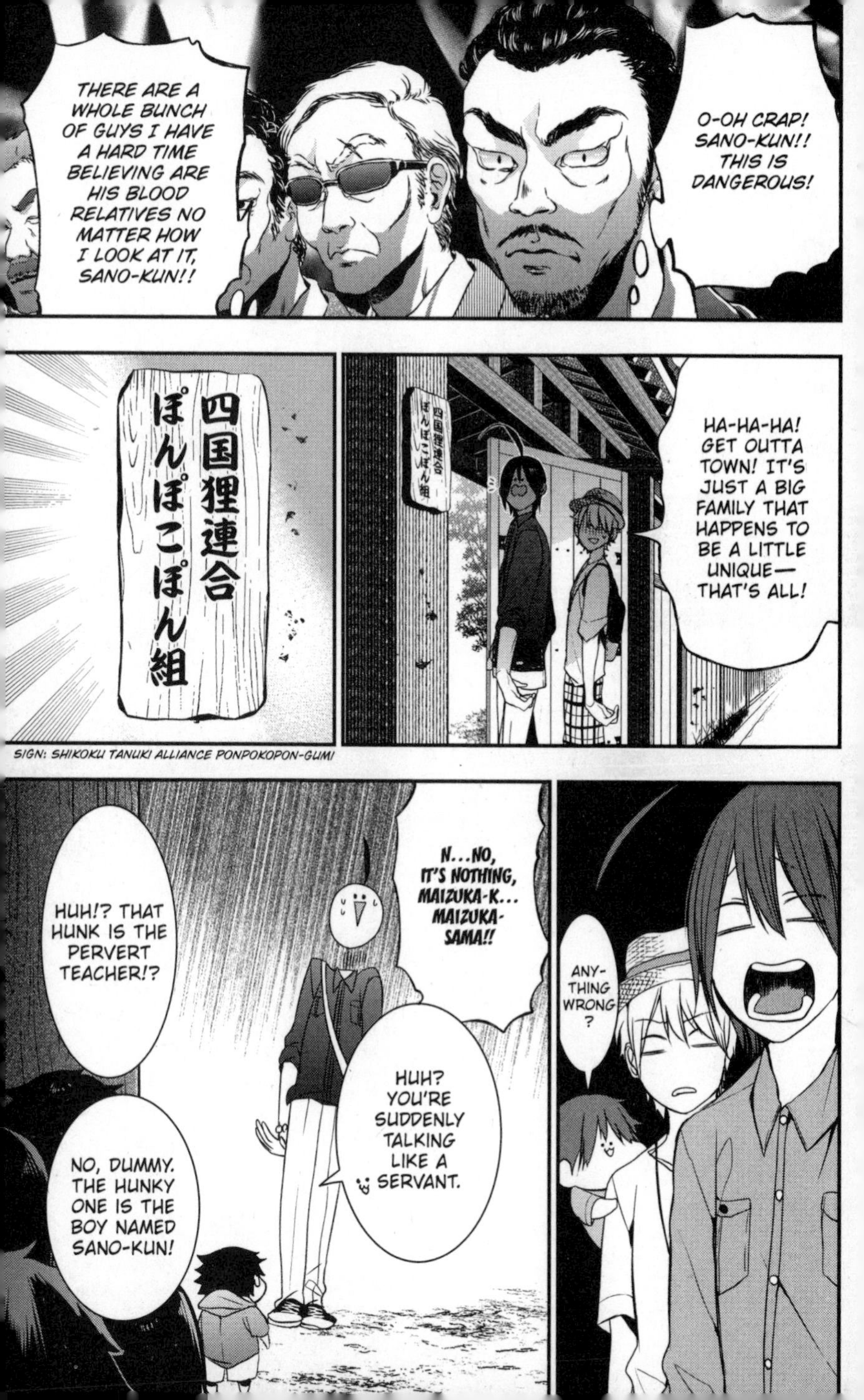
O-OH CRAP! SANO-KUN!! THIS IS DANGEROUS!
THERE ARE A WHOLE BUNCH OF GUYS I HAVE A HARD TIME BELIEVING ARE HIS BLOOD RELATIVES NO MATTER HOW I LOOK AT IT, SANO-KUN!!
HA-HA-HA! GET OUTTA TOWN! IT'S JUST A BIG FAMILY THAT HAPPENS TO BE A LITTLE UNIQUE—THAT'S ALL!
四国狸連合
ぽんぽこぽん組
ANYTHING WRONG?
N...NO, IT'S NOTHING, MAIZUKA-K... MAIZUKA-SAMA!!
HUH? YOU'RE SUDDENLY TALKING LIKE A SERVANT.
HUH!? THAT HUNK IS THE PERVERT TEACHER!?
NO, DUMMY. THE HUNKY ONE IS THE BOY NAMED SANO-KUN!

SIGN: SHIKOKU TANUKI ALLIANCE PONPOKOPON-GUMI

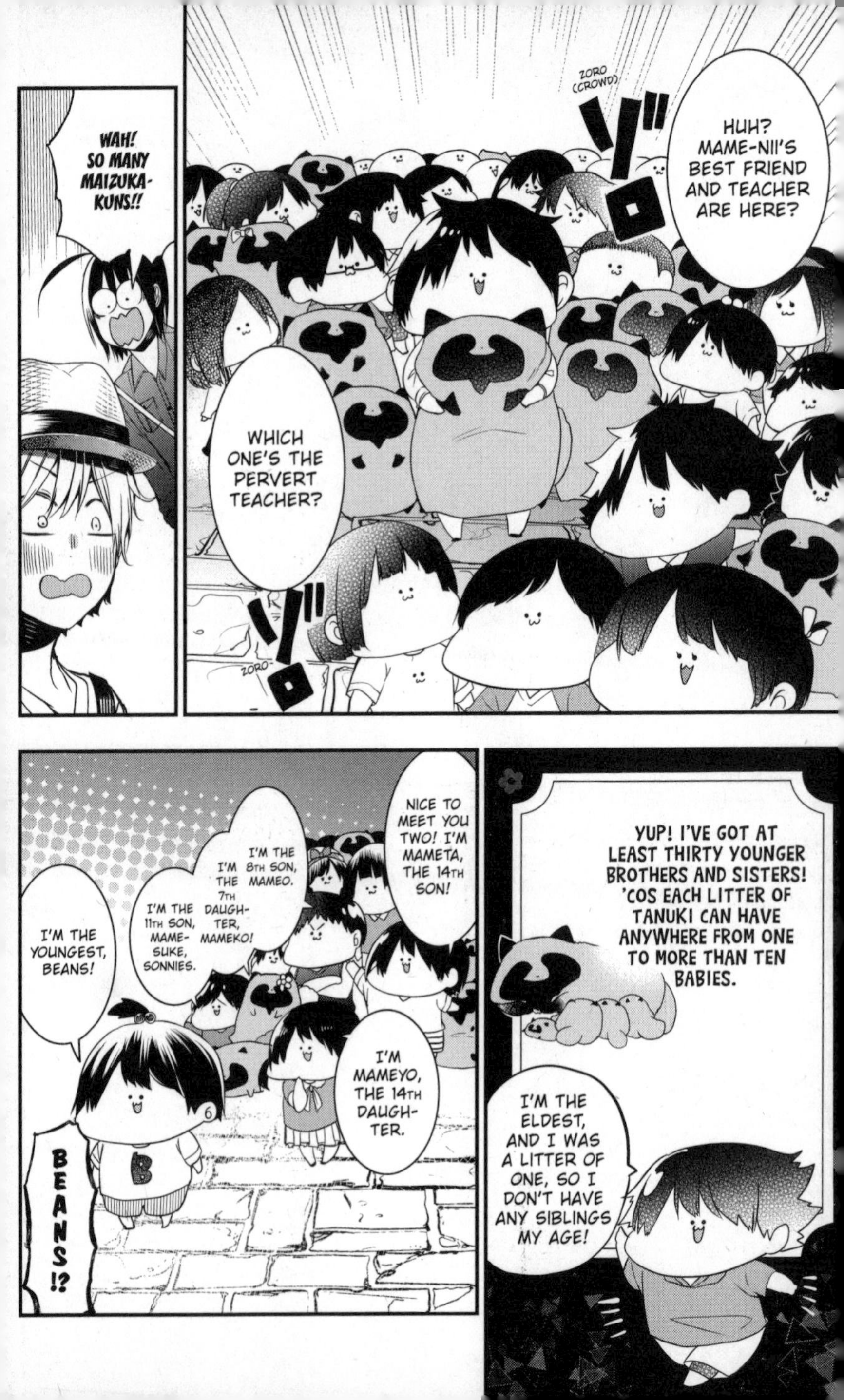
ZORO (CROWD)
HUH? MAME-NII'S BEST FRIEND AND TEACHER ARE HERE?
WHICH ONE'S THE PERVERT TEACHER?
ZORO
WAH! SO MANY MAIZUKA-KUNS!!
YUP! I'VE GOT AT LEAST THIRTY YOUNGER BROTHERS AND SISTERS! 'COS EACH LITTER OF TANUKI CAN HAVE ANYWHERE FROM ONE TO MORE THAN TEN BABIES.
I'M THE ELDEST, AND I WAS A LITTER OF ONE, SO I DON'T HAVE ANY SIBLINGS MY AGE!
NICE TO MEET YOU TWO! I'M MAMETA, THE 14TH SON!
I'M THE 8TH SON, MAMEO.
I'M THE 7TH DAUGHTER, MAMEKO!
I'M THE 11TH SON, MAMESUKE, SONNIES.
I'M MAMEYO, THE 14TH DAUGHTER.
I'M THE YOUNGEST, BEANS!
BEANS!?

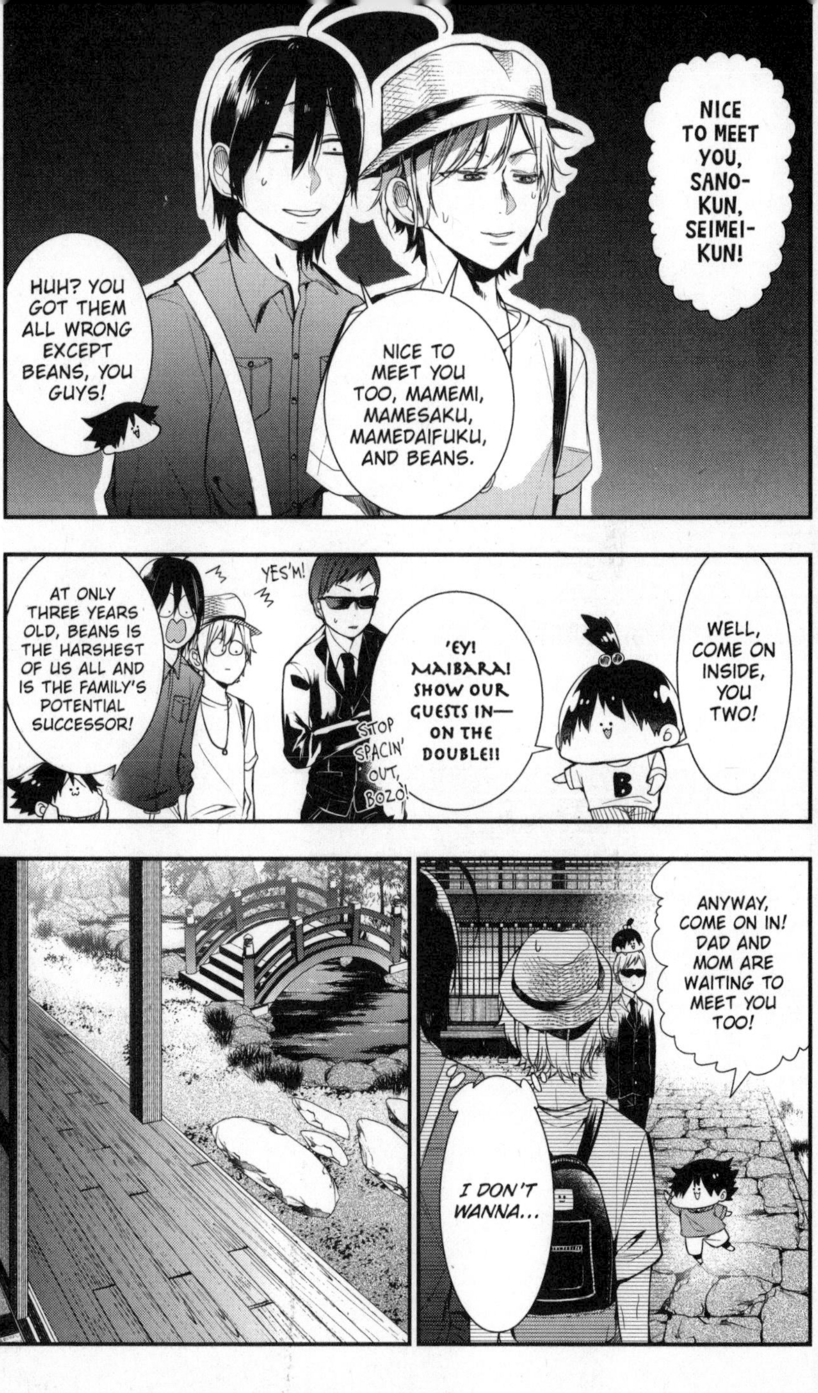
NICE TO MEET YOU, SANO-KUN, SEIMEI-KUN!
NICE TO MEET YOU TOO, MAMEMI, MAMESAKU, MAMEDAIFUKU, AND BEANS.
HUH? YOU GOT THEM ALL WRONG EXCEPT BEANS, YOU GUYS!
WELL, COME ON INSIDE, YOU TWO!
'EY! MAIBARA! SHOW OUR GUESTS IN—ON THE DOUBLE!!
STOP SPACIN' OUT, BOZO!
YES'M!
AT ONLY THREE YEARS OLD, BEANS IS THE HARSHEST OF US ALL AND IS THE FAMILY'S POTENTIAL SUCCESSOR!
ANYWAY, COME ON IN! DAD AND MOM ARE WAITING TO MEET YOU TOO!
I DON'T WANNA...

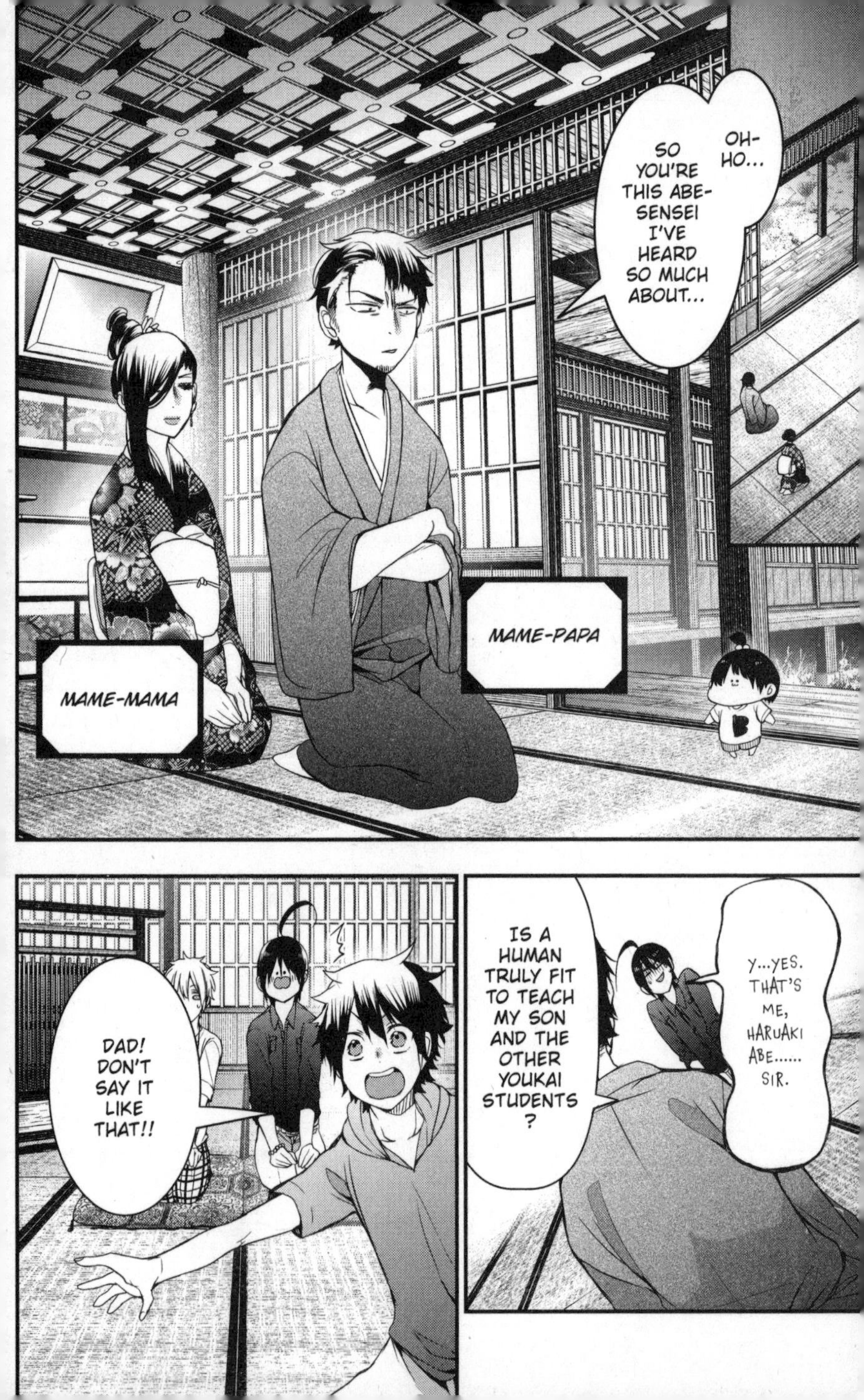
OH-HO... SO YOU'RE THIS ABE-SENSEI I'VE HEARD SO MUCH ABOUT...
MAME-PAPA
MAME-MAMA
Y...YES. THAT'S ME, HARUAKI ABE...... SIR.
IS A HUMAN TRULY FIT TO TEACH MY SON AND THE OTHER YOUKAI STUDENTS?
DAD! DON'T SAY IT LIKE THAT!!

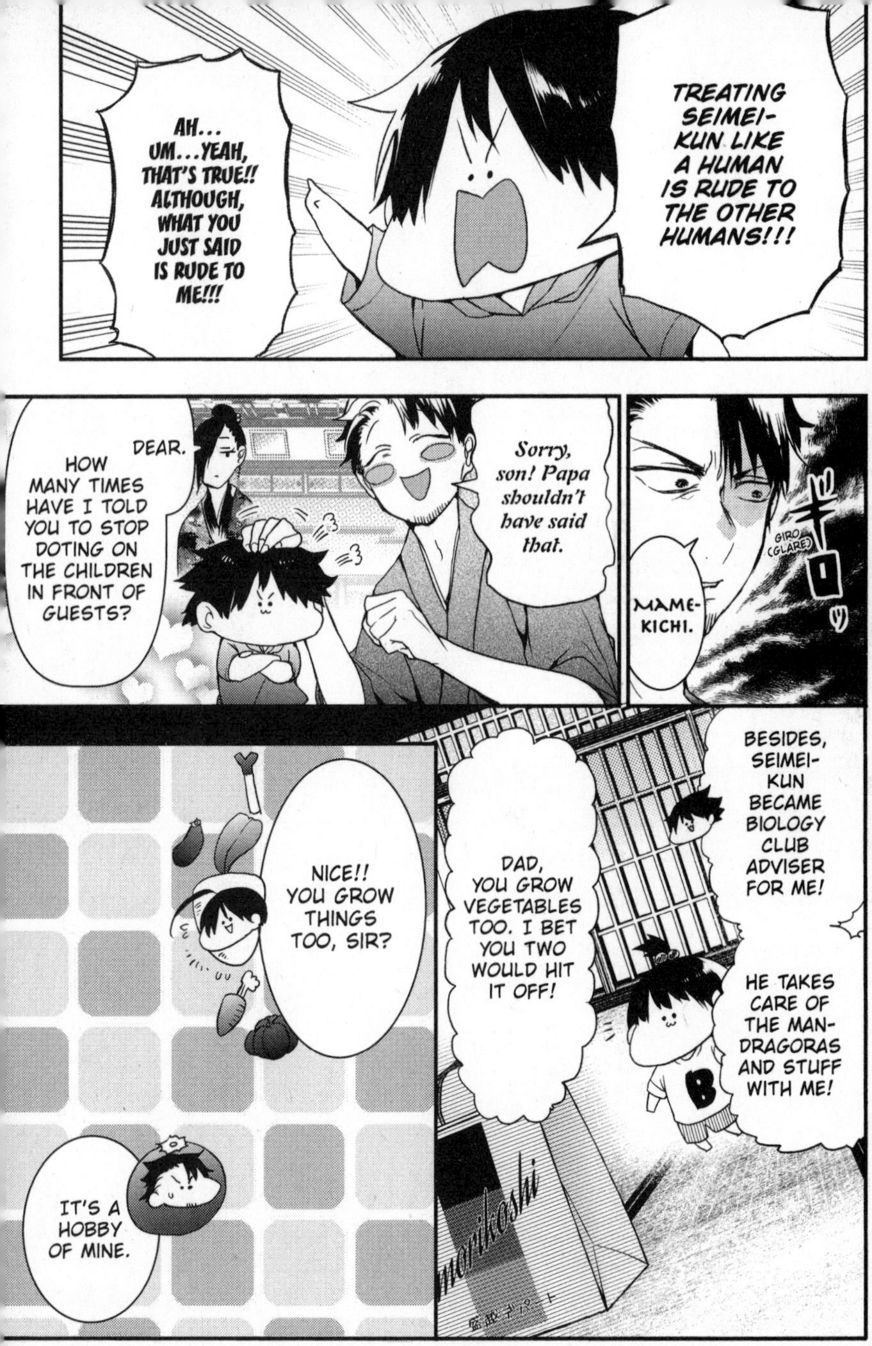
TREATING SEIMEI-KUN LIKE A HUMAN IS RUDE TO THE OTHER HUMANS!!!
AH... UM...YEAH, THAT'S TRUE!! ALTHOUGH, WHAT YOU JUST SAID IS RUDE TO ME!!!
GIRO (GLARE)
MAME-KICHI.
Sorry, son! Papa shouldn't have said that.
DEAR.
HOW MANY TIMES HAVE I TOLD YOU TO STOP DOTING ON THE CHILDREN IN FRONT OF GUESTS?
BESIDES, SEIMEI-KUN BECAME BIOLOGY CLUB ADVISER FOR ME!
HE TAKES CARE OF THE MAN-DRAGORAS AND STUFF WITH ME!
DAD, YOU GROW VEGETABLES TOO. I BET YOU TWO WOULD HIT IT OFF!
morikoshi
NICE!! YOU GROW THINGS TOO, SIR?
IT'S A HOBBY OF MINE.

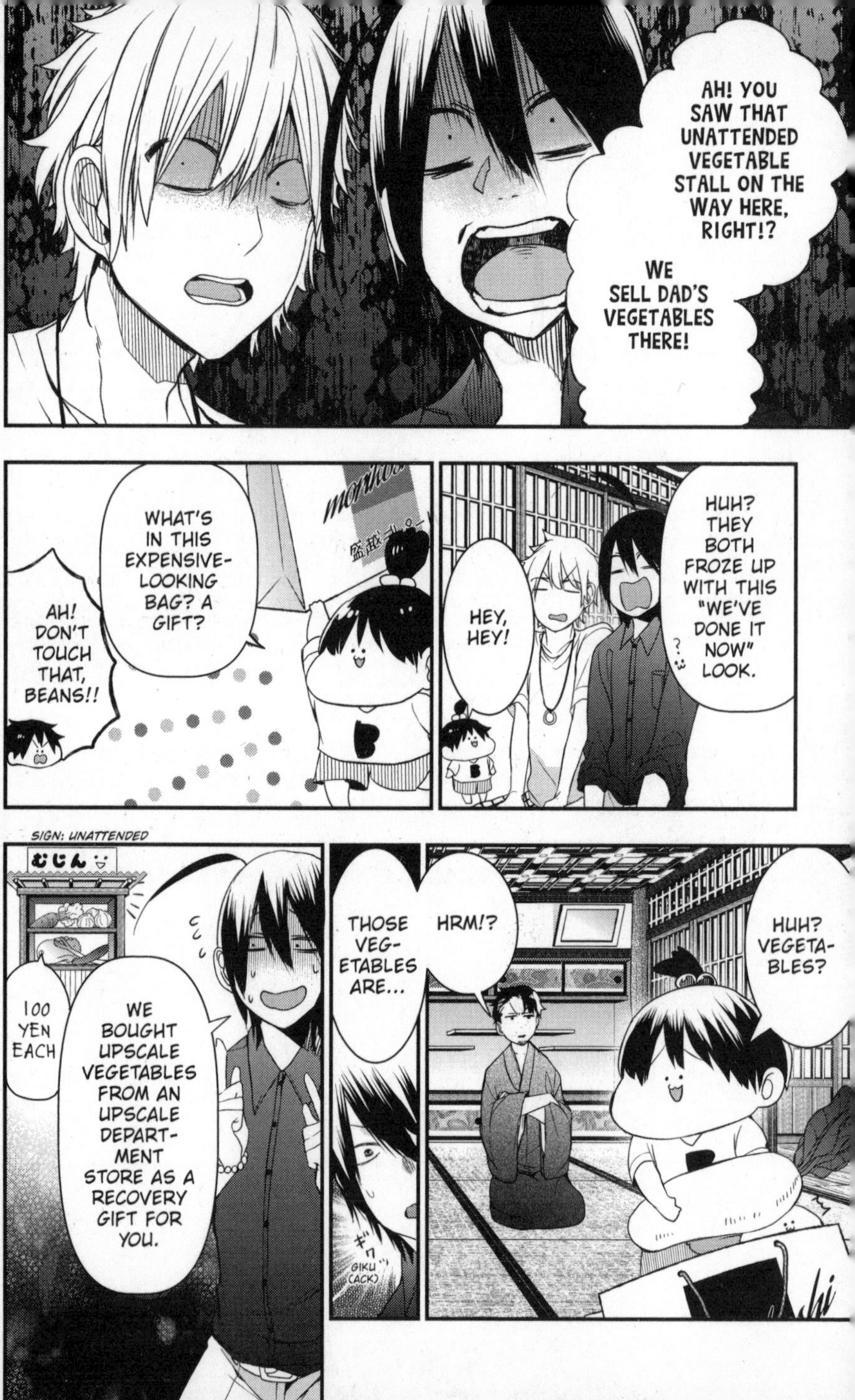
AH! YOU SAW THAT UNATTENDED VEGETABLE STALL ON THE WAY HERE, RIGHT!?
WE SELL DAD'S VEGETABLES THERE!
HUH? THEY BOTH FROZE UP WITH THIS "WE'VE DONE IT NOW" LOOK.
HEY, HEY!
WHAT'S IN THIS EXPENSIVE-LOOKING BAG? A GIFT?
AH! DON'T TOUCH THAT, BEANS!!
HUH? VEGETA-BLES?
HRM!?
THOSE VEG-ETABLES ARE...
GIKU (ACK)
SIGN: UNATTENDED
むじん
WE BOUGHT UPSCALE VEGETABLES FROM AN UPSCALE DEPART-MENT STORE AS A RECOVERY GIFT FOR YOU.
100 YEN EACH

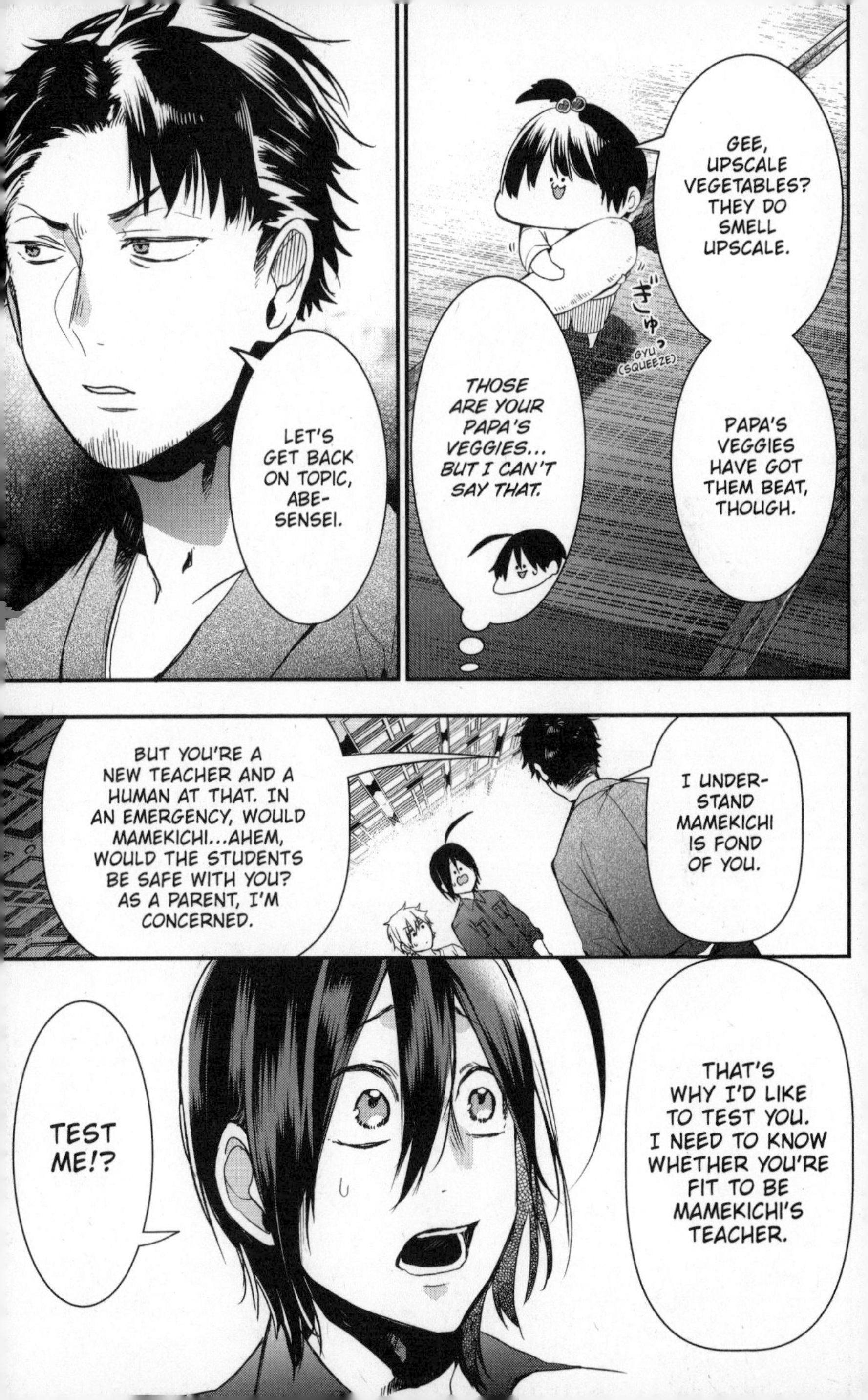
GEE, UPSCALE VEGETABLES? THEY DO SMELL UPSCALE.
PAPA'S VEGGIES HAVE GOT THEM BEAT, THOUGH.
GYU (SQUEEZE)
THOSE ARE YOUR PAPA'S VEGGIES... BUT I CAN'T SAY THAT.
LET'S GET BACK ON TOPIC, ABE-SENSEI.
I UNDER-STAND MAMEKICHI IS FOND OF YOU.
BUT YOU'RE A NEW TEACHER AND A HUMAN AT THAT. IN AN EMERGENCY, WOULD MAMEKICHI...AHEM, WOULD THE STUDENTS BE SAFE WITH YOU? AS A PARENT, I'M CONCERNED.
THAT'S WHY I'D LIKE TO TEST YOU. I NEED TO KNOW WHETHER YOU'RE FIT TO BE MAMEKICHI'S TEACHER.
TEST ME!?

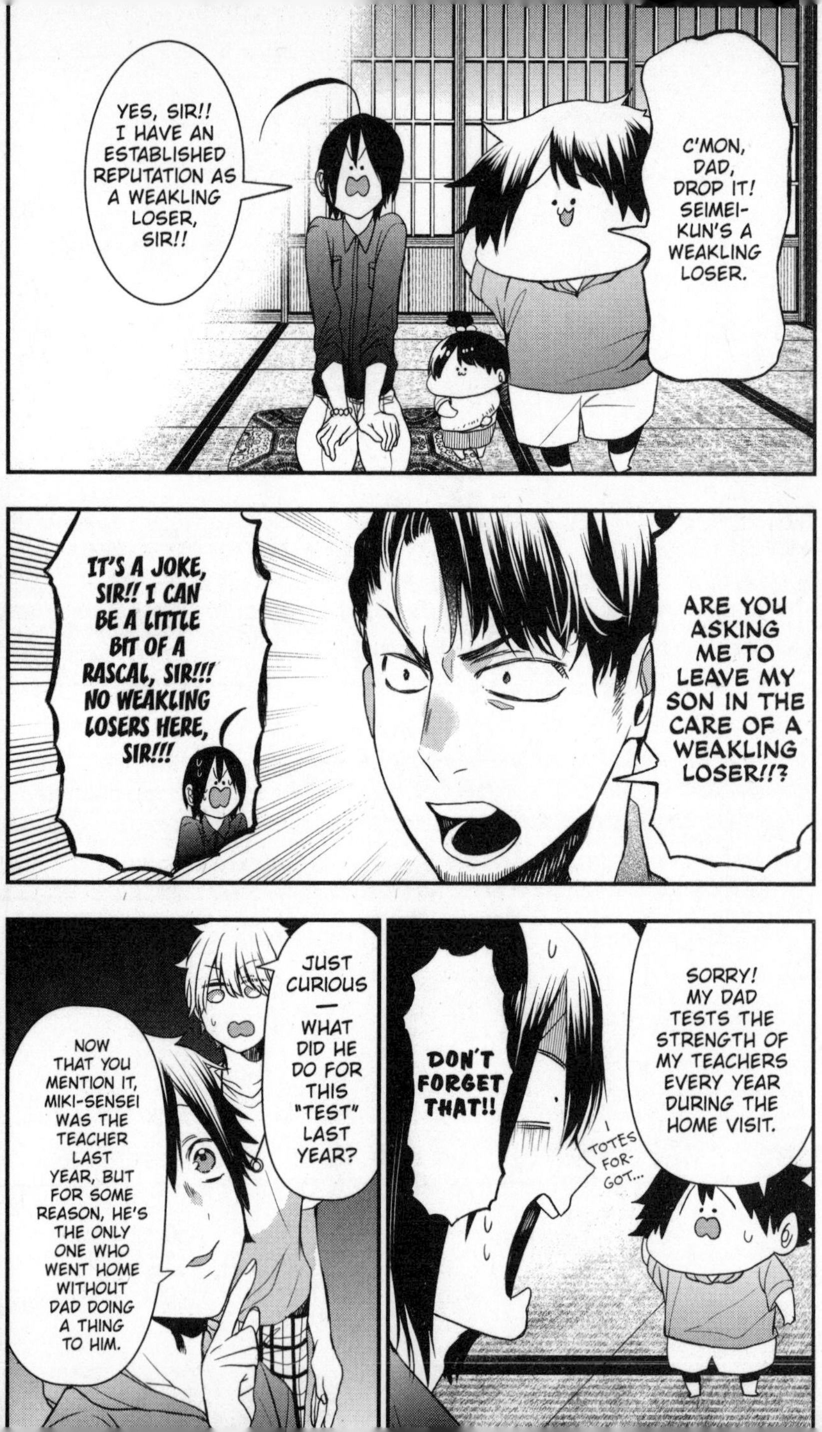
C'MON, DAD, DROP IT! SEIMEI-KUN'S A WEAKLING LOSER.
YES, SIR!! I HAVE AN ESTABLISHED REPUTATION AS A WEAKLING LOSER, SIR!!
ARE YOU ASKING ME TO LEAVE MY SON IN THE CARE OF A WEAKLING LOSER!!?
IT'S A JOKE, SIR!! I CAN BE A LITTLE BIT OF A RASCAL, SIR!!! NO WEAKLING LOSERS HERE, SIR!!!
SORRY! MY DAD TESTS THE STRENGTH OF MY TEACHERS EVERY YEAR DURING THE HOME VISIT.
DON'T FORGET THAT!!
I TOTES FOR-GOT...
JUST CURIOUS — WHAT DID HE DO FOR THIS "TEST" LAST YEAR?
NOW THAT YOU MENTION IT, MIKI-SENSEI WAS THE TEACHER LAST YEAR, BUT FOR SOME REASON, HE'S THE ONLY ONE WHO WENT HOME WITHOUT DAD DOING A THING TO HIM.

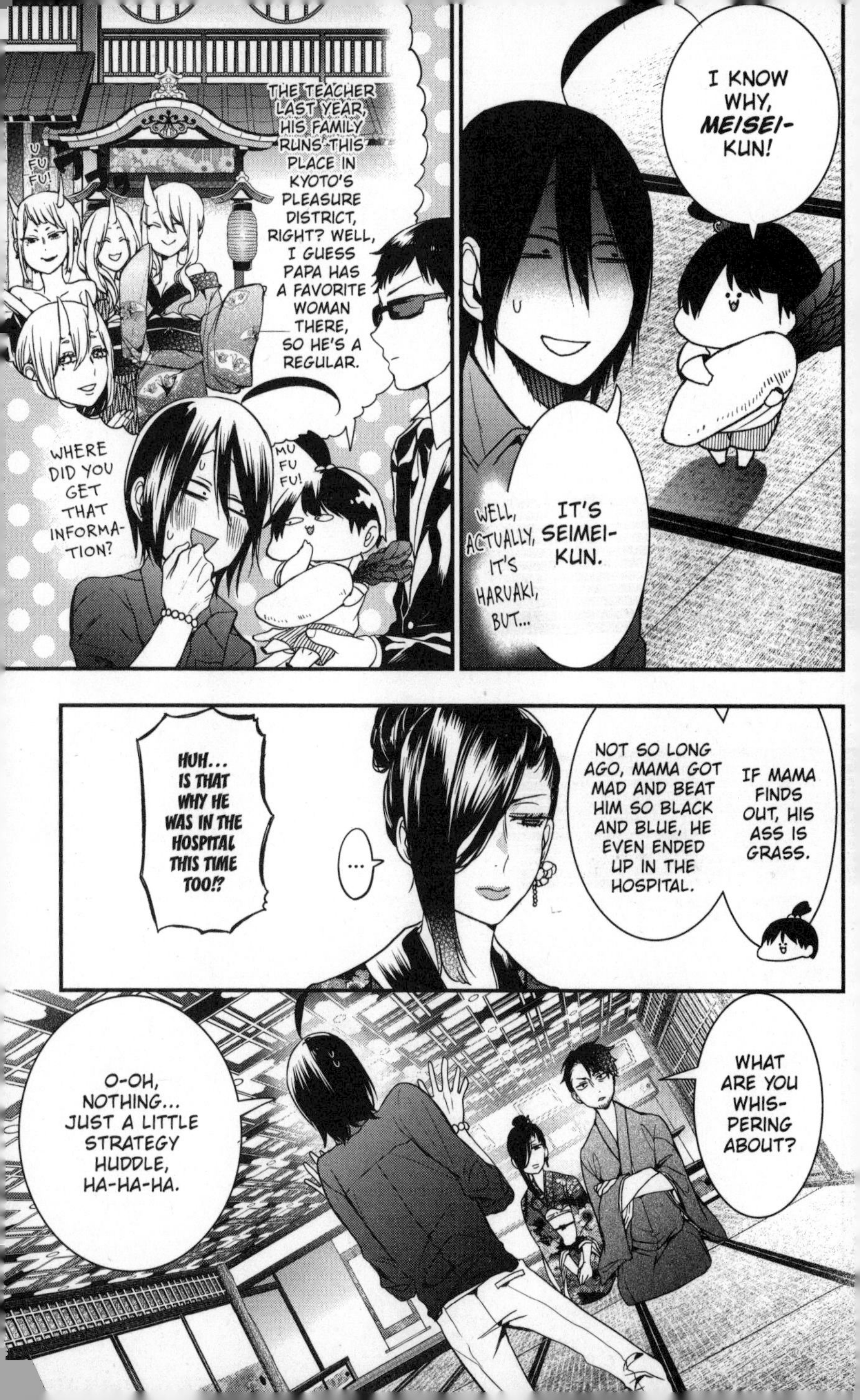
I KNOW WHY, *MEISEI*-KUN!
IT'S SEIMEI-KUN.
WELL, ACTUALLY, IT'S HARUAKI, BUT...
THE TEACHER LAST YEAR, HIS FAMILY RUNS THIS PLACE IN KYOTO'S PLEASURE DISTRICT, RIGHT? WELL, I GUESS PAPA HAS A FAVORITE WOMAN THERE, SO HE'S A REGULAR.
U FU FU!
MU FU FU!
WHERE DID YOU GET THAT INFORMATION?
NOT SO LONG AGO, MAMA GOT MAD AND BEAT HIM SO BLACK AND BLUE, HE EVEN ENDED UP IN THE HOSPITAL.
IF MAMA FINDS OUT, HIS ASS IS GRASS.
...
HUH... IS THAT WHY HE WAS IN THE HOSPITAL THIS TIME TOO!?
WHAT ARE YOU WHISPERING ABOUT?
O-OH, NOTHING... JUST A LITTLE STRATEGY HUDDLE, HA-HA-HA.

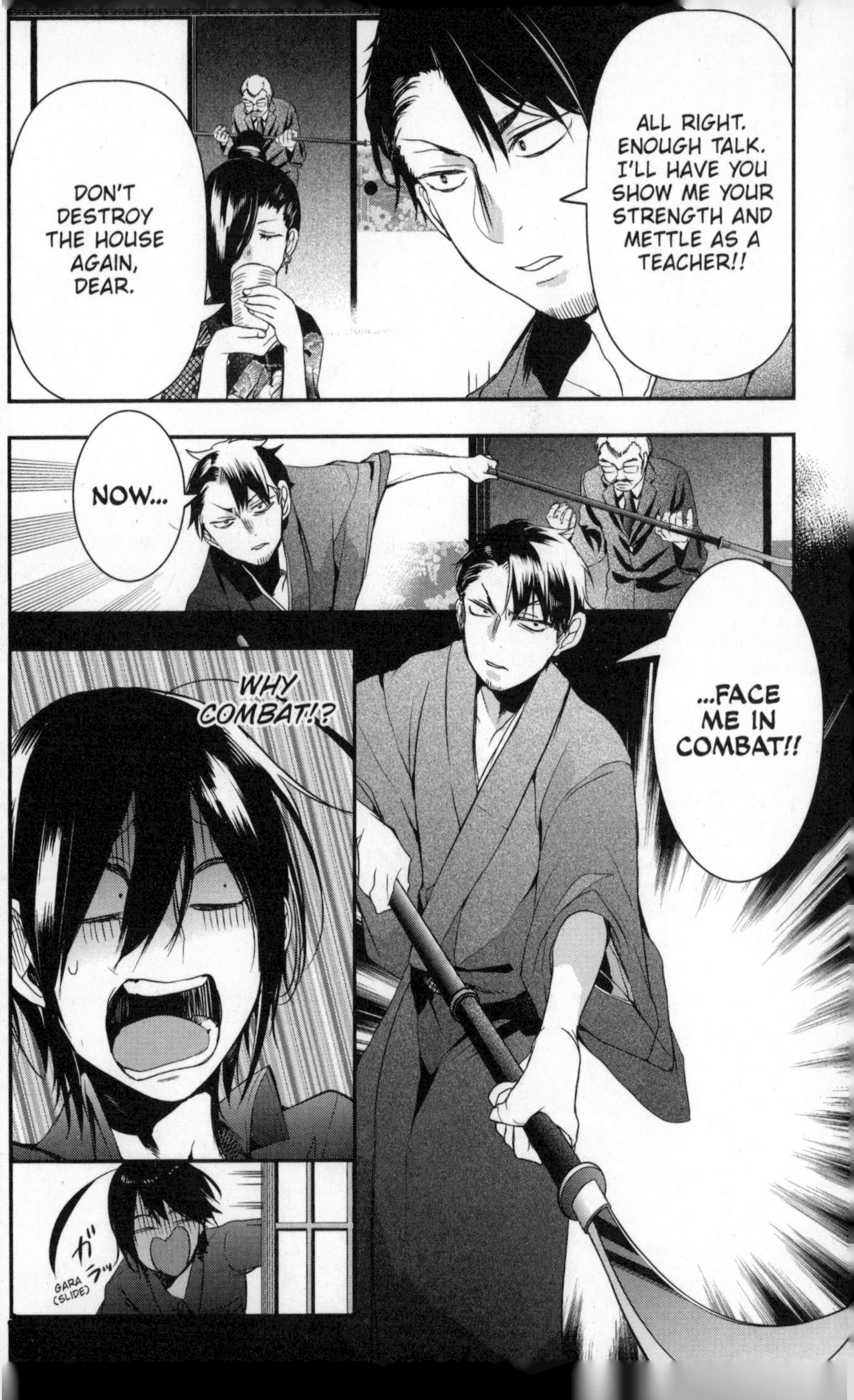
ALL RIGHT. ENOUGH TALK. I'LL HAVE YOU SHOW ME YOUR STRENGTH AND METTLE AS A TEACHER!!
DON'T DESTROY THE HOUSE AGAIN, DEAR.
NOW...
...FACE ME IN COMBAT!!
WHY COMBAT!?
ガラッ
GARA (SLIDE)

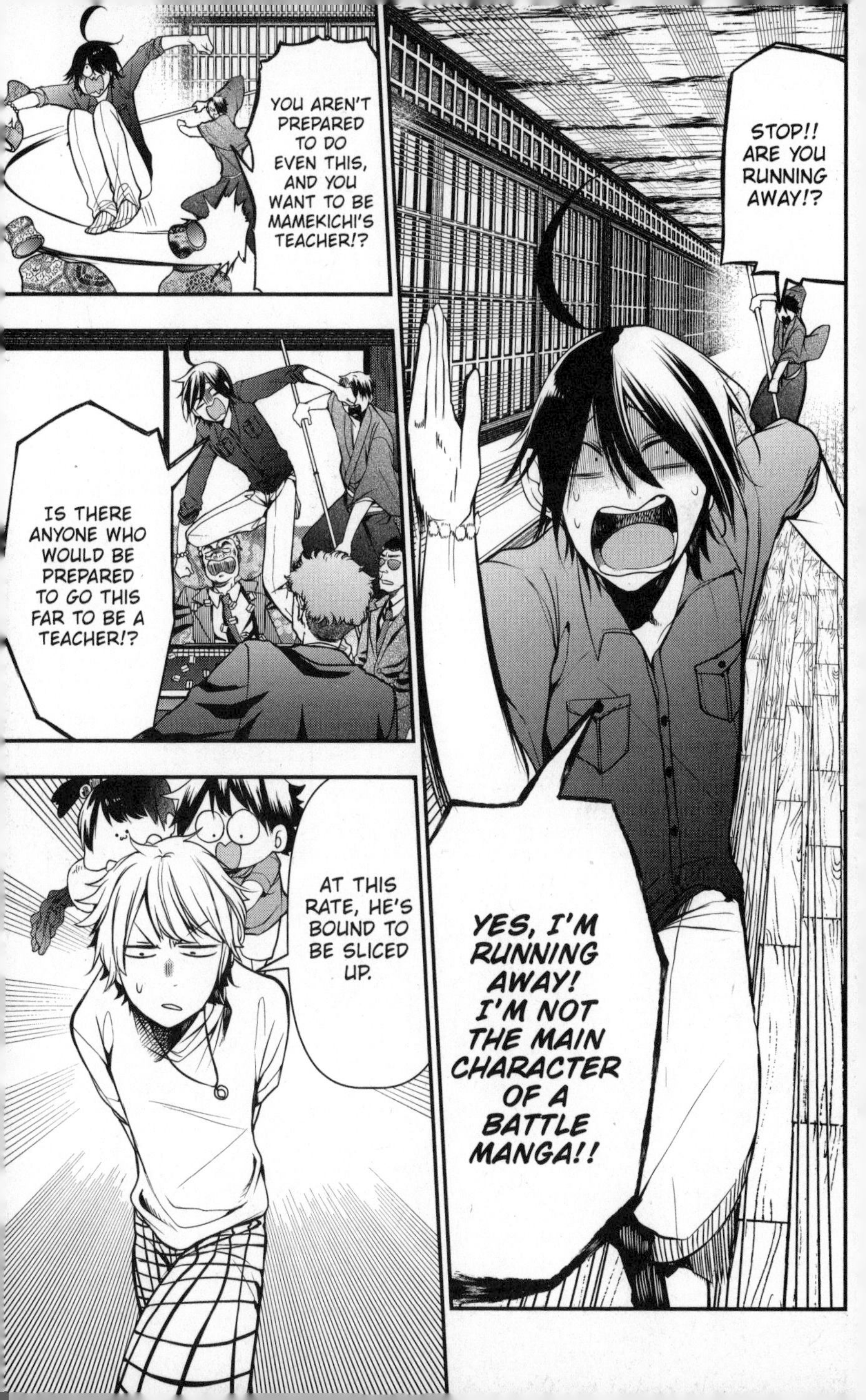
STOP!! ARE YOU RUNNING AWAY!?
YES, I'M RUNNING AWAY! I'M NOT THE MAIN CHARACTER OF A BATTLE MANGA!!
YOU AREN'T PREPARED TO DO EVEN THIS, AND YOU WANT TO BE MAMEKICHI'S TEACHER!?
IS THERE ANYONE WHO WOULD BE PREPARED TO GO THIS FAR TO BE A TEACHER!?
AT THIS RATE, HE'S BOUND TO BE SLICED UP.

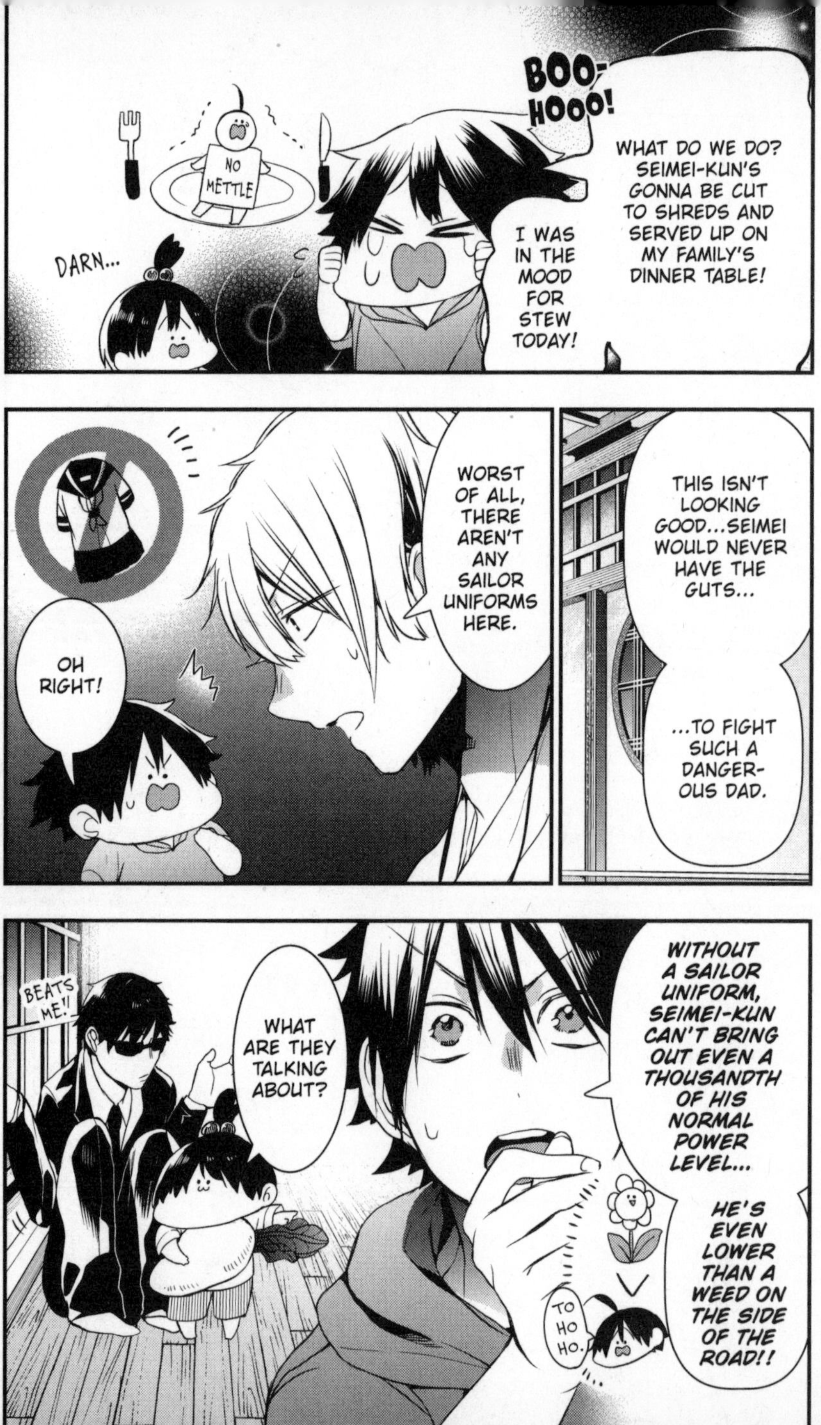
BOO-HOOO!
WHAT DO WE DO? SEIMEI-KUN'S GONNA BE CUT TO SHREDS AND SERVED UP ON MY FAMILY'S DINNER TABLE!
I WAS IN THE MOOD FOR STEW TODAY!
NO METTLE
DARN...
THIS ISN'T LOOKING GOOD...SEIMEI WOULD NEVER HAVE THE GUTS...
...TO FIGHT SUCH A DANGER-OUS DAD.
WORST OF ALL, THERE AREN'T ANY SAILOR UNIFORMS HERE.
OH RIGHT!
WITHOUT A SAILOR UNIFORM, SEIMEI-KUN CAN'T BRING OUT EVEN A THOUSANDTH OF HIS NORMAL POWER LEVEL...
HE'S EVEN LOWER THAN A WEED ON THE SIDE OF THE ROAD!!
TO HO HO.
WHAT ARE THEY TALKING ABOUT?
BEATS ME!!

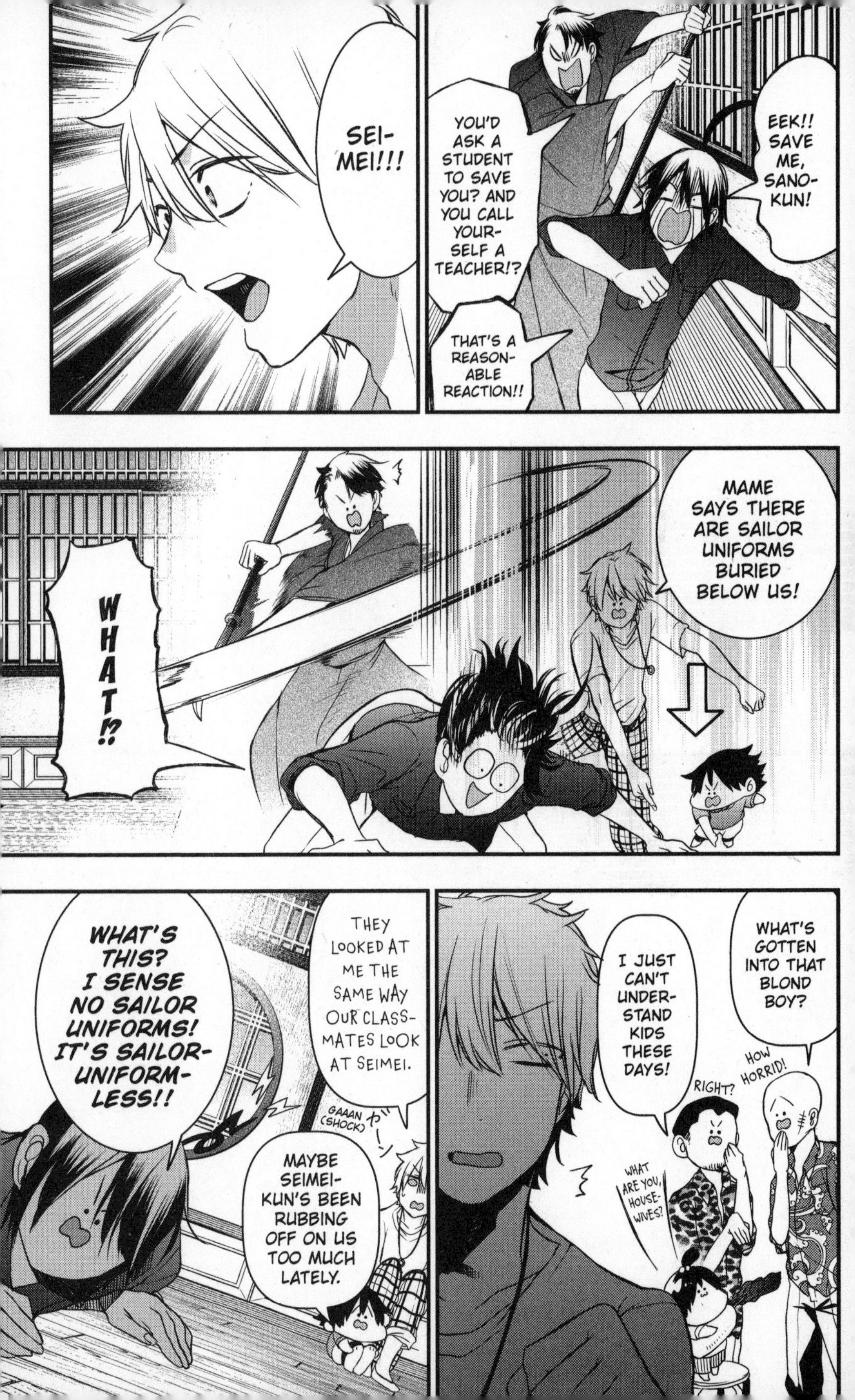
EEK!! SAVE ME, SANO-KUN!
YOU'D ASK A STUDENT TO SAVE YOU? AND YOU CALL YOURSELF A TEACHER!?
THAT'S A REASONABLE REACTION!!
SEI-MEI!!!
MAME SAYS THERE ARE SAILOR UNIFORMS BURIED BELOW US!
WHAT!?
WHAT'S GOTTEN INTO THAT BLOND BOY?
HOW HORRID!
I JUST CAN'T UNDERSTAND KIDS THESE DAYS!
RIGHT?
WHAT ARE YOU, HOUSEWIVES?
THEY LOOKED AT ME THE SAME WAY OUR CLASSMATES LOOK AT SEIMEI.
WHAT'S THIS? I SENSE NO SAILOR UNIFORMS! IT'S SAILOR-UNIFORMLESS!!
GAAAN (SHOCK)
MAYBE SEIMEI-KUN'S BEEN RUBBING OFF ON US TOO MUCH LATELY.

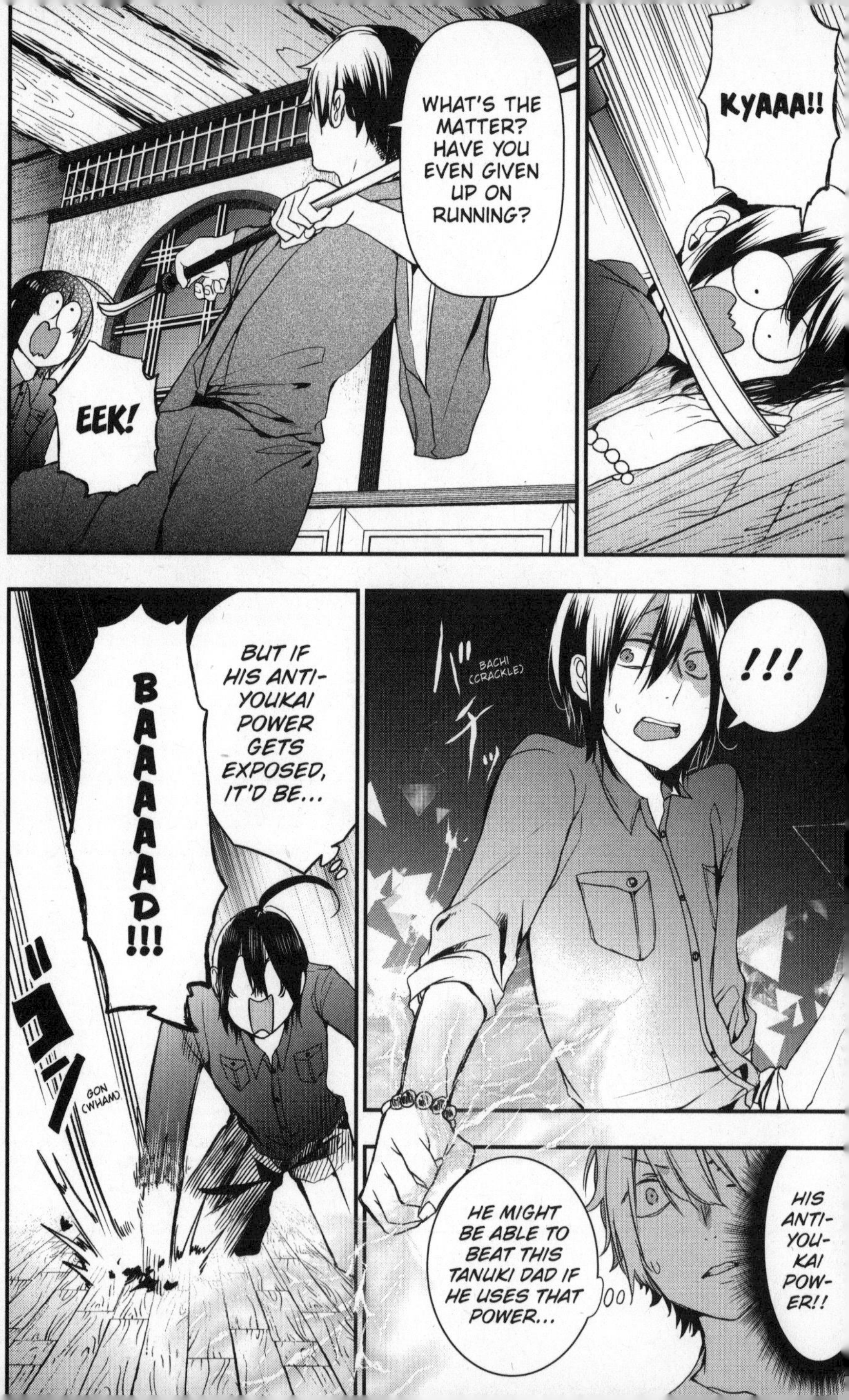
KYAAA!!
WHAT'S THE MATTER? HAVE YOU EVEN GIVEN UP ON RUNNING?
EEK!
BACHI (CRACKLE)
!!!
HIS ANTI-YOU-KAI POW-ER!!
HE MIGHT BE ABLE TO BEAT THIS TANUKI DAD IF HE USES THAT POWER...
BUT IF HIS ANTI-YOUKAI POWER GETS EXPOSED, IT'D BE...
BAAAAAAD!!!
GON (WHAM)

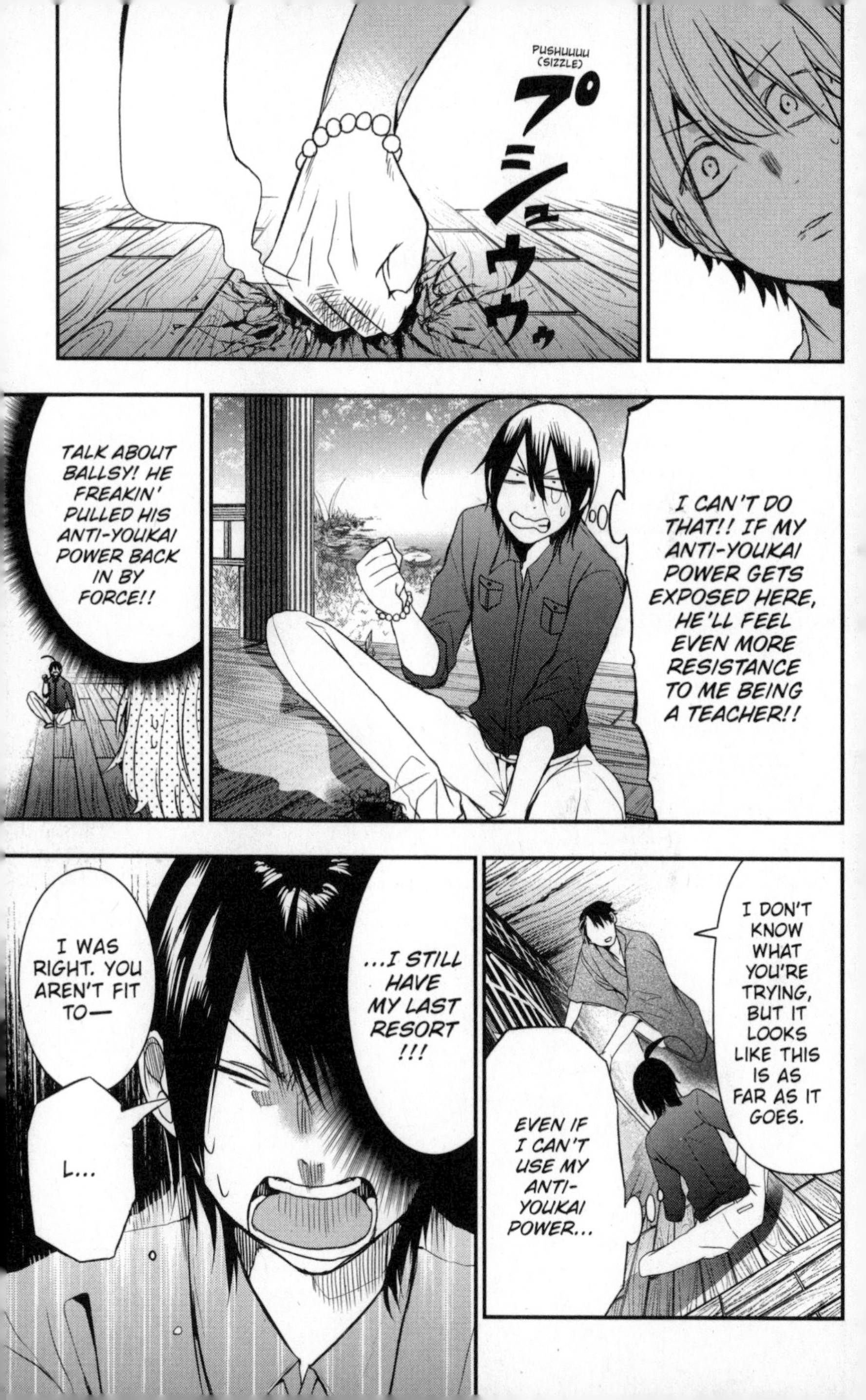
PUSHUUUU (SIZZLE)
プシュウウゥ
I CAN'T DO THAT!! IF MY ANTI-YOUKAI POWER GETS EXPOSED HERE, HE'LL FEEL EVEN MORE RESISTANCE TO ME BEING A TEACHER!!
TALK ABOUT BALLSY! HE FREAKIN' PULLED HIS ANTI-YOUKAI POWER BACK IN BY FORCE!!
I DON'T KNOW WHAT YOU'RE TRYING, BUT IT LOOKS LIKE THIS IS AS FAR AS IT GOES.
EVEN IF I CAN'T USE MY ANTI-YOUKAI POWER...
...I STILL HAVE MY LAST RESORT!!!
I WAS RIGHT. YOU AREN'T FIT TO—
L...

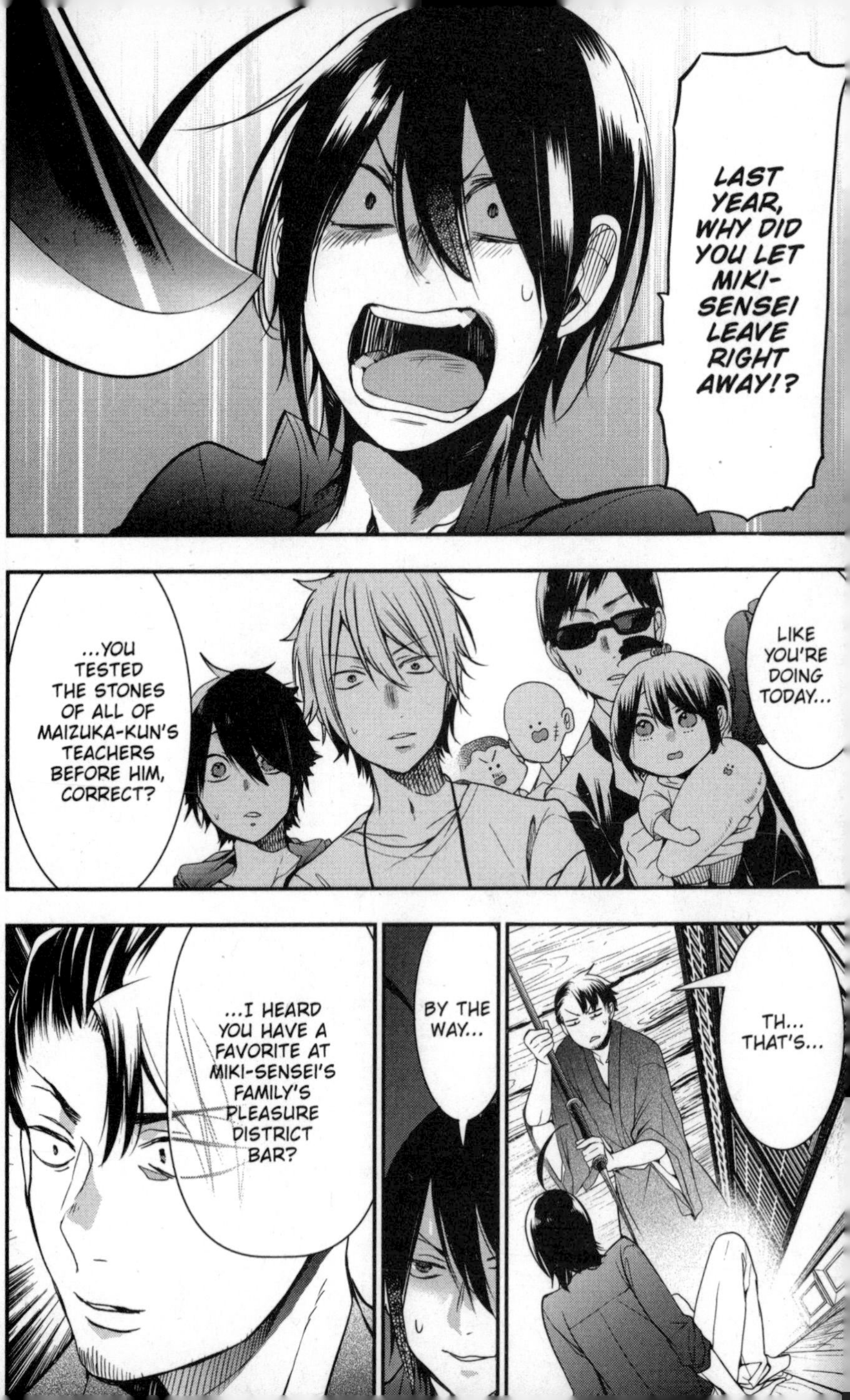
LAST YEAR, WHY DID YOU LET MIKI-SENSEI LEAVE RIGHT AWAY!?
LIKE YOU'RE DOING TODAY...
...YOU TESTED THE STONES OF ALL OF MAIZUKA-KUN'S TEACHERS BEFORE HIM, CORRECT?
TH... THAT'S...
BY THE WAY...
...I HEARD YOU HAVE A FAVORITE AT MIKI-SENSEI'S FAMILY'S PLEASURE DISTRICT BAR?

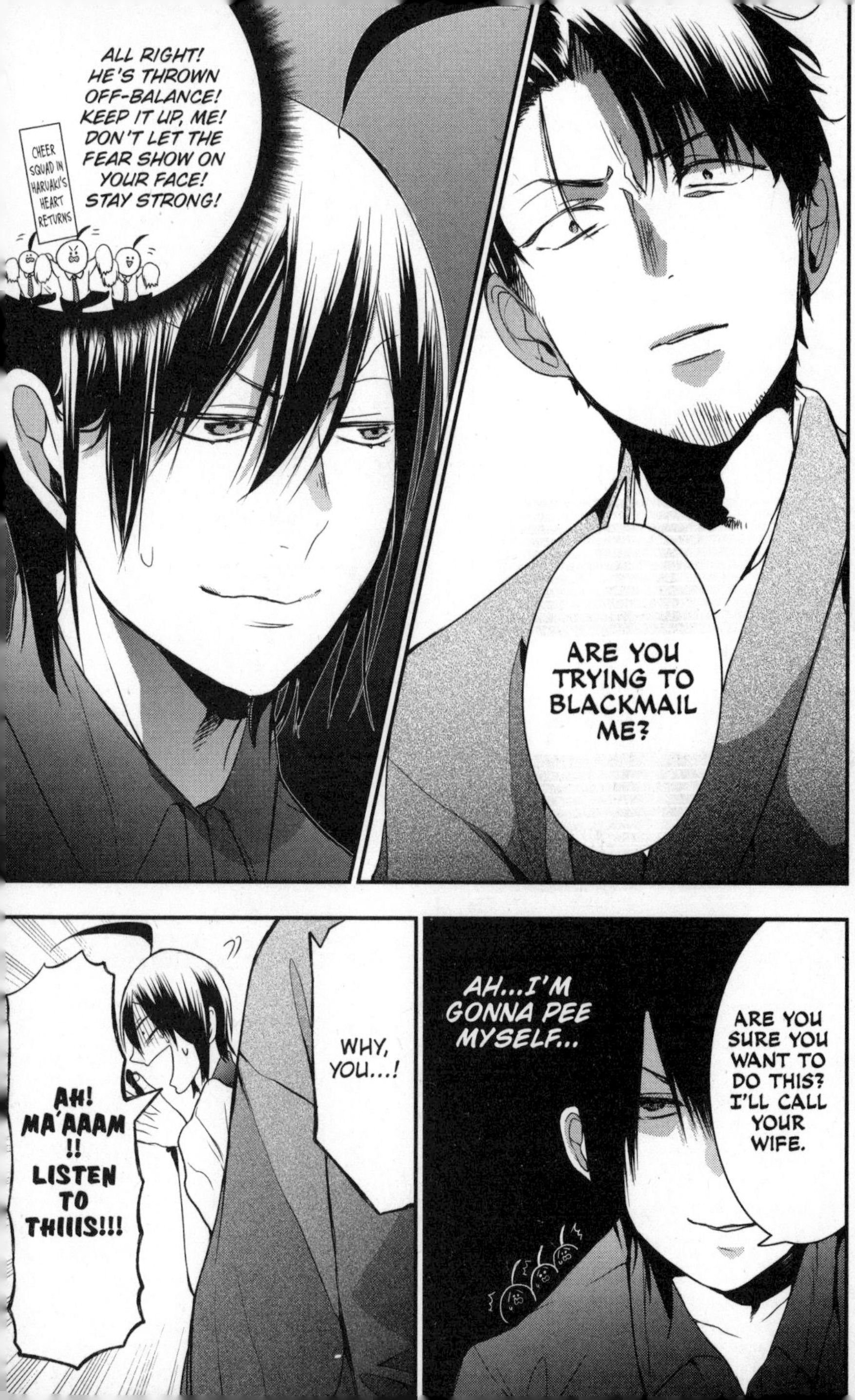
ARE YOU TRYING TO BLACKMAIL ME?
ALL RIGHT! HE'S THROWN OFF-BALANCE! KEEP IT UP, ME! DON'T LET THE FEAR SHOW ON YOUR FACE! STAY STRONG!
CHEER SQUAD IN HARUAKI'S HEART RETURNS
ARE YOU SURE YOU WANT TO DO THIS? I'LL CALL YOUR WIFE.
AH...I'M GONNA PEE MYSELF...
WHY, YOU...!
AH! MA'AAAM!! LISTEN TO THIIIS!!!

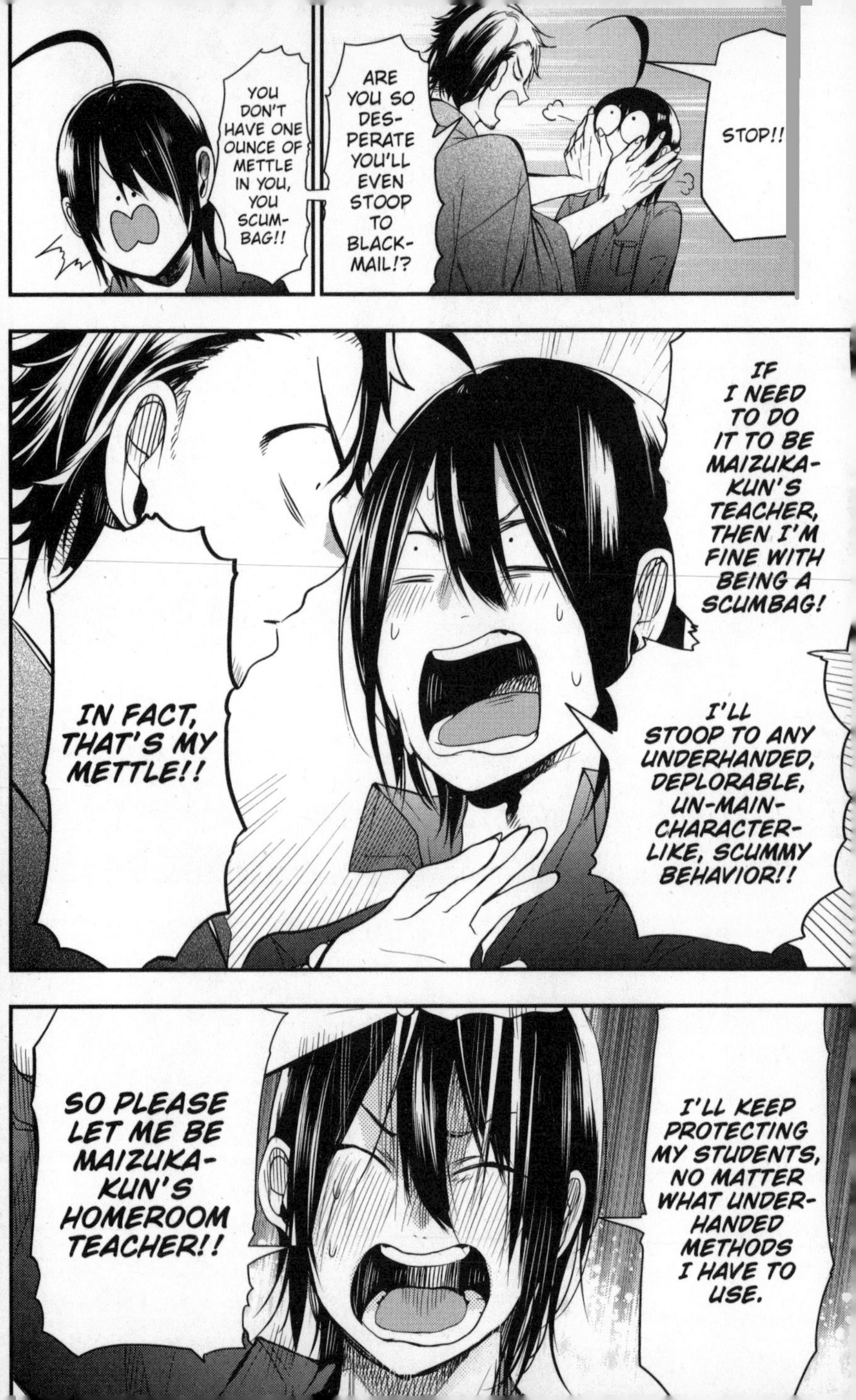
STOP!!
ARE YOU SO DESPERATE YOU'LL EVEN STOOP TO BLACKMAIL!?
YOU DON'T HAVE ONE OUNCE OF METTLE IN YOU, YOU SCUMBAG!!
IF I NEED TO DO IT TO BE MAIZUKA-KUN'S TEACHER, THEN I'M FINE WITH BEING A SCUMBAG!
I'LL STOOP TO ANY UNDERHANDED, DEPLORABLE, UN-MAIN-CHARACTER-LIKE, SCUMMY BEHAVIOR!!
IN FACT, THAT'S MY METTLE!!
I'LL KEEP PROTECTING MY STUDENTS, NO MATTER WHAT UNDERHANDED METHODS I HAVE TO USE.
SO PLEASE LET ME BE MAIZUKA-KUN'S HOMEROOM TEACHER!!

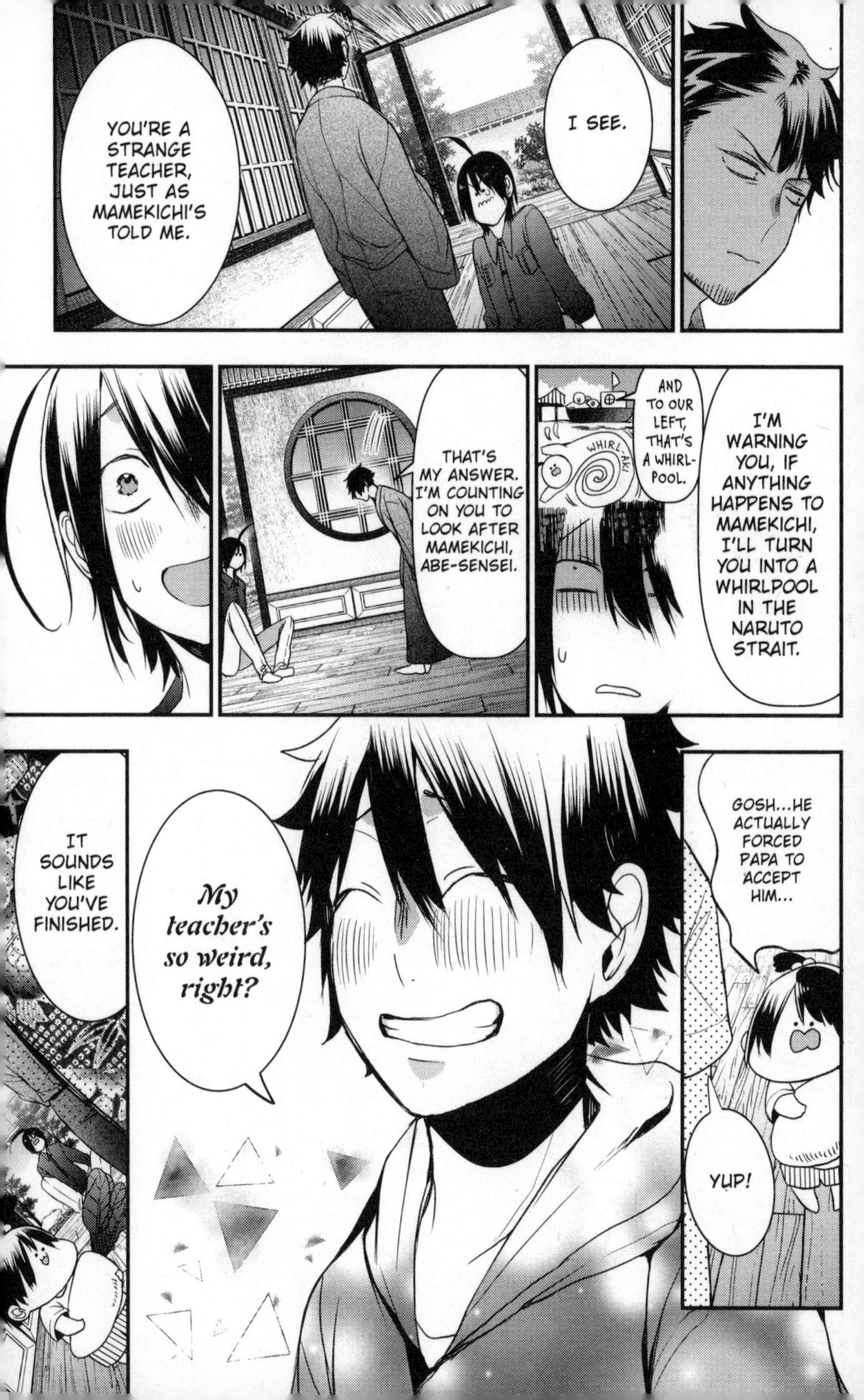
I SEE.
YOU'RE A STRANGE TEACHER, JUST AS MAMEKICHI'S TOLD ME.
I'M WARNING YOU, IF ANYTHING HAPPENS TO MAMEKICHI, I'LL TURN YOU INTO A WHIRLPOOL IN THE NARUTO STRAIT.
AND TO OUR LEFT, THAT'S A WHIRLPOOL.
WHIRL-AKI
THAT'S MY ANSWER. I'M COUNTING ON YOU TO LOOK AFTER MAMEKICHI, ABE-SENSEI.
GOSH...HE ACTUALLY FORCED PAPA TO ACCEPT HIM...
YUP!
My teacher's so weird, right?
IT SOUNDS LIKE YOU'VE FINISHED.

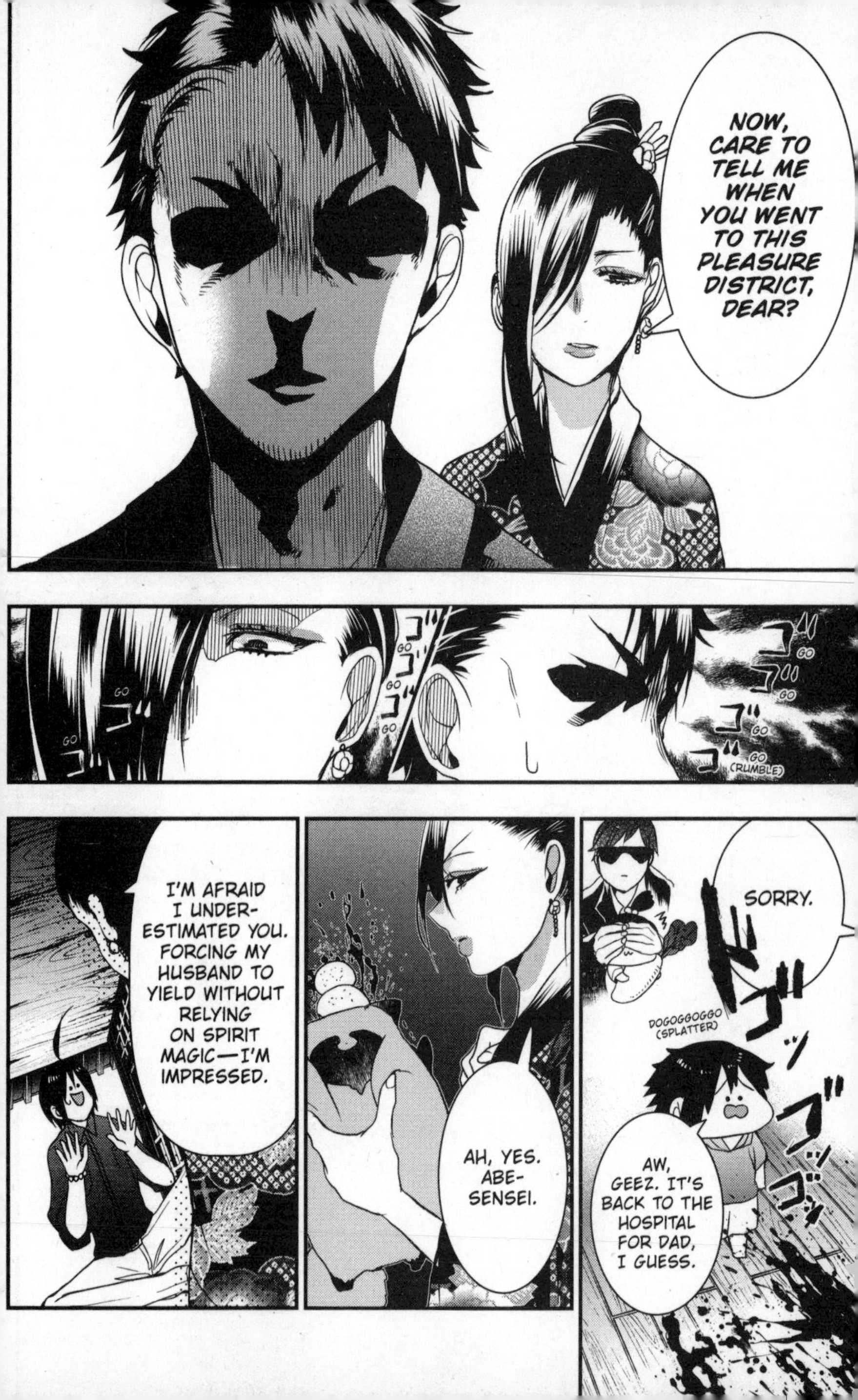
NOW, CARE TO TELL ME WHEN YOU WENT TO THIS PLEASURE DISTRICT, DEAR?
GO GO GO GO (RUMBLE)
GO GO GO GO
SORRY.
DOGOGGOGGO (SPLATTER)
AW, GEEZ. IT'S BACK TO THE HOSPITAL FOR DAD, I GUESS.
AH, YES. ABE-SENSEI.
I'M AFRAID I UNDER-ESTIMATED YOU. FORCING MY HUSBAND TO YIELD WITHOUT RELYING ON SPIRIT MAGIC—I'M IMPRESSED.

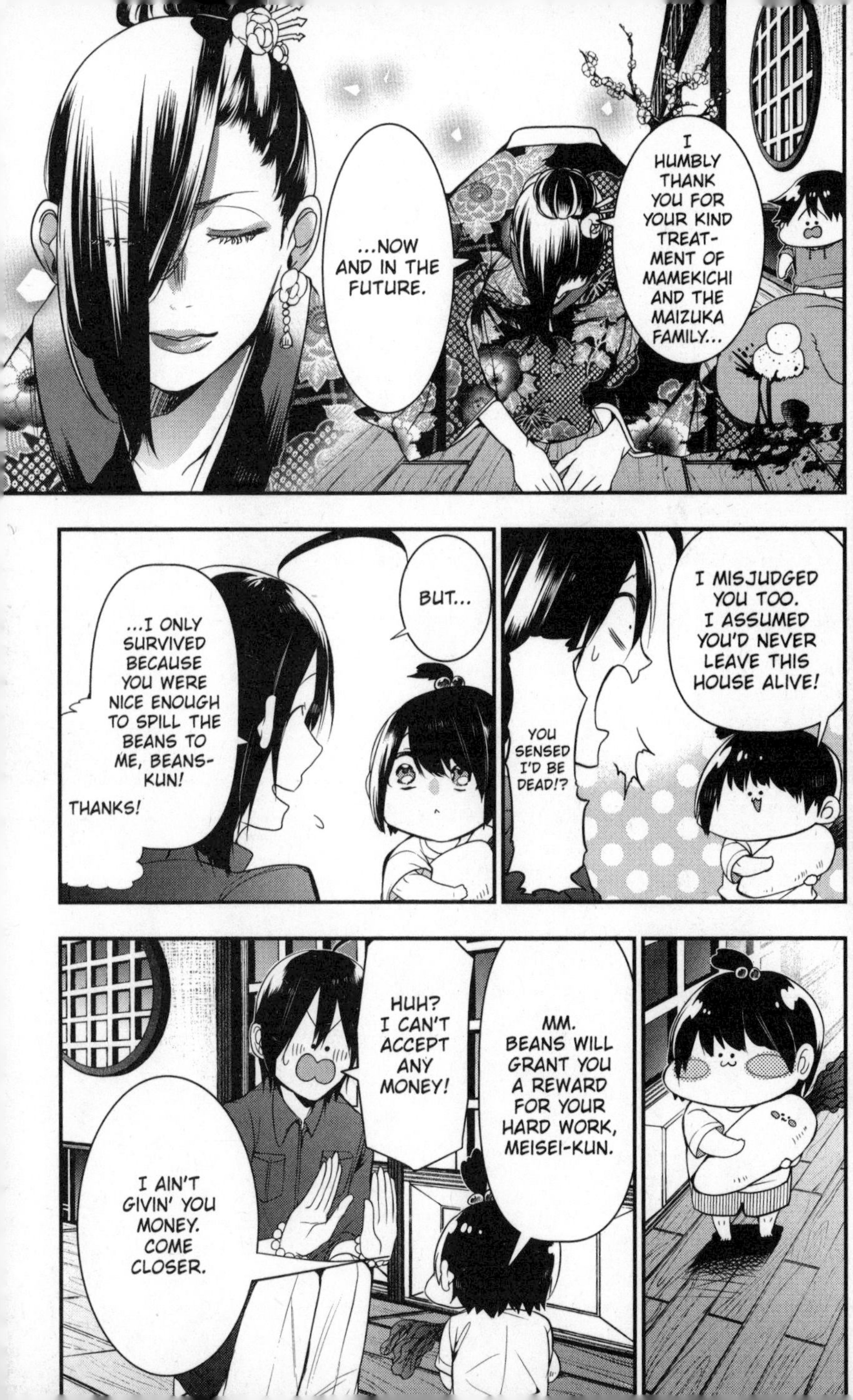
I HUMBLY THANK YOU FOR YOUR KIND TREATMENT OF MAMEKICHI AND THE MAIZUKA FAMILY...
...NOW AND IN THE FUTURE.
I MISJUDGED YOU TOO. I ASSUMED YOU'D NEVER LEAVE THIS HOUSE ALIVE!
YOU SENSED I'D BE DEAD!?
BUT...
...I ONLY SURVIVED BECAUSE YOU WERE NICE ENOUGH TO SPILL THE BEANS TO ME, BEANS-KUN!
THANKS!
MM. BEANS WILL GRANT YOU A REWARD FOR YOUR HARD WORK, MEISEI-KUN.
HUH? I CAN'T ACCEPT ANY MONEY!
I AIN'T GIVIN' YOU MONEY. COME CLOSER.

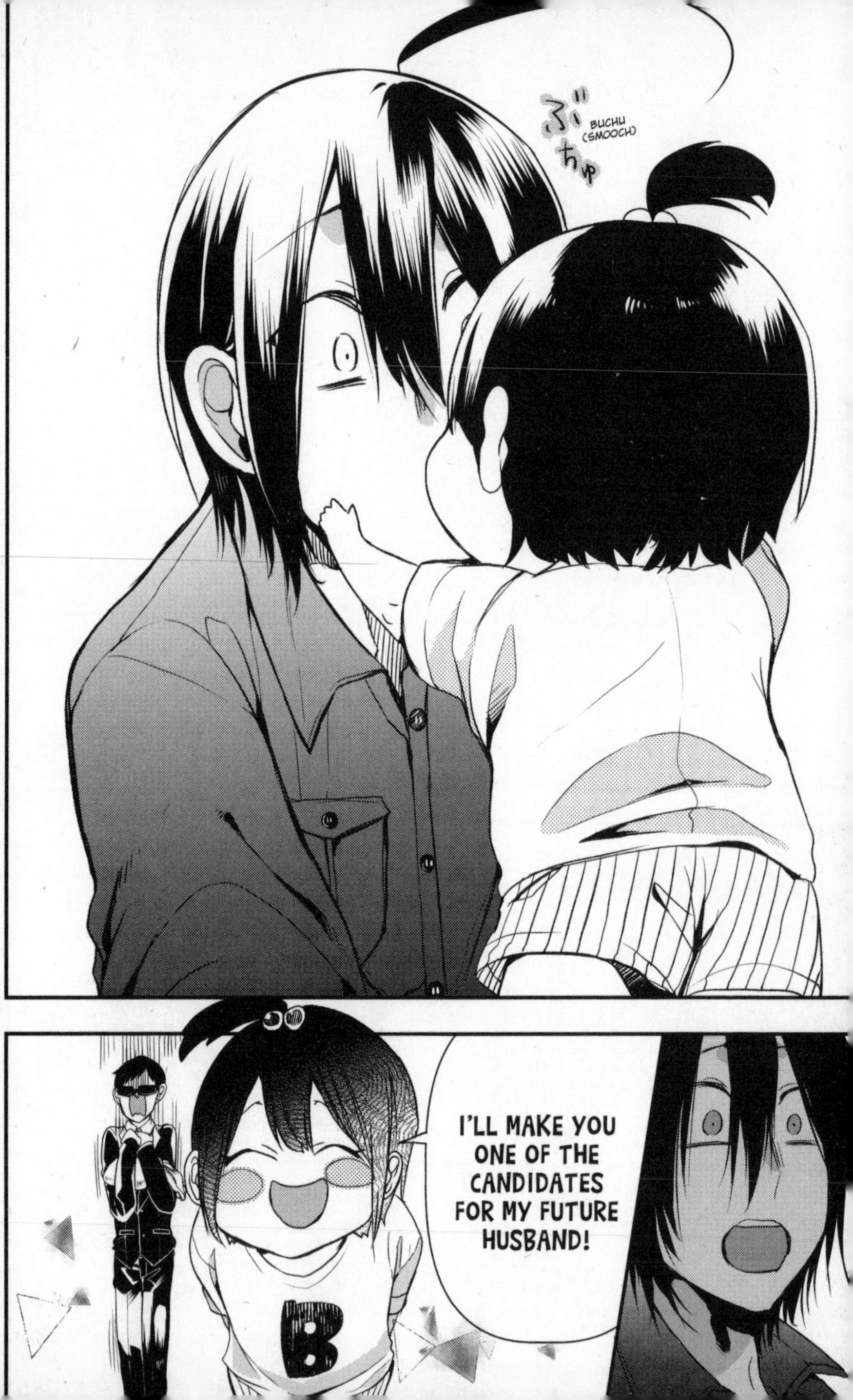
ぶちゅ
BUCHU (SMOOCH)
I'LL MAKE YOU ONE OF THE CANDIDATES FOR MY FUTURE HUSBAND!

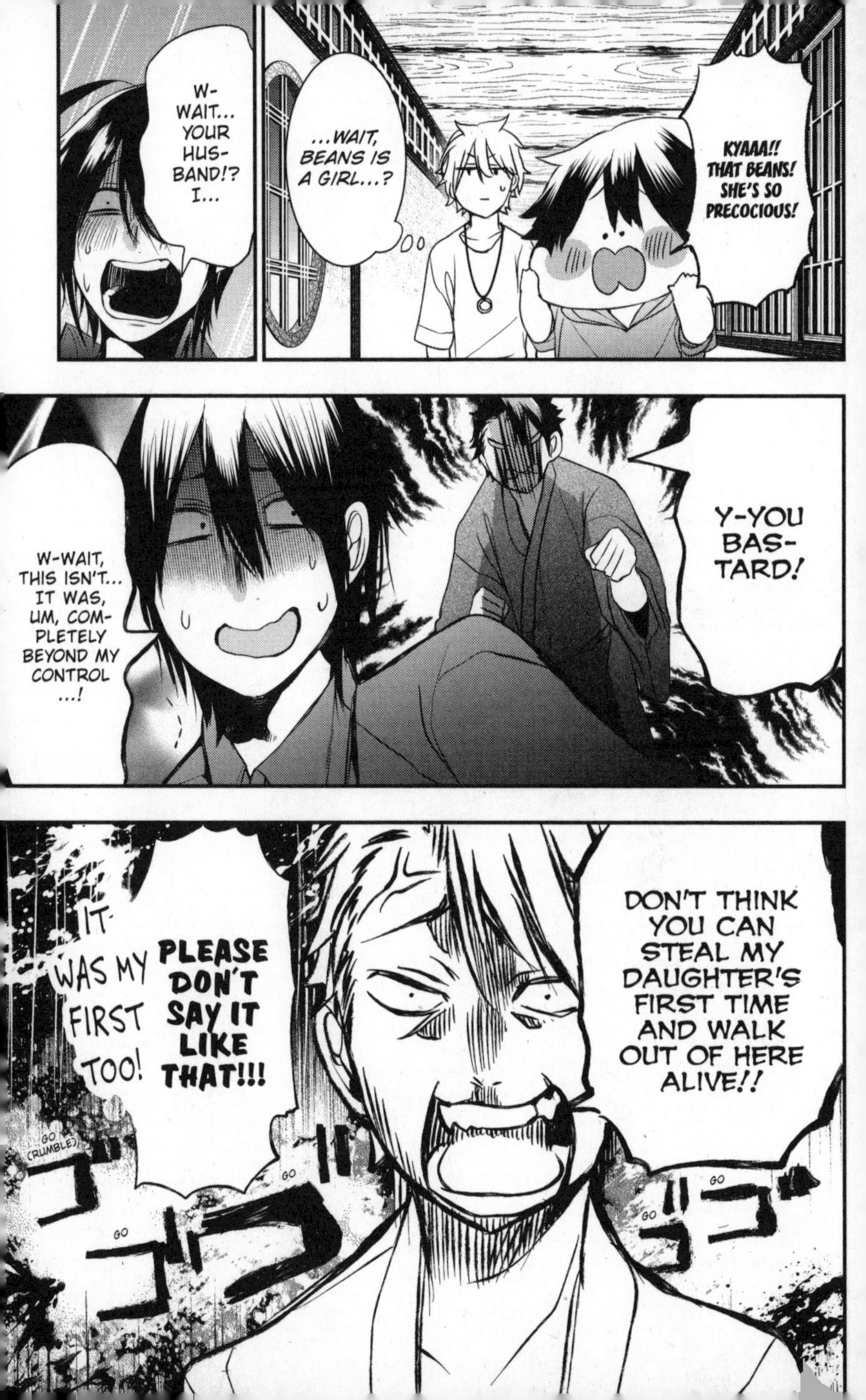
KYAAA!! THAT BEANS! SHE'S SO PRECOCIOUS!
...WAIT, BEANS IS A GIRL...?
W-WAIT... YOUR HUS-BAND!? I...
Y-YOU BAS-TARD!
W-WAIT, THIS ISN'T... IT WAS, UM, COM-PLETELY BEYOND MY CONTROL ...!
DON'T THINK YOU CAN STEAL MY DAUGHTER'S FIRST TIME AND WALK OUT OF HERE ALIVE!!
IT WAS MY FIRST TOO!
PLEASE DON'T SAY IT LIKE THAT!!!
GO
GO
GO
GO
GO (RUMBLE)

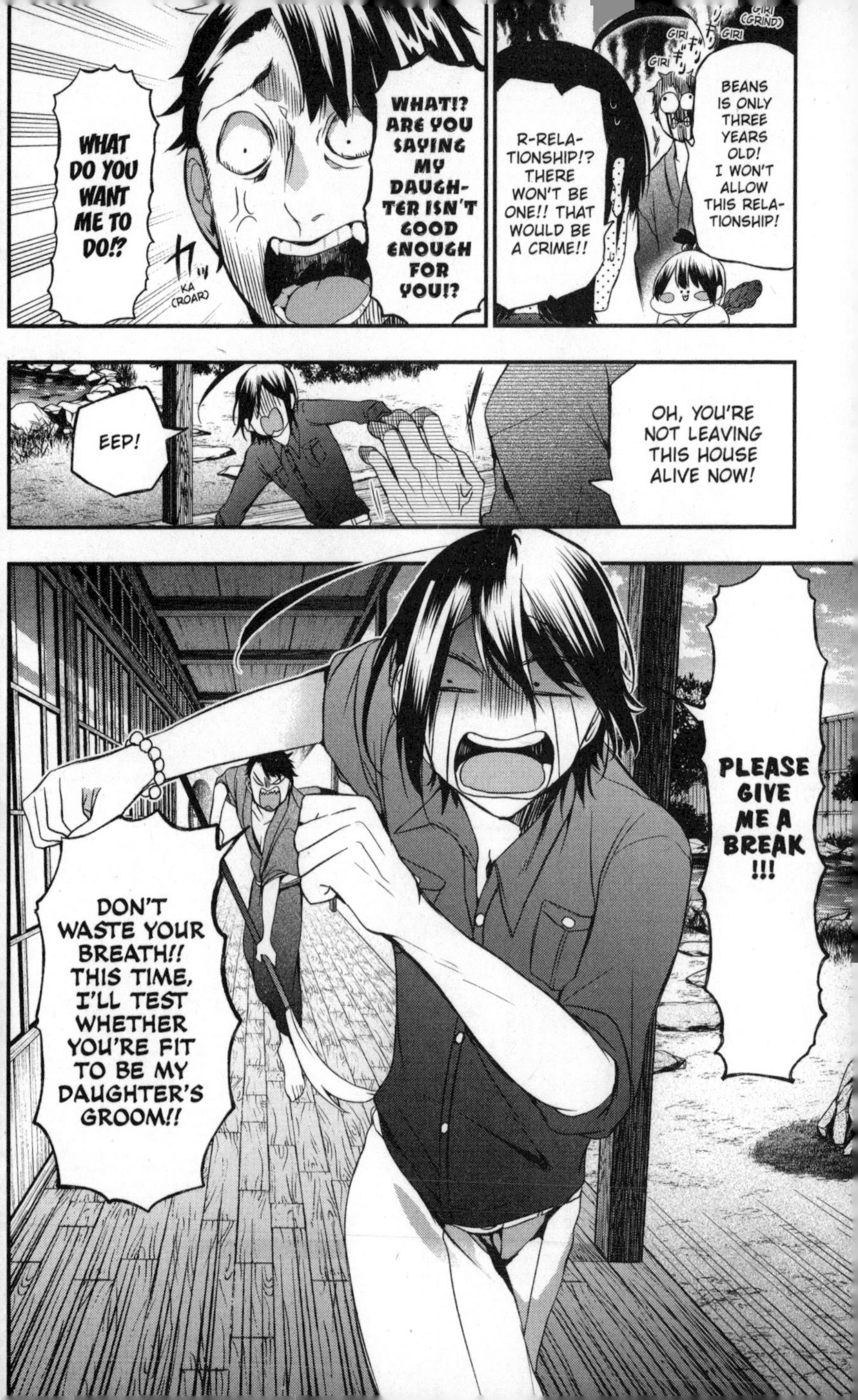
GIRI (GRIND)
GIRI
GIRI
GIRI
BEANS IS ONLY THREE YEARS OLD! I WON'T ALLOW THIS RELATIONSHIP!
R-RELATIONSHIP!? THERE WON'T BE ONE!! THAT WOULD BE A CRIME!!
WHAT!? ARE YOU SAYING MY DAUGHTER ISN'T GOOD ENOUGH FOR YOU!?
KA (ROAR)
WHAT DO YOU WANT ME TO DO!?
OH, YOU'RE NOT LEAVING THIS HOUSE ALIVE NOW!
EEP!
PLEASE GIVE ME A BREAK!!!
DON'T WASTE YOUR BREATH!! THIS TIME, I'LL TEST WHETHER YOU'RE FIT TO BE MY DAUGHTER'S GROOM!!

Thirty-Third Period Prying into Haruaki's Problem!

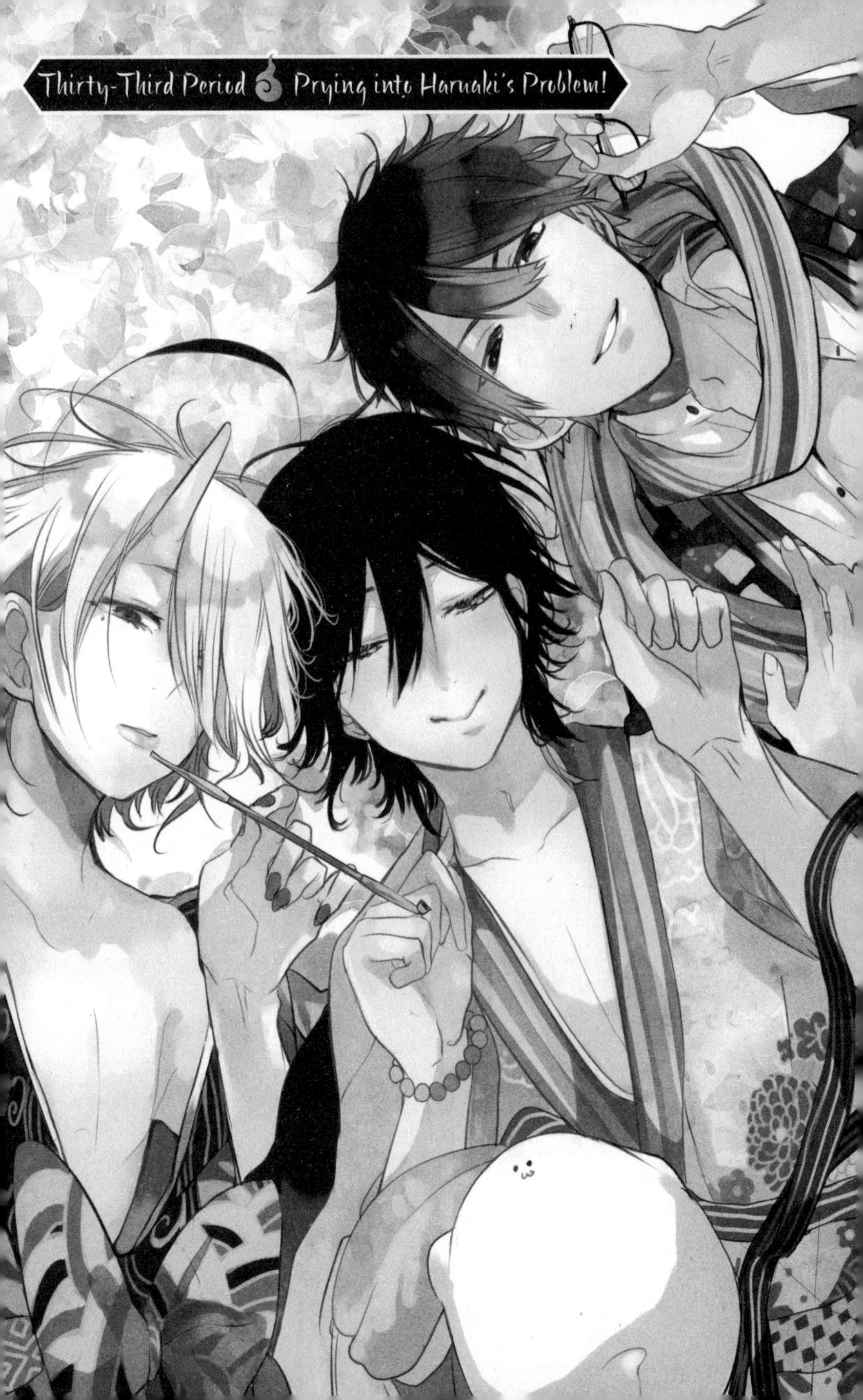

GHOUL SCHOOL TOP SECRET CHARACTER PROFILES

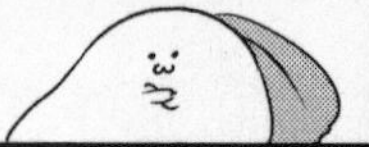

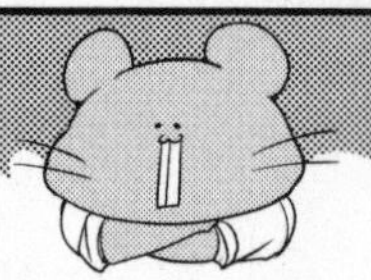

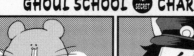

MOUSE-SENSEI
Birthday: ??
13 cm
Top Secret: As a Hyakki Academy teacher, he was homeroom teacher to the principal, followed by the two old-timers below.

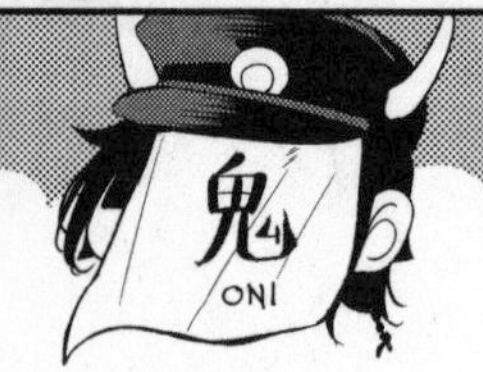
鬼
ONI

??? OGOSO
Birthday: June 10
172 cm
Top Secret: As of this point (through Ch. 33), thinks of Fuji as shallow and scary.

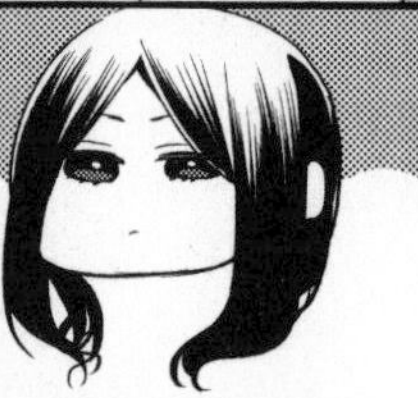

YURI RENJOU
Birthday: January 1
165 cm
Top Secret: Has a crush on someone in class...?

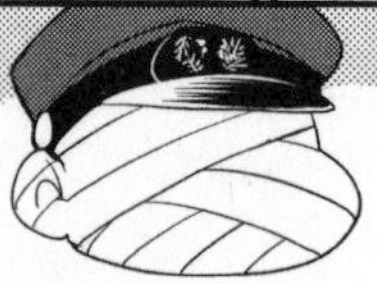

MAKOTO YAMAZAKI
Birthday: ??
176 cm
Top Secret: When he takes others' forms, he imitates not only how they look on the outside but how they are on the inside too—so if it's someone who's totally honest, he's exactly like them, but if they hide their real feelings, he seems like a different person.

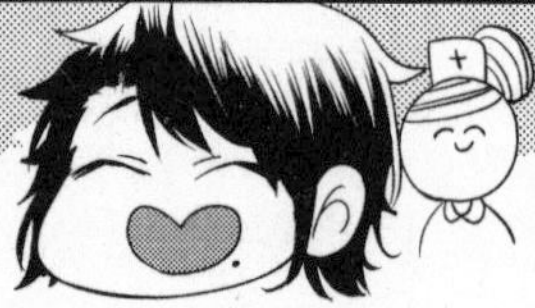

AKIRA TAKAHASHI
Birthday: ??
180 cm
Top Secret: The way he's always smiling is actually scary. According to the doctor, his nurses are his greatest creation.

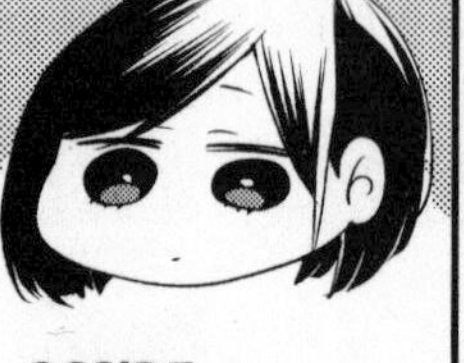

SCRIBE (TENMARU KARASUMA)
160 cm
Top Secret: Acts calm, but he's extremely into (2-D) women. Closet pervert.

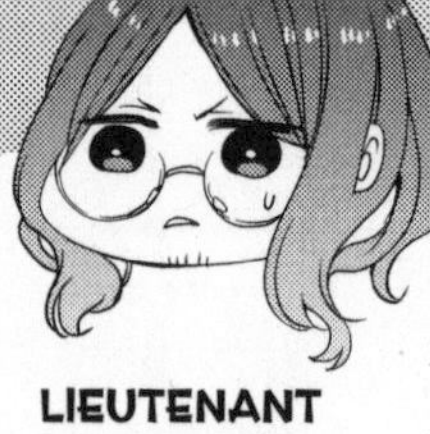

LIEUTENANT (BONMARU KARASUMA)
176 cm
Top Secret: Has a mother's nature—he's good at cooking and sewing.

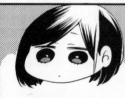

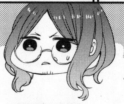

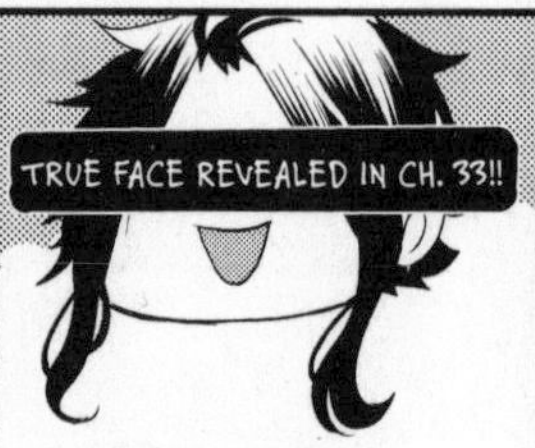
TRUE FACE REVEALED IN CH. 33!!

CAPTAIN (REAL NAME UNKNOWN)
178 cm
Top Secret: According to the principal: "He seems like he's empty-headed, when in actuality, his brain is always turning...is what he wants you to think, but the real truth is nothing's going on in there."

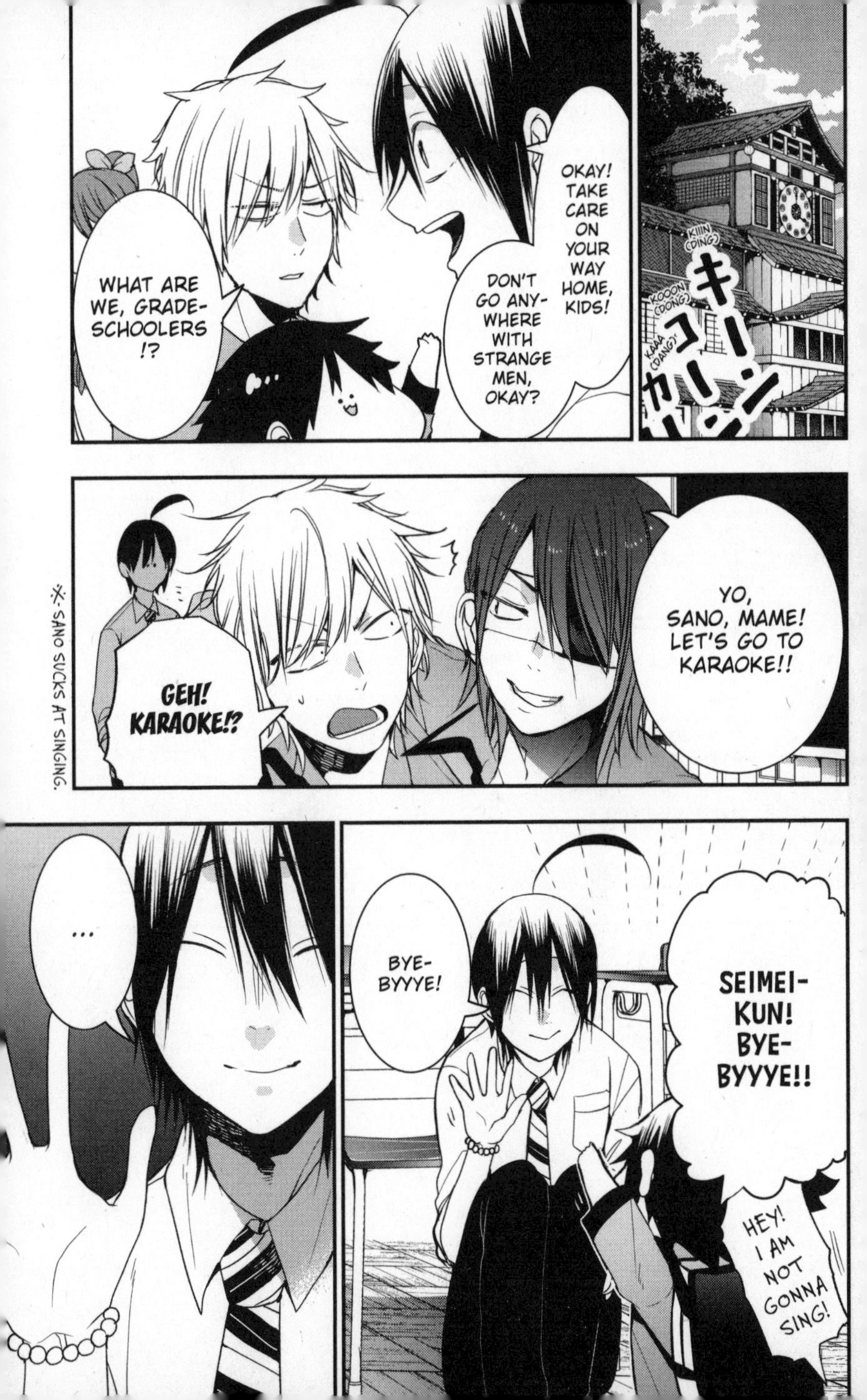
KIIN (DING)
KOOON (DONG)
KAAA (DANG)
OKAY! TAKE CARE ON YOUR WAY HOME, KIDS!
DON'T GO ANY-WHERE WITH STRANGE MEN, OKAY?
WHAT ARE WE, GRADE-SCHOOLERS!?
YO, SANO, MAME! LET'S GO TO KARAOKE!!
GEH! KARAOKE!?
※-SANO SUCKS AT SINGING.
SEIMEI-KUN! BYE-BYYYE!!
BYE-BYYYE!
HEY! I AM NOT GONNA SING!
...

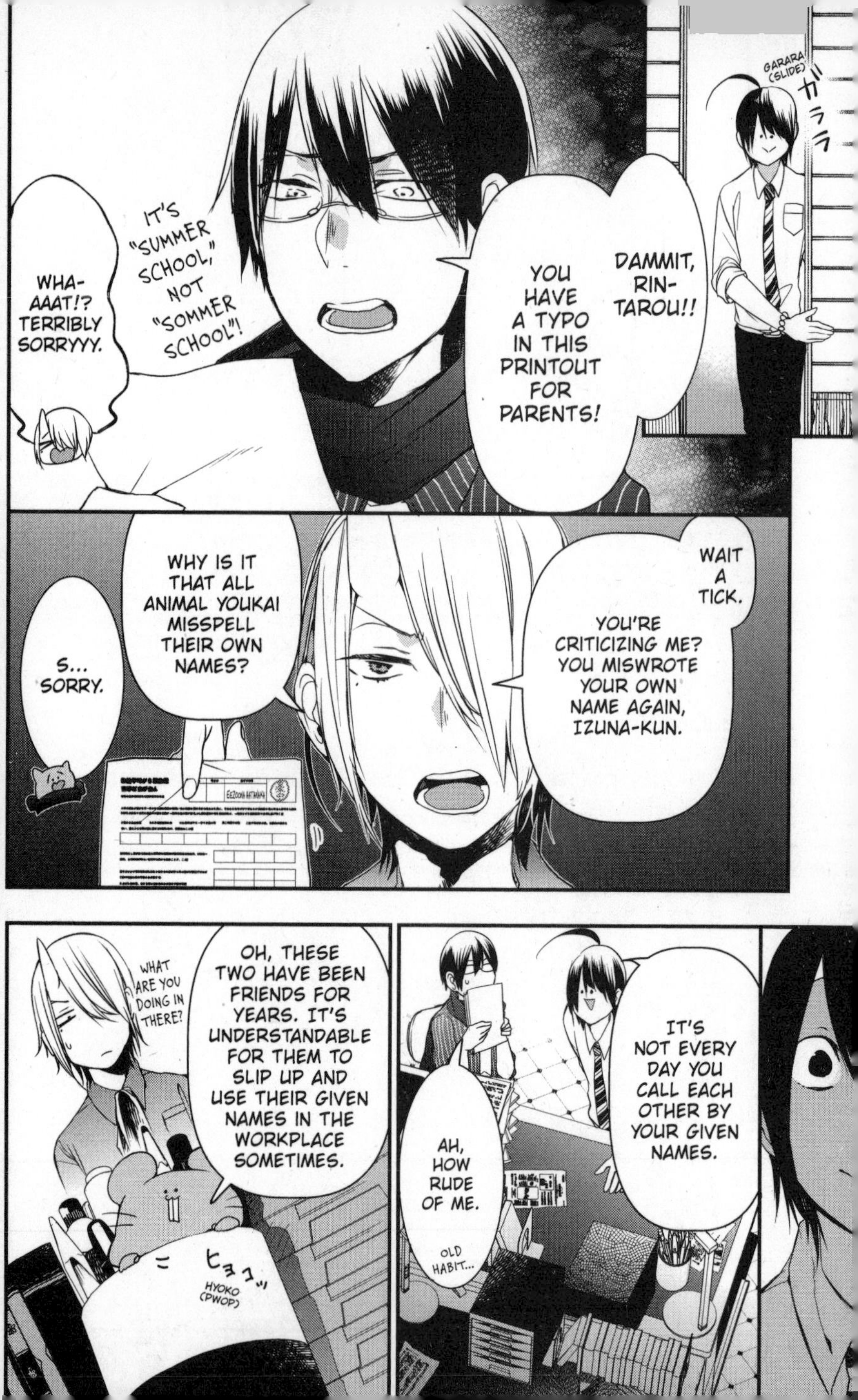
GARARA (SLIDE)
ガララ
DAMMIT, RIN-TAROU!!
YOU HAVE A TYPO IN THIS PRINTOUT FOR PARENTS!
IT'S "SUMMER SCHOOL," NOT "SOMMER SCHOOL"!
WHA-AAAT!? TERRIBLY SORRYYY.
WAIT A TICK.
YOU'RE CRITICIZING ME? YOU MISWROTE YOUR OWN NAME AGAIN, IZUNA-KUN.
WHY IS IT THAT ALL ANIMAL YOUKAI MISSPELL THEIR OWN NAMES?
S... SORRY.
IT'S NOT EVERY DAY YOU CALL EACH OTHER BY YOUR GIVEN NAMES.
AH, HOW RUDE OF ME.
OLD HABIT...
OH, THESE TWO HAVE BEEN FRIENDS FOR YEARS. IT'S UNDERSTANDABLE FOR THEM TO SLIP UP AND USE THEIR GIVEN NAMES IN THE WORKPLACE SOMETIMES.
WHAT ARE YOU DOING IN THERE?
ヒョコッ
HYOKO (PWOP)

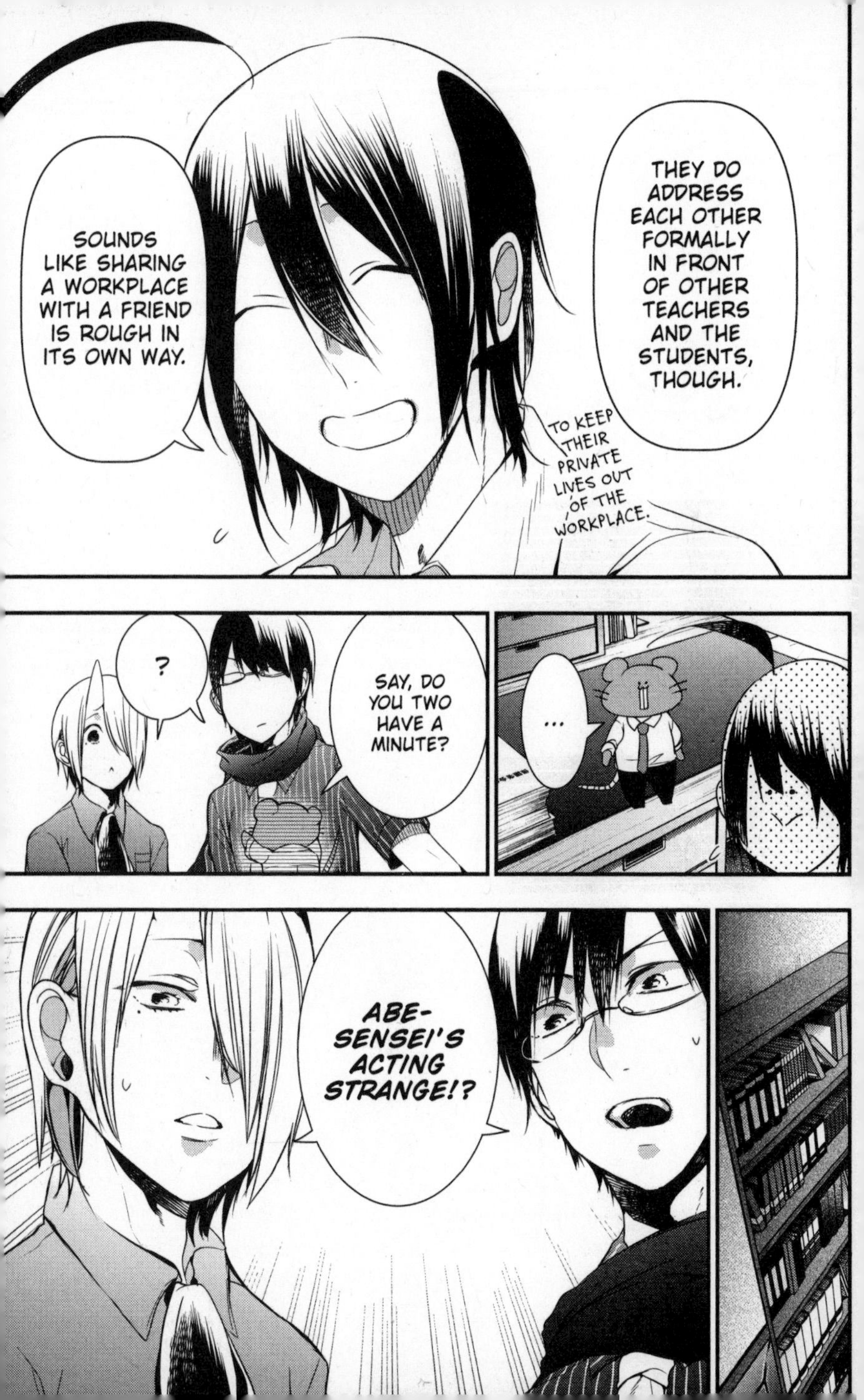
THEY DO ADDRESS EACH OTHER FORMALLY IN FRONT OF OTHER TEACHERS AND THE STUDENTS, THOUGH.
TO KEEP THEIR PRIVATE LIVES OUT OF THE WORKPLACE.
SOUNDS LIKE SHARING A WORKPLACE WITH A FRIEND IS ROUGH IN ITS OWN WAY.
...
SAY, DO YOU TWO HAVE A MINUTE?
?
ABE-SENSEI'S ACTING STRANGE!?

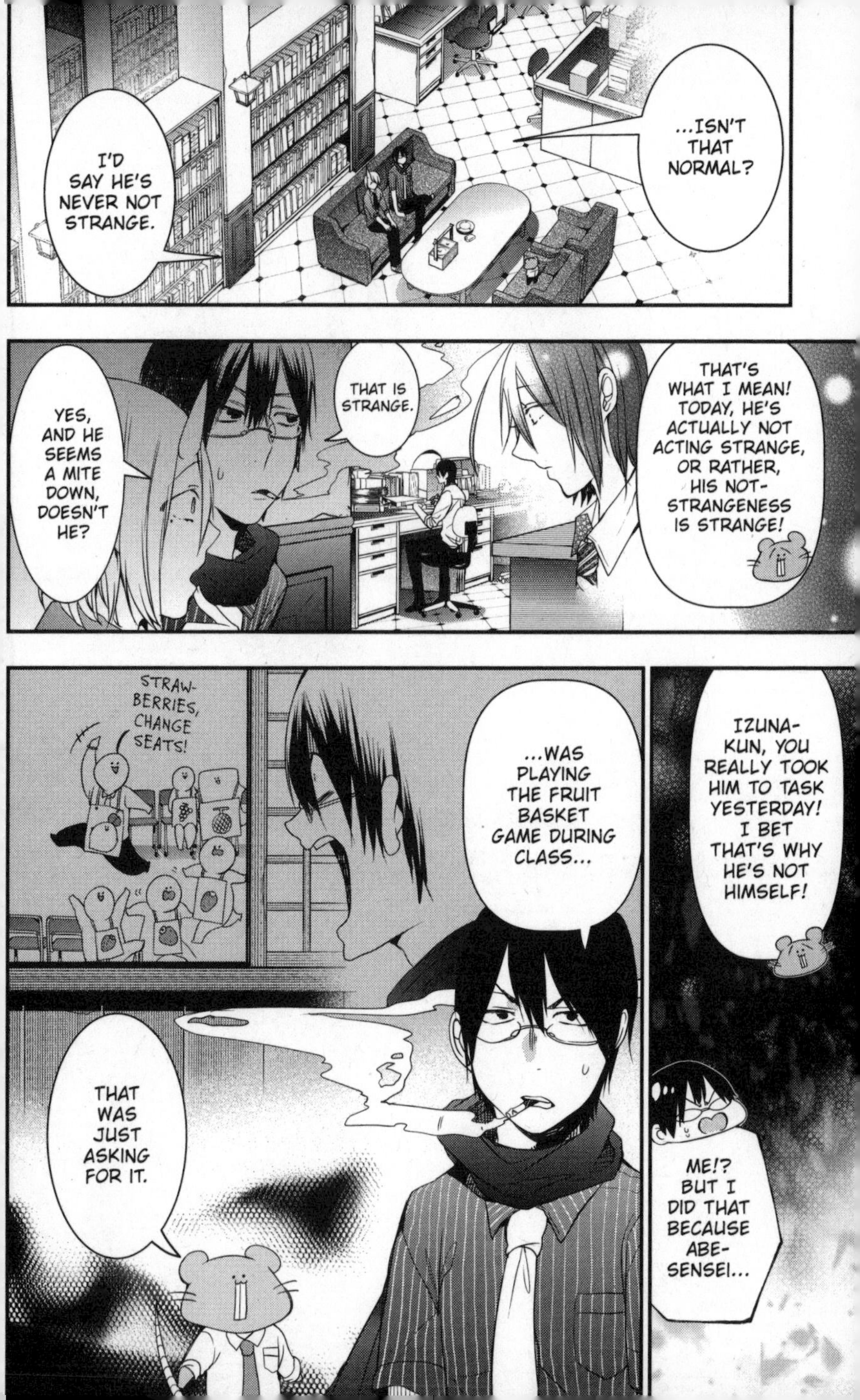
...ISN'T THAT NORMAL?
I'D SAY HE'S NEVER NOT STRANGE.
THAT'S WHAT I MEAN! TODAY, HE'S ACTUALLY NOT ACTING STRANGE, OR RATHER, HIS NOT-STRANGENESS IS STRANGE!
THAT IS STRANGE.
YES, AND HE SEEMS A MITE DOWN, DOESN'T HE?
IZUNA-KUN, YOU REALLY TOOK HIM TO TASK YESTERDAY! I BET THAT'S WHY HE'S NOT HIMSELF!
ME!? BUT I DID THAT BECAUSE ABE-SENSEI...
...WAS PLAYING THE FRUIT BASKET GAME DURING CLASS...
STRAWBERRIES, CHANGE SEATS!
THAT WAS JUST ASKING FOR IT.

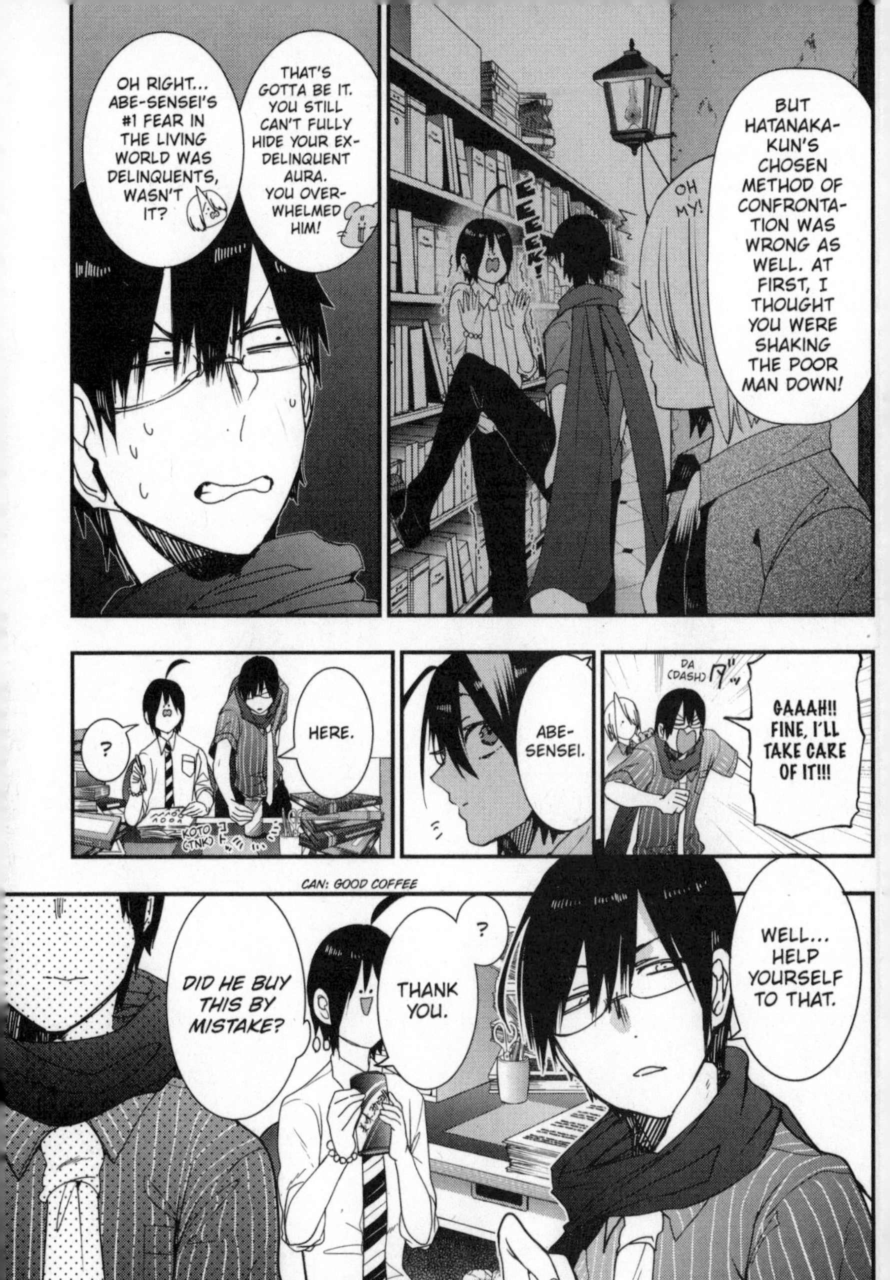
BUT HATANAKA-KUN'S CHOSEN METHOD OF CONFRONTATION WAS WRONG AS WELL. AT FIRST, I THOUGHT YOU WERE SHAKING THE POOR MAN DOWN!
OH MY!
EEEEK!
THAT'S GOTTA BE IT. YOU STILL CAN'T FULLY HIDE YOUR EX-DELINQUENT AURA. YOU OVER-WHELMED HIM!
OH RIGHT... ABE-SENSEI'S #1 FEAR IN THE LIVING WORLD WAS DELINQUENTS, WASN'T IT?
DA (DASH)
GAAAH!! FINE, I'LL TAKE CARE OF IT!!!
ABE-SENSEI.
HERE.
?
KOTO (TNK)
CAN: GOOD COFFEE
WELL... HELP YOURSELF TO THAT.
?
THANK YOU.
DID HE BUY THIS BY MISTAKE?

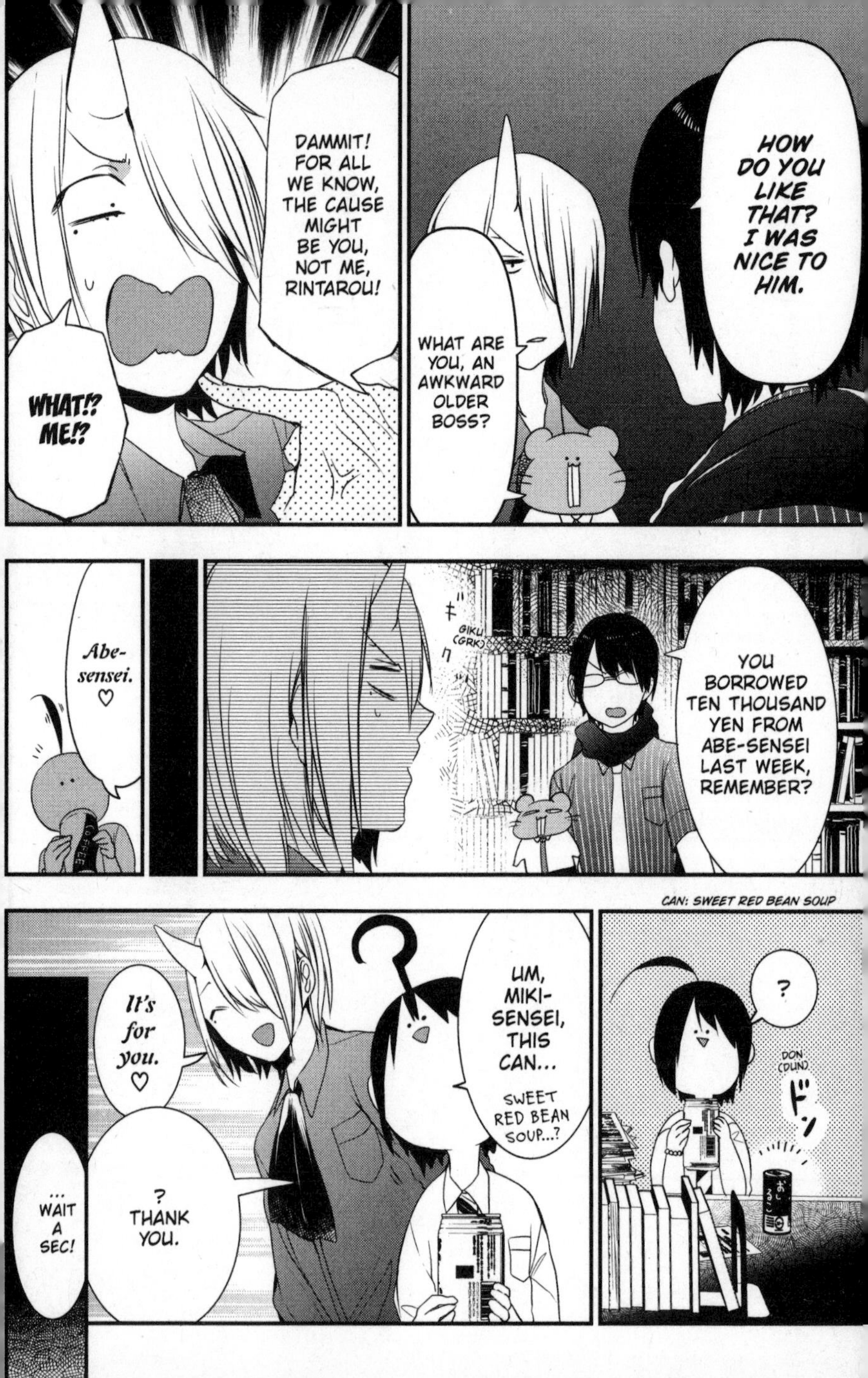
HOW DO YOU LIKE THAT? I WAS NICE TO HIM.
WHAT ARE YOU, AN AWKWARD OLDER BOSS?
DAMMIT! FOR ALL WE KNOW, THE CAUSE MIGHT BE YOU, NOT ME, RINTAROU!
WHAT!? ME!?
YOU BORROWED TEN THOUSAND YEN FROM ABE-SENSEI LAST WEEK, REMEMBER?
GIKU (GRK)
Abe-sensei. ♡
COFFEE
CAN: SWEET RED BEAN SOUP
?
DON (DUN)
UM, MIKI-SENSEI, THIS CAN...
SWEET RED BEAN SOUP...?
It's for you. ♡
? THANK YOU.
... WAIT A SEC!

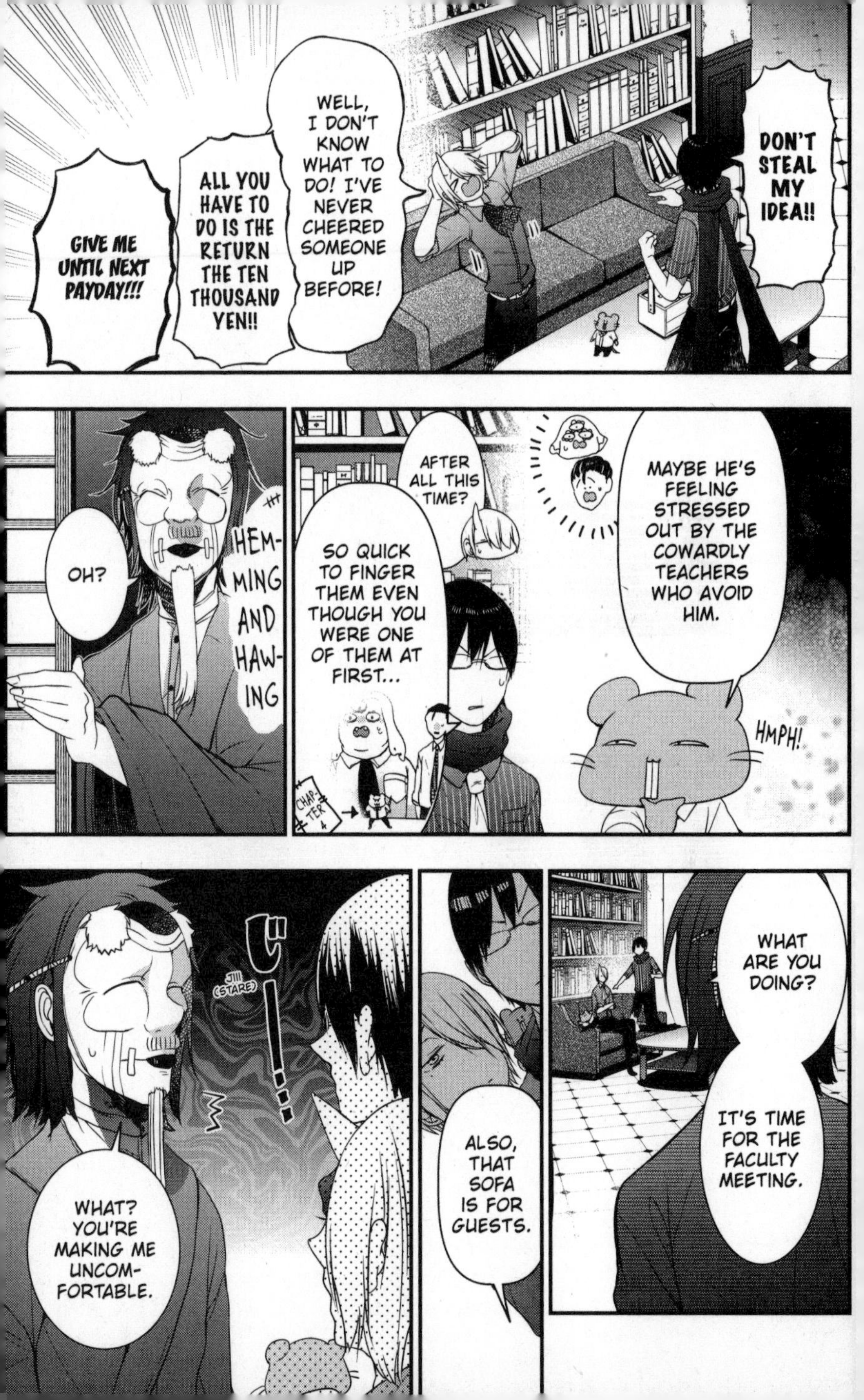
DON'T STEAL MY IDEA!!
WELL, I DON'T KNOW WHAT TO DO! I'VE NEVER CHEERED SOMEONE UP BEFORE!
ALL YOU HAVE TO DO IS THE RETURN THE TEN THOUSAND YEN!!
GIVE ME UNTIL NEXT PAYDAY!!!
MAYBE HE'S FEELING STRESSED OUT BY THE COWARDLY TEACHERS WHO AVOID HIM.
HMPH!
AFTER ALL THIS TIME?
SO QUICK TO FINGER THEM EVEN THOUGH YOU WERE ONE OF THEM AT FIRST...
CHAPTER 4
OH?
HEM-MING AND HAW-ING
WHAT ARE YOU DOING?
IT'S TIME FOR THE FACULTY MEETING.
ALSO, THAT SOFA IS FOR GUESTS.
JIII (STARE)
WHAT? YOU'RE MAKING ME UNCOM-FORTABLE.

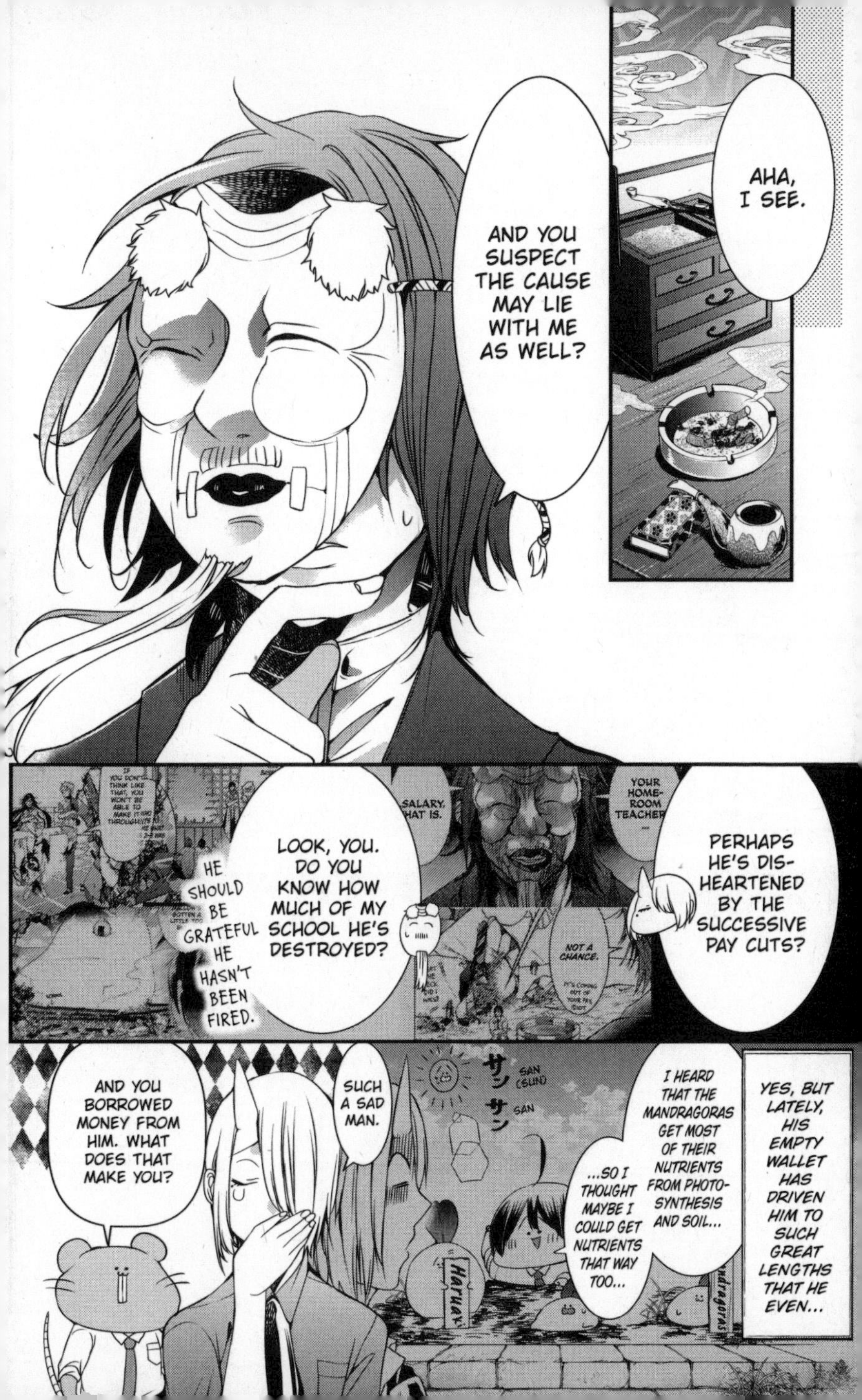
AHA, I SEE.
AND YOU SUSPECT THE CAUSE MAY LIE WITH ME AS WELL?
PERHAPS HE'S DIS-HEARTENED BY THE SUCCESSIVE PAY CUTS?
YOUR HOME-ROOM TEACHER...
SALARY, THAT IS.
NOT A CHANCE.
LOOK, YOU. DO YOU KNOW HOW MUCH OF MY SCHOOL HE'S DESTROYED?
HE SHOULD BE GRATEFUL HE HASN'T BEEN FIRED.
YES, BUT LATELY, HIS EMPTY WALLET HAS DRIVEN HIM TO SUCH GREAT LENGTHS THAT HE EVEN...
I HEARD THAT THE MANDRAGORAS GET MOST OF THEIR NUTRIENTS FROM PHOTO-SYNTHESIS AND SOIL...
...SO I THOUGHT MAYBE I COULD GET NUTRIENTS THAT WAY TOO...
サン SAN (SUN)
サン SAN
SUCH A SAD MAN.
AND YOU BORROWED MONEY FROM HIM. WHAT DOES THAT MAKE YOU?

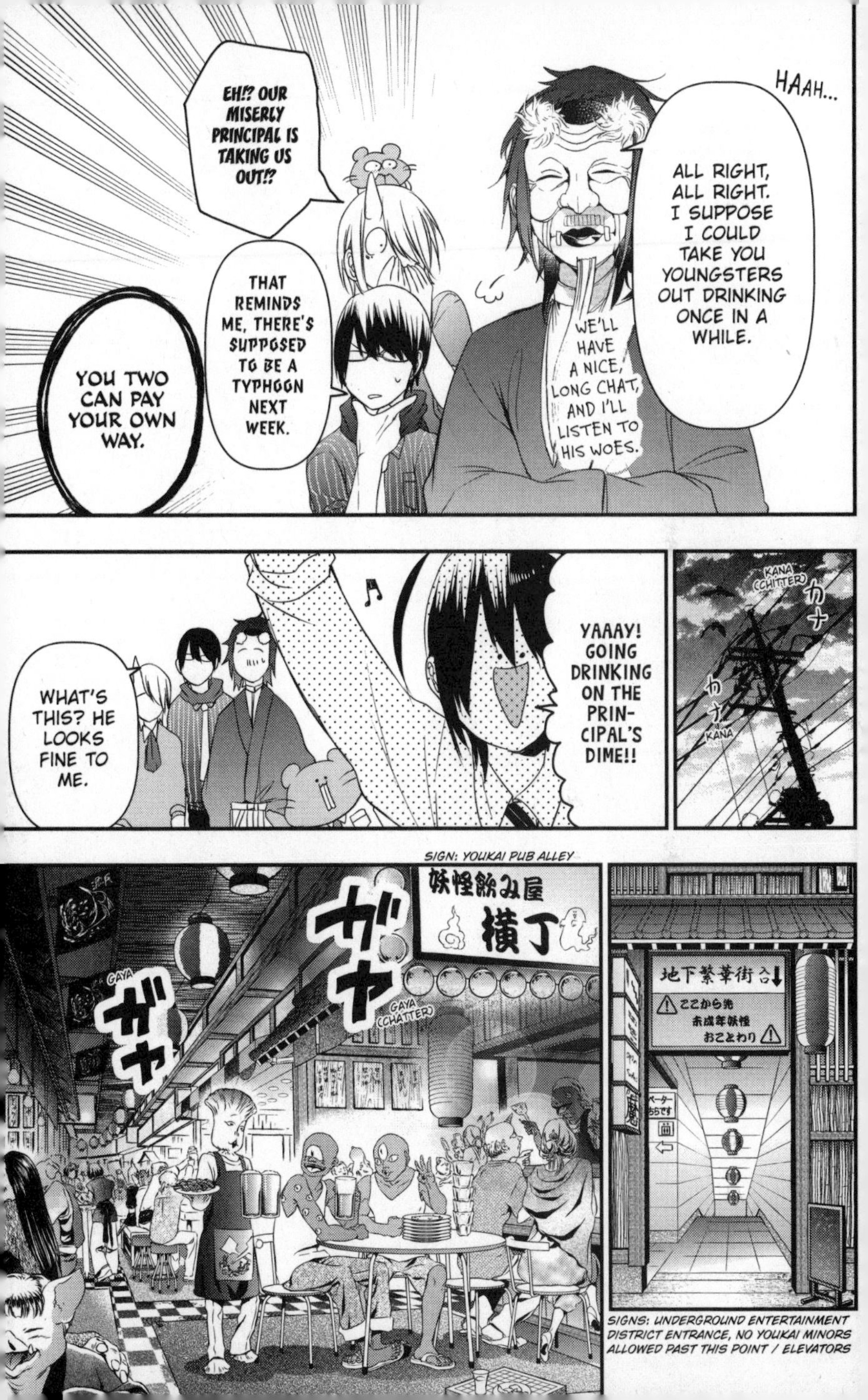
HAAH...
ALL RIGHT, ALL RIGHT. I SUPPOSE I COULD TAKE YOU YOUNGSTERS OUT DRINKING ONCE IN A WHILE.
WE'LL HAVE A NICE, LONG CHAT, AND I'LL LISTEN TO HIS WOES.
EH!? OUR MISERLY PRINCIPAL IS TAKING US OUT!?
THAT REMINDS ME, THERE'S SUPPOSED TO BE A TYPHOON NEXT WEEK.
YOU TWO CAN PAY YOUR OWN WAY.
KANA (CHATTER) カナ
カナ KANA
YAAAY! GOING DRINKING ON THE PRIN-CIPAL'S DIME!!
WHAT'S THIS? HE LOOKS FINE TO ME.
SIGNS: UNDERGROUND ENTERTAINMENT DISTRICT ENTRANCE, NO YOUKAI MINORS ALLOWED PAST THIS POINT / ELEVATORS
SIGN: YOUKAI PUB ALLEY
妖怪飲み屋 横丁
ガヤ GAYA (CHATTER)
GAYA ガヤ

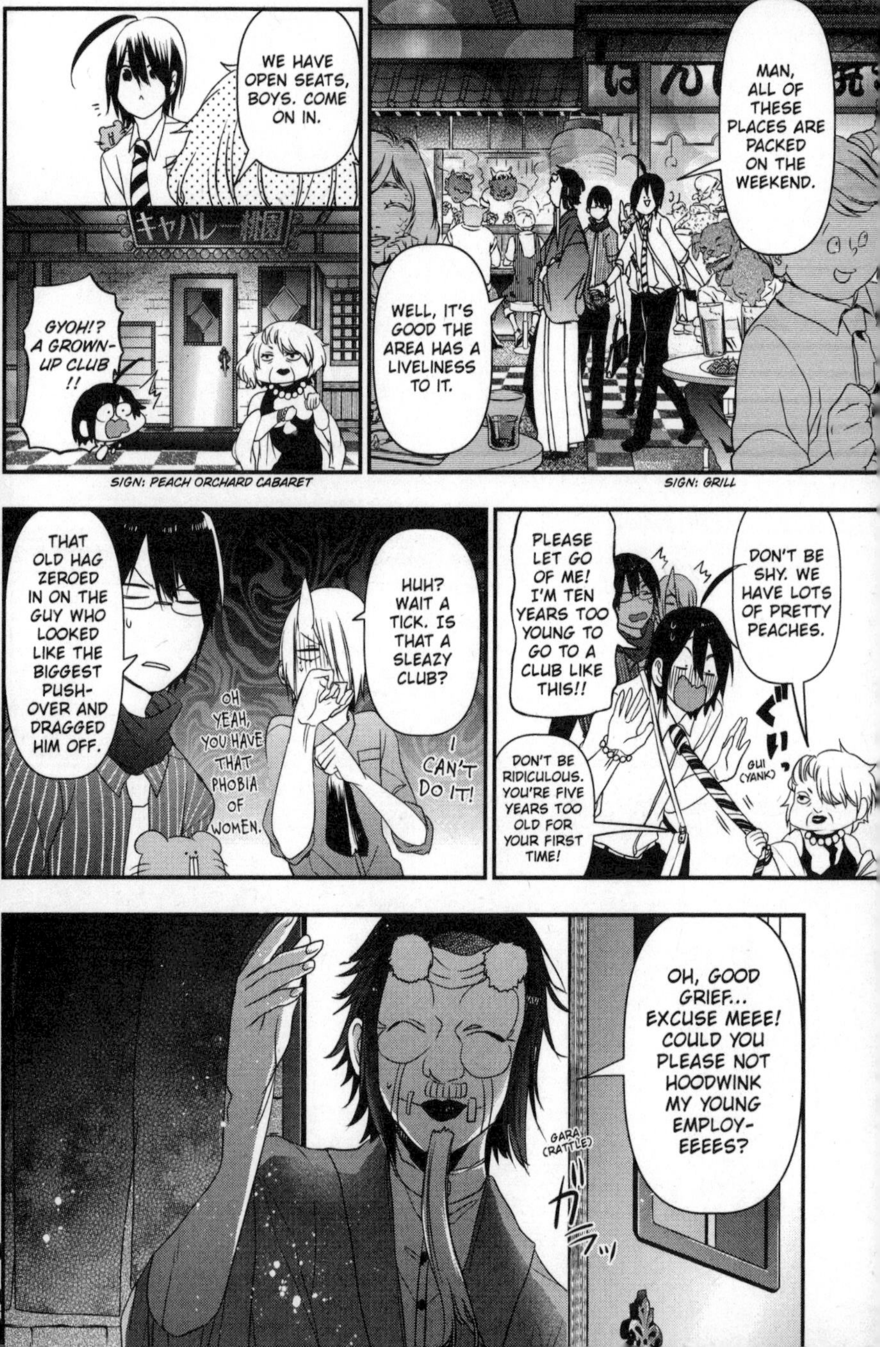
MAN, ALL OF THESE PLACES ARE PACKED ON THE WEEKEND.
WELL, IT'S GOOD THE AREA HAS A LIVELINESS TO IT.
SIGN: GRILL
WE HAVE OPEN SEATS, BOYS. COME ON IN.
GYOH!? A GROWN-UP CLUB!!
SIGN: PEACH ORCHARD CABARET
DON'T BE SHY. WE HAVE LOTS OF PRETTY PEACHES.
PLEASE LET GO OF ME! I'M TEN YEARS TOO YOUNG TO GO TO A CLUB LIKE THIS!!
DON'T BE RIDICULOUS. YOU'RE FIVE YEARS TOO OLD FOR YOUR FIRST TIME!
GUI (YANK)
HUH? WAIT A TICK. IS THAT A SLEAZY CLUB?
I CAN'T DO IT!
THAT OLD HAG ZEROED IN ON THE GUY WHO LOOKED LIKE THE BIGGEST PUSH-OVER AND DRAGGED HIM OFF.
OH YEAH, YOU HAVE THAT PHOBIA OF WOMEN.
OH, GOOD GRIEF... EXCUSE MEEE! COULD YOU PLEASE NOT HOODWINK MY YOUNG EMPLOY-EEEES?
GARA (RATTLE)

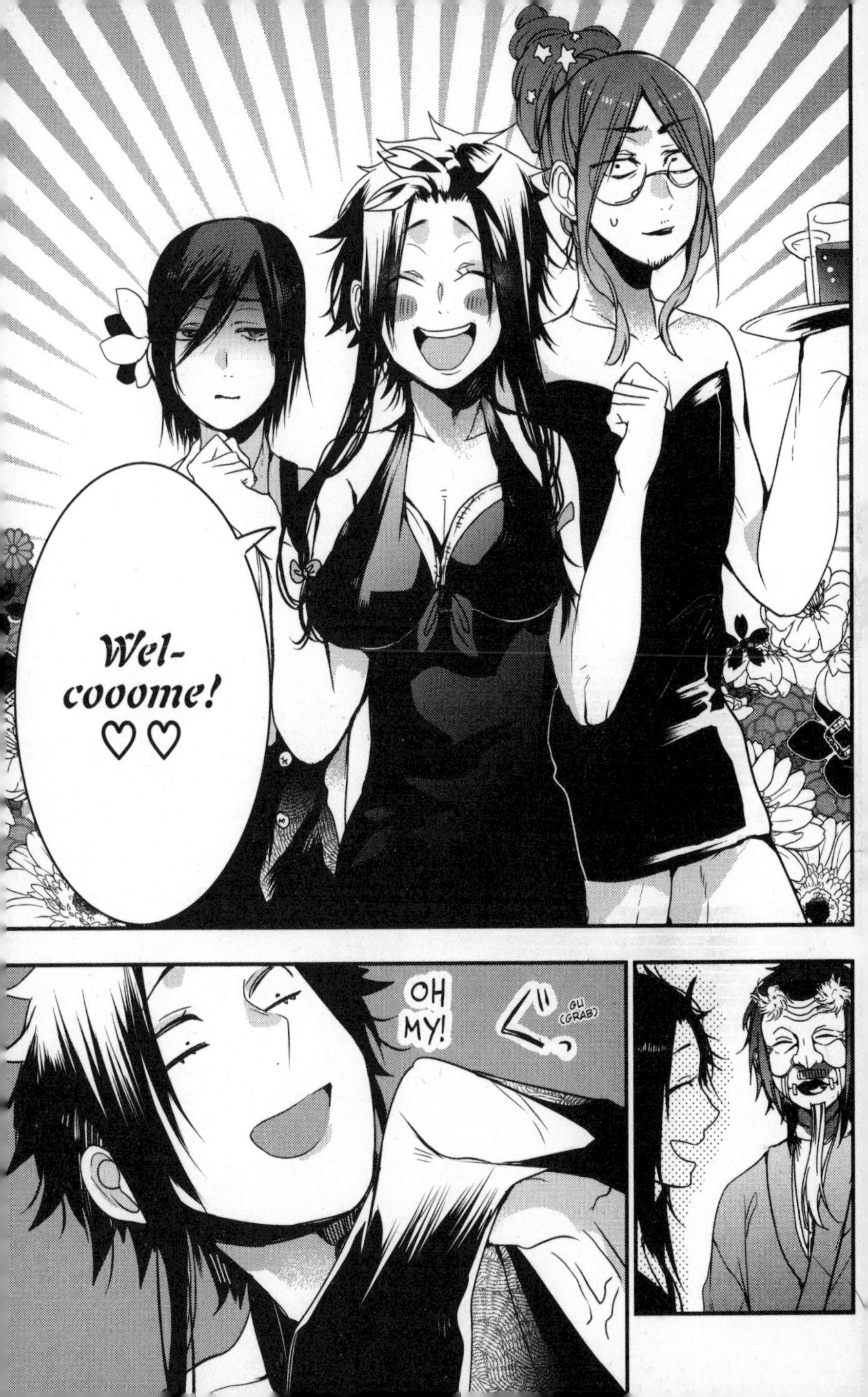
Wel-cooome! ♡ ♡
GU (GRAB)
OH MY!

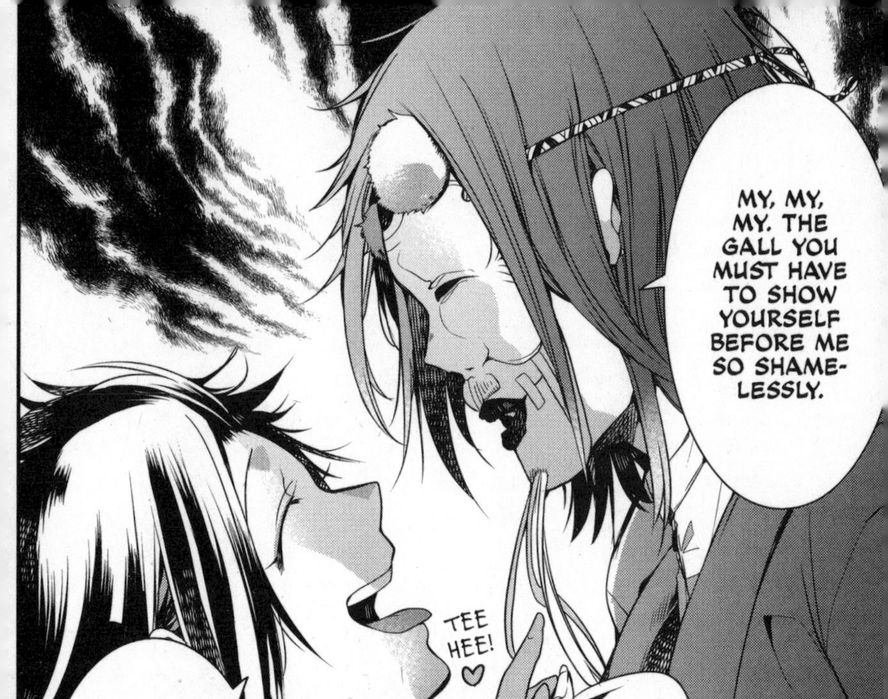
MY, MY, MY. THE GALL YOU MUST HAVE TO SHOW YOURSELF BEFORE ME SO SHAMELESSLY.
TEE HEE! ♡
Oh gosh. Aren't we friends, Acchan? ♡

TAG: BREAST PADDING

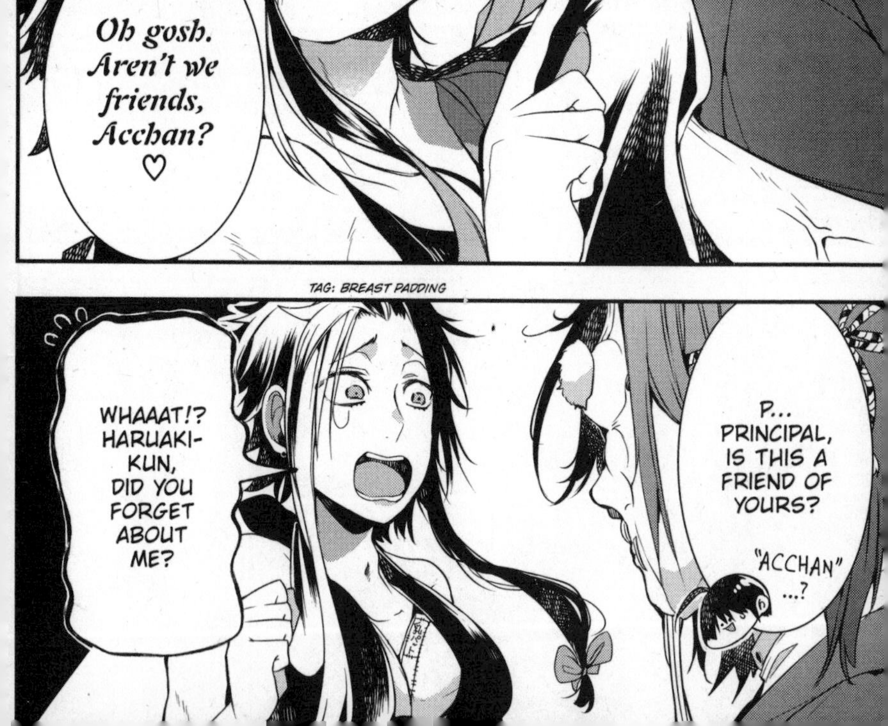
P... PRINCIPAL, IS THIS A FRIEND OF YOURS?
"ACCHAN" ...?
WHAAAT!? HARUAKI-KUN, DID YOU FORGET ABOUT ME?

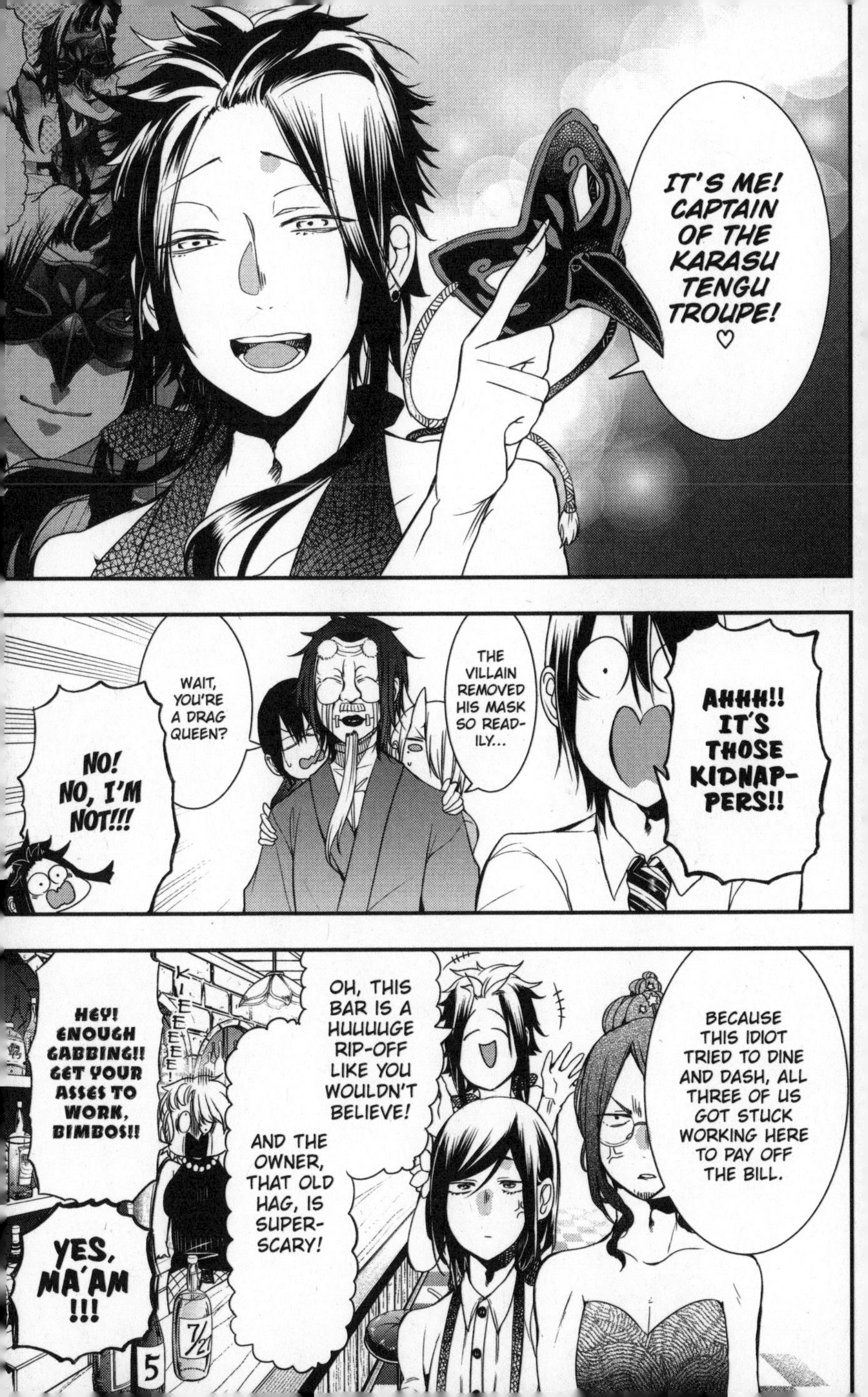
IT'S ME! CAPTAIN OF THE KARASU TENGU TROUPE! ♡
AHHH!! IT'S THOSE KIDNAPPERS!!
THE VILLAIN REMOVED HIS MASK SO READILY...
WAIT, YOU'RE A DRAG QUEEN?
NO! NO, I'M NOT!!!
BECAUSE THIS IDIOT TRIED TO DINE AND DASH, ALL THREE OF US GOT STUCK WORKING HERE TO PAY OFF THE BILL.
OH, THIS BAR IS A HUUUUGE RIP-OFF LIKE YOU WOULDN'T BELIEVE!
AND THE OWNER, THAT OLD HAG, IS SUPER-SCARY!
KIEEEEE!
HEY! ENOUGH GABBING!! GET YOUR ASSES TO WORK, BIMBOS!!
YES, MA'AM!!!

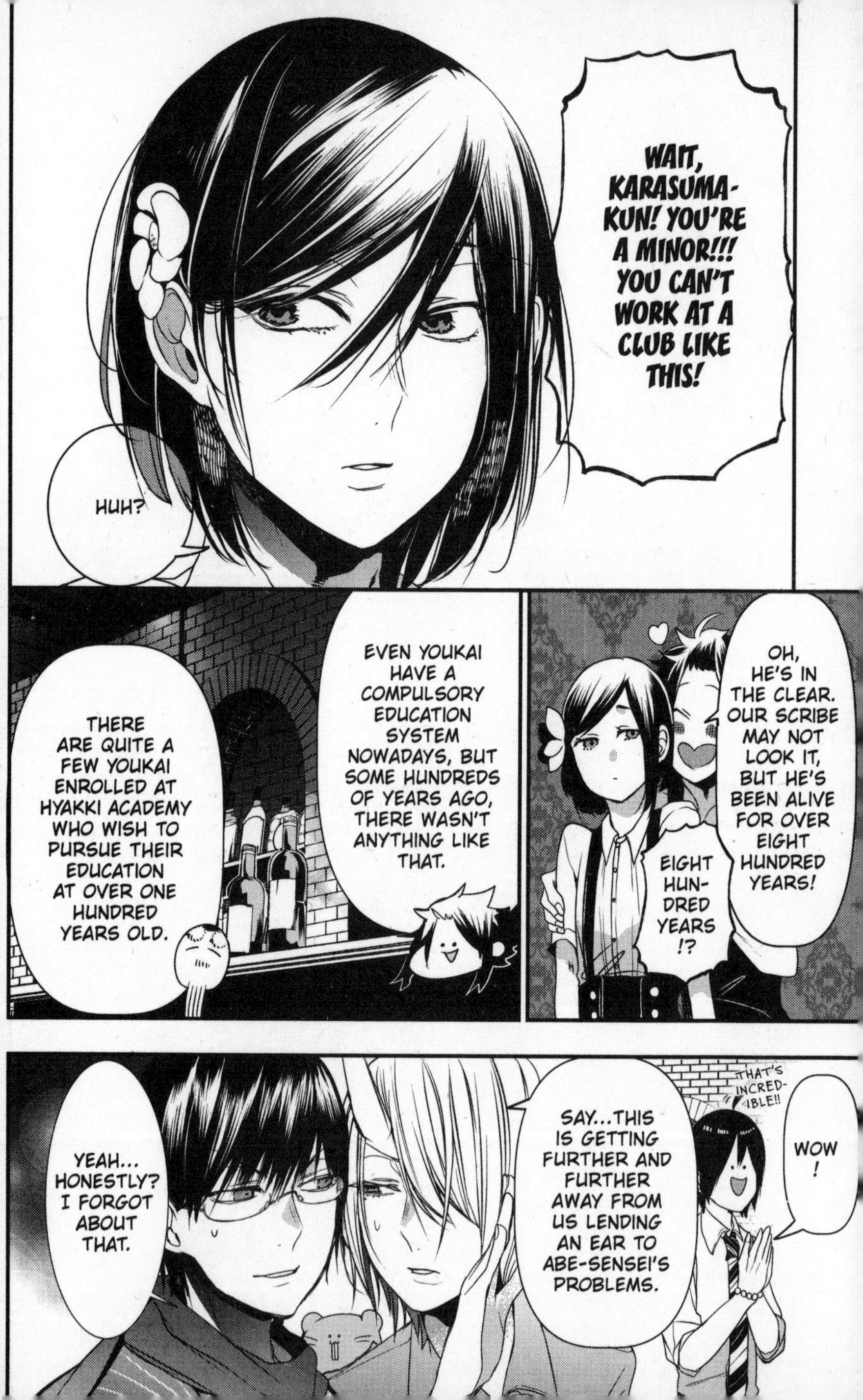
WAIT, KARASUMA-KUN! YOU'RE A MINOR!!! YOU CAN'T WORK AT A CLUB LIKE THIS!
HUH?
OH, HE'S IN THE CLEAR. OUR SCRIBE MAY NOT LOOK IT, BUT HE'S BEEN ALIVE FOR OVER EIGHT HUNDRED YEARS!
EIGHT HUN-DRED YEARS !?
EVEN YOUKAI HAVE A COMPULSORY EDUCATION SYSTEM NOWADAYS, BUT SOME HUNDREDS OF YEARS AGO, THERE WASN'T ANYTHING LIKE THAT.
THERE ARE QUITE A FEW YOUKAI ENROLLED AT HYAKKI ACADEMY WHO WISH TO PURSUE THEIR EDUCATION AT OVER ONE HUNDRED YEARS OLD.
THAT'S INCRED-IBLE!!
WOW!
SAY...THIS IS GETTING FURTHER AND FURTHER AWAY FROM US LENDING AN EAR TO ABE-SENSEI'S PROBLEMS.
YEAH... HONESTLY? I FORGOT ABOUT THAT.

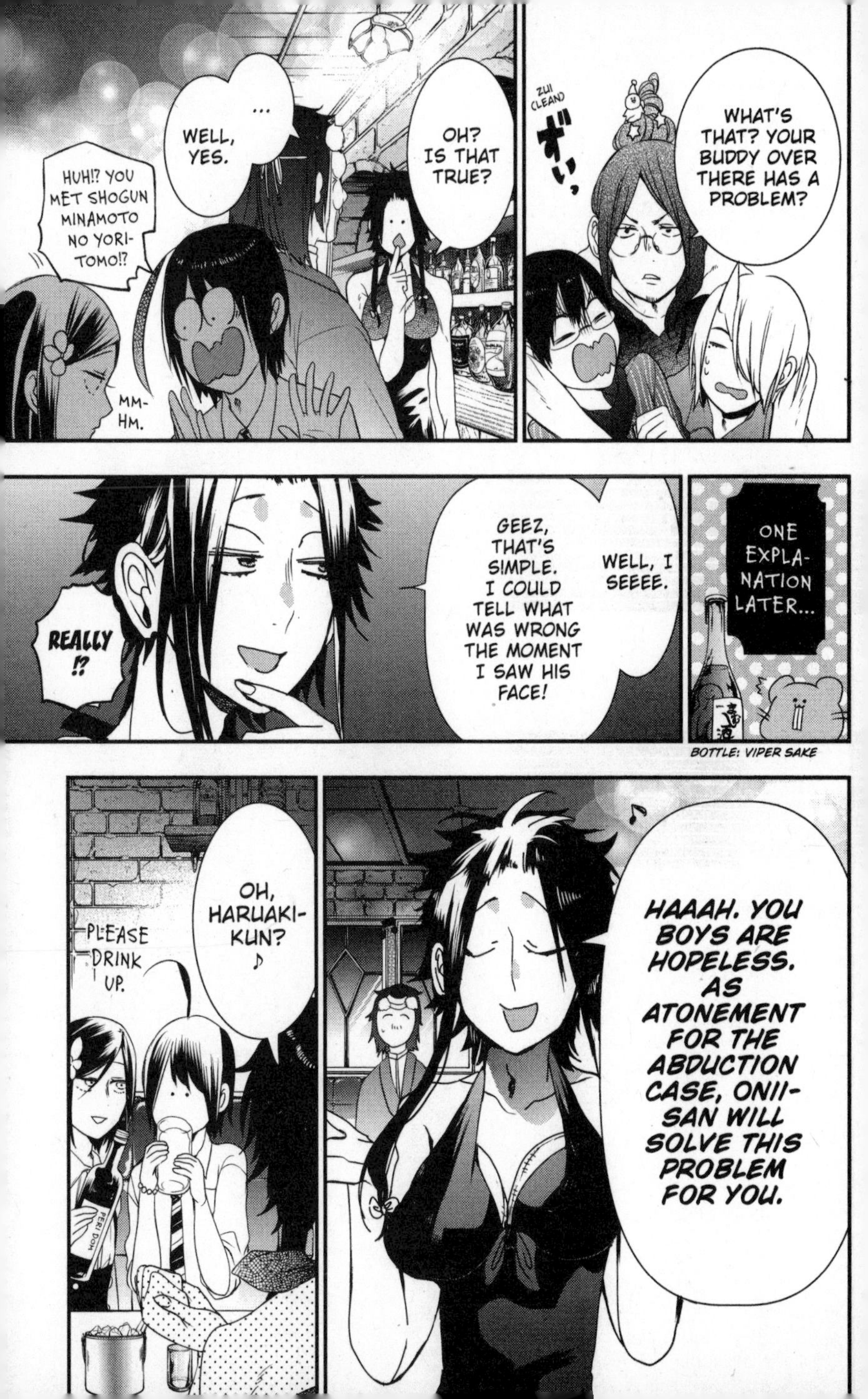
ZUI (LEAN)
WHAT'S THAT? YOUR BUDDY OVER THERE HAS A PROBLEM?
OH? IS THAT TRUE?
... WELL, YES.
HUH!? YOU MET SHOGUN MINAMOTO NO YORI-TOMO!?
MM-HM.
ONE EXPLANATION LATER...
WELL, I SEEEE.
GEEZ, THAT'S SIMPLE. I COULD TELL WHAT WAS WRONG THE MOMENT I SAW HIS FACE!
REALLY!?
BOTTLE: VIPER SAKE
HAAAH. YOU BOYS ARE HOPELESS. AS ATONEMENT FOR THE ABDUCTION CASE, ONII-SAN WILL SOLVE THIS PROBLEM FOR YOU.
OH, HARUAKI-KUN? ♪
PLEASE DRINK UP.
PERI DOM

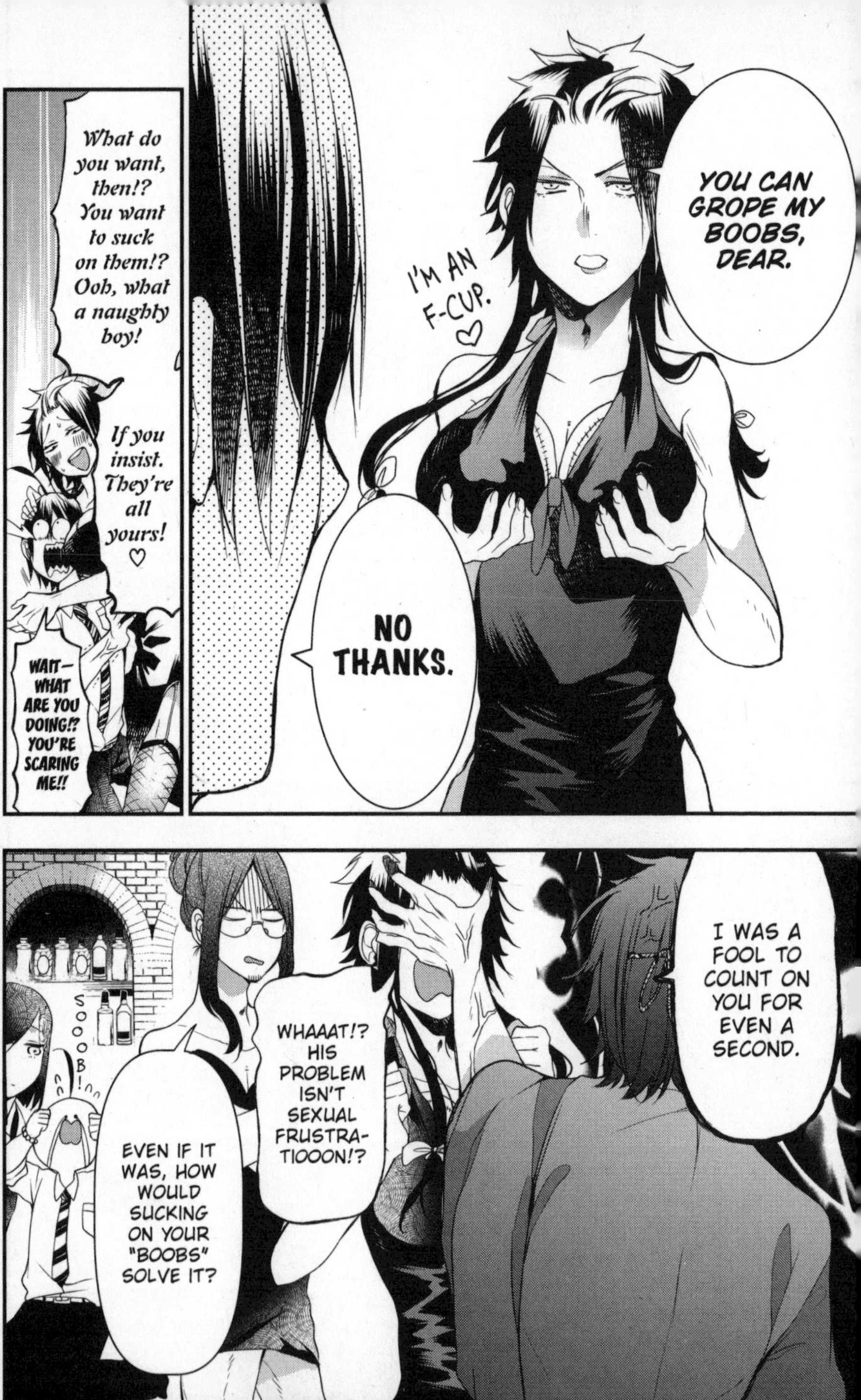
YOU CAN GROPE MY BOOBS, DEAR.
I'M AN F-CUP. ♡
NO THANKS.
What do you want, then!? You want to suck on them!? Ooh, what a naughty boy!
If you insist. They're all yours! ♡
WAIT— WHAT ARE YOU DOING!? YOU'RE SCARING ME!!
I WAS A FOOL TO COUNT ON YOU FOR EVEN A SECOND.
WHAAAT!? HIS PROBLEM ISN'T SEXUAL FRUSTRA-TIOOON!?
EVEN IF IT WAS, HOW WOULD SUCKING ON YOUR "BOOBS" SOLVE IT?
SOOOOB!

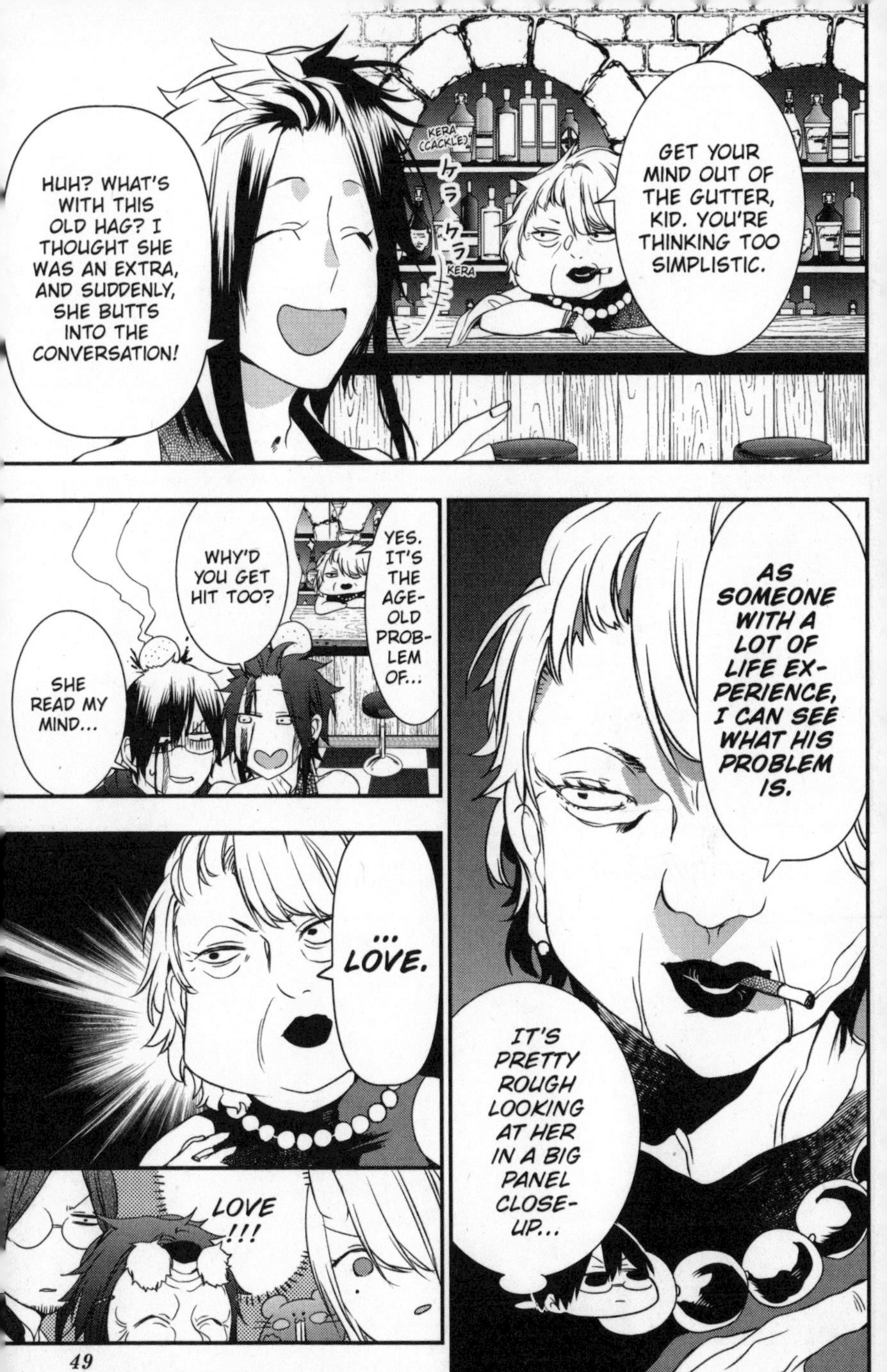
GET YOUR MIND OUT OF THE GUTTER, KID. YOU'RE THINKING TOO SIMPLISTIC.
KERA (CACKLE)
ケラケラ
KERA
HUH? WHAT'S WITH THIS OLD HAG? I THOUGHT SHE WAS AN EXTRA, AND SUDDENLY, SHE BUTTS INTO THE CONVERSATION!
AS SOMEONE WITH A LOT OF LIFE EXPERIENCE, I CAN SEE WHAT HIS PROBLEM IS.
IT'S PRETTY ROUGH LOOKING AT HER IN A BIG PANEL CLOSE-UP...
YES. IT'S THE AGE-OLD PROBLEM OF...
WHY'D YOU GET HIT TOO?
SHE READ MY MIND...
... LOVE.
LOVE !!!

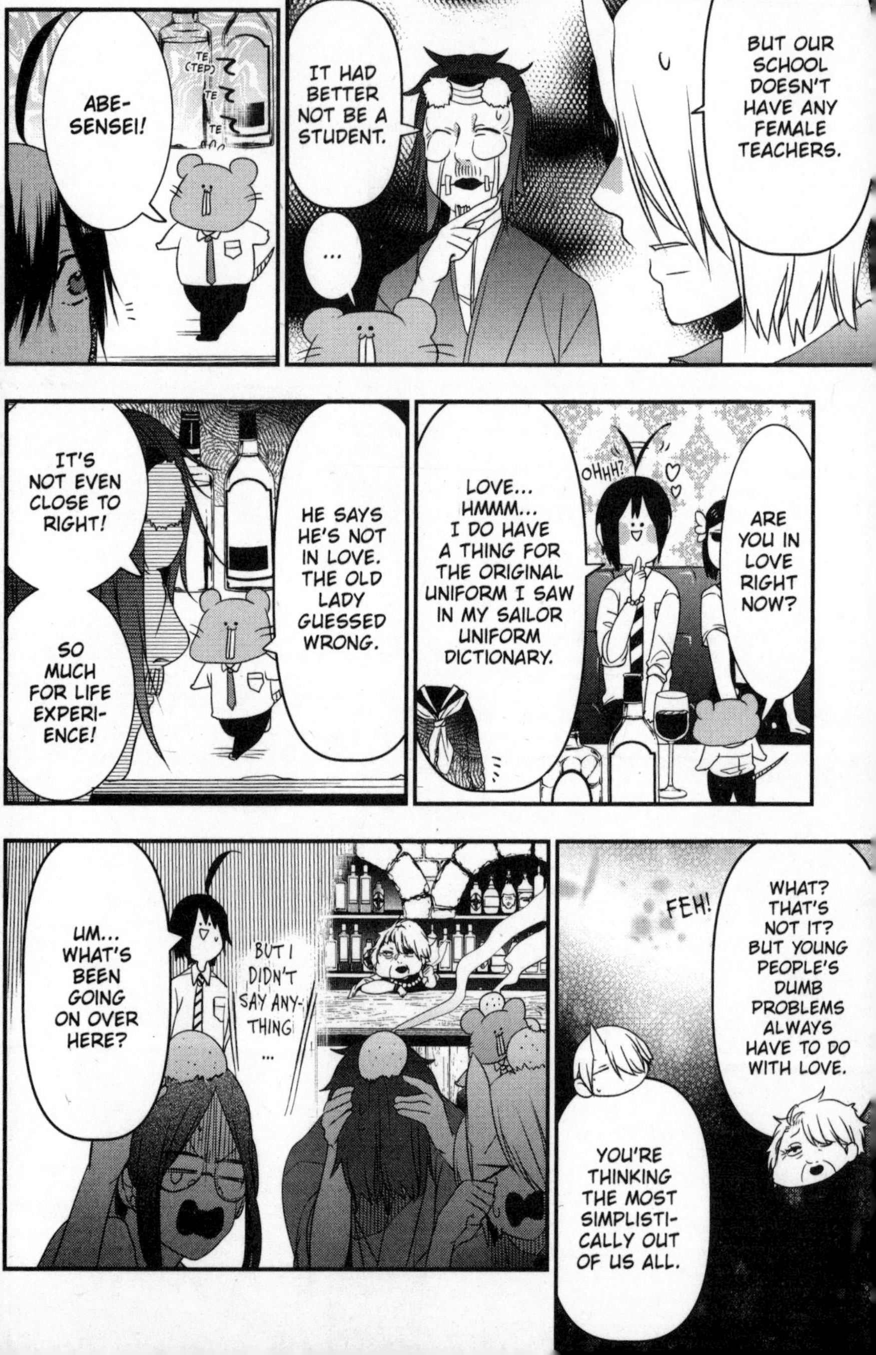
BUT OUR SCHOOL DOESN'T HAVE ANY FEMALE TEACHERS.
IT HAD BETTER NOT BE A STUDENT.
...
TE (TEP) TE TE
ABE-SENSEI!
ARE YOU IN LOVE RIGHT NOW?
OHHH?
LOVE... HMMM... I DO HAVE A THING FOR THE ORIGINAL UNIFORM I SAW IN MY SAILOR UNIFORM DICTIONARY.
HE SAYS HE'S NOT IN LOVE. THE OLD LADY GUESSED WRONG.
IT'S NOT EVEN CLOSE TO RIGHT!
SO MUCH FOR LIFE EXPERI-ENCE!
WHAT? THAT'S NOT IT? BUT YOUNG PEOPLE'S DUMB PROBLEMS ALWAYS HAVE TO DO WITH LOVE.
FEH!
YOU'RE THINKING THE MOST SIMPLISTI-CALLY OUT OF US ALL.
BUT I DIDN'T SAY ANY-THING...
UM... WHAT'S BEEN GOING ON OVER HERE?

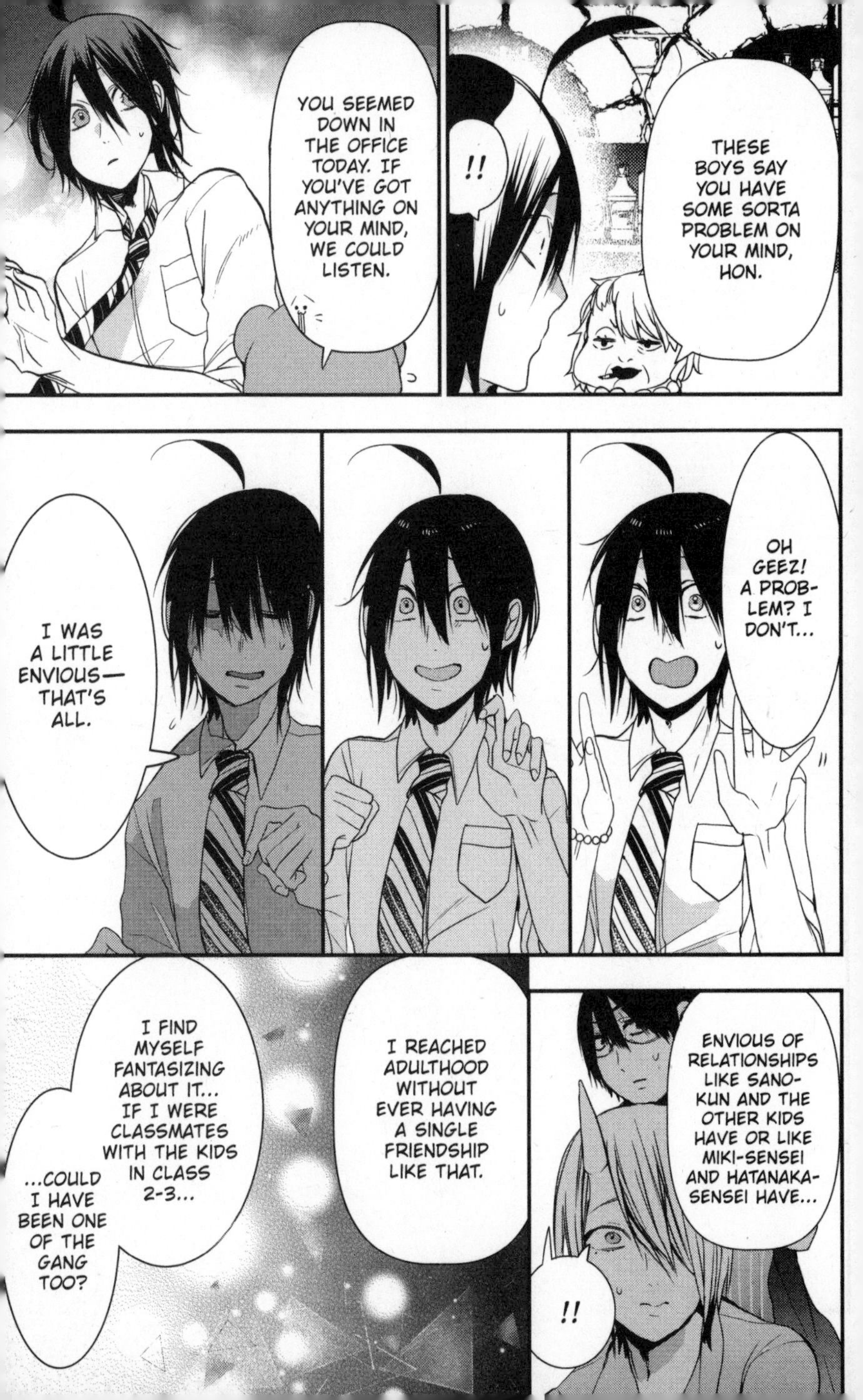
THESE BOYS SAY YOU HAVE SOME SORTA PROBLEM ON YOUR MIND, HON.
!!
YOU SEEMED DOWN IN THE OFFICE TODAY. IF YOU'VE GOT ANYTHING ON YOUR MIND, WE COULD LISTEN.
OH GEEZ! A PROB-LEM? I DON'T...
I WAS A LITTLE ENVIOUS—THAT'S ALL.
ENVIOUS OF RELATIONSHIPS LIKE SANO-KUN AND THE OTHER KIDS HAVE OR LIKE MIKI-SENSEI AND HATANAKA-SENSEI HAVE...
!!
I REACHED ADULTHOOD WITHOUT EVER HAVING A SINGLE FRIENDSHIP LIKE THAT.
I FIND MYSELF FANTASIZING ABOUT IT... IF I WERE CLASSMATES WITH THE KIDS IN CLASS 2-3...
...COULD I HAVE BEEN ONE OF THE GANG TOO?

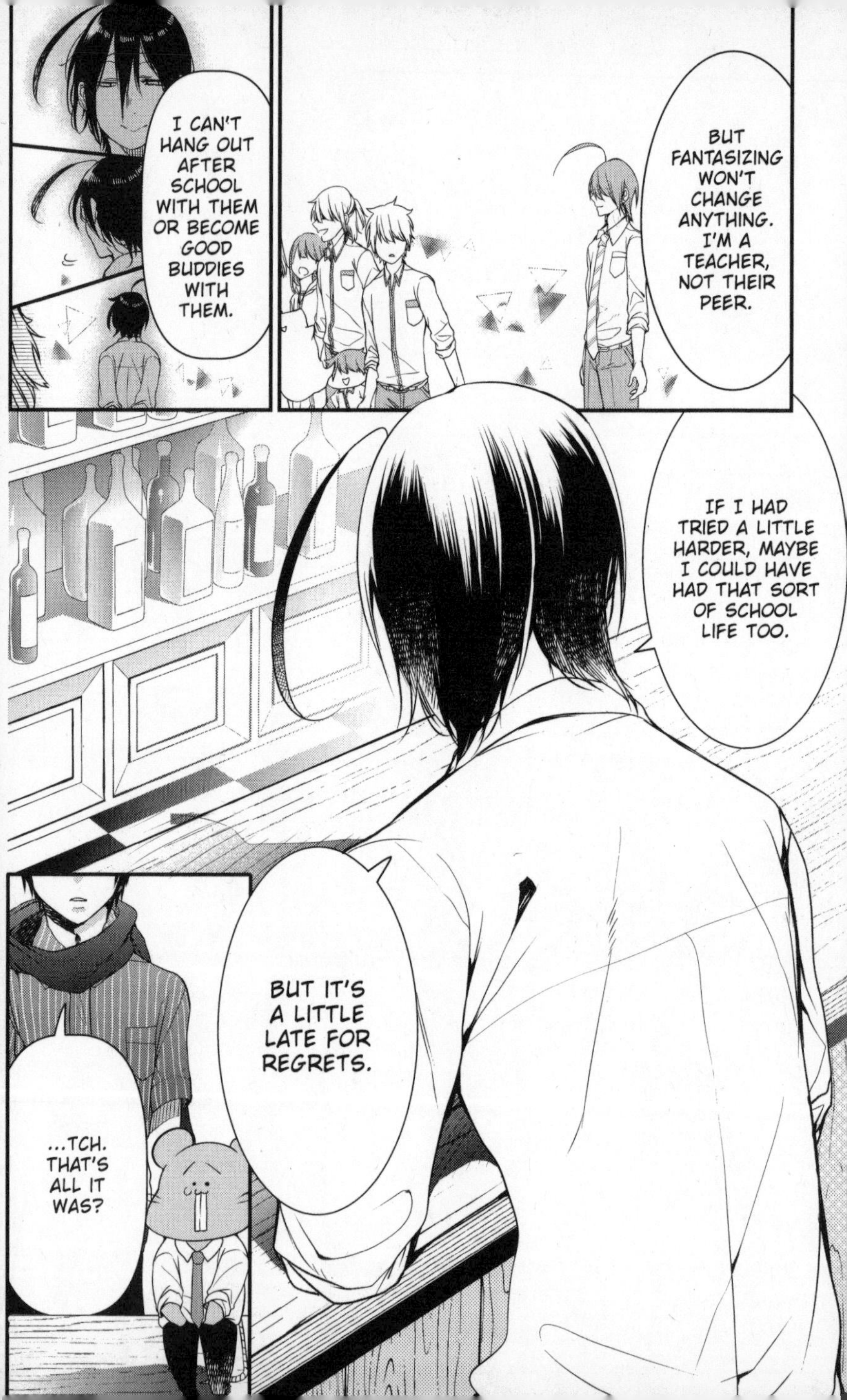
BUT FANTASIZING WON'T CHANGE ANYTHING. I'M A TEACHER, NOT THEIR PEER.
I CAN'T HANG OUT AFTER SCHOOL WITH THEM OR BECOME GOOD BUDDIES WITH THEM.
IF I HAD TRIED A LITTLE HARDER, MAYBE I COULD HAVE HAD THAT SORT OF SCHOOL LIFE TOO.
BUT IT'S A LITTLE LATE FOR REGRETS.
...TCH. THAT'S ALL IT WAS?

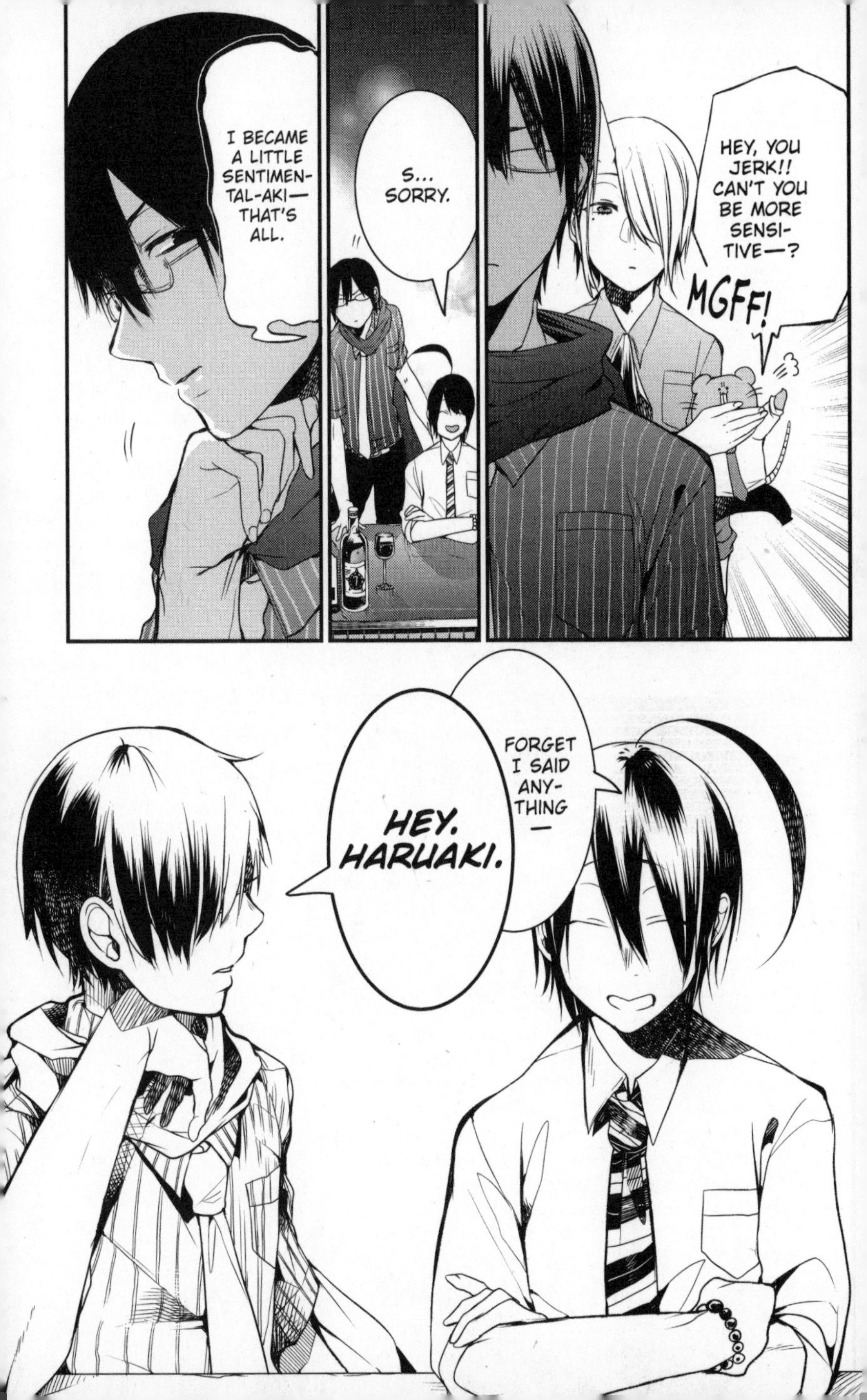
HEY, YOU JERK!! CAN'T YOU BE MORE SENSI-TIVE—?
MGFF!
S... SORRY.
I BECAME A LITTLE SENTIMEN-TAL-AKI— THAT'S ALL.
FORGET I SAID ANY-THING —
HEY. HARUAKI.

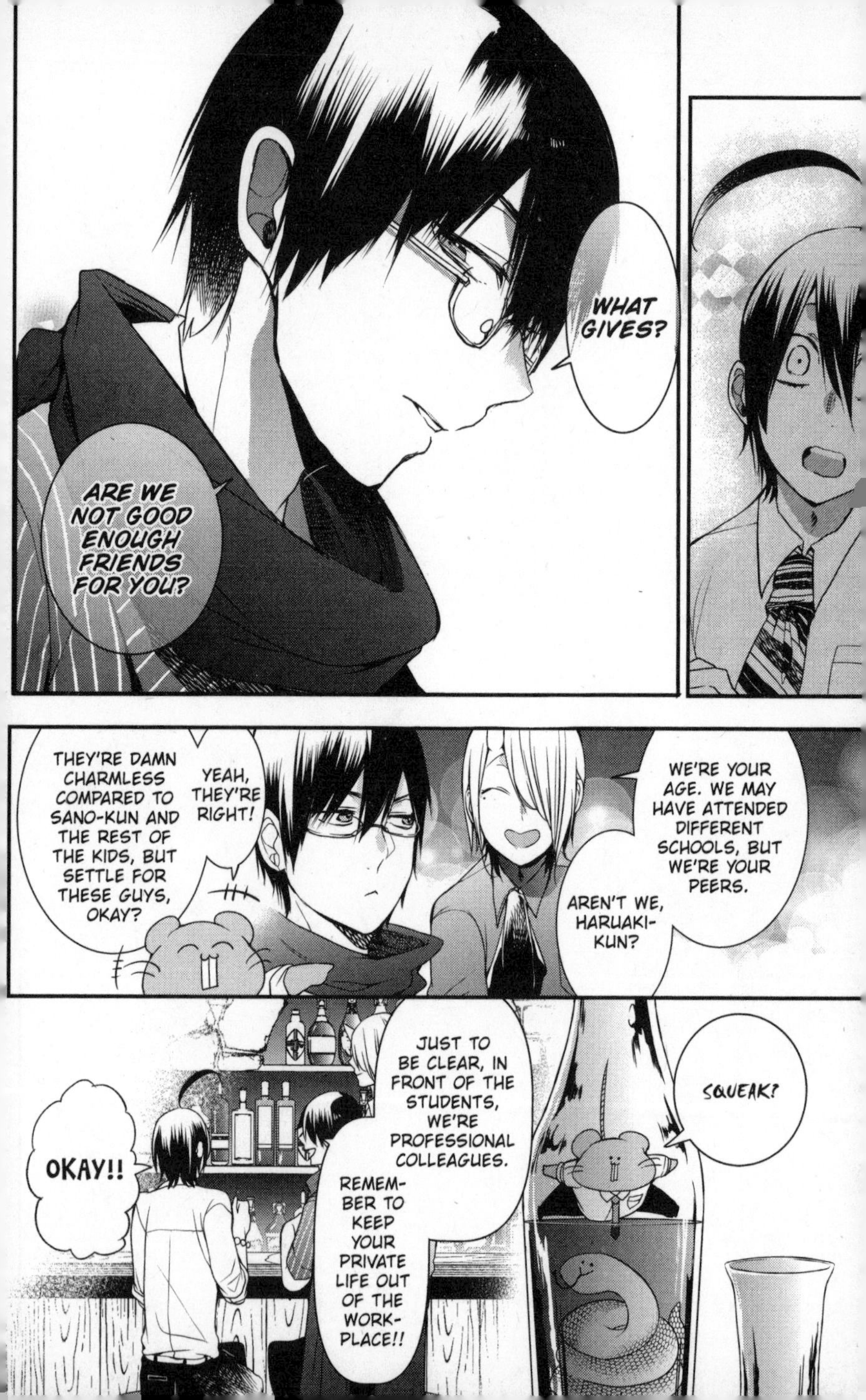
WHAT GIVES?
ARE WE NOT GOOD ENOUGH FRIENDS FOR YOU?
WE'RE YOUR AGE. WE MAY HAVE ATTENDED DIFFERENT SCHOOLS, BUT WE'RE YOUR PEERS.
AREN'T WE, HARUAKI-KUN?
YEAH, THEY'RE RIGHT!
THEY'RE DAMN CHARMLESS COMPARED TO SANO-KUN AND THE REST OF THE KIDS, BUT SETTLE FOR THESE GUYS, OKAY?
SQUEAK?
JUST TO BE CLEAR, IN FRONT OF THE STUDENTS, WE'RE PROFESSIONAL COLLEAGUES.
REMEMBER TO KEEP YOUR PRIVATE LIFE OUT OF THE WORKPLACE!!
OKAY!!

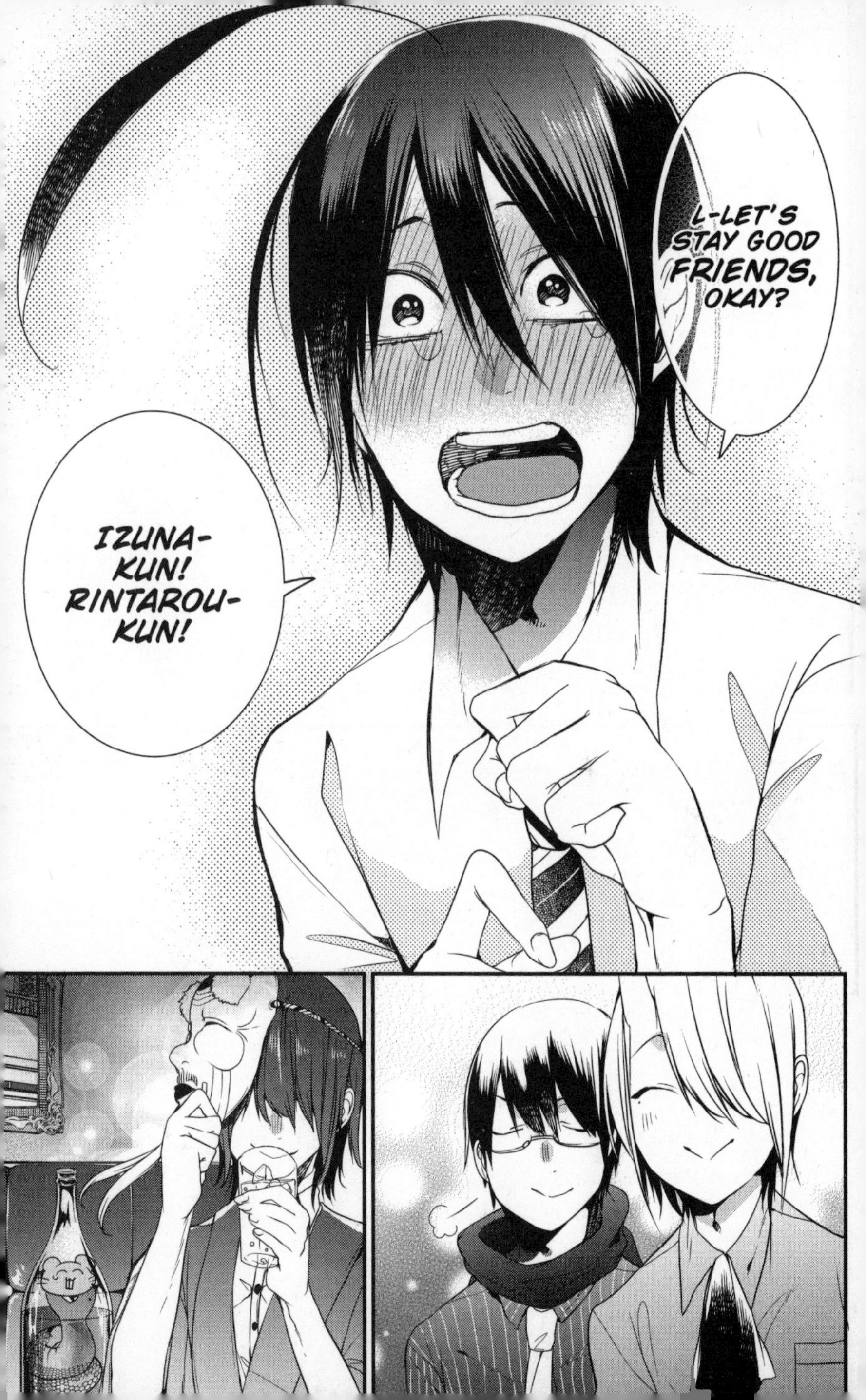
L-LET'S STAY GOOD FRIENDS, OKAY?
IZUNA-KUN! RINTAROU-KUN!

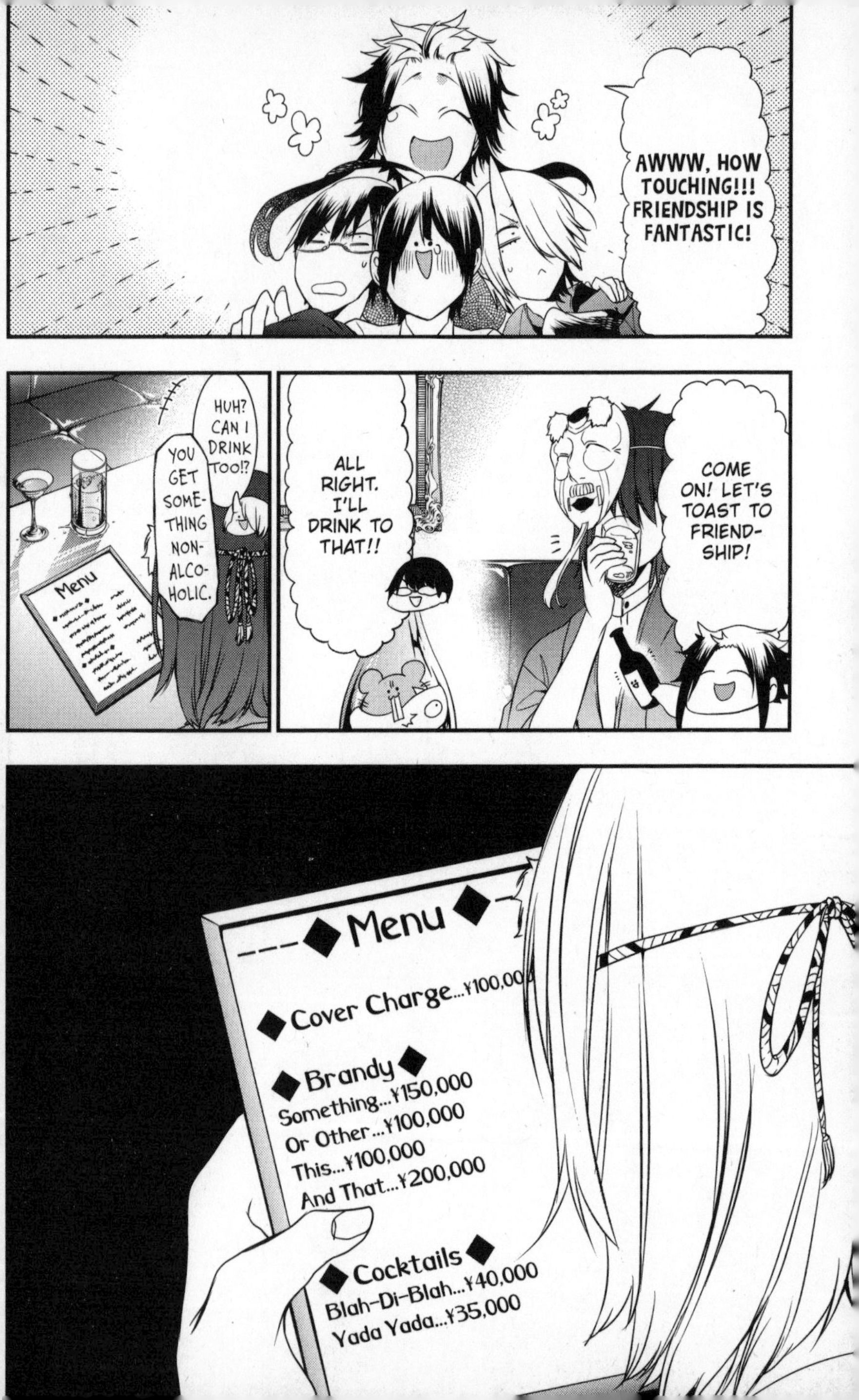
AWWW, HOW TOUCHING!!! FRIENDSHIP IS FANTASTIC!
COME ON! LET'S TOAST TO FRIEND-SHIP!
ALL RIGHT. I'LL DRINK TO THAT!!
HUH? CAN I DRINK TOO!?
YOU GET SOME-THING NON-ALCO-HOLIC.
Menu
Menu
Cover Charge...¥100,00
Brandy
Something...¥150,000
Or Other...¥100,000
This...¥100,000
And That...¥200,000
Cocktails
Blah-Di-Blah...¥40,000
Yada Yada...¥35,000

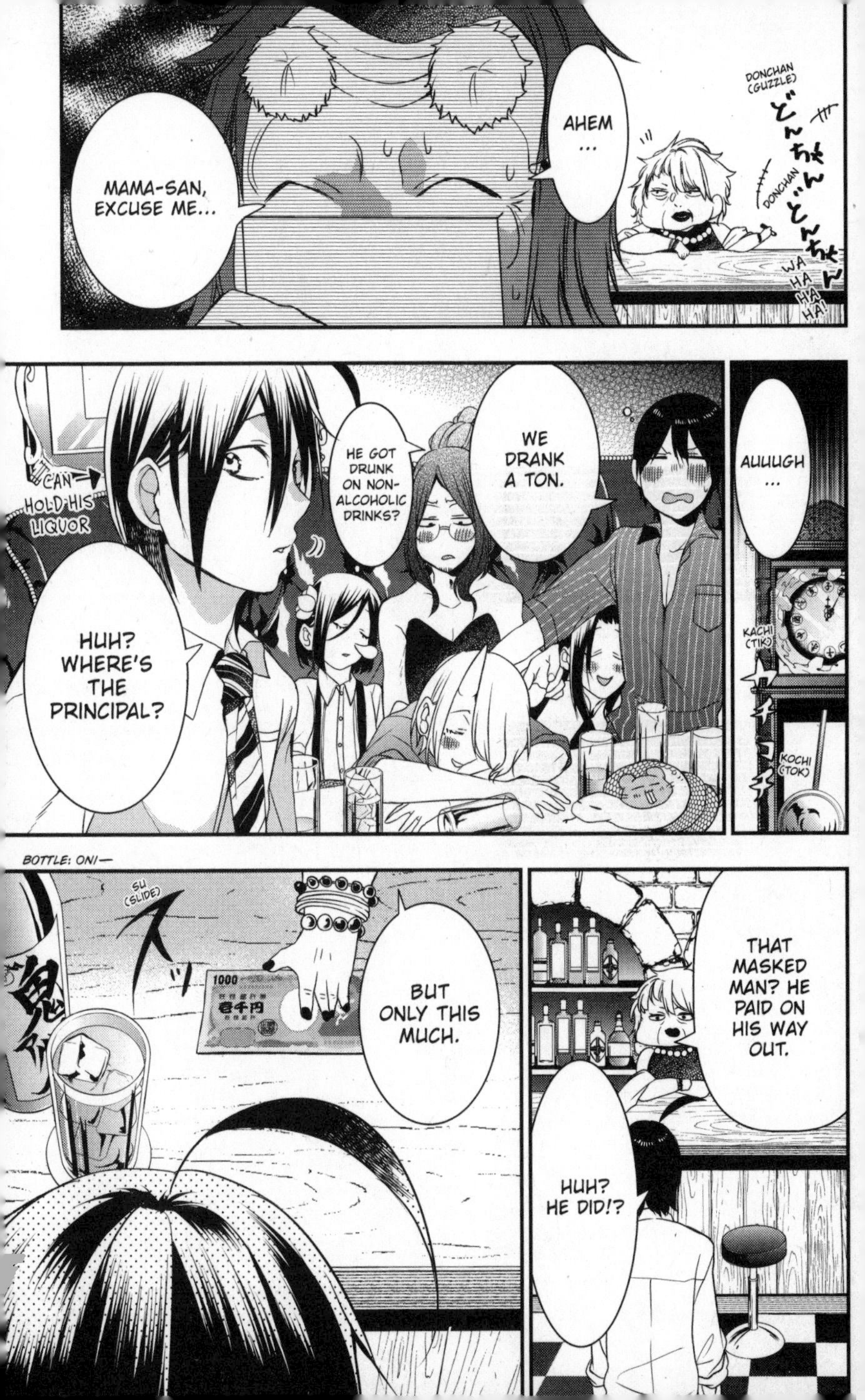
DONCHAN (GUZZLE)
どんちゃんどんちゃん
DONCHAN
WA HA HA HA!
AHEM ...
MAMA-SAN, EXCUSE ME...
AUUUGH ...
KACHI (TIK)
KOCHI (TOK)
WE DRANK A TON.
HE GOT DRUNK ON NON-ALCOHOLIC DRINKS?
CAN HOLD HIS LIQUOR
HUH? WHERE'S THE PRINCIPAL?
BOTTLE: ONI—
THAT MASKED MAN? HE PAID ON HIS WAY OUT.
HUH? HE DID!?
BUT ONLY THIS MUCH.
SU (SLIDE)
1000
壱千円

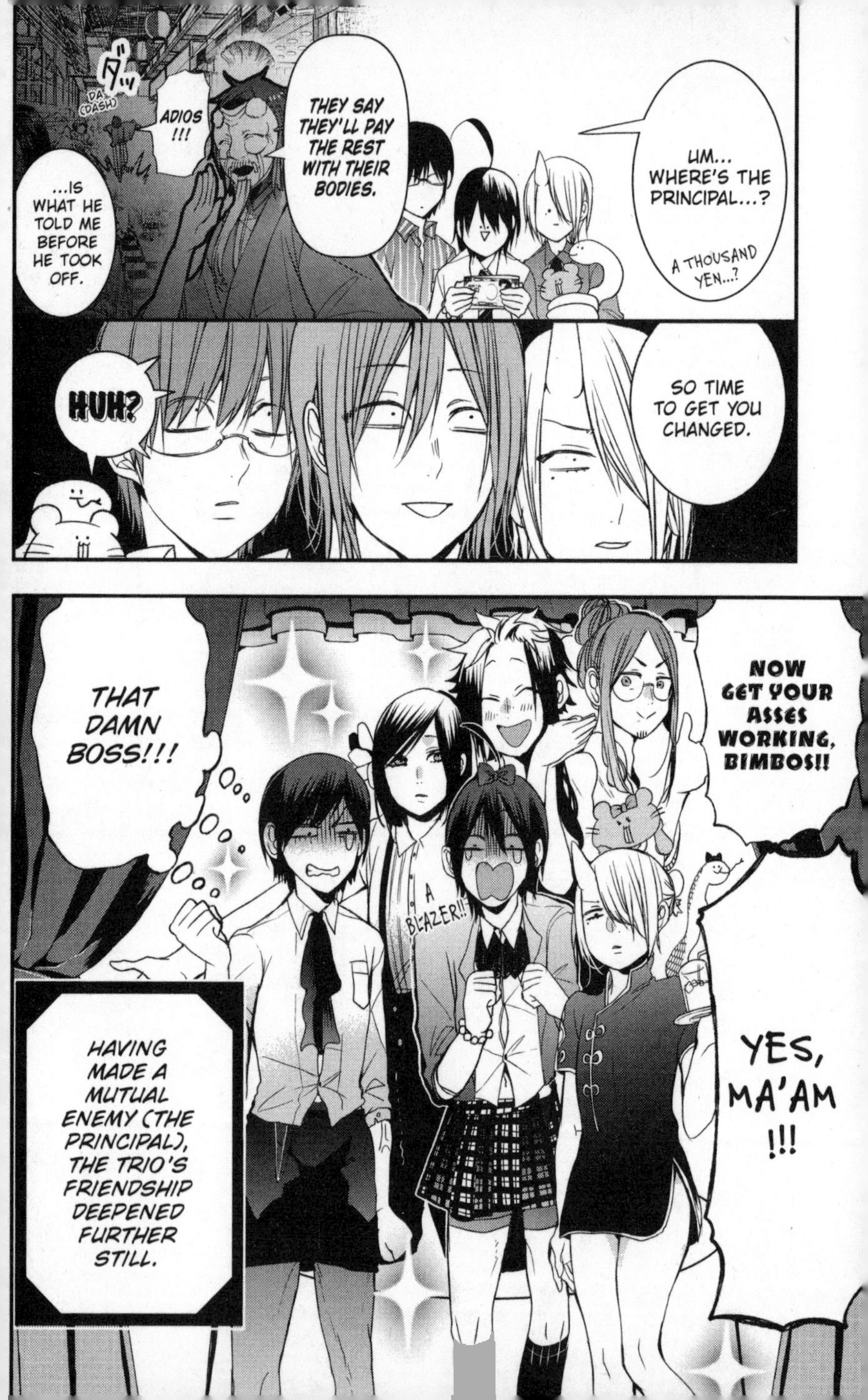
UM... WHERE'S THE PRINCIPAL...?
A THOUSAND YEN...?
THEY SAY THEY'LL PAY THE REST WITH THEIR BODIES.
ADIOS !!!
(DASH)
...IS WHAT HE TOLD ME BEFORE HE TOOK OFF.
SO TIME TO GET YOU CHANGED.
HUH?
NOW GET YOUR ASSES WORKING, BIMBOS!!
YES, MA'AM !!!
A BLAZER!!
THAT DAMN BOSS!!!
HAVING MADE A MUTUAL ENEMY (THE PRINCIPAL), THE TRIO'S FRIENDSHIP DEEPENED FURTHER STILL.

Thirty-Fourth Period

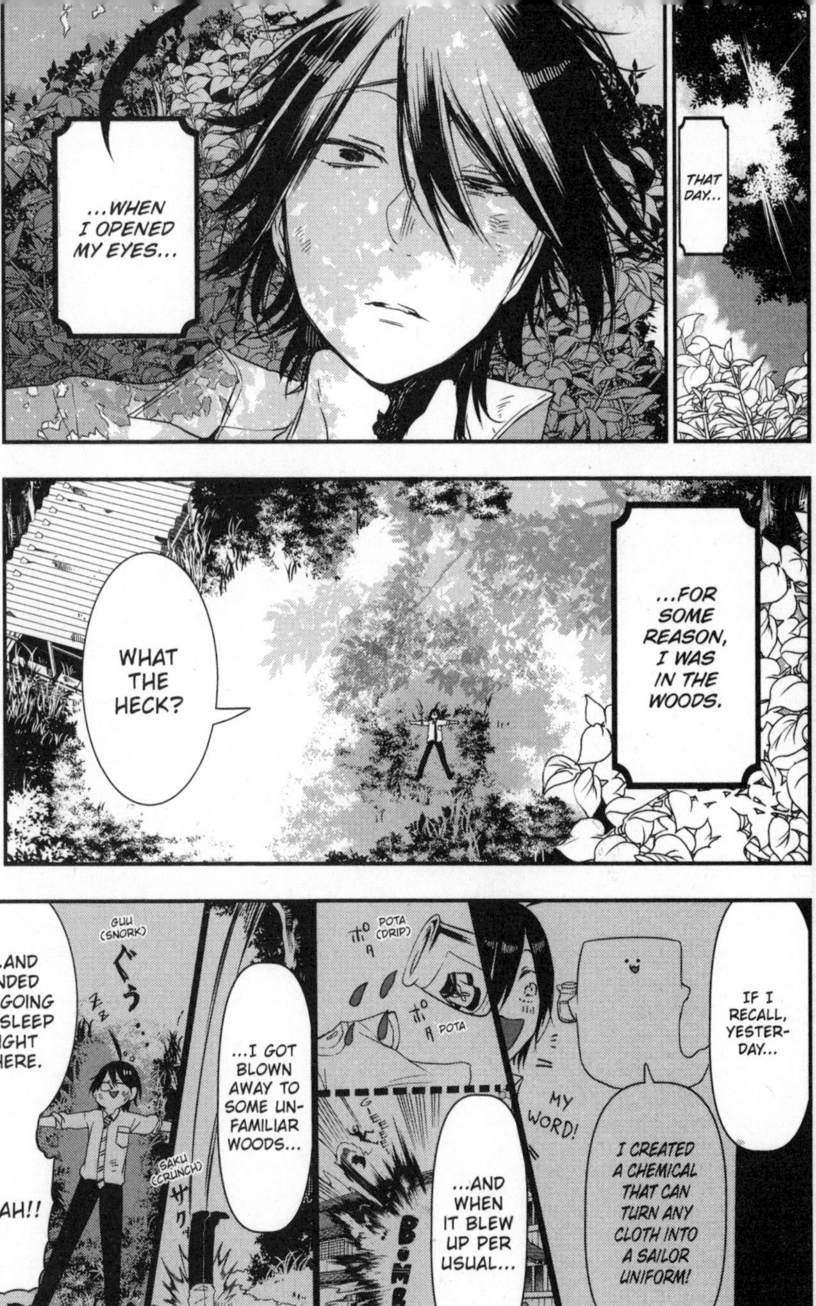
THAT DAY...
...WHEN I OPENED MY EYES...
...FOR SOME REASON, I WAS IN THE WOODS.
WHAT THE HECK?
IF I RECALL, YESTERDAY...
I CREATED A CHEMICAL THAT CAN TURN ANY CLOTH INTO A SAILOR UNIFORM!
POTA (DRIP)
POTA
MY WORD!
...AND WHEN IT BLEW UP PER USUAL...
BOMB!
...I GOT BLOWN AWAY TO SOME UN-FAMILIAR WOODS...
SAKU (CRUNCH)
GUU (SNORK)
...AND ENDED UP GOING TO SLEEP RIGHT THERE.
...AH!!

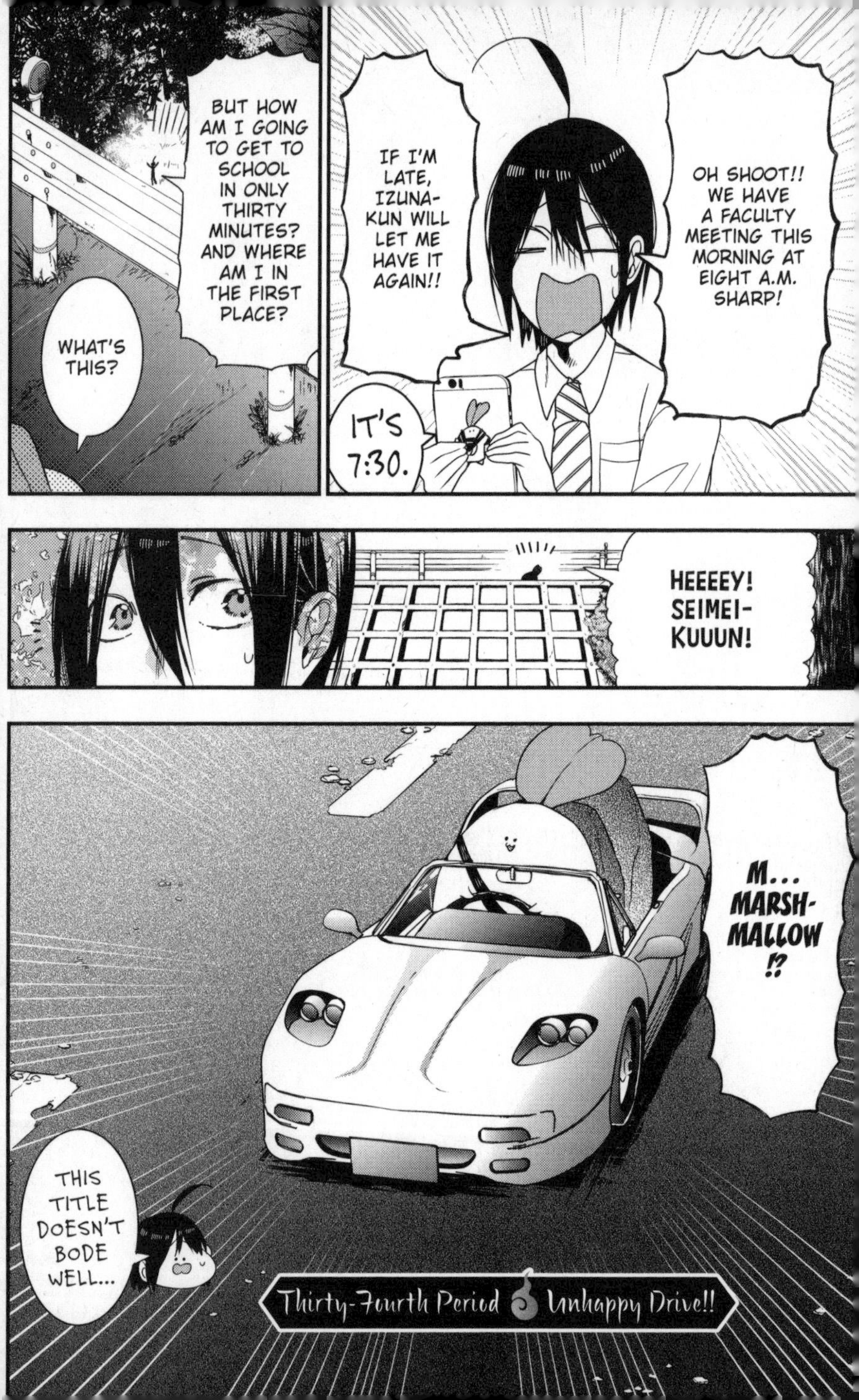
OH SHOOT!! WE HAVE A FACULTY MEETING THIS MORNING AT EIGHT A.M. SHARP!
IF I'M LATE, IZUNA-KUN WILL LET ME HAVE IT AGAIN!!
IT'S 7:30.
BUT HOW AM I GOING TO GET TO SCHOOL IN ONLY THIRTY MINUTES? AND WHERE AM I IN THE FIRST PLACE?
WHAT'S THIS?
HEEEEY! SEIMEI-KUUUN!
M... MARSH-MALLOW!?
THIS TITLE DOESN'T BODE WELL...
Thirty-Fourth Period Unhappy Drive!!

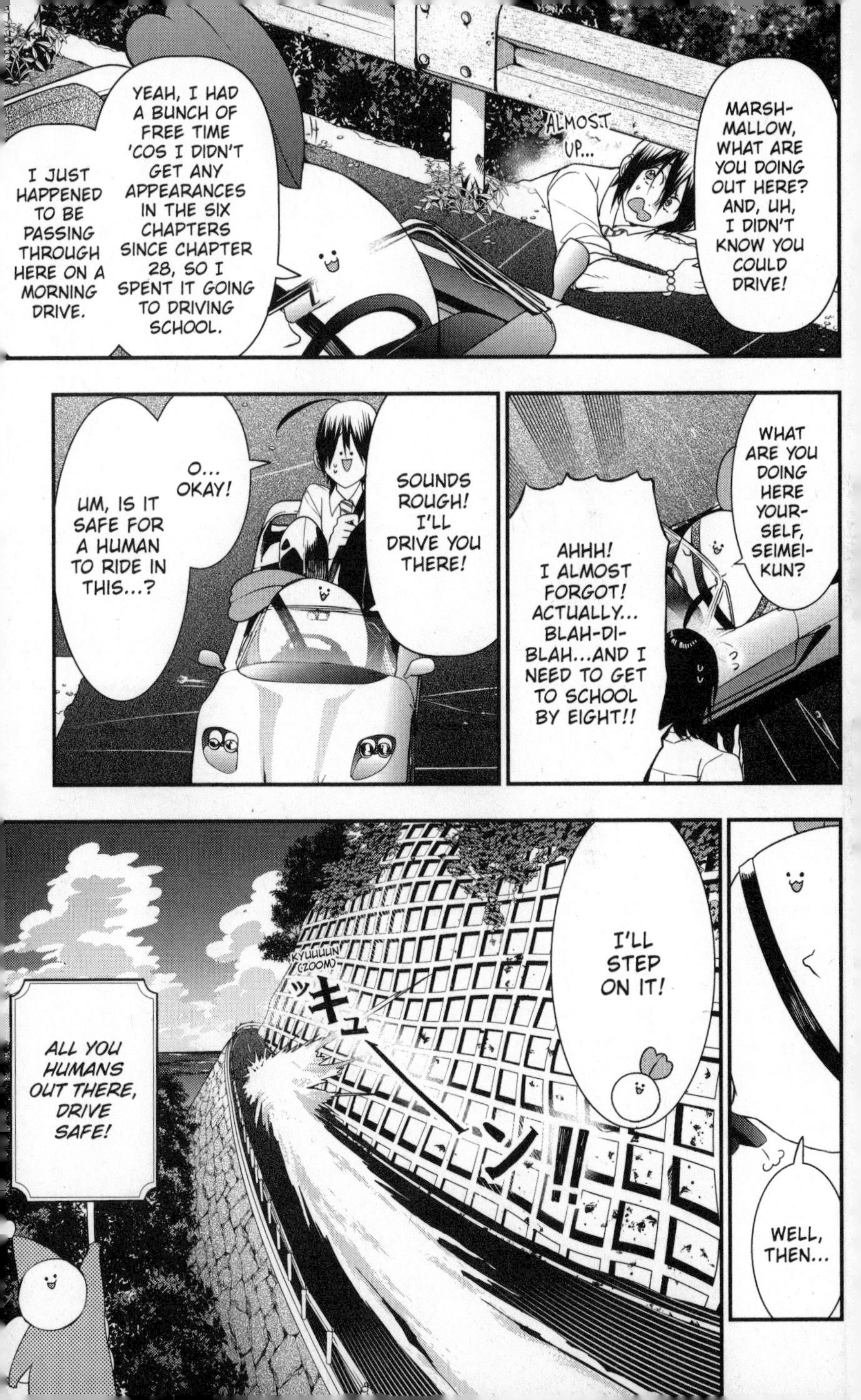
MARSH-MALLOW, WHAT ARE YOU DOING OUT HERE? AND, UH, I DIDN'T KNOW YOU COULD DRIVE!
ALMOST UP...
YEAH, I HAD A BUNCH OF FREE TIME 'COS I DIDN'T GET ANY APPEARANCES IN THE SIX CHAPTERS SINCE CHAPTER 28, SO I SPENT IT GOING TO DRIVING SCHOOL.
I JUST HAPPENED TO BE PASSING THROUGH HERE ON A MORNING DRIVE.
WHAT ARE YOU DOING HERE YOURSELF, SEIMEI-KUN?
AHHH! I ALMOST FORGOT! ACTUALLY... BLAH-DI-BLAH...AND I NEED TO GET TO SCHOOL BY EIGHT!!
SOUNDS ROUGH! I'LL DRIVE YOU THERE!
O... OKAY!
UM, IS IT SAFE FOR A HUMAN TO RIDE IN THIS...?
WELL, THEN...
I'LL STEP ON IT!
KYUUUUN (ZOOM)
ツキューン!!
ALL YOU HUMANS OUT THERE, DRIVE SAFE!

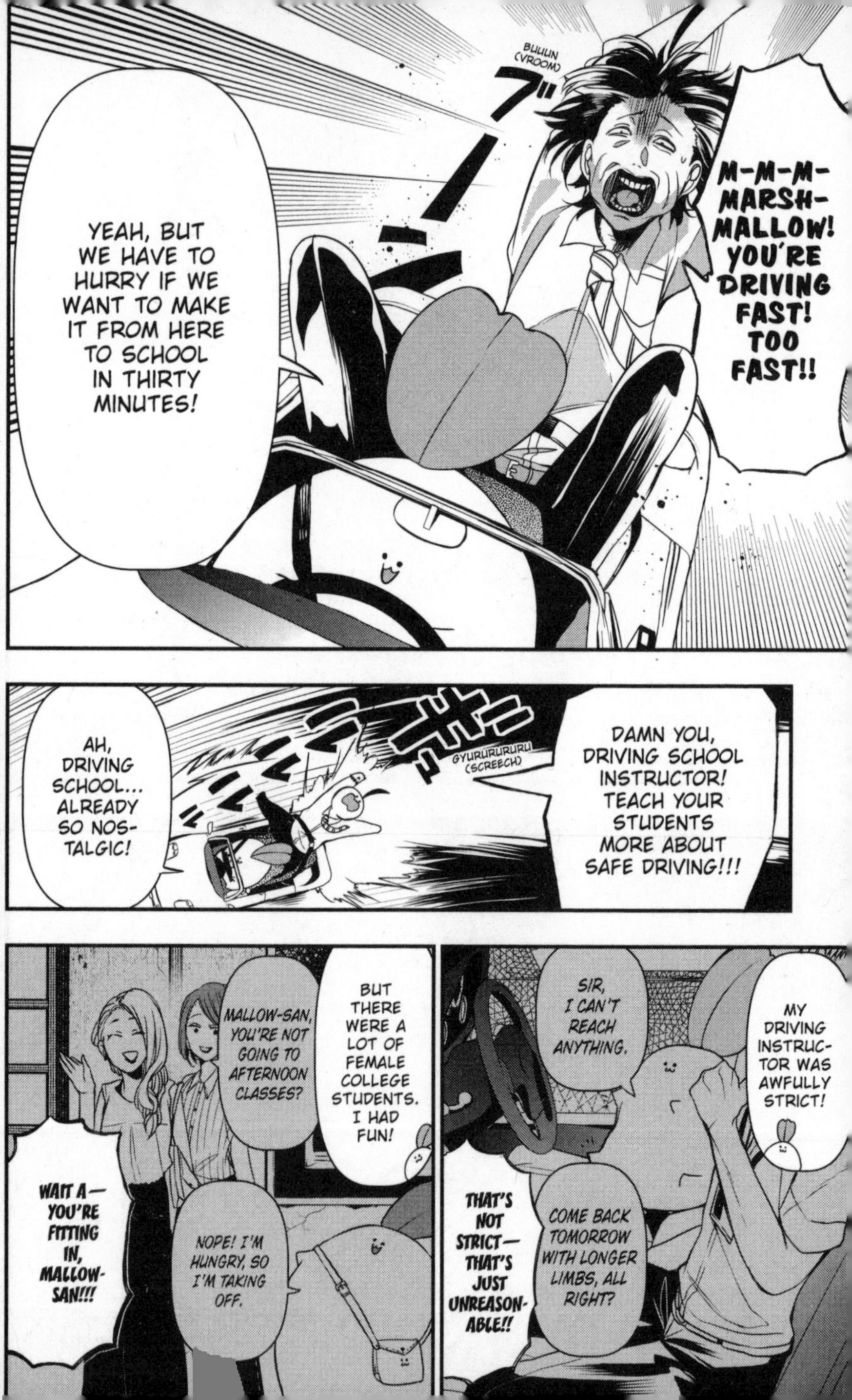
BUUUN (VROOM)
M-M-M-MARSH-MALLOW! YOU'RE DRIVING FAST! TOO FAST!!
YEAH, BUT WE HAVE TO HURRY IF WE WANT TO MAKE IT FROM HERE TO SCHOOL IN THIRTY MINUTES!
DAMN YOU, DRIVING SCHOOL INSTRUCTOR! TEACH YOUR STUDENTS MORE ABOUT SAFE DRIVING!!!
GYURURURURU (SCREECH)
AH, DRIVING SCHOOL... ALREADY SO NOS-TALGIC!
MY DRIVING INSTRUC-TOR WAS AWFULLY STRICT!
SIR, I CAN'T REACH ANYTHING.
COME BACK TOMORROW WITH LONGER LIMBS, ALL RIGHT?
THAT'S NOT STRICT—THAT'S JUST UNREASON-ABLE!!
BUT THERE WERE A LOT OF FEMALE COLLEGE STUDENTS. I HAD FUN!
MALLOW-SAN, YOU'RE NOT GOING TO AFTERNOON CLASSES?
NOPE! I'M HUNGRY, SO I'M TAKING OFF.
WAIT A— YOU'RE FITTING IN, MALLOW-SAN!!!

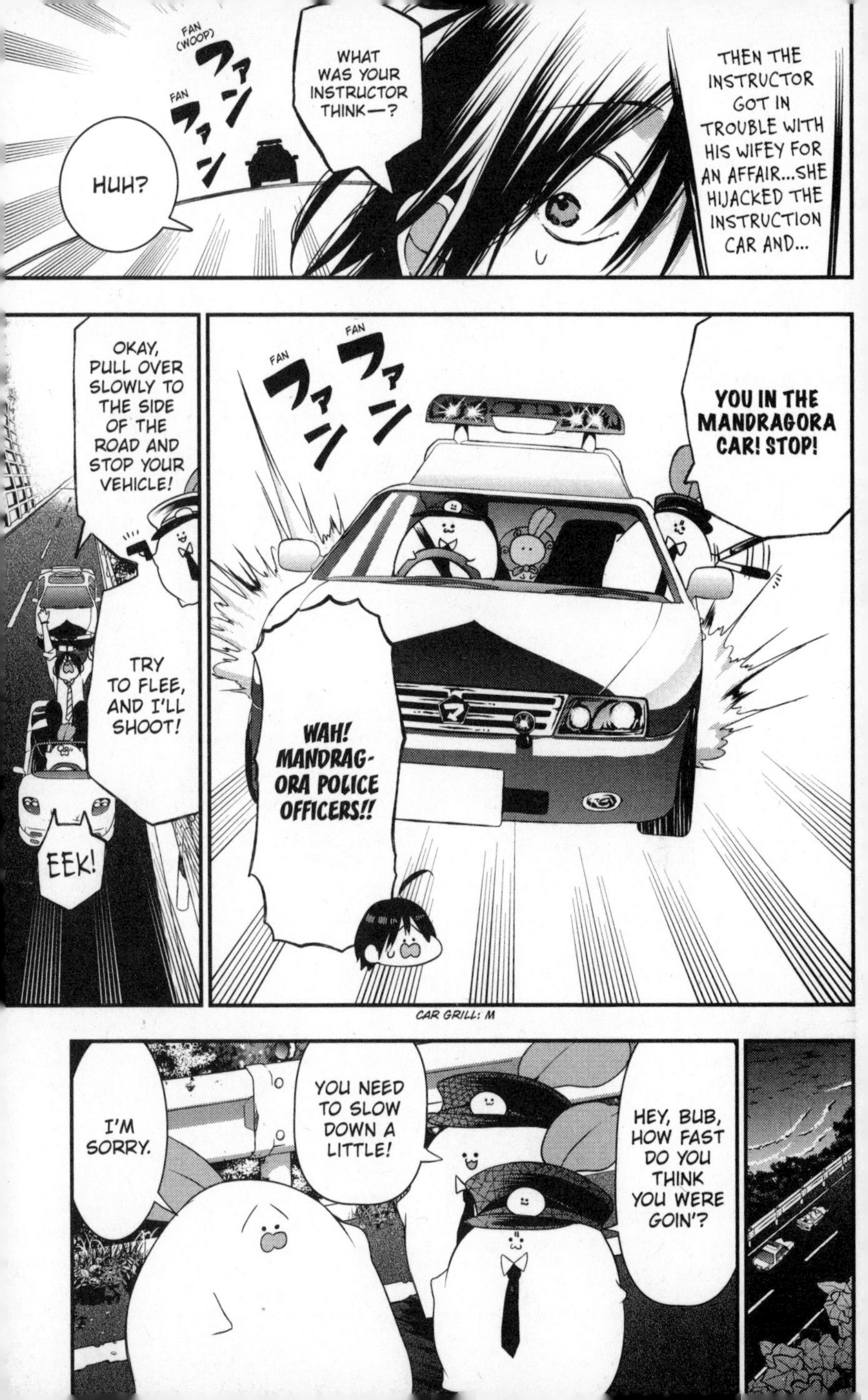
THEN THE INSTRUCTOR GOT IN TROUBLE WITH HIS WIFEY FOR AN AFFAIR...SHE HIJACKED THE INSTRUCTION CAR AND...
WHAT WAS YOUR INSTRUCTOR THINK—?
FAN (WOOP)
ファン
FAN
ファン
HUH?
YOU IN THE MANDRAGORA CAR! STOP!
FAN
ファン
FAN
ファン
WAH! MANDRAG-ORA POLICE OFFICERS!!
OKAY, PULL OVER SLOWLY TO THE SIDE OF THE ROAD AND STOP YOUR VEHICLE!
TRY TO FLEE, AND I'LL SHOOT!
EEK!
HEY, BUB, HOW FAST DO YOU THINK YOU WERE GOIN'?
YOU NEED TO SLOW DOWN A LITTLE!
I'M SORRY.
CAR GRILL: M

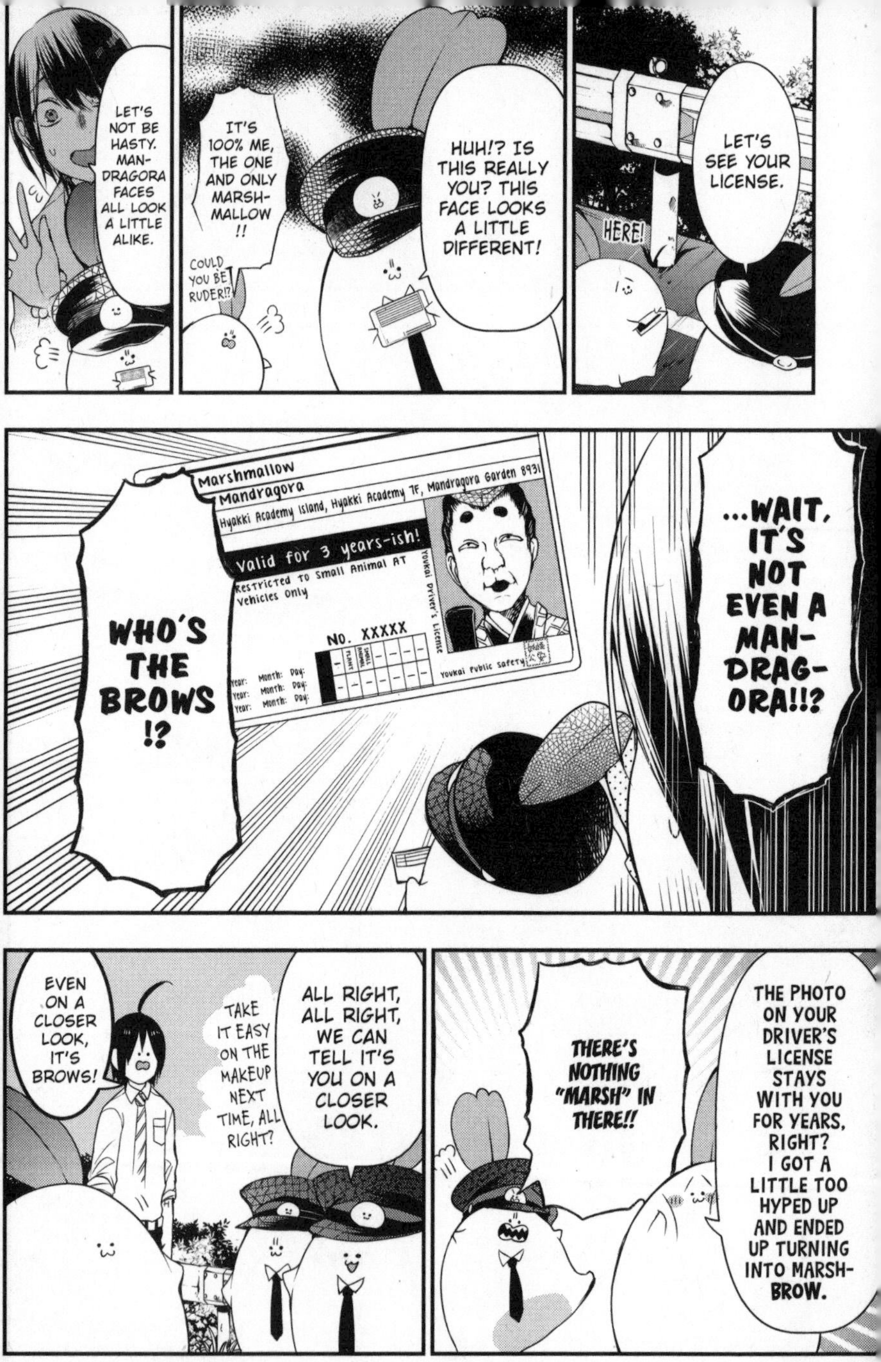
LET'S SEE YOUR LICENSE.
HERE!
HUH!? IS THIS REALLY YOU? THIS FACE LOOKS A LITTLE DIFFERENT!
IT'S 100% ME, THE ONE AND ONLY MARSH-MALLOW!!
COULD YOU BE RUDER!?
LET'S NOT BE HASTY. MAN-DRAGORA FACES ALL LOOK A LITTLE ALIKE.
...WAIT, IT'S NOT EVEN A MAN-DRAG-ORA!!?
Marshmallow
Mandragora
Hyakki Academy Island, Hyakki Academy 7F, Mandragora Garden 8931
Valid for 3 years-ish!
Restricted to Small Animal AT Vehicles Only
NO. XXXXX
PLANT
SMALL ANIMAL
Year: Month: Day:
Year: Month: Day:
Year: Month: Day:
Youkai Driver's License
Youkai Public Safety
WHO'S THE BROWS!?
THE PHOTO ON YOUR DRIVER'S LICENSE STAYS WITH YOU FOR YEARS, RIGHT? I GOT A LITTLE TOO HYPED UP AND ENDED UP TURNING INTO MARSH-BROW.
THERE'S NOTHING "MARSH" IN THERE!!
ALL RIGHT, ALL RIGHT, WE CAN TELL IT'S YOU ON A CLOSER LOOK.
TAKE IT EASY ON THE MAKEUP NEXT TIME, ALL RIGHT?
EVEN ON A CLOSER LOOK, IT'S BROWS!

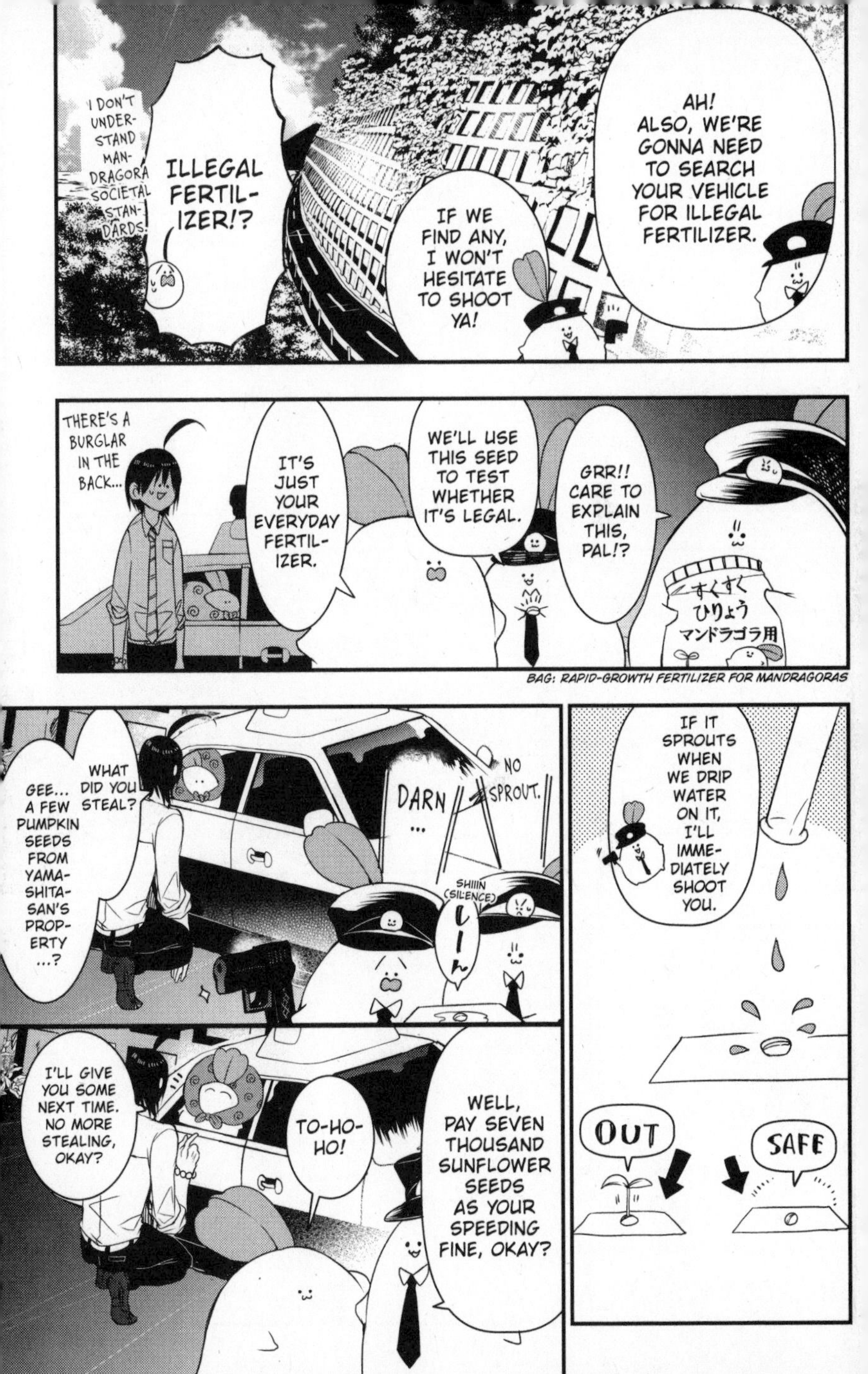
AH! ALSO, WE'RE GONNA NEED TO SEARCH YOUR VEHICLE FOR ILLEGAL FERTILIZER.
IF WE FIND ANY, I WON'T HESITATE TO SHOOT YA!
ILLEGAL FERTILIZER!?
I DON'T UNDERSTAND MANDRAGORA SOCIETAL STANDARDS!
GRR!! CARE TO EXPLAIN THIS, PAL!?
すくすく ひりょう マンドラゴラ用
WE'LL USE THIS SEED TO TEST WHETHER IT'S LEGAL.
IT'S JUST YOUR EVERYDAY FERTILIZER.
THERE'S A BURGLAR IN THE BACK...
BAG: RAPID-GROWTH FERTILIZER FOR MANDRAGORAS
IF IT SPROUTS WHEN WE DRIP WATER ON IT, I'LL IMMEDIATELY SHOOT YOU.
OUT
SAFE
NO SPROUT.
DARN...
SHIIIN (SILENCE)
しーん
WHAT DID YOU STEAL?
GEE... A FEW PUMPKIN SEEDS FROM YAMASHITA-SAN'S PROPERTY...?
WELL, PAY SEVEN THOUSAND SUNFLOWER SEEDS AS YOUR SPEEDING FINE, OKAY?
TO-HO-HO!
I'LL GIVE YOU SOME NEXT TIME. NO MORE STEALING, OKAY?

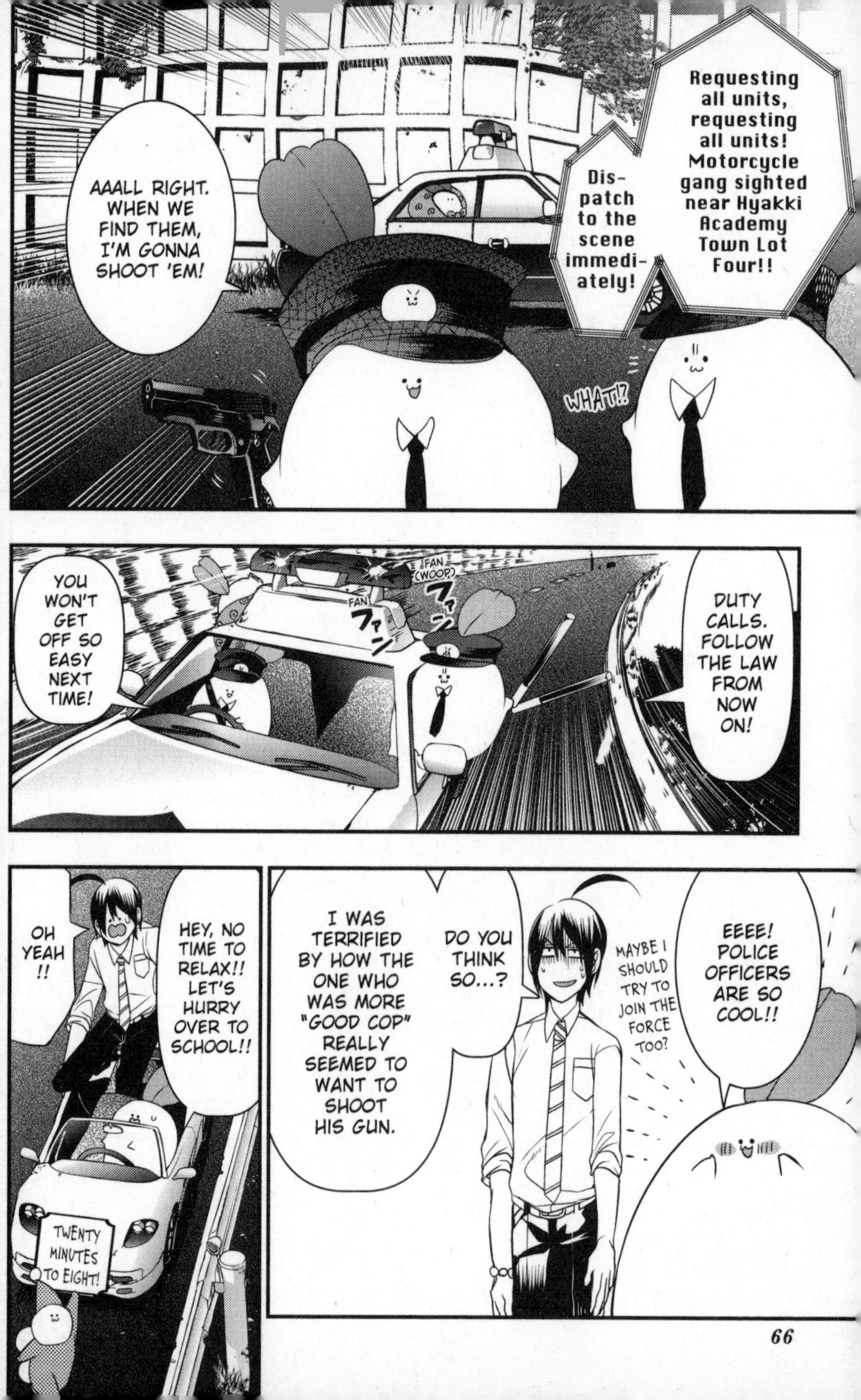
Requesting all units, requesting all units! Motorcycle gang sighted near Hyakki Academy Town Lot Four!!
Dis-patch to the scene immedi-ately!
WHAT!?
AAALL RIGHT. WHEN WE FIND THEM, I'M GONNA SHOOT 'EM!
DUTY CALLS. FOLLOW THE LAW FROM NOW ON!
FAN (WOOP)
ファン
FAN
ファン
YOU WON'T GET OFF SO EASY NEXT TIME!
EEEE! POLICE OFFICERS ARE SO COOL!!
MAYBE I SHOULD TRY TO JOIN THE FORCE TOO?
DO YOU THINK SO...?
I WAS TERRIFIED BY HOW THE ONE WHO WAS MORE "GOOD COP" REALLY SEEMED TO WANT TO SHOOT HIS GUN.
HEY, NO TIME TO RELAX!! LET'S HURRY OVER TO SCHOOL!!
OH YEAH!!
TWENTY MINUTES TO EIGHT!

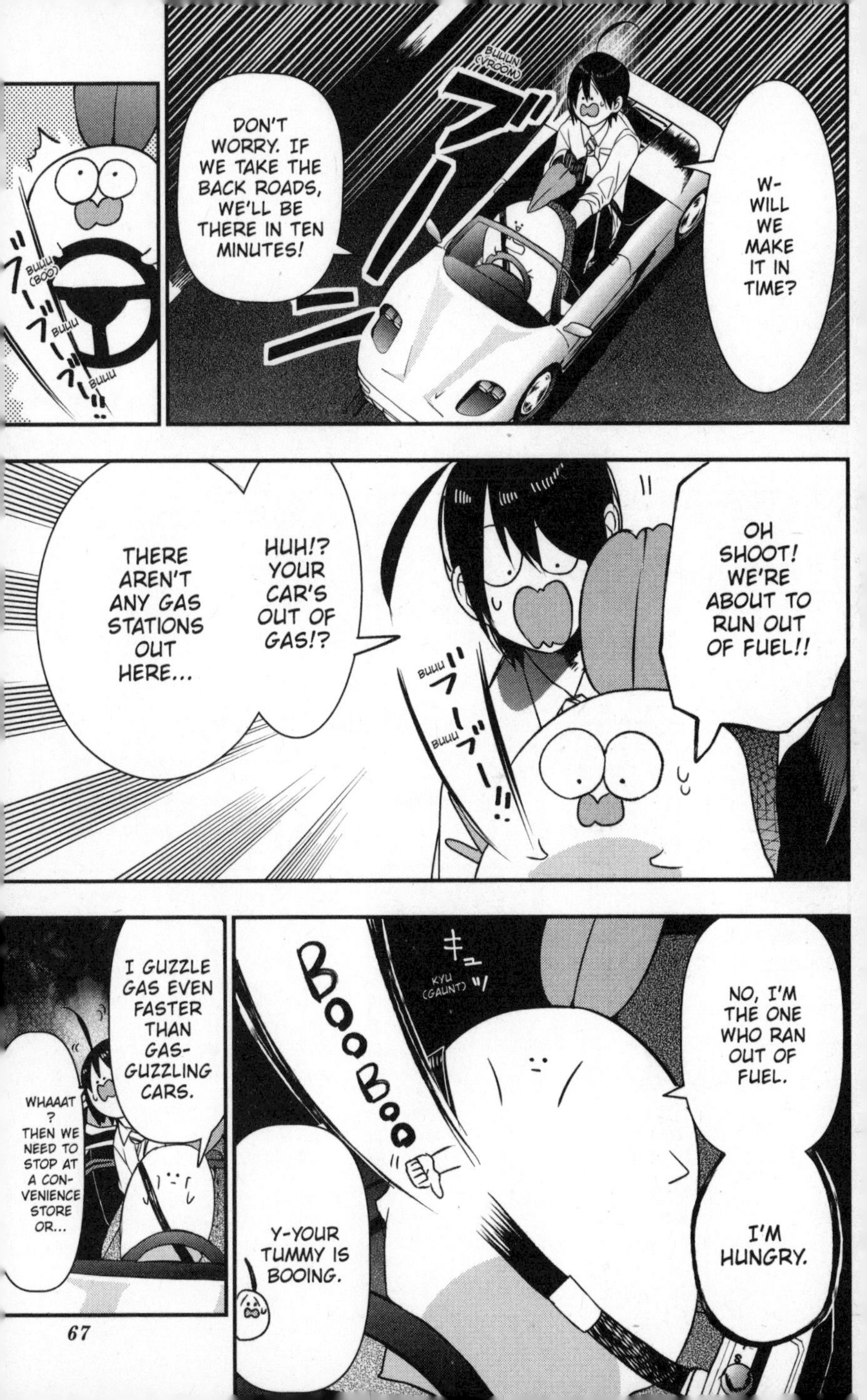
BUUUN (VROOM)
W-WILL WE MAKE IT IN TIME?
DON'T WORRY. IF WE TAKE THE BACK ROADS, WE'LL BE THERE IN TEN MINUTES!
BUUU (BOO)
BUUU
BUUU
OH SHOOT! WE'RE ABOUT TO RUN OUT OF FUEL!!
HUH!? YOUR CAR'S OUT OF GAS!?
THERE AREN'T ANY GAS STATIONS OUT HERE...
BUUU
BUUU
KYU (GAUNT)
NO, I'M THE ONE WHO RAN OUT OF FUEL.
BOOBOO
I'M HUNGRY.
Y-YOUR TUMMY IS BOOING.
I GUZZLE GAS EVEN FASTER THAN GAS-GUZZLING CARS.
WHAAAT? THEN WE NEED TO STOP AT A CONVENIENCE STORE OR...

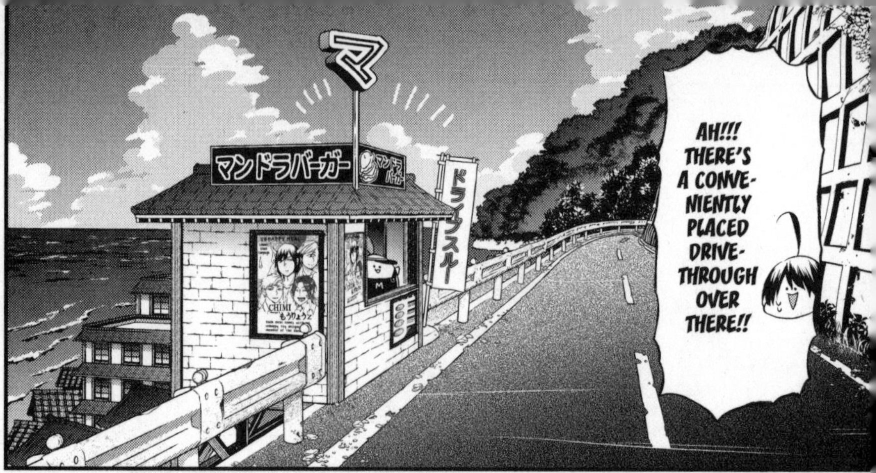
マンドラバーガー
ドライブスルー
AH!!! THERE'S A CONVENIENTLY PLACED DRIVE-THROUGH OVER THERE!!

BANNER: DRIVE-THROUGH / SIGNS: M; MANDRABURGER

APRON: MANDRABURGER

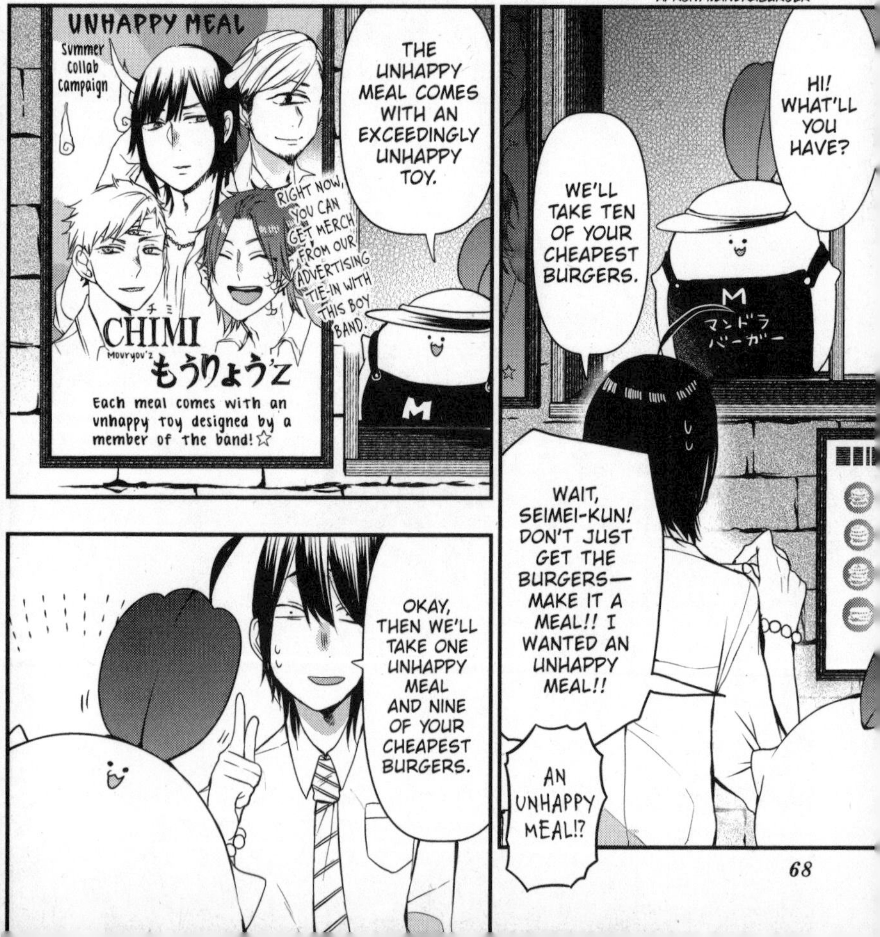
HI! WHAT'LL YOU HAVE?
WE'LL TAKE TEN OF YOUR CHEAPEST BURGERS.
M
マンドラバーガー
WAIT, SEIMEI-KUN! DON'T JUST GET THE BURGERS—MAKE IT A MEAL!! I WANTED AN UNHAPPY MEAL!!
AN UNHAPPY MEAL!?
UNHAPPY MEAL
Summer Collab Campaign
CHIMI
チミ
Movryov'z
もうりょう'Z
Each meal comes with an vnhappy toy designed by a member of the band!☆
THE UNHAPPY MEAL COMES WITH AN EXCEEDINGLY UNHAPPY TOY.
RIGHT NOW, YOU CAN GET MERCH FROM OUR ADVERTISING TIE-IN WITH THIS BOY BAND.
OKAY, THEN WE'LL TAKE ONE UNHAPPY MEAL AND NINE OF YOUR CHEAPEST BURGERS.

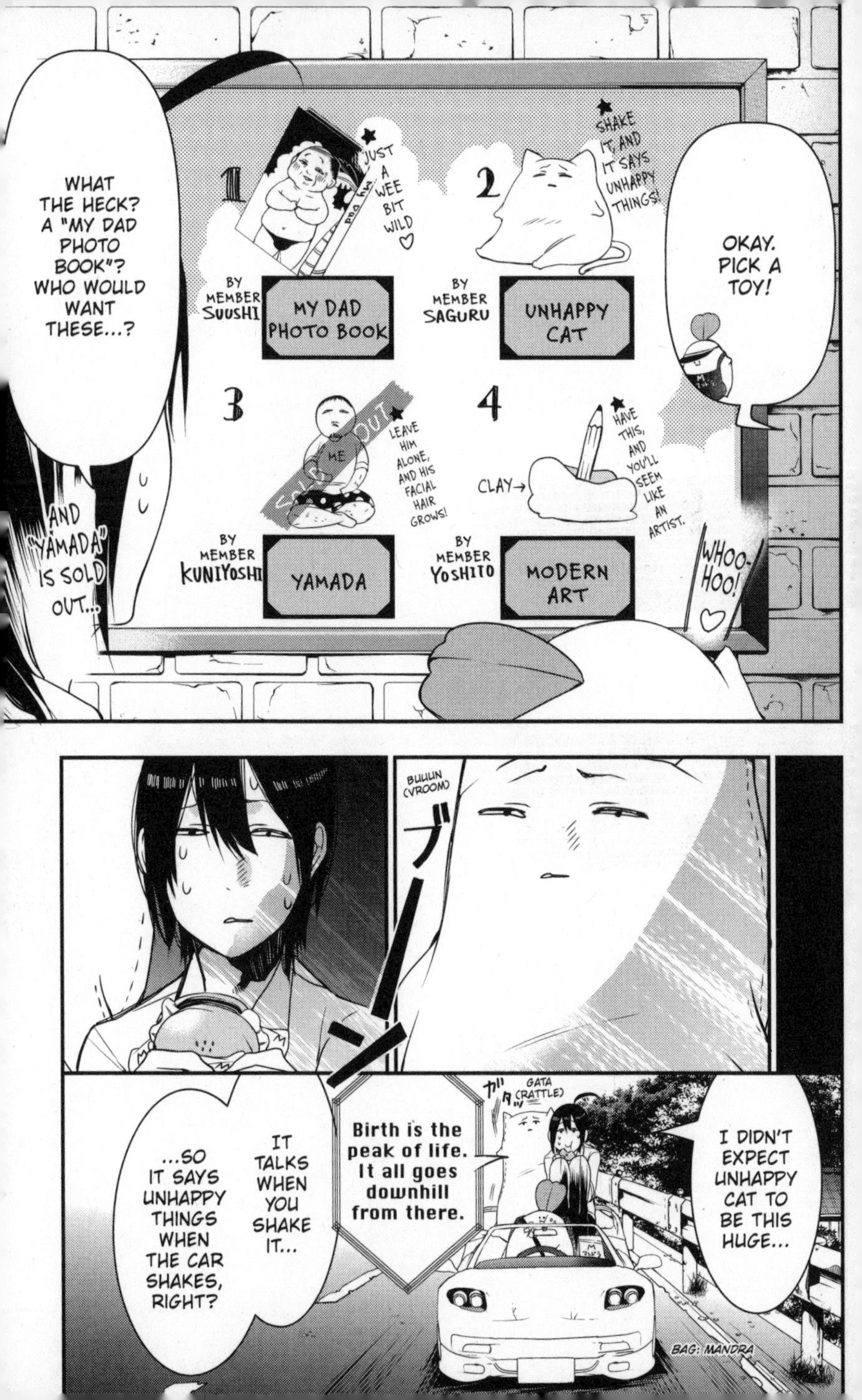
OKAY. PICK A TOY!
WHOO-HOO!
2
SHAKE IT, AND IT SAYS UNHAPPY THINGS!
BY MEMBER SAGURU
UNHAPPY CAT
1
JUST A WEE BIT WILD
BY MEMBER SUUSHI
MY DAD PHOTO BOOK
4
HAVE THIS, AND YOU'LL SEEM LIKE AN ARTIST.
CLAY→
BY MEMBER YOSHITO
MODERN ART
3
SOLD OUT
LEAVE HIM ALONE, AND HIS FACIAL HAIR GROWS!
ME
BY MEMBER KUNIYOSHI
YAMADA
WHAT THE HECK? A "MY DAD PHOTO BOOK"? WHO WOULD WANT THESE...?
AND "YAMADA" IS SOLD OUT...
BUUUN (VROOM)
I DIDN'T EXPECT UNHAPPY CAT TO BE THIS HUGE...
GATA (RATTLE)
Birth is the peak of life. It all goes downhill from there.
IT TALKS WHEN YOU SHAKE IT...
...SO IT SAYS UNHAPPY THINGS WHEN THE CAR SHAKES, RIGHT?
BAG: MANDRA

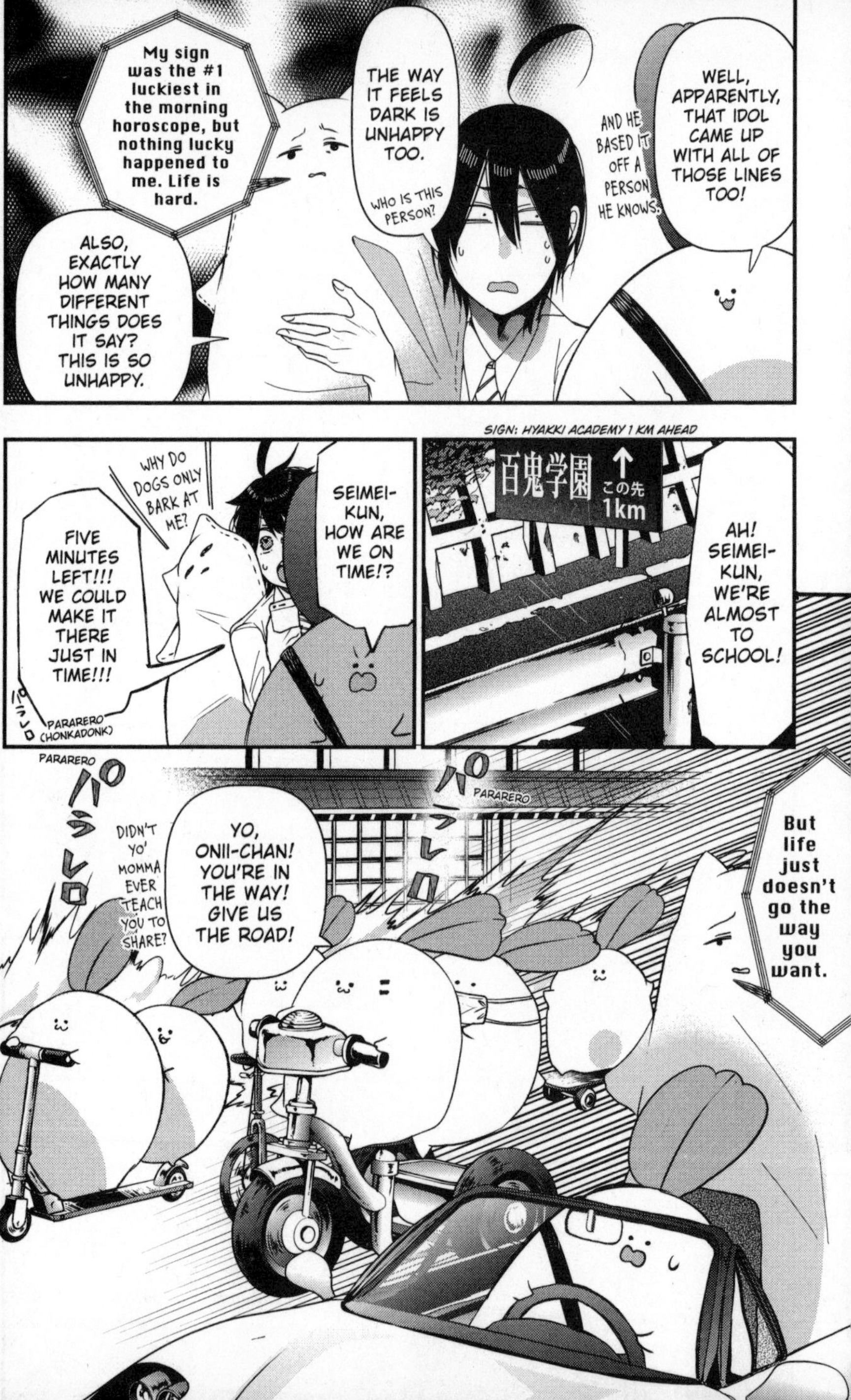
WELL, APPARENTLY, THAT IDOL CAME UP WITH ALL OF THOSE LINES TOO!
AND HE BASED IT OFF A PERSON HE KNOWS.
THE WAY IT FEELS DARK IS UNHAPPY TOO.
WHO IS THIS PERSON?
My sign was the #1 luckiest in the morning horoscope, but nothing lucky happened to me. Life is hard.
ALSO, EXACTLY HOW MANY DIFFERENT THINGS DOES IT SAY? THIS IS SO UNHAPPY.
SIGN: HYAKKI ACADEMY 1 KM AHEAD
百鬼学園
この先
1km
AH! SEIMEI-KUN, WE'RE ALMOST TO SCHOOL!
SEIMEI-KUN, HOW ARE WE ON TIME!?
WHY DO DOGS ONLY BARK AT ME?
FIVE MINUTES LEFT!!! WE COULD MAKE IT THERE JUST IN TIME!!!
パラレロ
PARARERO (HONKADONK)
But life just doesn't go the way you want.
パラレロ
PARARERO
YO, ONII-CHAN! YOU'RE IN THE WAY! GIVE US THE ROAD!
DIDN'T YO' MOMMA EVER TEACH YOU TO SHARE?
パラレロ
PARARERO

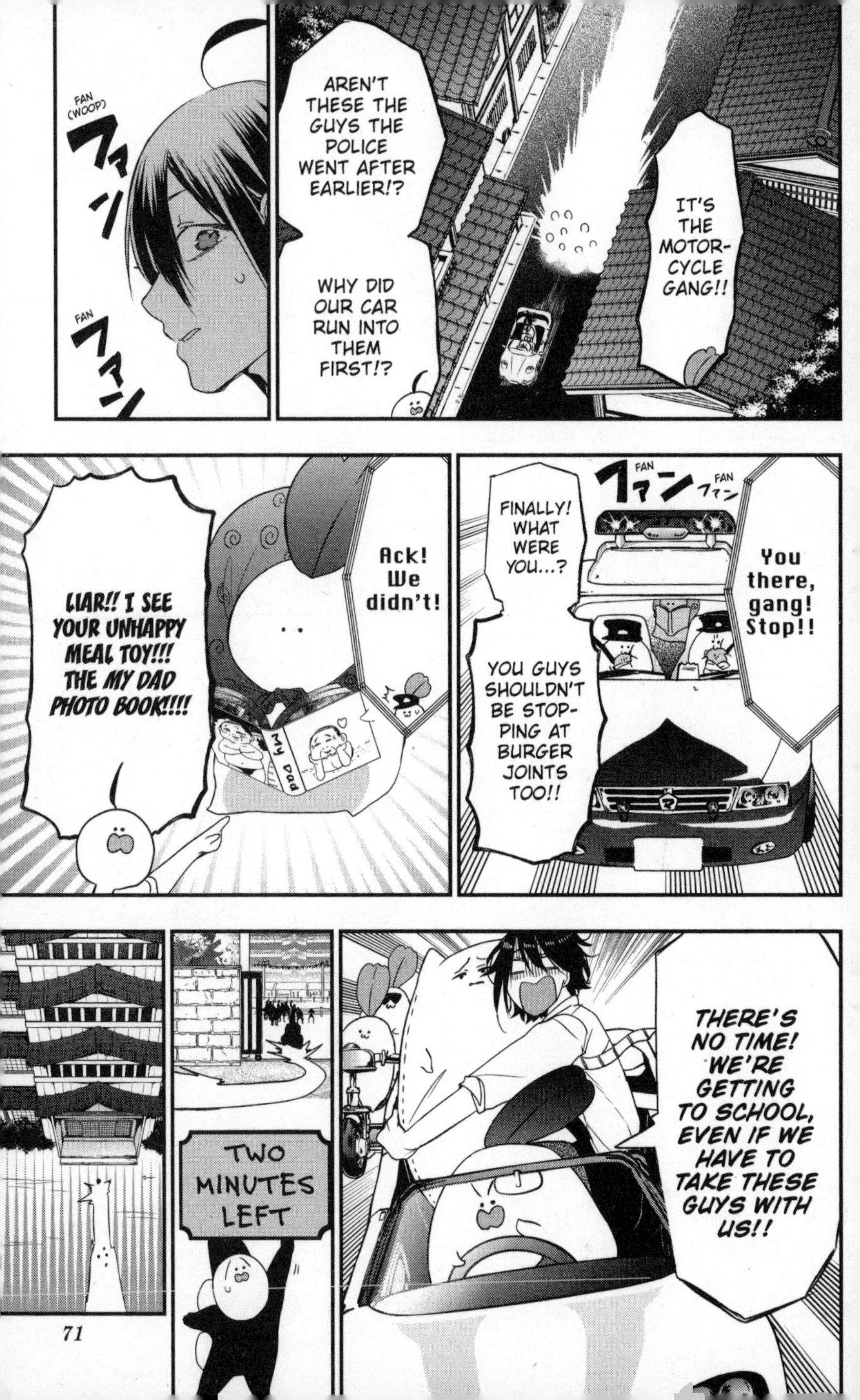
IT'S THE MOTORCYCLE GANG!!
AREN'T THESE THE GUYS THE POLICE WENT AFTER EARLIER!?
WHY DID OUR CAR RUN INTO THEM FIRST!?
FAN (WOOP)
FAN
FAN
FAN
You there, gang! Stop!!
FINALLY! WHAT WERE YOU...?
YOU GUYS SHOULDN'T BE STOP-PING AT BURGER JOINTS TOO!!
Ack! We didn't!
LIAR!! I SEE YOUR UNHAPPY MEAL TOY!!! THE MY DAD PHOTO BOOK!!!!
My Dad
THERE'S NO TIME! WE'RE GETTING TO SCHOOL, EVEN IF WE HAVE TO TAKE THESE GUYS WITH US!!
TWO MINUTES LEFT

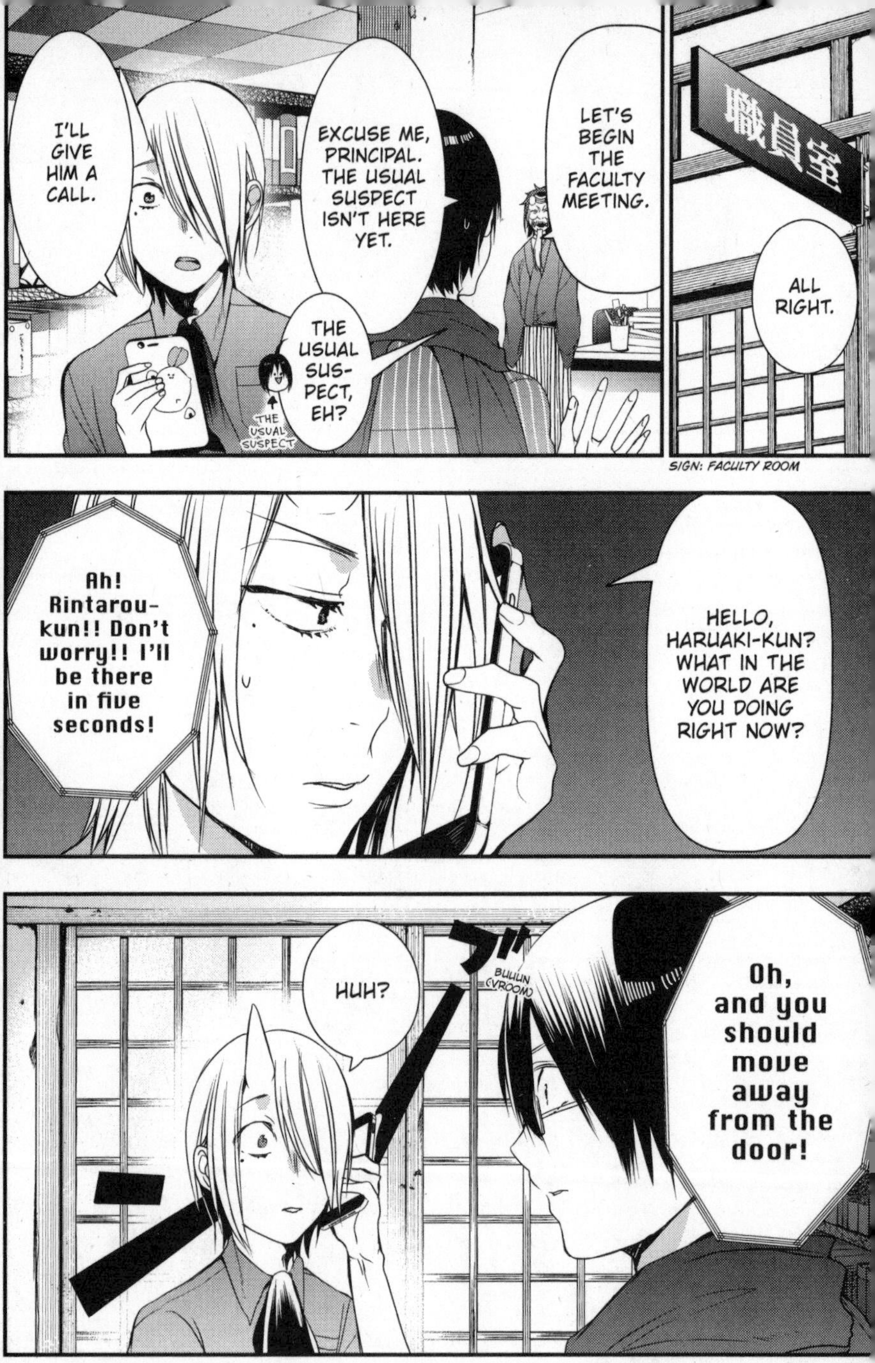
職員室
ALL RIGHT.
SIGN: FACULTY ROOM
LET'S BEGIN THE FACULTY MEETING.
EXCUSE ME, PRINCIPAL. THE USUAL SUSPECT ISN'T HERE YET.
THE USUAL SUS-PECT, EH?
I'LL GIVE HIM A CALL.
THE USUAL SUSPECT
HELLO, HARUAKI-KUN? WHAT IN THE WORLD ARE YOU DOING RIGHT NOW?
Ah! Rintarou-kun!! Don't worry!! I'll be there in five seconds!
Oh, and you should move away from the door!
BUUUN (VROOM)
HUH?

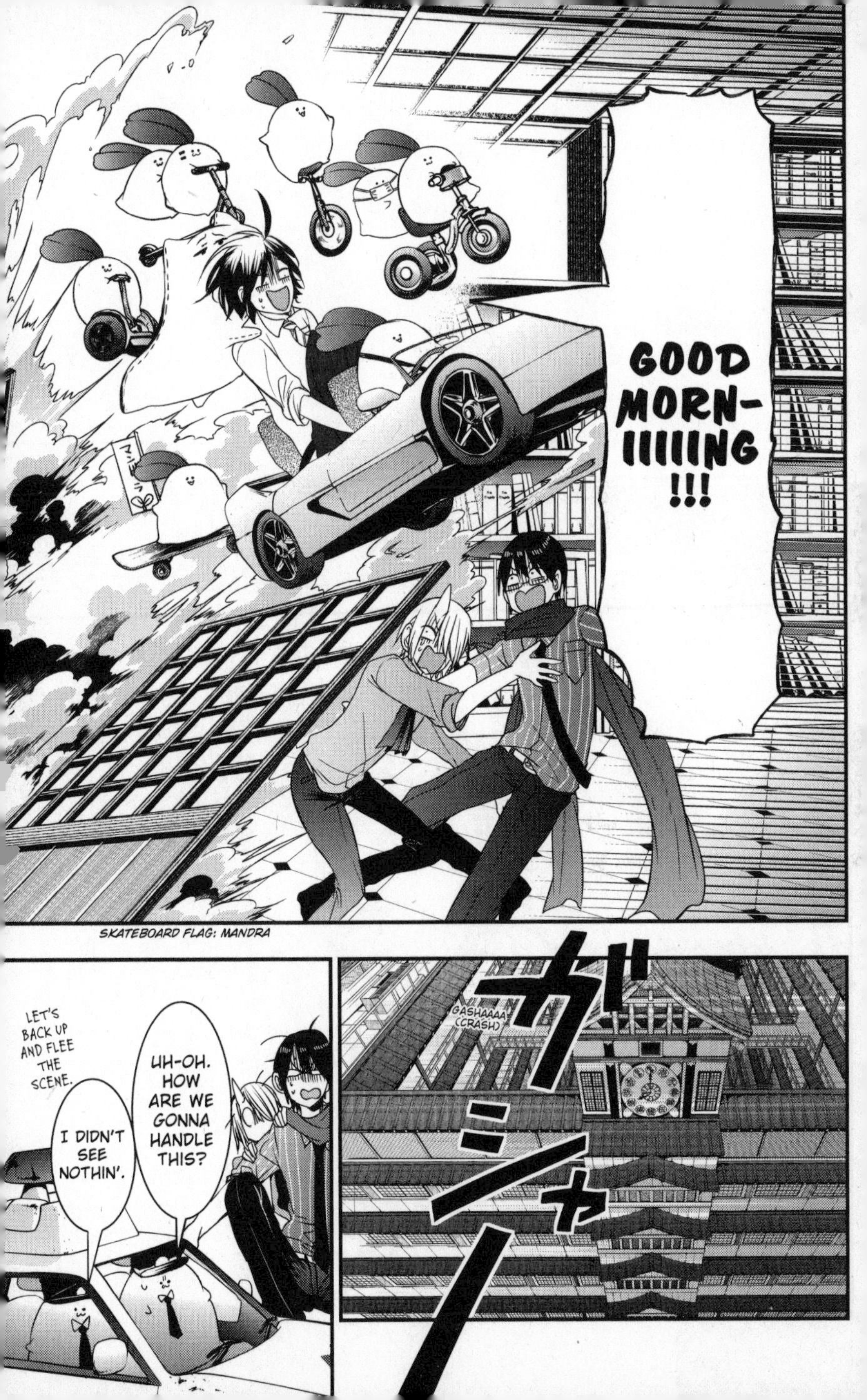
GOOD MORN-IIIIIING!!!
SKATEBOARD FLAG: MANDRA
GASHAAAA (CRASH)
UH-OH. HOW ARE WE GONNA HANDLE THIS?
LET'S BACK UP AND FLEE THE SCENE.
I DIDN'T SEE NOTHIN'.

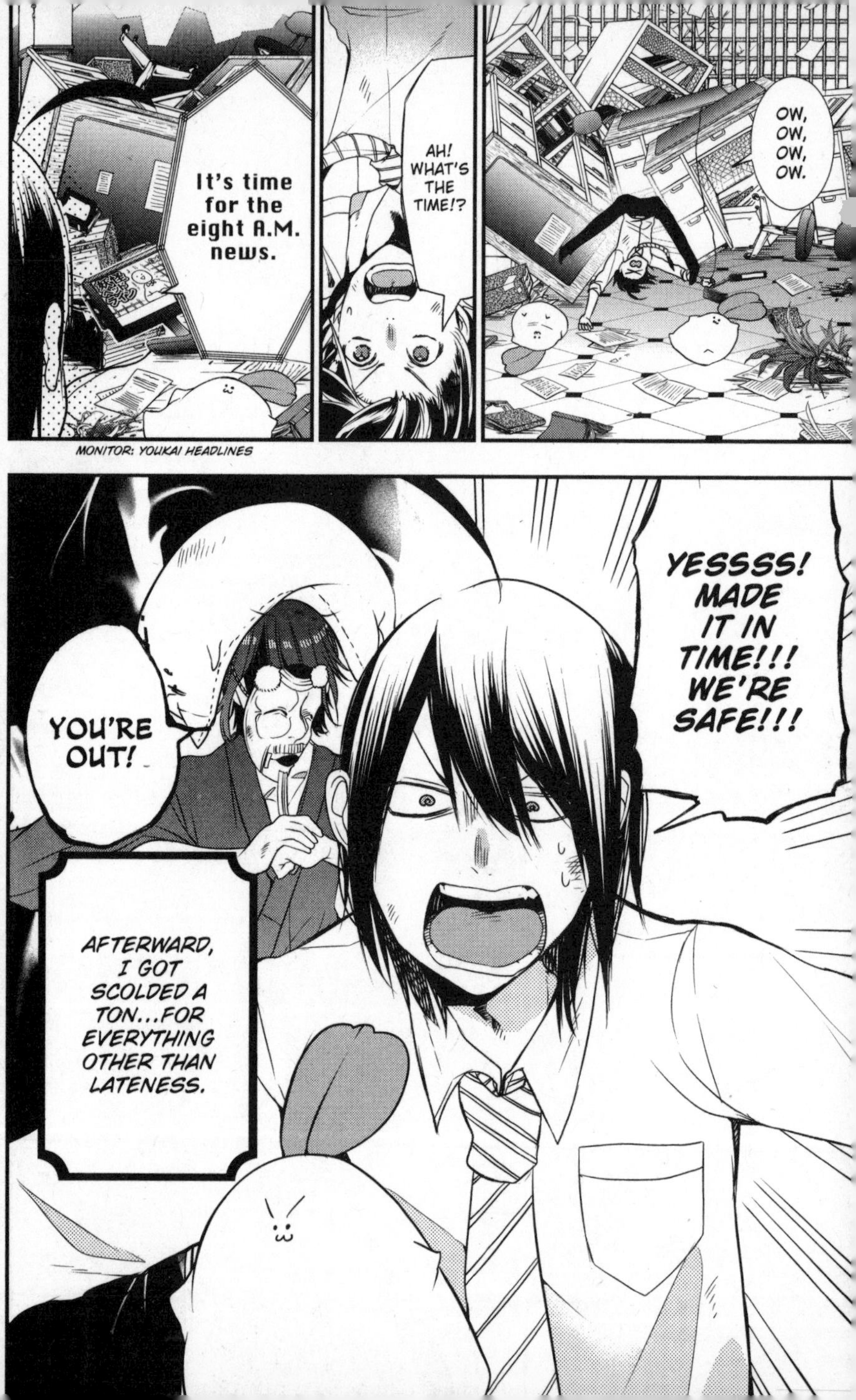
OW, OW, OW, OW.
AH! WHAT'S THE TIME!?
It's time for the eight A.M. news.
MONITOR: YOUKAI HEADLINES
YESSSS! MADE IT IN TIME!!! WE'RE SAFE!!!
YOU'RE OUT!
AFTERWARD, I GOT SCOLDED A TON...FOR EVERYTHING OTHER THAN LATENESS.

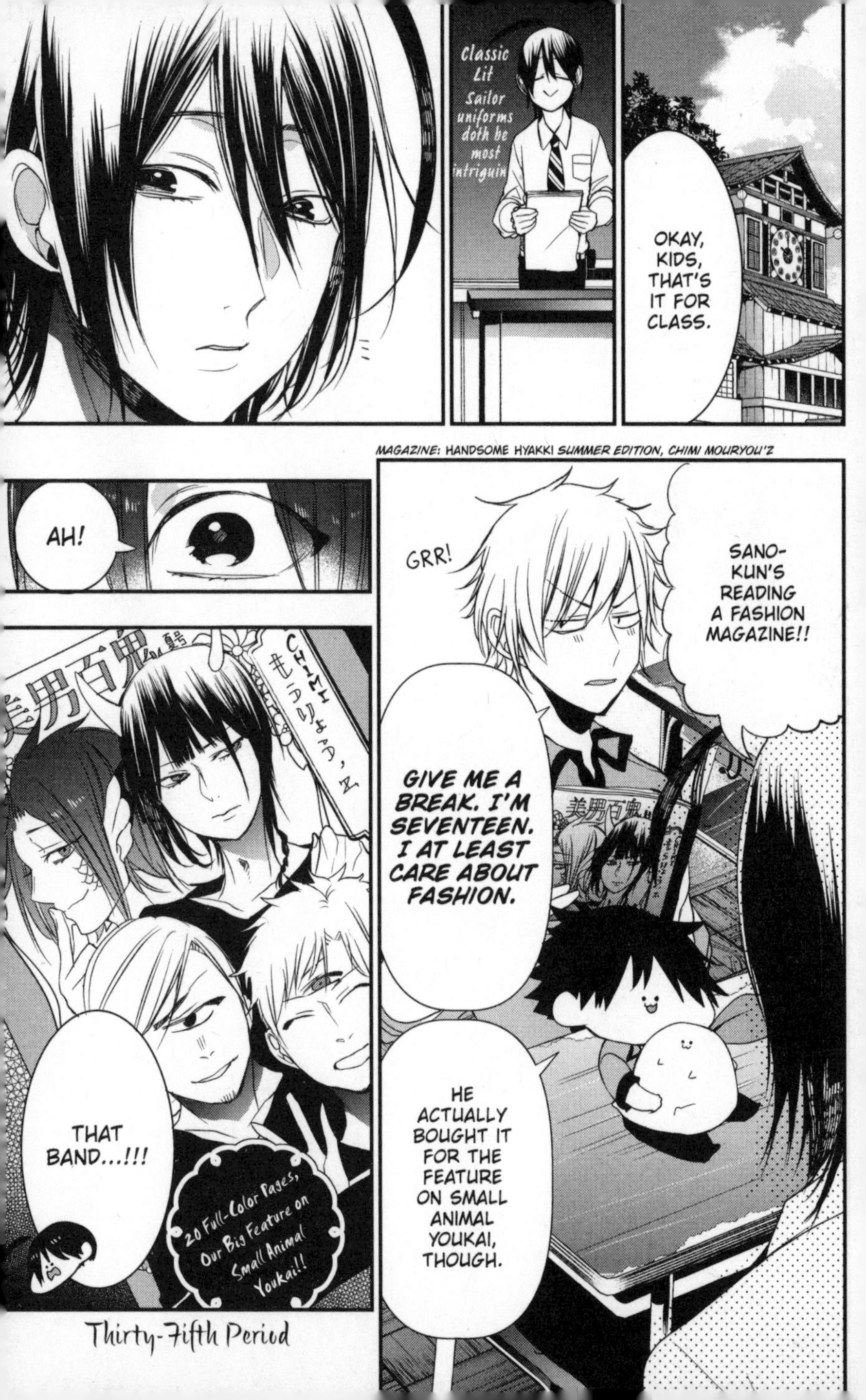
OKAY, KIDS, THAT'S IT FOR CLASS.
Classic Lit
Sailor uniforms doth be most intriguin
MAGAZINE: HANDSOME HYAKKI SUMMER EDITION, CHIMI MOURYOU'Z
SANO-KUN'S READING A FASHION MAGAZINE!!
GRR!
GIVE ME A BREAK. I'M SEVENTEEN. I AT LEAST CARE ABOUT FASHION.
HE ACTUALLY BOUGHT IT FOR THE FEATURE ON SMALL ANIMAL YOUKAI, THOUGH.
AH!
CHIMI
THAT BAND...!!!
20 Full-Color Pages, Our Big Feature on Small Animal Youkai!!

Thirty-Fifth Period

Thirty-Fifth Period Spy on the Class-3 Guys!!

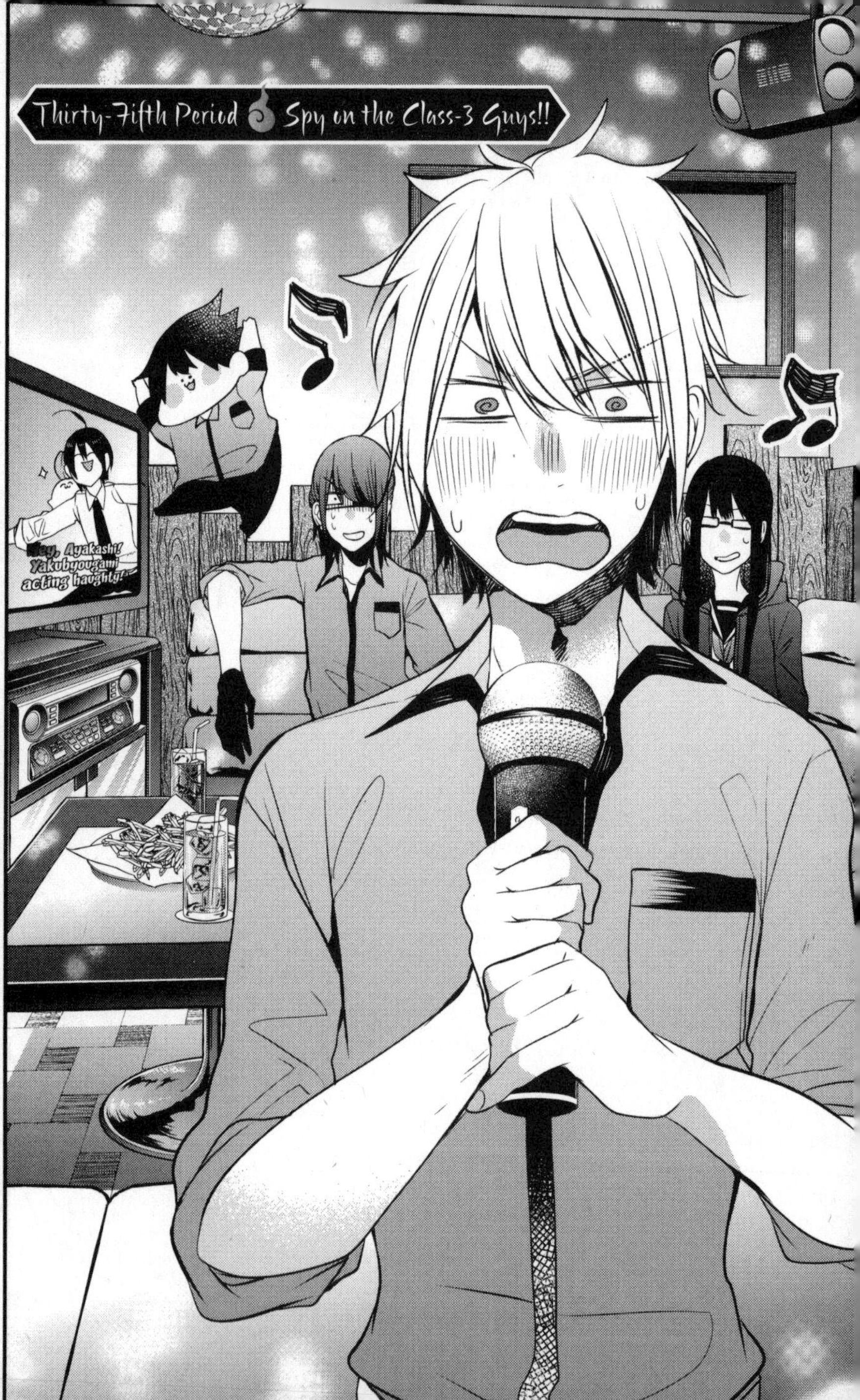
Hey, Ayakashi! Yakubyougami acting haughty!

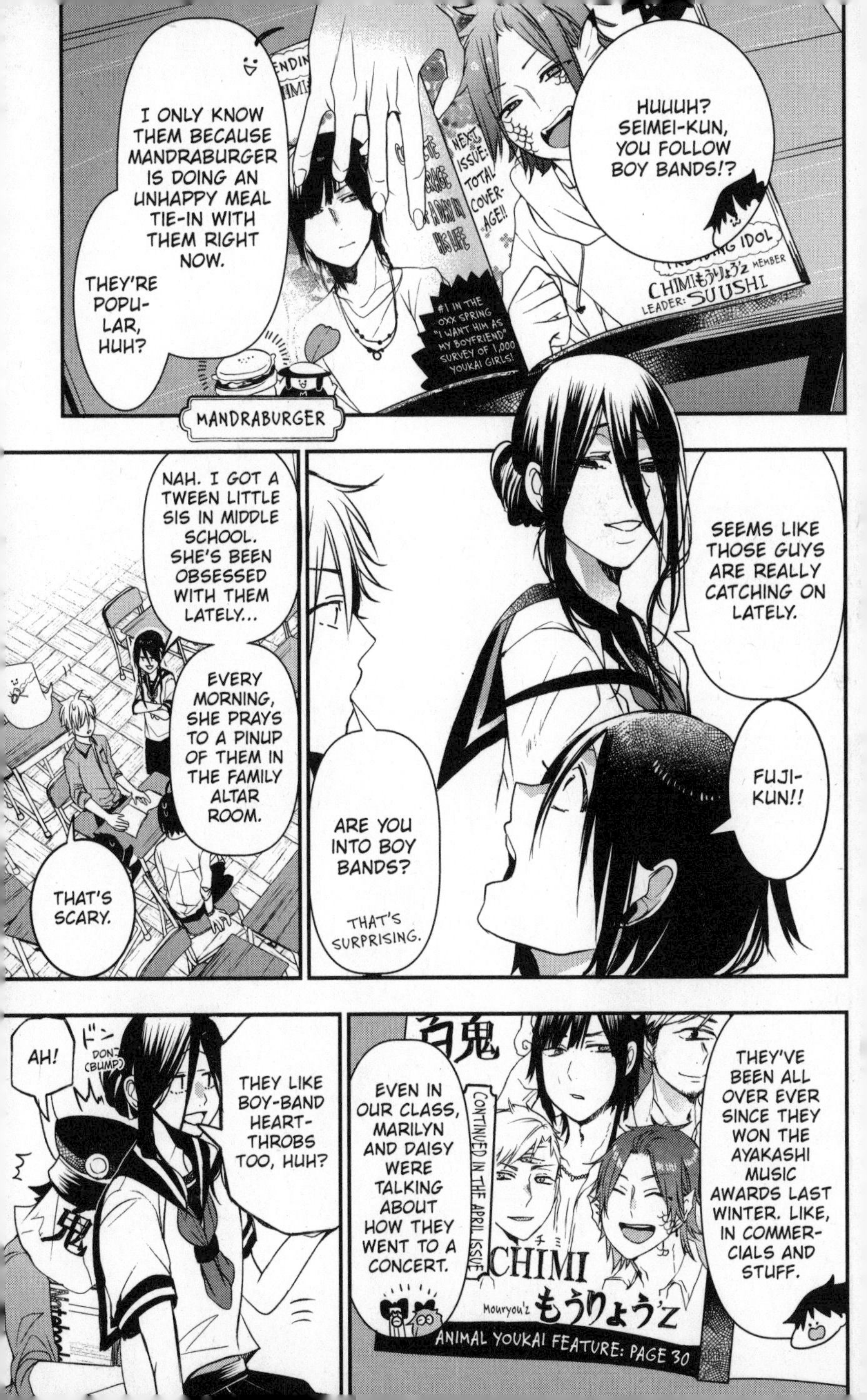
HUUUH? SEIMEI-KUN, YOU FOLLOW BOY BANDS!?
NEXT ISSUE: TOTAL COVERAGE!!
CHIMIもうりょう'z MEMBER
LEADER: SUUSHI
#1 IN THE OXX SPRING "I WANT HIM AS MY BOYFRIEND" SURVEY OF 1,000 YOUKAI GIRLS!
I ONLY KNOW THEM BECAUSE MANDRABURGER IS DOING AN UNHAPPY MEAL TIE-IN WITH THEM RIGHT NOW.
THEY'RE POPULAR, HUH?
MANDRABURGER
SEEMS LIKE THOSE GUYS ARE REALLY CATCHING ON LATELY.
FUJI-KUN!!
ARE YOU INTO BOY BANDS?
THAT'S SURPRISING.
NAH. I GOT A TWEEN LITTLE SIS IN MIDDLE SCHOOL. SHE'S BEEN OBSESSED WITH THEM LATELY...
EVERY MORNING, SHE PRAYS TO A PINUP OF THEM IN THE FAMILY ALTAR ROOM.
THAT'S SCARY.
THEY'VE BEEN ALL OVER EVER SINCE THEY WON THE AYAKASHI MUSIC AWARDS LAST WINTER. LIKE, IN COMMERCIALS AND STUFF.
EVEN IN OUR CLASS, MARILYN AND DAISY WERE TALKING ABOUT HOW THEY WENT TO A CONCERT.
CONTINUED IN THE APRIL ISSUE
CHIMI チミ
Mouryou'z もうりょう'z
ANIMAL YOUKAI FEATURE: PAGE 30
AH!
ドン DON (BUMP)
THEY LIKE BOY-BAND HEART-THROBS TOO, HUH?

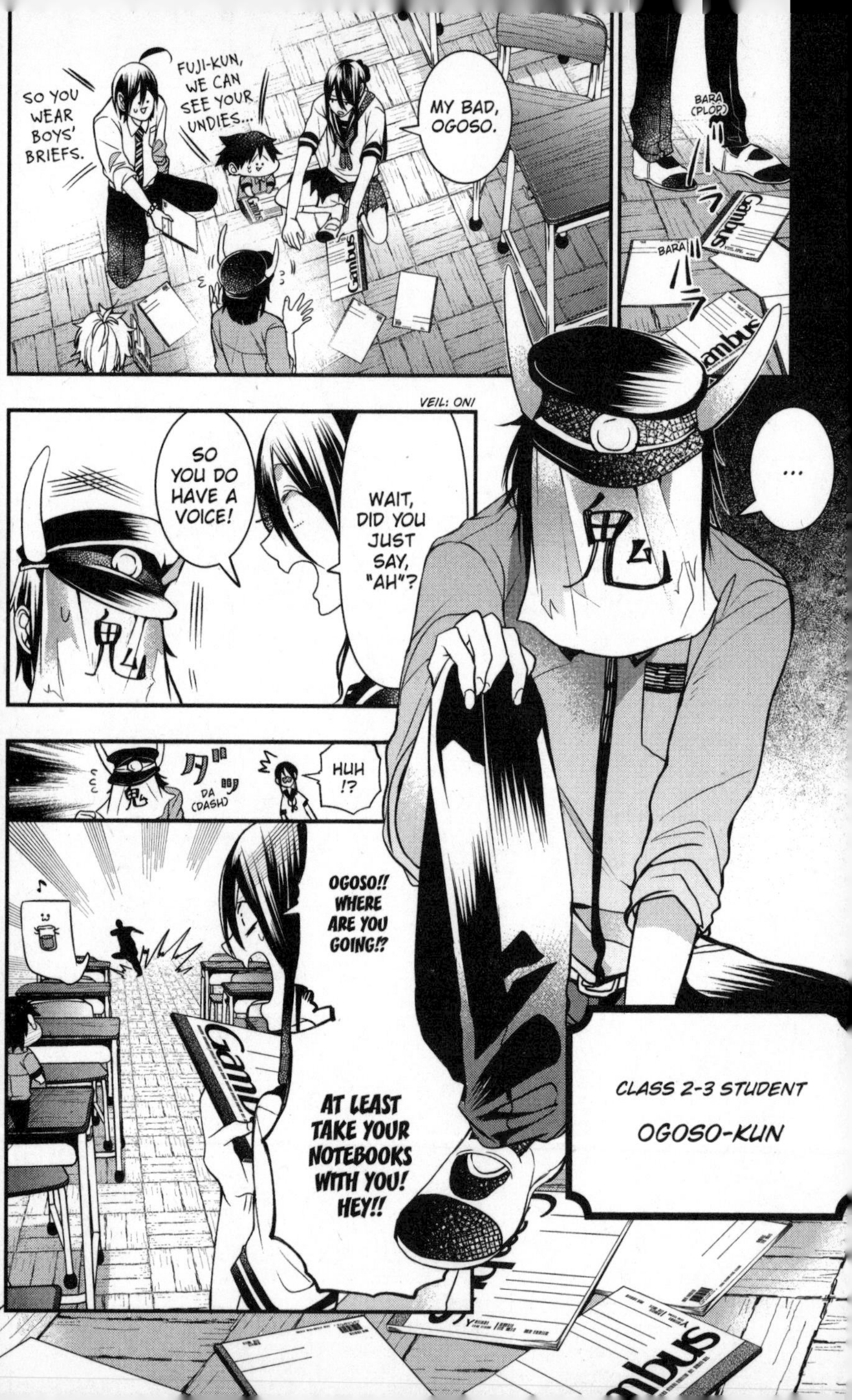
BARA (PLOP)
BARA
MY BAD, OGOSO.
FUJI-KUN, WE CAN SEE YOUR UNDIES...
SO YOU WEAR BOYS' BRIEFS.
VEIL: ONI
...
CLASS 2-3 STUDENT
OGOSO-KUN
WAIT, DID YOU JUST SAY, "AH"?
SO YOU DO HAVE A VOICE!
HUH !?
DA (DASH)
OGOSO!! WHERE ARE YOU GOING!?
AT LEAST TAKE YOUR NOTEBOOKS WITH YOU! HEY!!

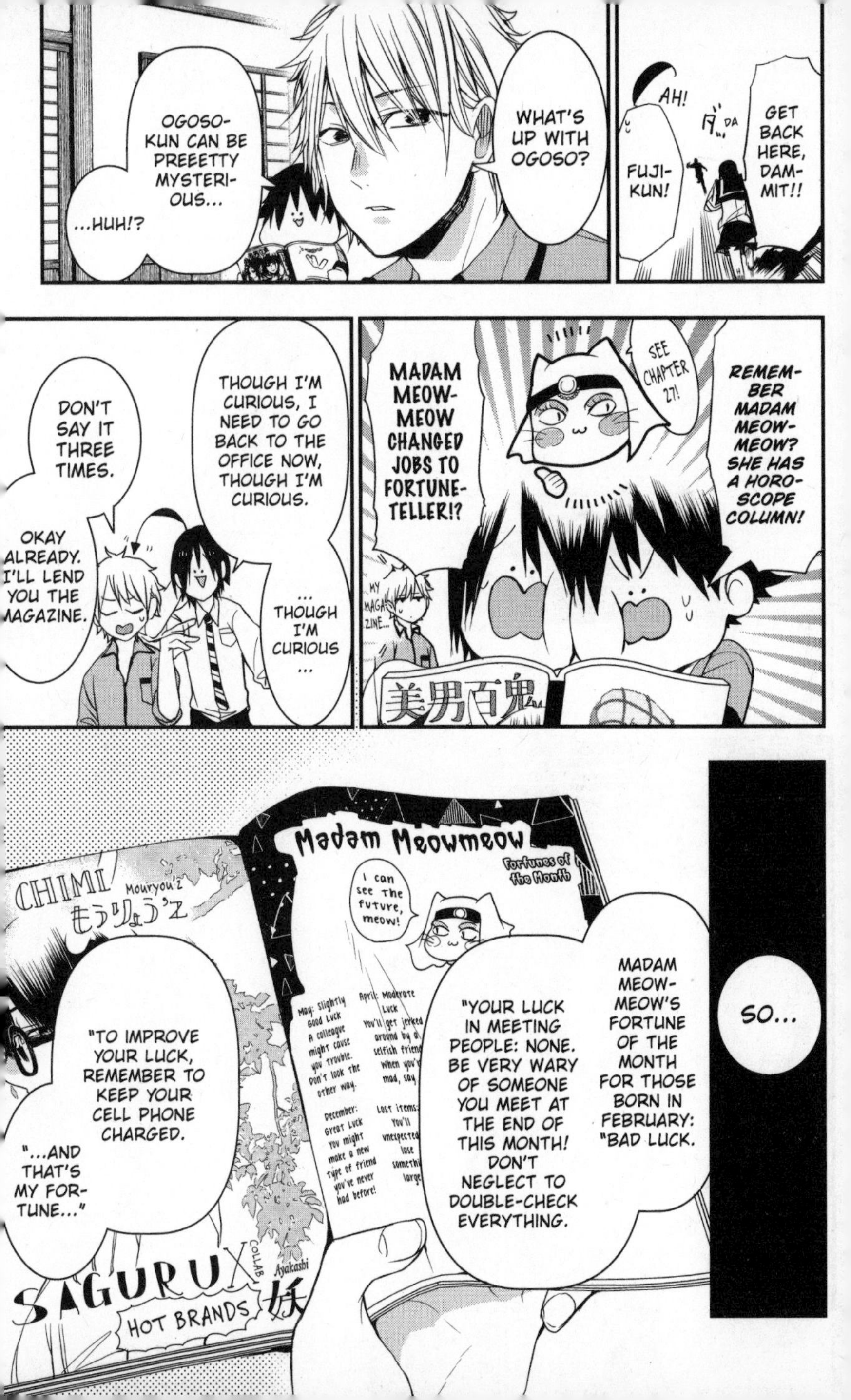
GET BACK HERE, DAMMIT!!
DA
AH!
FUJI-KUN!
WHAT'S UP WITH OGOSO?
OGOSO-KUN CAN BE PREEETTY MYSTERIOUS...
...HUH!?
REMEMBER MADAM MEOW-MEOW? SHE HAS A HOROSCOPE COLUMN!
SEE CHAPTER 27!
MADAM MEOW-MEOW CHANGED JOBS TO FORTUNE-TELLER!?
MY MAGAZINE...
美男百鬼
THOUGH I'M CURIOUS, I NEED TO GO BACK TO THE OFFICE NOW, THOUGH I'M CURIOUS.
DON'T SAY IT THREE TIMES.
...THOUGH I'M CURIOUS...
OKAY ALREADY. I'LL LEND YOU THE MAGAZINE.
SO...
MADAM MEOW-MEOW'S FORTUNE OF THE MONTH FOR THOSE BORN IN FEBRUARY: "BAD LUCK.
"YOUR LUCK IN MEETING PEOPLE: NONE. BE VERY WARY OF SOMEONE YOU MEET AT THE END OF THIS MONTH! DON'T NEGLECT TO DOUBLE-CHECK EVERYTHING.
Madam Meowmeow
Fortunes of the Month
I can see the future, meow!
April: Moderate Luck You'll get jerked around by a selfish friend. When you're mad, say
May: Slightly Good Luck A colleague might cause you trouble. Don't look the other way.
Lost items: You'll unexpectedly lose something large
December: Great Luck You might make a new type of friend you've never had before!
CHIMI Mouryou'z もうりょう'ズ
"TO IMPROVE YOUR LUCK, REMEMBER TO KEEP YOUR CELL PHONE CHARGED.
"...AND THAT'S MY FORTUNE..."
SAGURU X COLLAB Ayakashi 妖
HOT BRANDS

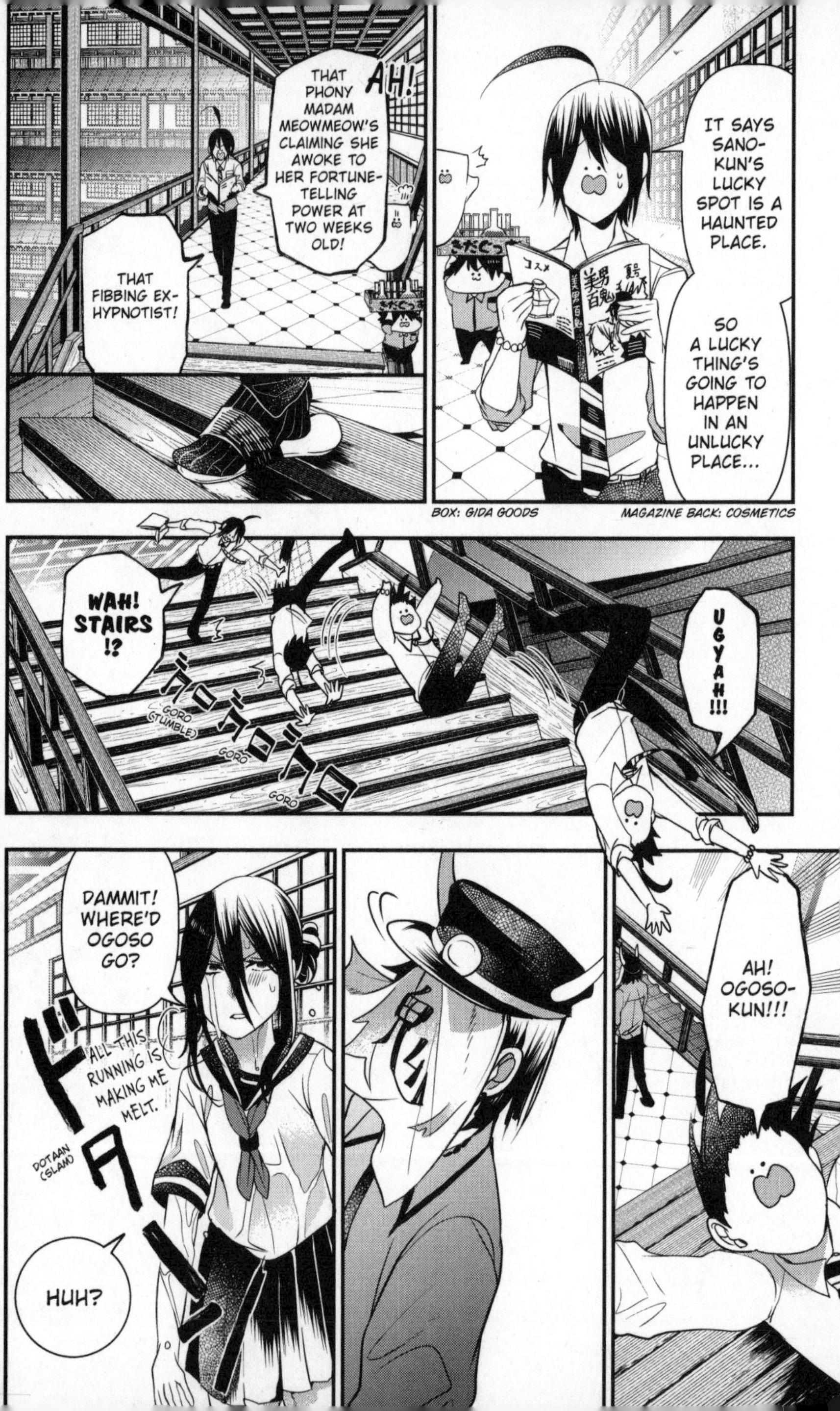
IT SAYS SANO-KUN'S LUCKY SPOT IS A HAUNTED PLACE.
SO A LUCKY THING'S GOING TO HAPPEN IN AN UNLUCKY PLACE...
AH!
THAT PHONY MADAM MEOWMEOW'S CLAIMING SHE AWOKE TO HER FORTUNE-TELLING POWER AT TWO WEEKS OLD!
THAT FIBBING EX-HYPNOTIST!
BOX: GIDA GOODS
MAGAZINE BACK: COSMETICS
UGYAH!!!
WAH! STAIRS!?
GORO (TUMBLE)
GORO
GORO
AH! OGOSO-KUN!!!
DAMMIT! WHERE'D OGOSO GO?
ALL THIS RUNNING IS MAKING ME MELT.
DOTAAN (SLAM)
HUH?

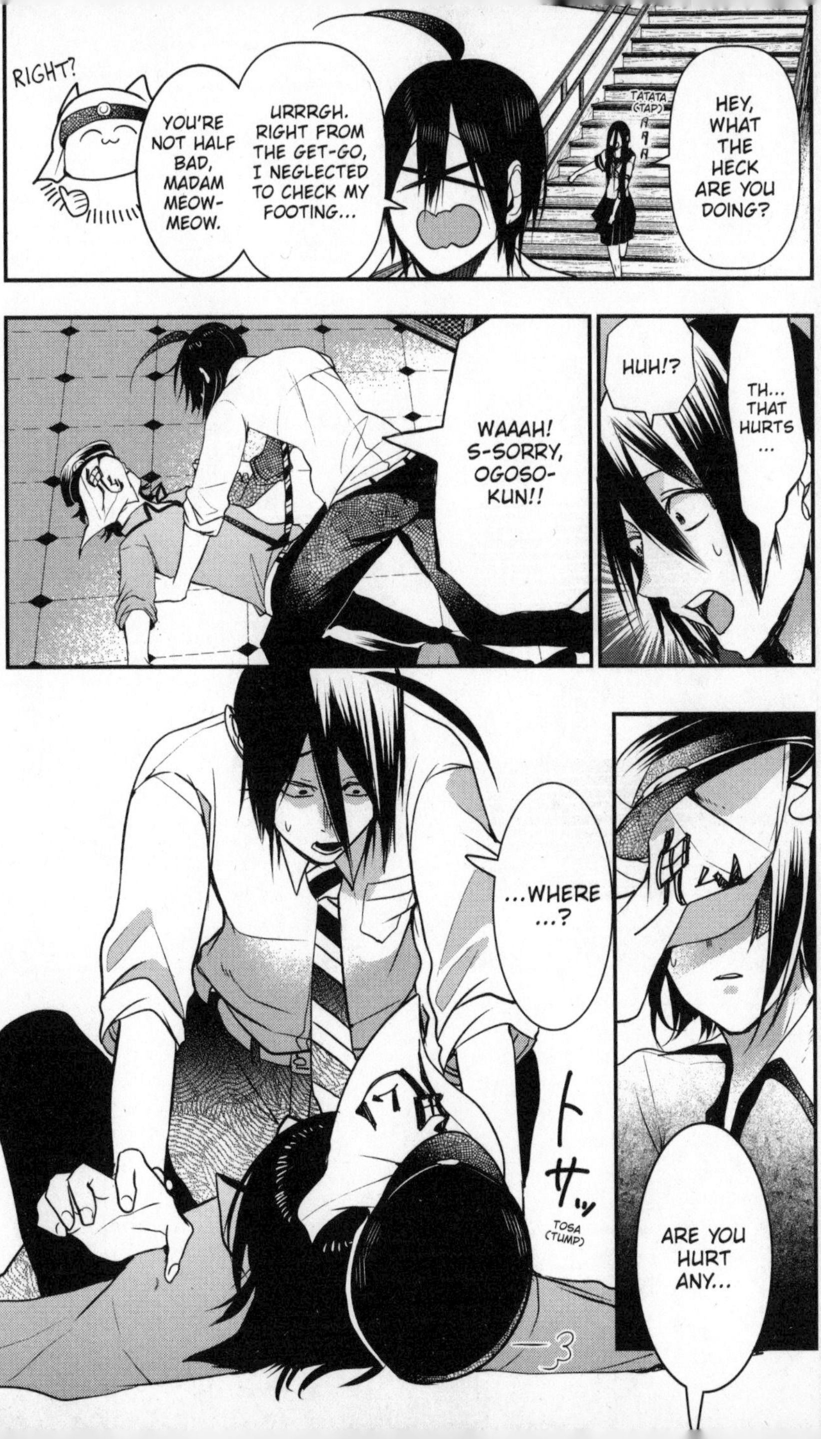
HEY, WHAT THE HECK ARE YOU DOING?
TATATA (TAP)
URRRGH. RIGHT FROM THE GET-GO, I NEGLECTED TO CHECK MY FOOTING...
YOU'RE NOT HALF BAD, MADAM MEOW-MEOW.
RIGHT?
TH... THAT HURTS ...
HUH!?
WAAAH! S-SORRY, OGOSO-KUN!!
ARE YOU HURT ANY...
...WHERE ...?
TOSA (TUMP)

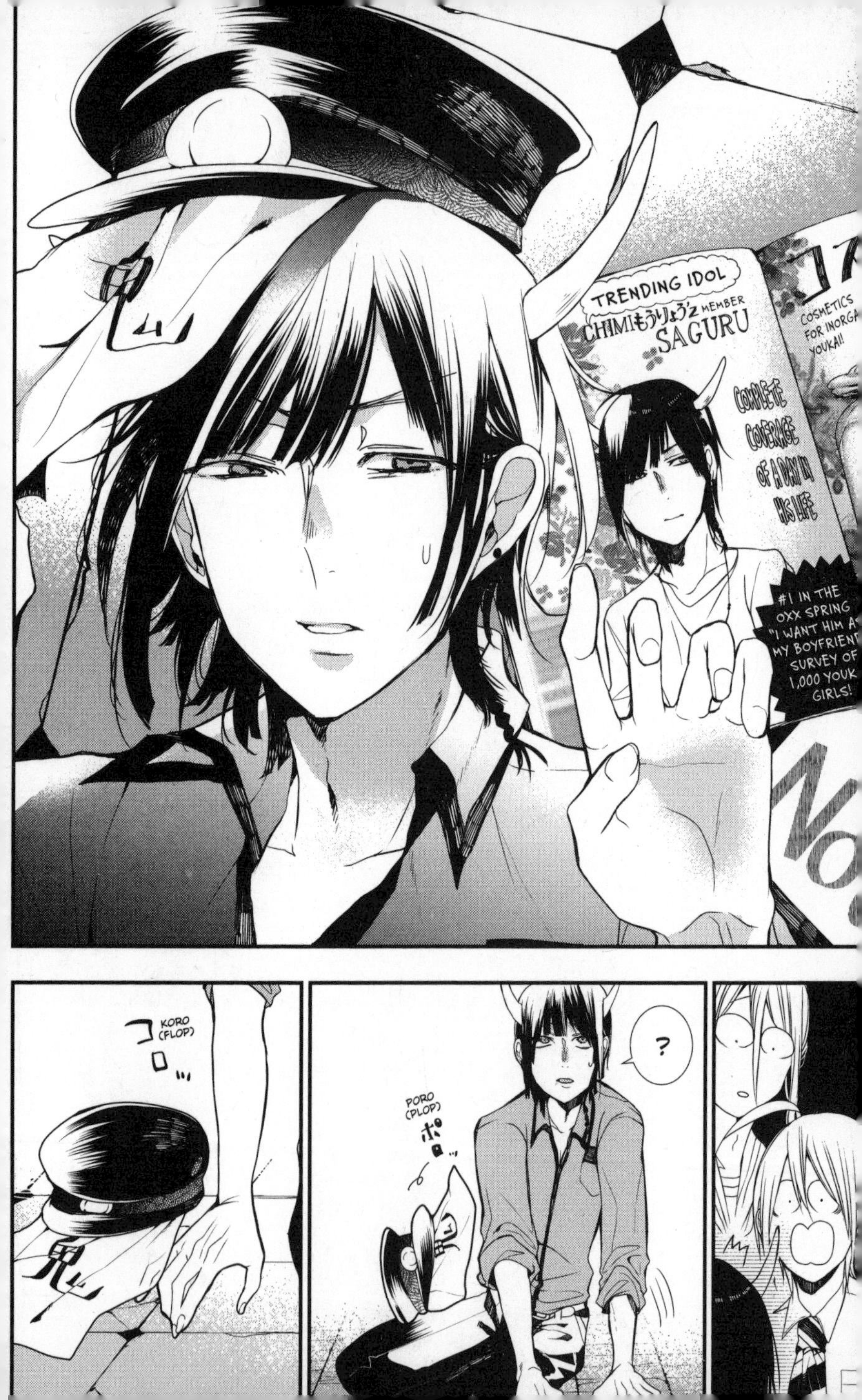

コス
COSMETICS FOR INORGA YOUKAI!
TRENDING IDOL
CHIMIもうりょう'z MEMBER
SAGURU
COMPLETE COVERAGE OF A DAY IN HIS LIFE
#1 IN THE OXX SPRING "I WANT HIM A MY BOYFRIEND SURVEY OF 1,000 YOUK GIRLS!
?
ポロッ
PORO (PLOP)
コロッ
KORO (FLOP)

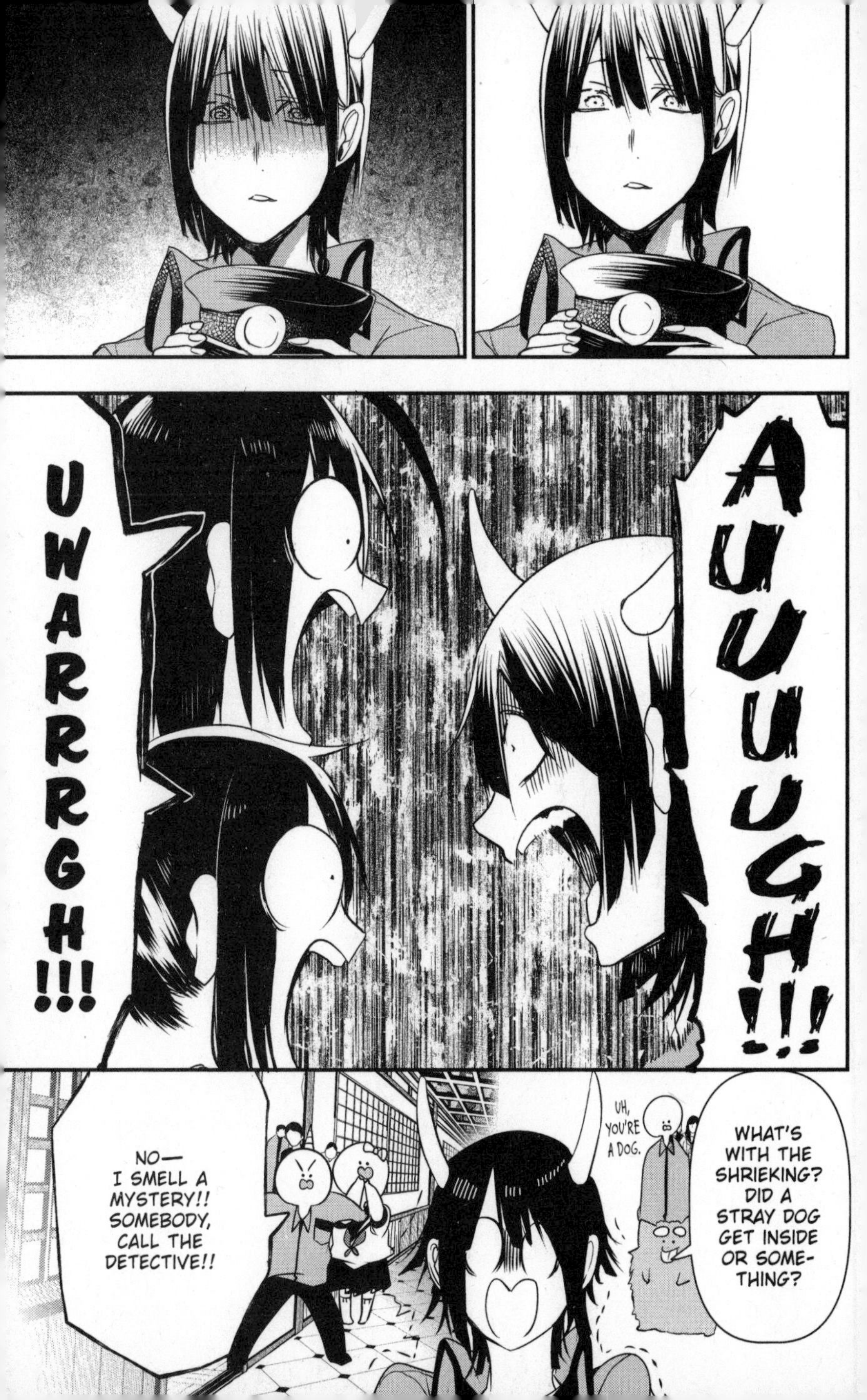
AUUUGH!!
UWARRRGH!!!
WHAT'S WITH THE SHRIEKING? DID A STRAY DOG GET INSIDE OR SOME-THING?
UH, YOU'RE A DOG.
NO— I SMELL A MYSTERY!! SOMEBODY, CALL THE DETECTIVE!!

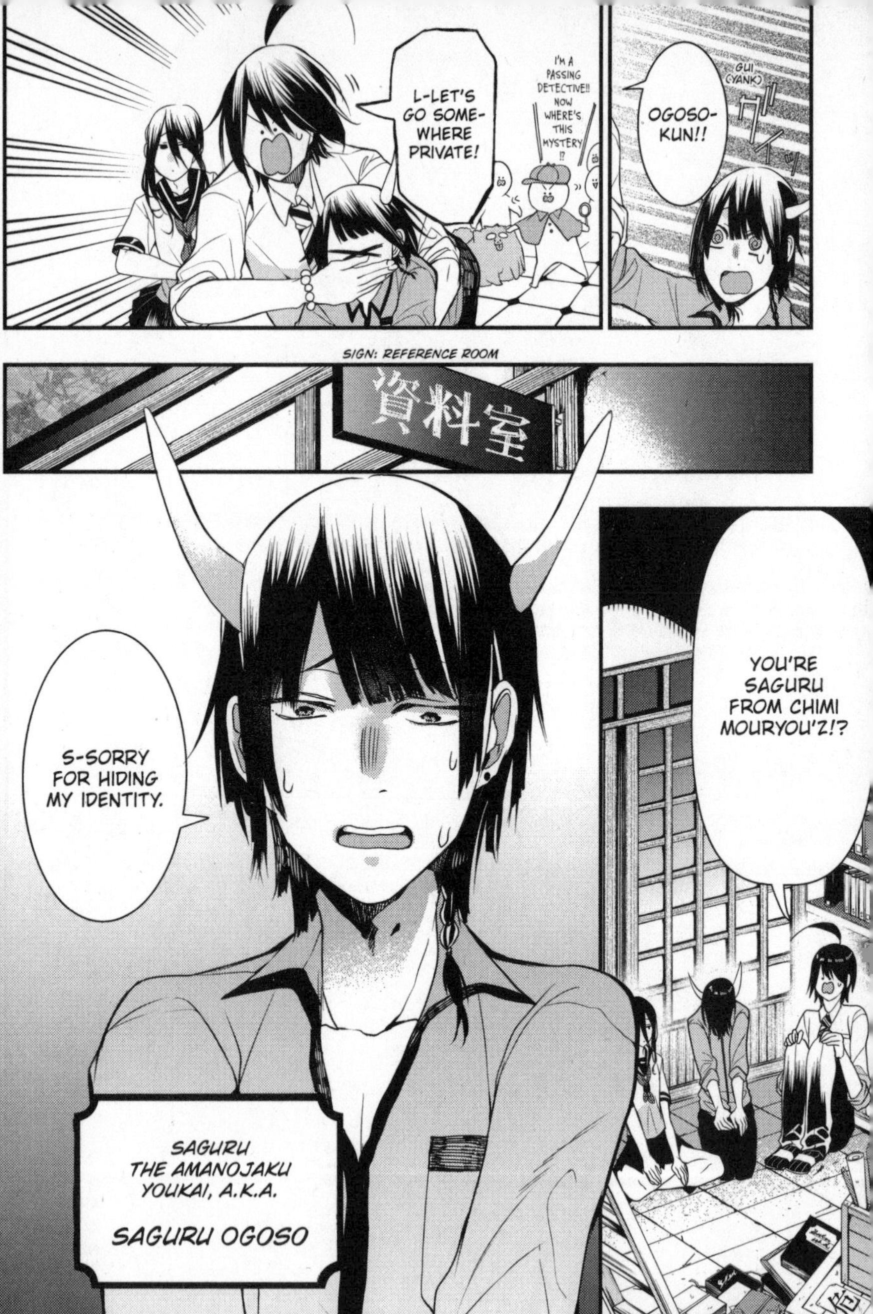

OGOSO-KUN!!
GUI (YANK)
L-LET'S GO SOME-WHERE PRIVATE!
I'M A PASSING DETECTIVE!! NOW WHERE'S THIS MYSTERY!?
SIGN: REFERENCE ROOM
資料室
YOU'RE SAGURU FROM CHIMI MOURYOU'Z!?
S-SORRY FOR HIDING MY IDENTITY.
SAGURU THE AMANOJAKU YOUKAI, A.K.A.
SAGURU OGOSO
BOX: DANGER

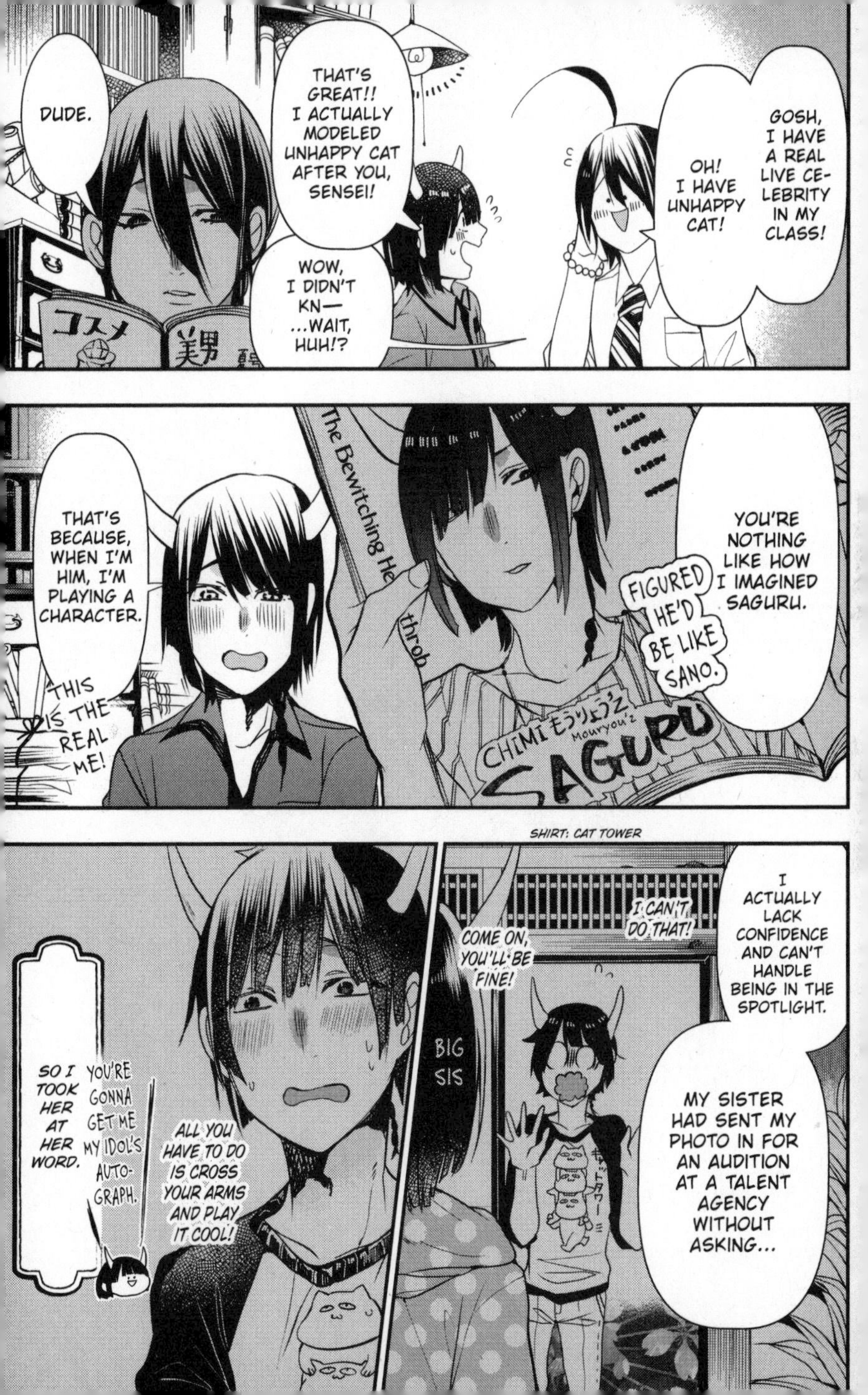
GOSH, I HAVE A REAL LIVE CELEBRITY IN MY CLASS!
OH! I HAVE UNHAPPY CAT!
THAT'S GREAT!! I ACTUALLY MODELED UNHAPPY CAT AFTER YOU, SENSEI!
WOW, I DIDN'T KN— ...WAIT, HUH!?
DUDE.
コスメ
美男
YOU'RE NOTHING LIKE HOW I IMAGINED SAGURU.
FIGURED HE'D BE LIKE SANO.
The Bewitching He
throb
CHIMI もうりょう'z Mouryou'z
SAGURU
THAT'S BECAUSE, WHEN I'M HIM, I'M PLAYING A CHARACTER.
THIS IS THE REAL ME!
SHIRT: CAT TOWER
I ACTUALLY LACK CONFIDENCE AND CAN'T HANDLE BEING IN THE SPOTLIGHT.
I CAN'T DO THAT!
MY SISTER HAD SENT MY PHOTO IN FOR AN AUDITION AT A TALENT AGENCY WITHOUT ASKING...
COME ON, YOU'LL BE FINE!
BIG SIS
ALL YOU HAVE TO DO IS CROSS YOUR ARMS AND PLAY IT COOL!
YOU'RE GONNA GET ME MY IDOL'S AUTOGRAPH.
SO I TOOK HER AT HER WORD.

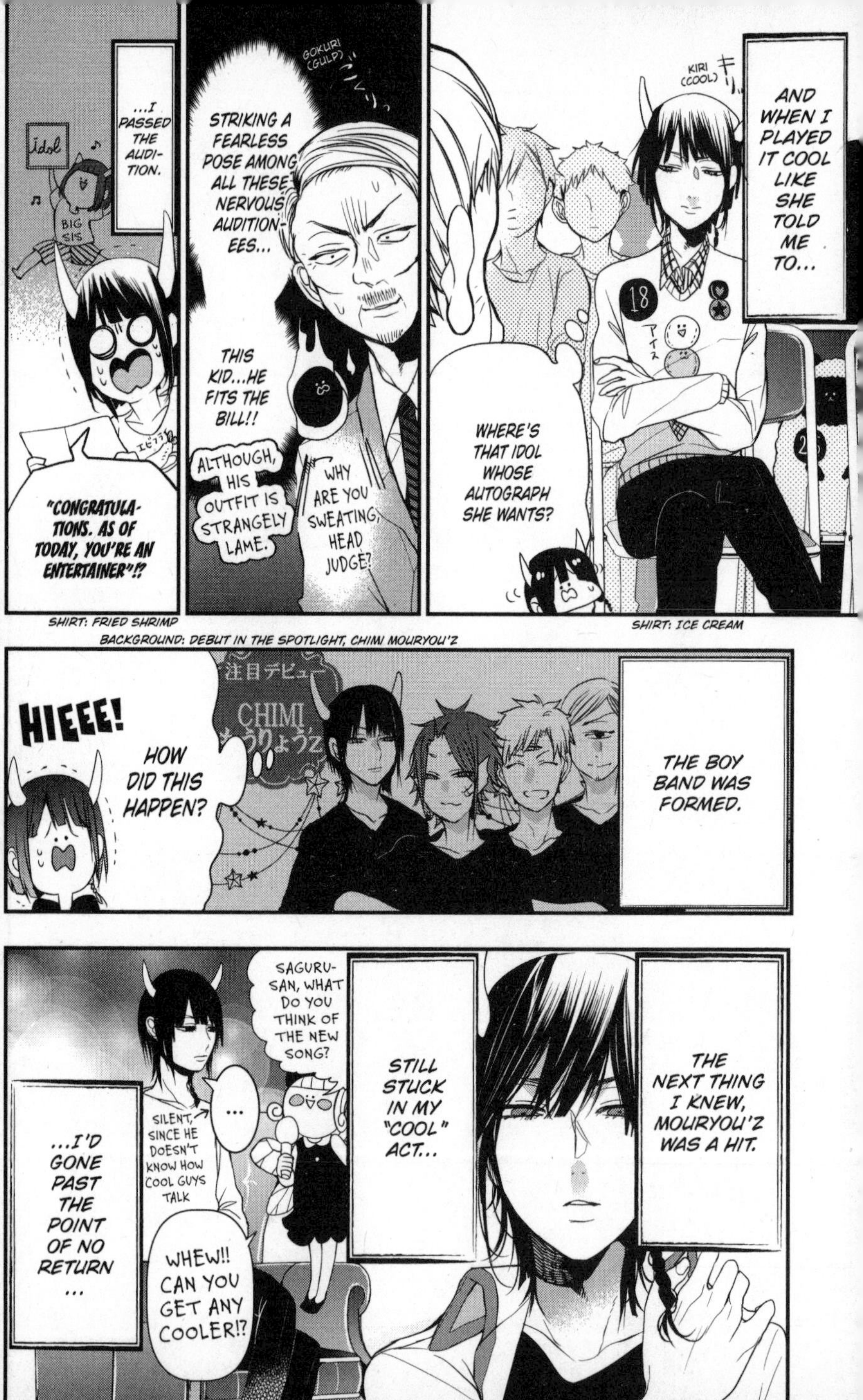
KIRI (COOL)
AND WHEN I PLAYED IT COOL LIKE SHE TOLD ME TO...
WHERE'S THAT IDOL WHOSE AUTOGRAPH SHE WANTS?
GOKURI (GULP)
STRIKING A FEARLESS POSE AMONG ALL THESE NERVOUS AUDITIONEES...
THIS KID...HE FITS THE BILL!!
WHY ARE YOU SWEATING, HEAD JUDGE?
ALTHOUGH, HIS OUTFIT IS STRANGELY LAME.
...I PASSED THE AUDITION.
idol
BIG SIS
"CONGRATULATIONS. AS OF TODAY, YOU'RE AN ENTERTAINER"!?
SHIRT: ICE CREAM
BACKGROUND: DEBUT IN THE SPOTLIGHT, CHIMI MOURYOU'Z
SHIRT: FRIED SHRIMP
THE BOY BAND WAS FORMED.
HOW DID THIS HAPPEN?
HIEEE!
THE NEXT THING I KNEW, MOURYOU'Z WAS A HIT.
STILL STUCK IN MY "COOL" ACT...
SAGURU-SAN, WHAT DO YOU THINK OF THE NEW SONG?
...
SILENT, SINCE HE DOESN'T KNOW HOW COOL GUYS TALK
WHEW!! CAN YOU GET ANY COOLER!?
...I'D GONE PAST THE POINT OF NO RETURN...

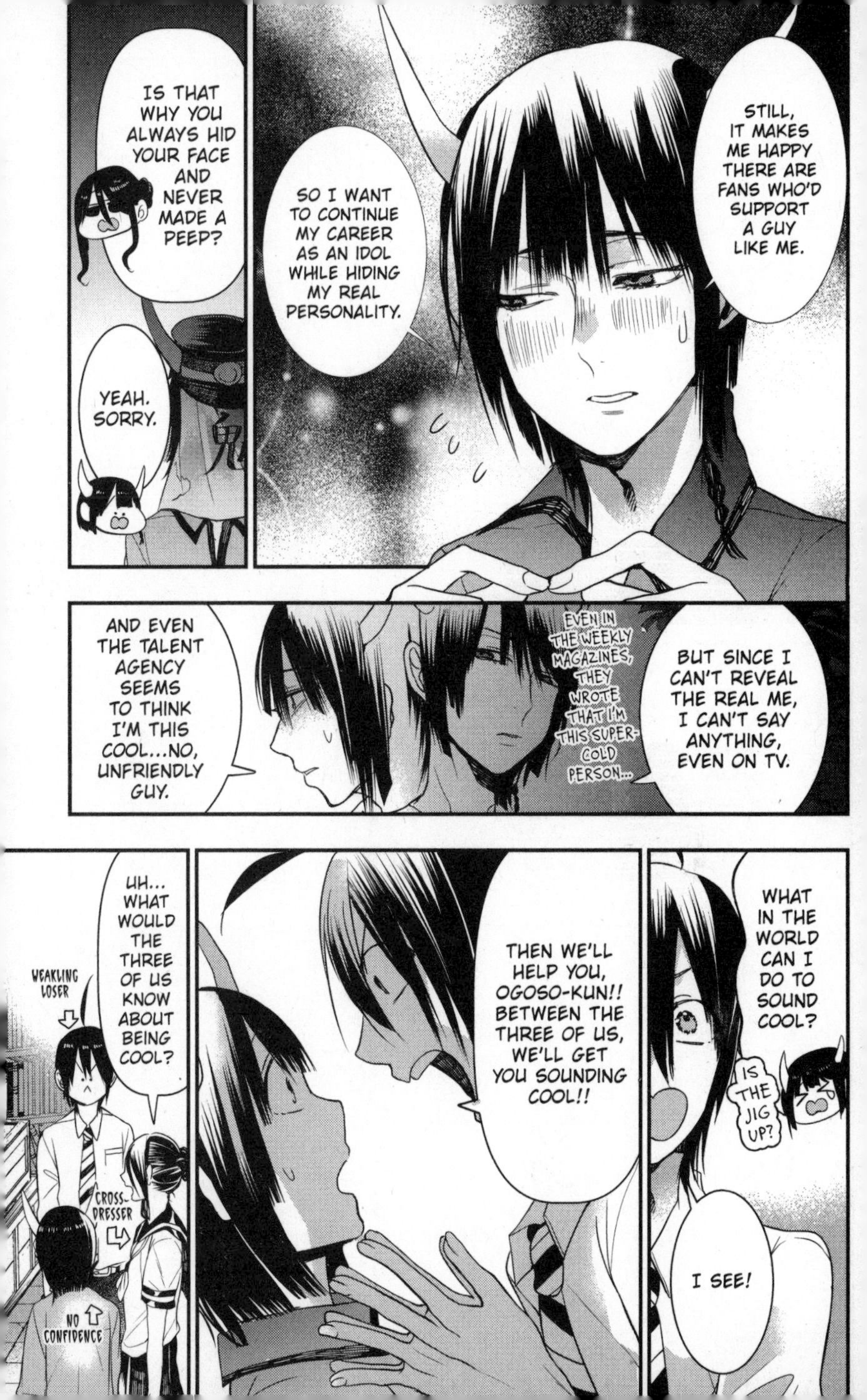
STILL, IT MAKES ME HAPPY THERE ARE FANS WHO'D SUPPORT A GUY LIKE ME.
SO I WANT TO CONTINUE MY CAREER AS AN IDOL WHILE HIDING MY REAL PERSONALITY.
IS THAT WHY YOU ALWAYS HID YOUR FACE AND NEVER MADE A PEEP?
YEAH. SORRY.
BUT SINCE I CAN'T REVEAL THE REAL ME, I CAN'T SAY ANYTHING, EVEN ON TV.
EVEN IN THE WEEKLY MAGAZINES, THEY WROTE THAT I'M THIS SUPER-COLD PERSON...
AND EVEN THE TALENT AGENCY SEEMS TO THINK I'M THIS COOL...NO, UNFRIENDLY GUY.
WHAT IN THE WORLD CAN I DO TO SOUND COOL?
IS THE JIG UP?
I SEE!
THEN WE'LL HELP YOU, OGOSO-KUN!! BETWEEN THE THREE OF US, WE'LL GET YOU SOUNDING COOL!!
UH... WHAT WOULD THE THREE OF US KNOW ABOUT BEING COOL?
WEAKLING LOSER
CROSS-DRESSER
NO CONFIDENCE

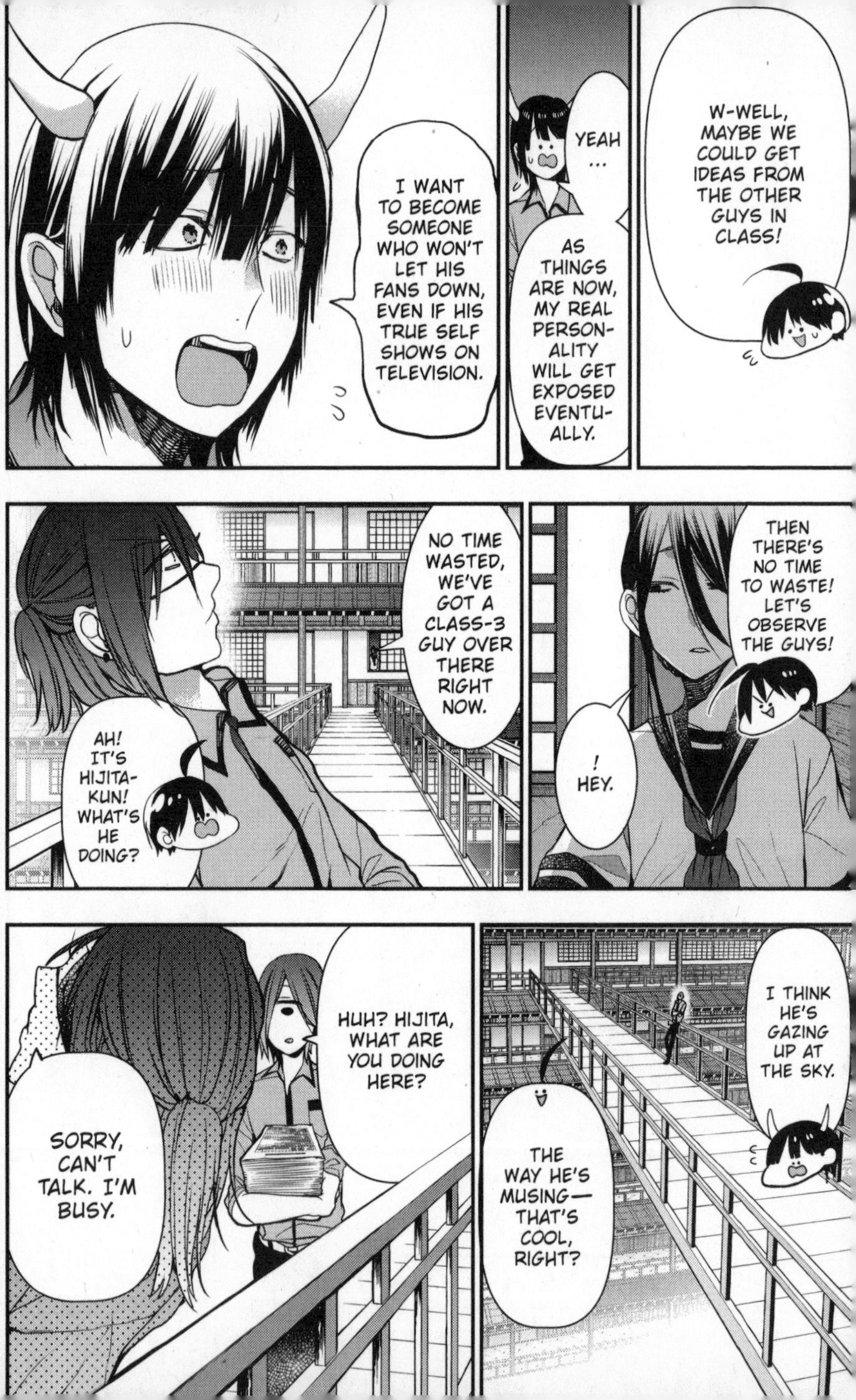
W-WELL, MAYBE WE COULD GET IDEAS FROM THE OTHER GUYS IN CLASS!
YEAH ...
AS THINGS ARE NOW, MY REAL PERSONALITY WILL GET EXPOSED EVENTUALLY.
I WANT TO BECOME SOMEONE WHO WON'T LET HIS FANS DOWN, EVEN IF HIS TRUE SELF SHOWS ON TELEVISION.
THEN THERE'S NO TIME TO WASTE! LET'S OBSERVE THE GUYS!
! HEY.
NO TIME WASTED, WE'VE GOT A CLASS-3 GUY OVER THERE RIGHT NOW.
AH! IT'S HIJITA-KUN! WHAT'S HE DOING?
I THINK HE'S GAZING UP AT THE SKY.
THE WAY HE'S MUSING—THAT'S COOL, RIGHT?
HUH? HIJITA, WHAT ARE YOU DOING HERE?
SORRY, CAN'T TALK. I'M BUSY.

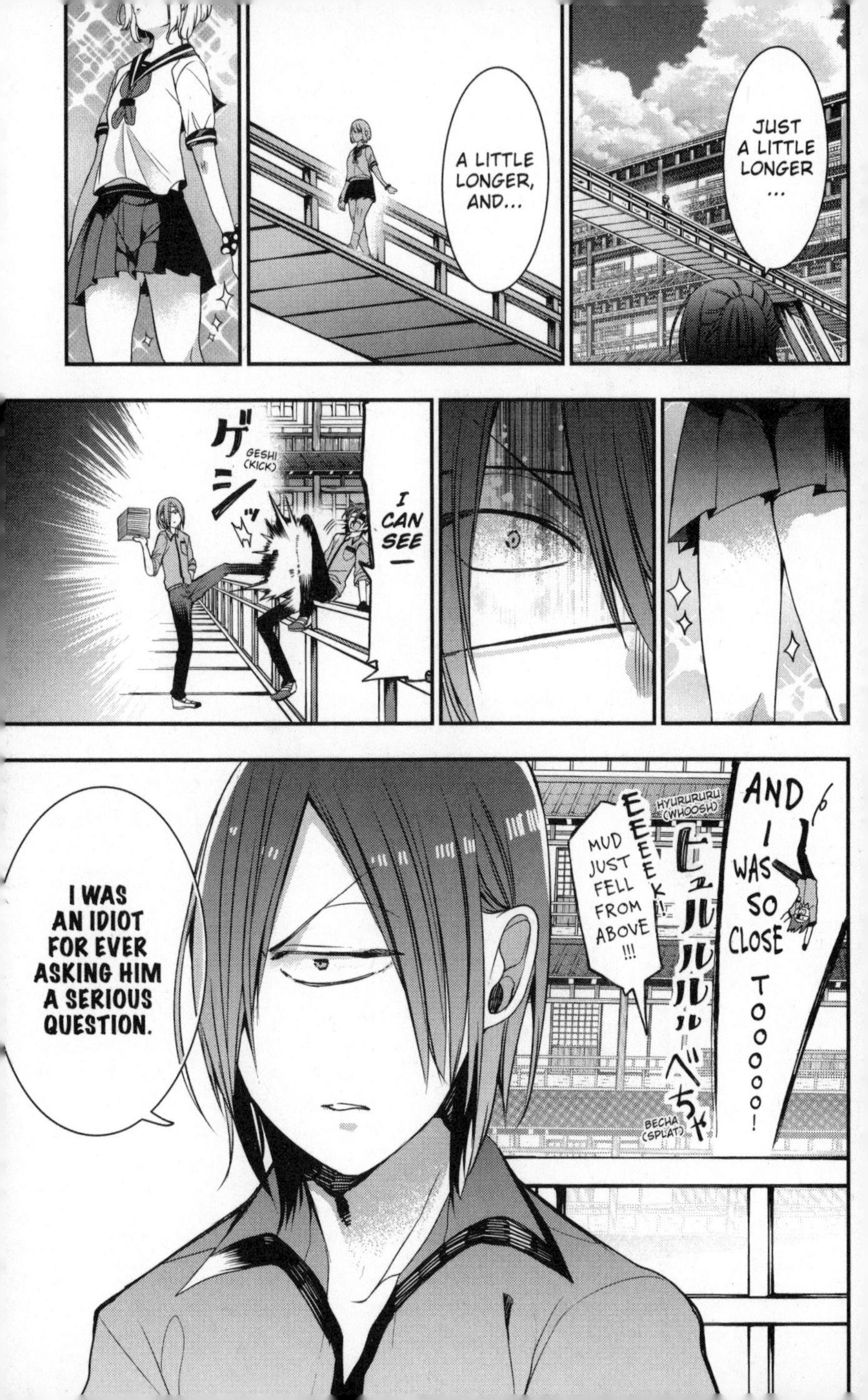
JUST A LITTLE LONGER ...
A LITTLE LONGER, AND...
I CAN SEE—
ゲシッ
GESHI (KICK)
AND I WAS SO CLOSE TOOOOO!
ヒュルルルル
HYURURURU (WHOOSH)
EEEEK!!
MUD JUST FELL FROM ABOVE!!!
べちゃ
BECHA (SPLAT)
I WAS AN IDIOT FOR EVER ASKING HIM A SERIOUS QUESTION.

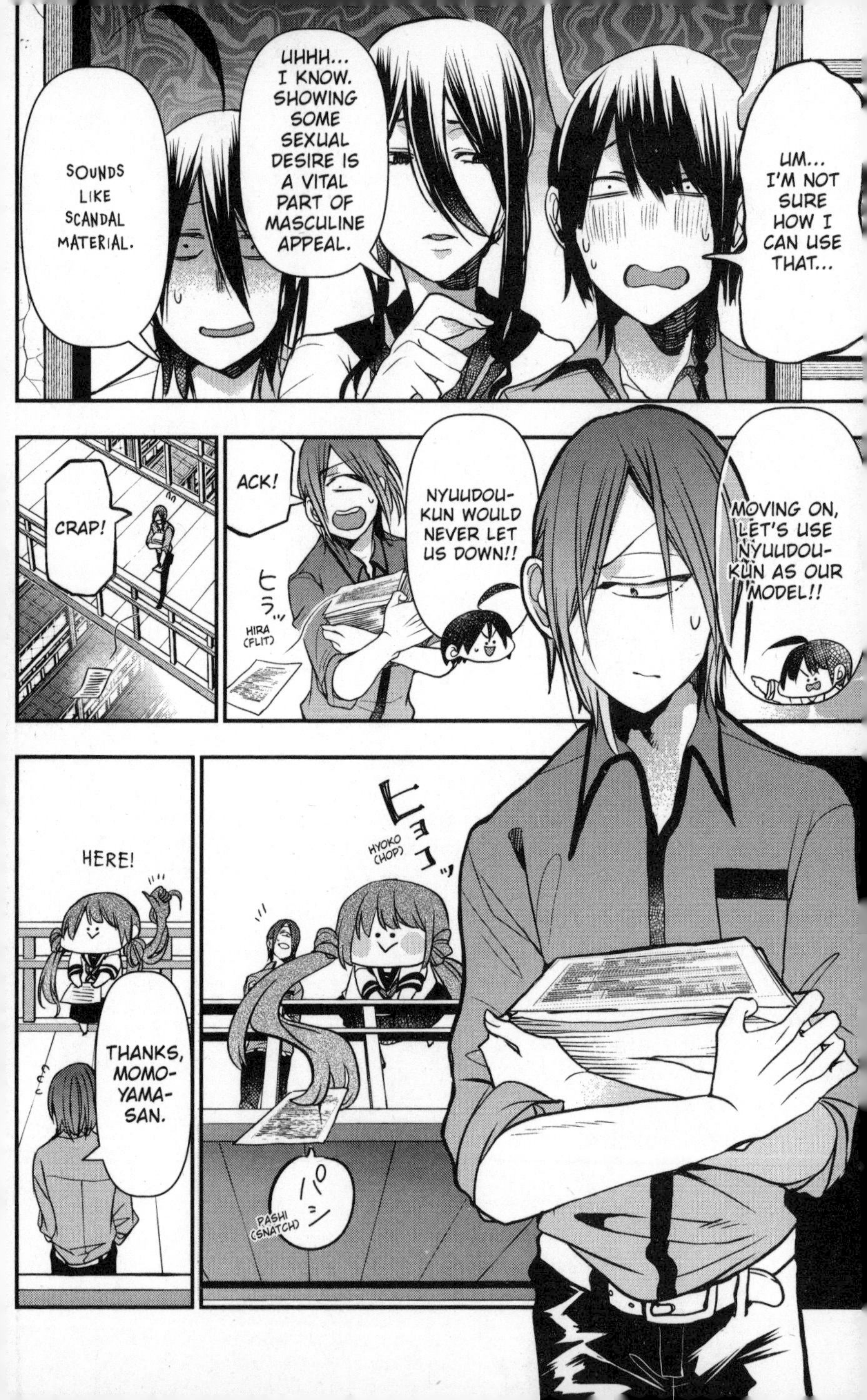
UM... I'M NOT SURE HOW I CAN USE THAT...
UHHH... I KNOW. SHOWING SOME SEXUAL DESIRE IS A VITAL PART OF MASCULINE APPEAL.
SOUNDS LIKE SCANDAL MATERIAL.
MOVING ON, LET'S USE NYUUDOU-KUN AS OUR MODEL!!
NYUUDOU-KUN WOULD NEVER LET US DOWN!!
ACK!
ヒラッ
HIRA (FLIT)
CRAP!
ヒョコッ
HYOKO (HOP)
パシ
PASHI (SNATCH)
HERE!
THANKS, MOMOYAMA-SAN.

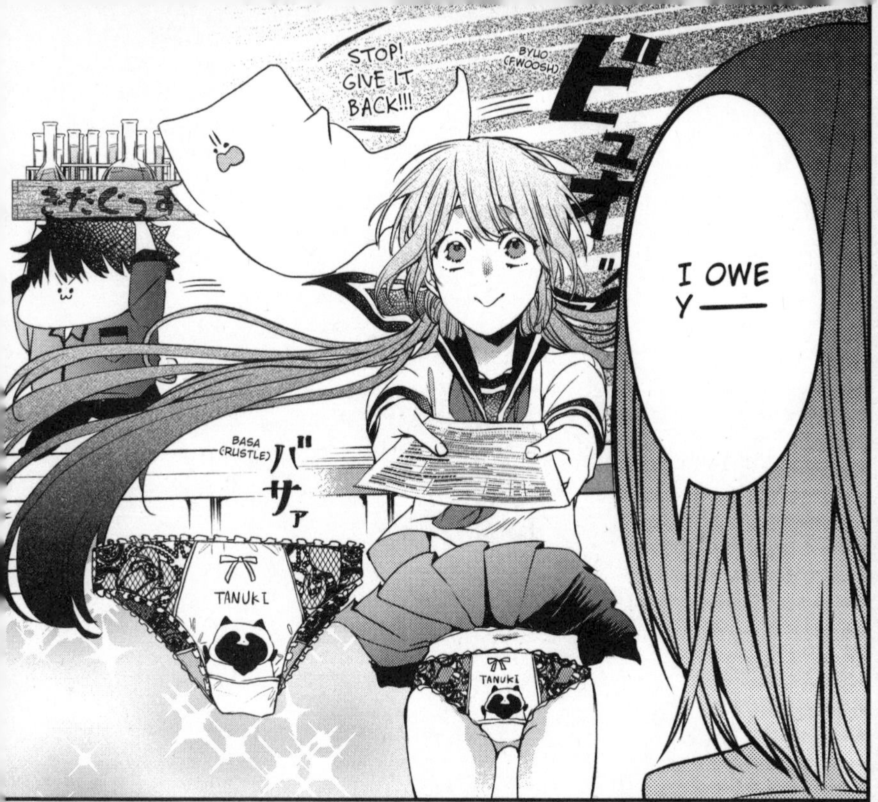
I OWE Y——
BYUO (FWOOSH)
STOP! GIVE IT BACK!!!
BASA (RUSTLE)
TANUKI
TANUKI

BOX: GIDA GOODS

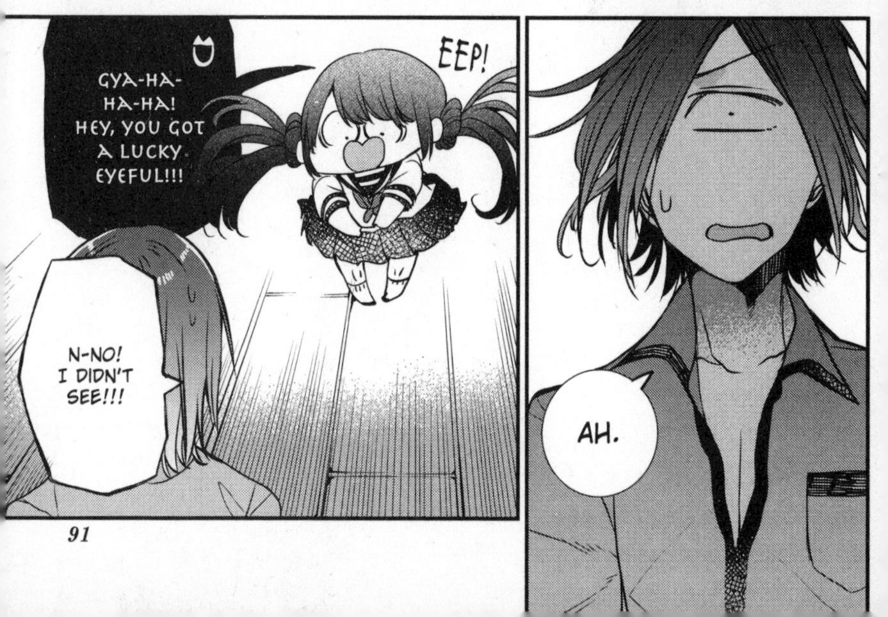
AH.
EEP!
GYA-HA-HA-HA! HEY, YOU GOT A LUCKY EYEFUL!!!
N-NO! I DIDN'T SEE!!!

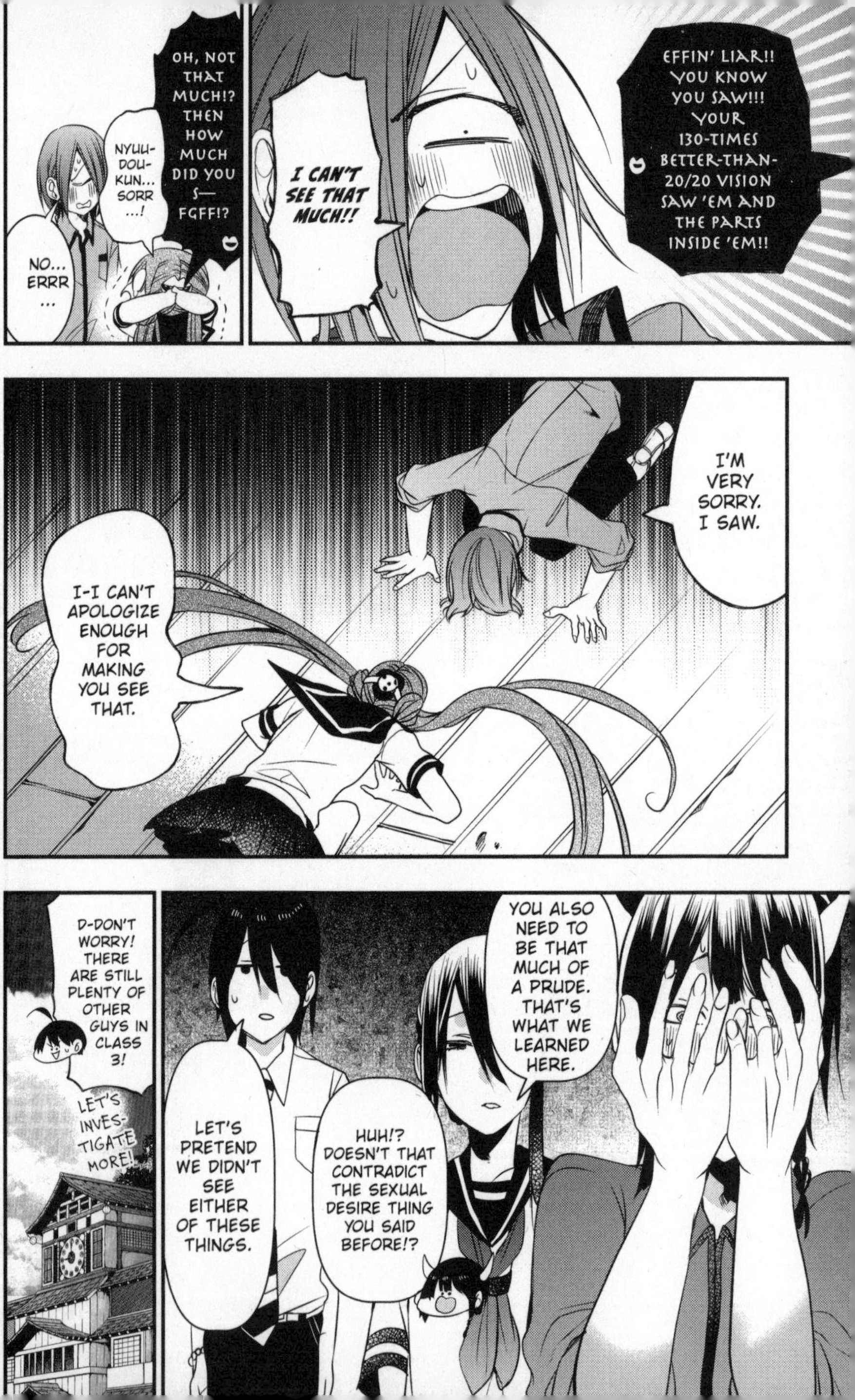
EFFIN' LIAR!! YOU KNOW YOU SAW!!! YOUR 130-TIMES BETTER-THAN-20/20 VISION SAW 'EM AND THE PARTS INSIDE 'EM!!
I CAN'T SEE THAT MUCH!!
OH, NOT THAT MUCH!? THEN HOW MUCH DID YOU S— FGFF!?
NYUU-DOU-KUN... SORR...!
NO... ERRR...
I'M VERY SORRY. I SAW.
I-I CAN'T APOLOGIZE ENOUGH FOR MAKING YOU SEE THAT.
YOU ALSO NEED TO BE THAT MUCH OF A PRUDE. THAT'S WHAT WE LEARNED HERE.
HUH!? DOESN'T THAT CONTRADICT THE SEXUAL DESIRE THING YOU SAID BEFORE!?
LET'S PRETEND WE DIDN'T SEE EITHER OF THESE THINGS.
D-DON'T WORRY! THERE ARE STILL PLENTY OF OTHER GUYS IN CLASS 3!
LET'S INVES-TIGATE MORE!

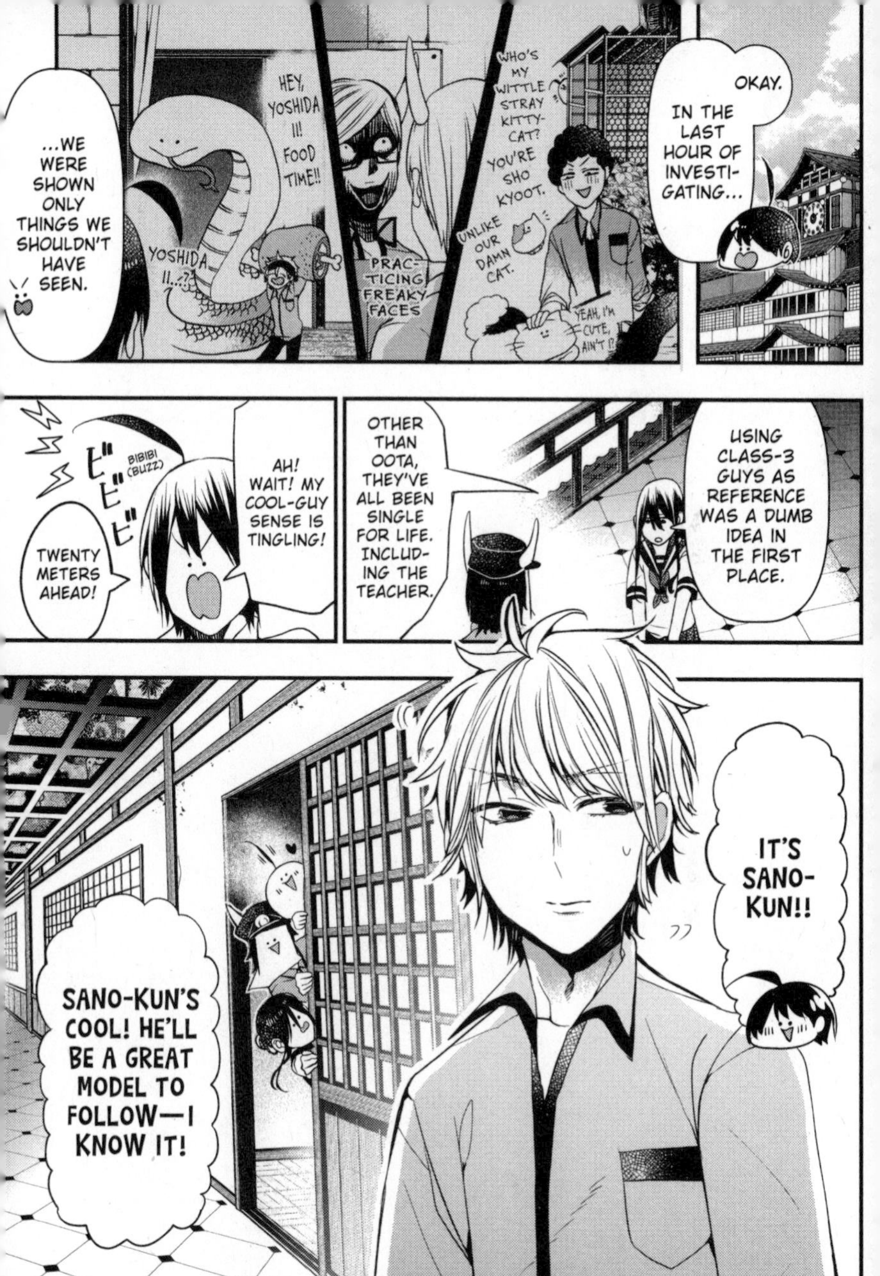

OKAY.
IN THE LAST HOUR OF INVESTI-GATING...
WHO'S MY WITTLE STRAY KITTY-CAT? YOU'RE SHO KYOOT.
UNLIKE OUR DAMN CAT.
YEAH, I'M CUTE, AIN'T I?
HEY, YOSHIDA II! FOOD TIME!!
PRAC-TICING FREAKY FACES
YOSHIDA II...?
...WE WERE SHOWN ONLY THINGS WE SHOULDN'T HAVE SEEN.
USING CLASS-3 GUYS AS REFERENCE WAS A DUMB IDEA IN THE FIRST PLACE.
OTHER THAN OOTA, THEY'VE ALL BEEN SINGLE FOR LIFE. INCLUD-ING THE TEACHER.
AH! WAIT! MY COOL-GUY SENSE IS TINGLING!
BIBIBI (BUZZ)
TWENTY METERS AHEAD!
IT'S SANO-KUN!!
SANO-KUN'S COOL! HE'LL BE A GREAT MODEL TO FOLLOW—I KNOW IT!

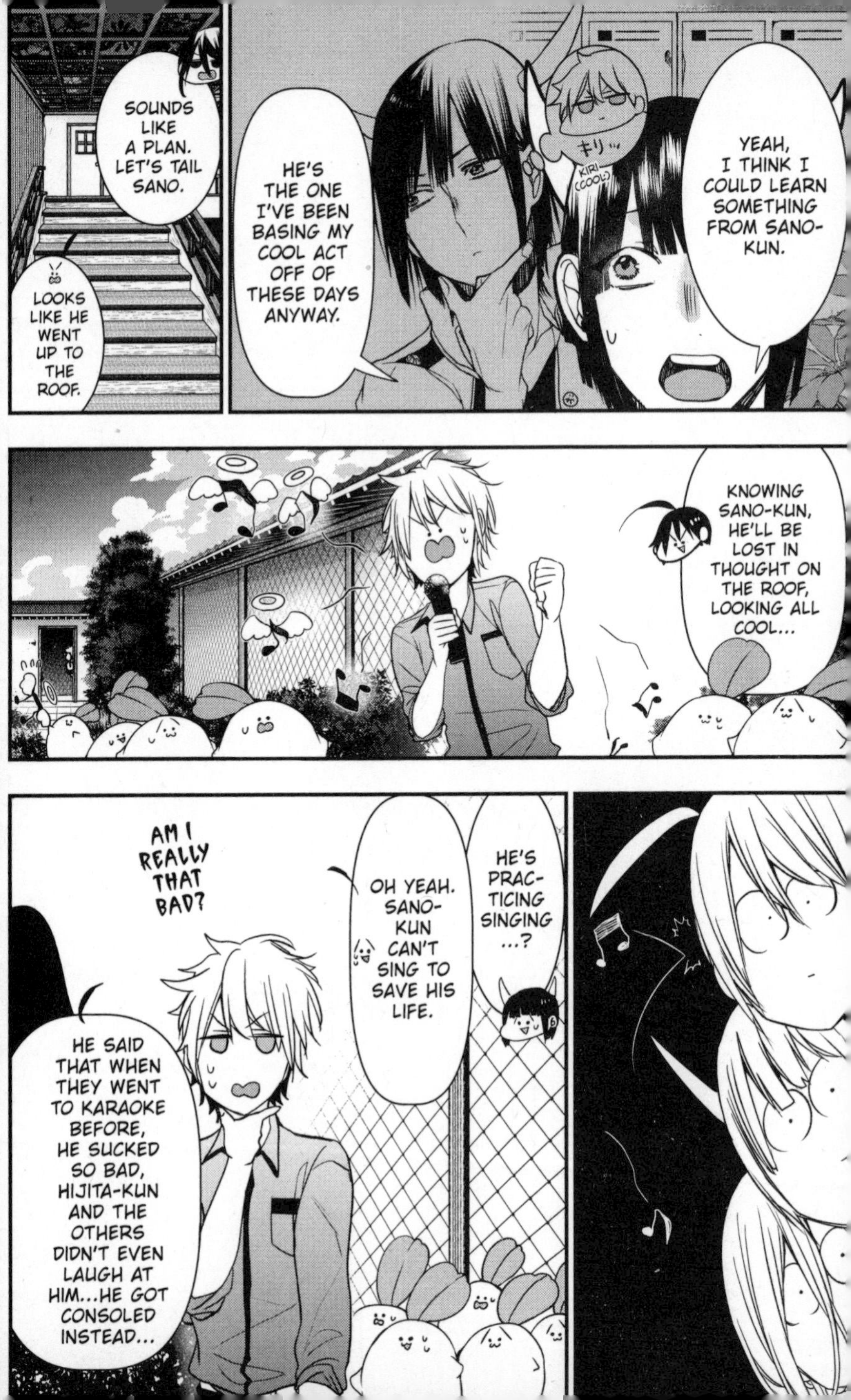
YEAH, I THINK I COULD LEARN SOMETHING FROM SANO-KUN.
キリッ
KIRI (COOL)
HE'S THE ONE I'VE BEEN BASING MY COOL ACT OFF OF THESE DAYS ANYWAY.
SOUNDS LIKE A PLAN. LET'S TAIL SANO.
LOOKS LIKE HE WENT UP TO THE ROOF.
KNOWING SANO-KUN, HE'LL BE LOST IN THOUGHT ON THE ROOF, LOOKING ALL COOL...
HE'S PRAC-TICING SINGING ...?
OH YEAH. SANO-KUN CAN'T SING TO SAVE HIS LIFE.
AM I REALLY THAT BAD?
HE SAID THAT WHEN THEY WENT TO KARAOKE BEFORE, HE SUCKED SO BAD, HIJITA-KUN AND THE OTHERS DIDN'T EVEN LAUGH AT HIM...HE GOT CONSOLED INSTEAD...

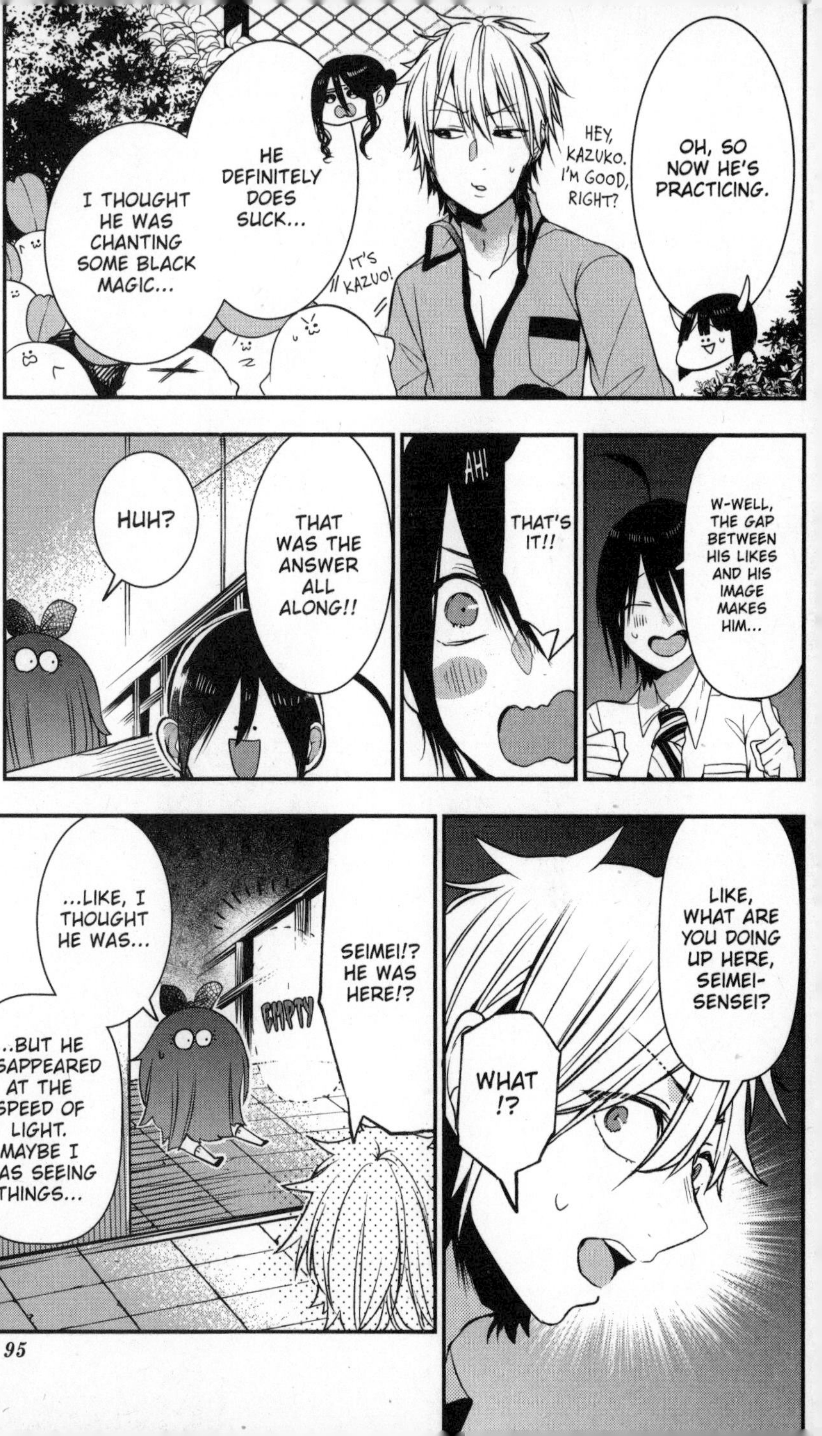
OH, SO NOW HE'S PRACTICING.
HEY, KAZUKO. I'M GOOD, RIGHT?
HE DEFINITELY DOES SUCK...
IT'S KAZUO!
I THOUGHT HE WAS CHANTING SOME BLACK MAGIC...
W-WELL, THE GAP BETWEEN HIS LIKES AND HIS IMAGE MAKES HIM...
AH!
THAT'S IT!!
THAT WAS THE ANSWER ALL ALONG!!
HUH?
LIKE, WHAT ARE YOU DOING UP HERE, SEIMEI-SENSEI?
WHAT!?
SEIMEI!? HE WAS HERE!?
...LIKE, I THOUGHT HE WAS...
...BUT HE DISAPPEARED AT THE SPEED OF LIGHT. MAYBE I WAS SEEING THINGS...

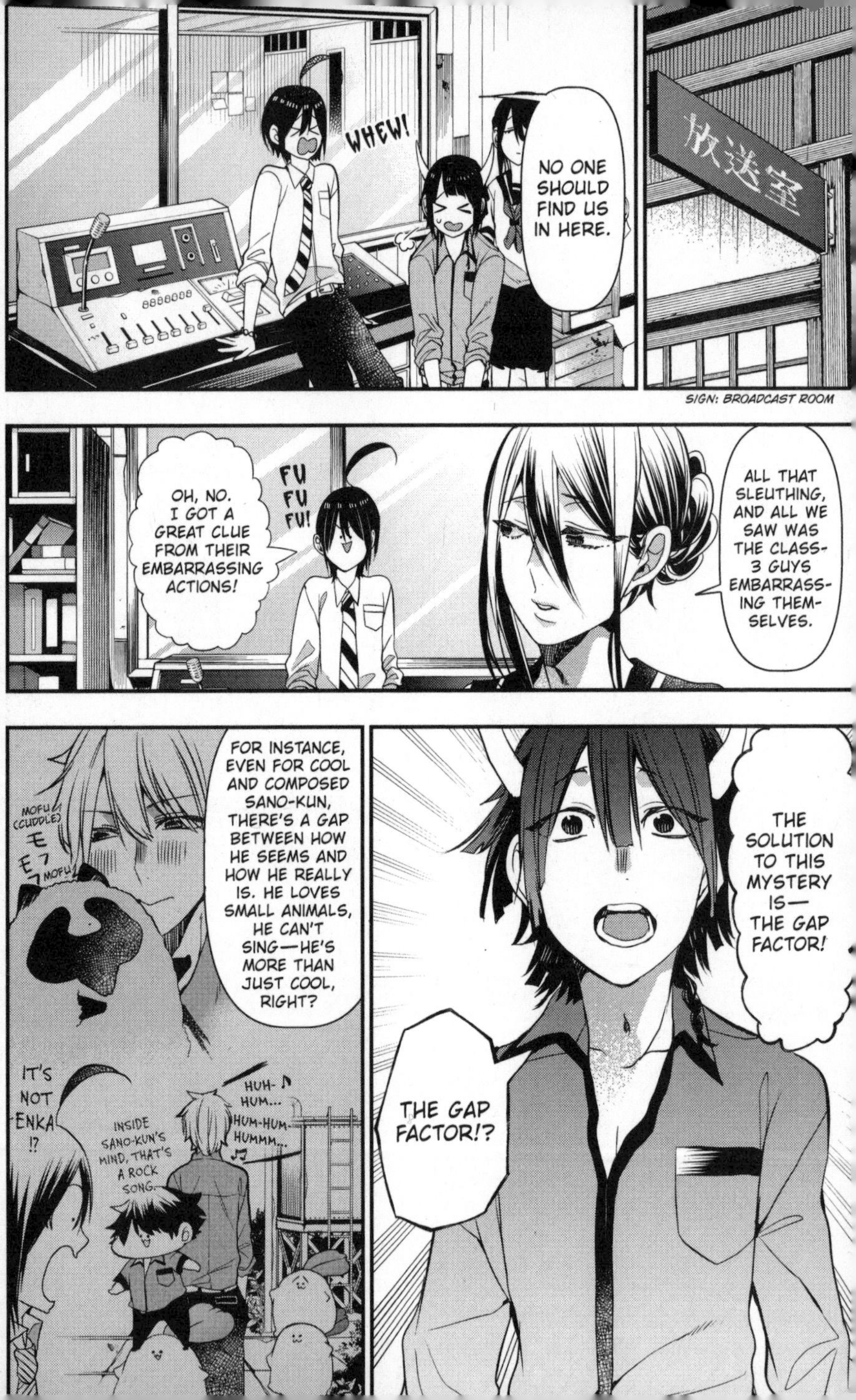
放送室
SIGN: BROADCAST ROOM
NO ONE SHOULD FIND US IN HERE.
WHEW!
ALL THAT SLEUTHING, AND ALL WE SAW WAS THE CLASS-3 GUYS EMBARRASSING THEMSELVES.
FU FU FU!
OH, NO. I GOT A GREAT CLUE FROM THEIR EMBARRASSING ACTIONS!
THE SOLUTION TO THIS MYSTERY IS— THE GAP FACTOR!
THE GAP FACTOR!?
FOR INSTANCE, EVEN FOR COOL AND COMPOSED SANO-KUN, THERE'S A GAP BETWEEN HOW HE SEEMS AND HOW HE REALLY IS. HE LOVES SMALL ANIMALS, HE CAN'T SING—HE'S MORE THAN JUST COOL, RIGHT?
MOFU (CUDDLE)
モフ
モフ
MOFU
HUH-HUM... HUM-HUM-HUMMM...
INSIDE SANO-KUN'S MIND, THAT'S A ROCK SONG.
IT'S NOT ENKA!?

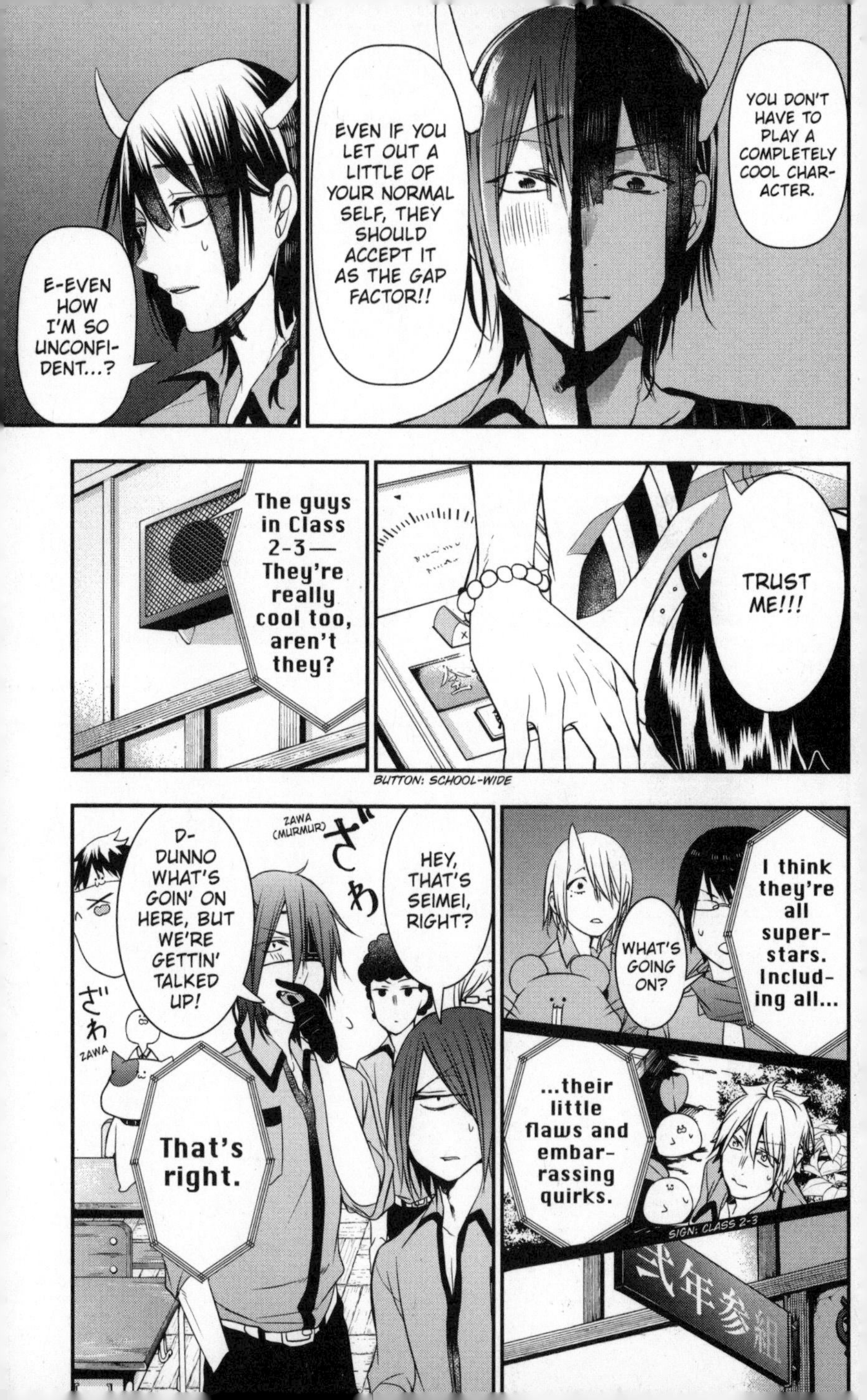
YOU DON'T HAVE TO PLAY A COMPLETELY COOL CHARACTER.
EVEN IF YOU LET OUT A LITTLE OF YOUR NORMAL SELF, THEY SHOULD ACCEPT IT AS THE GAP FACTOR!!
E-EVEN HOW I'M SO UNCONFIDENT...?
TRUST ME!!!
BUTTON: SCHOOL-WIDE
The guys in Class 2-3— They're really cool too, aren't they?
I think they're all superstars. Including all...
WHAT'S GOING ON?
...their little flaws and embarrassing quirks.
SIGN: CLASS 2-3
HEY, THAT'S SEIMEI, RIGHT?
ZAWA (MURMUR)
D-DUNNO WHAT'S GOIN' ON HERE, BUT WE'RE GETTIN' TALKED UP!
ZAWA
That's right.

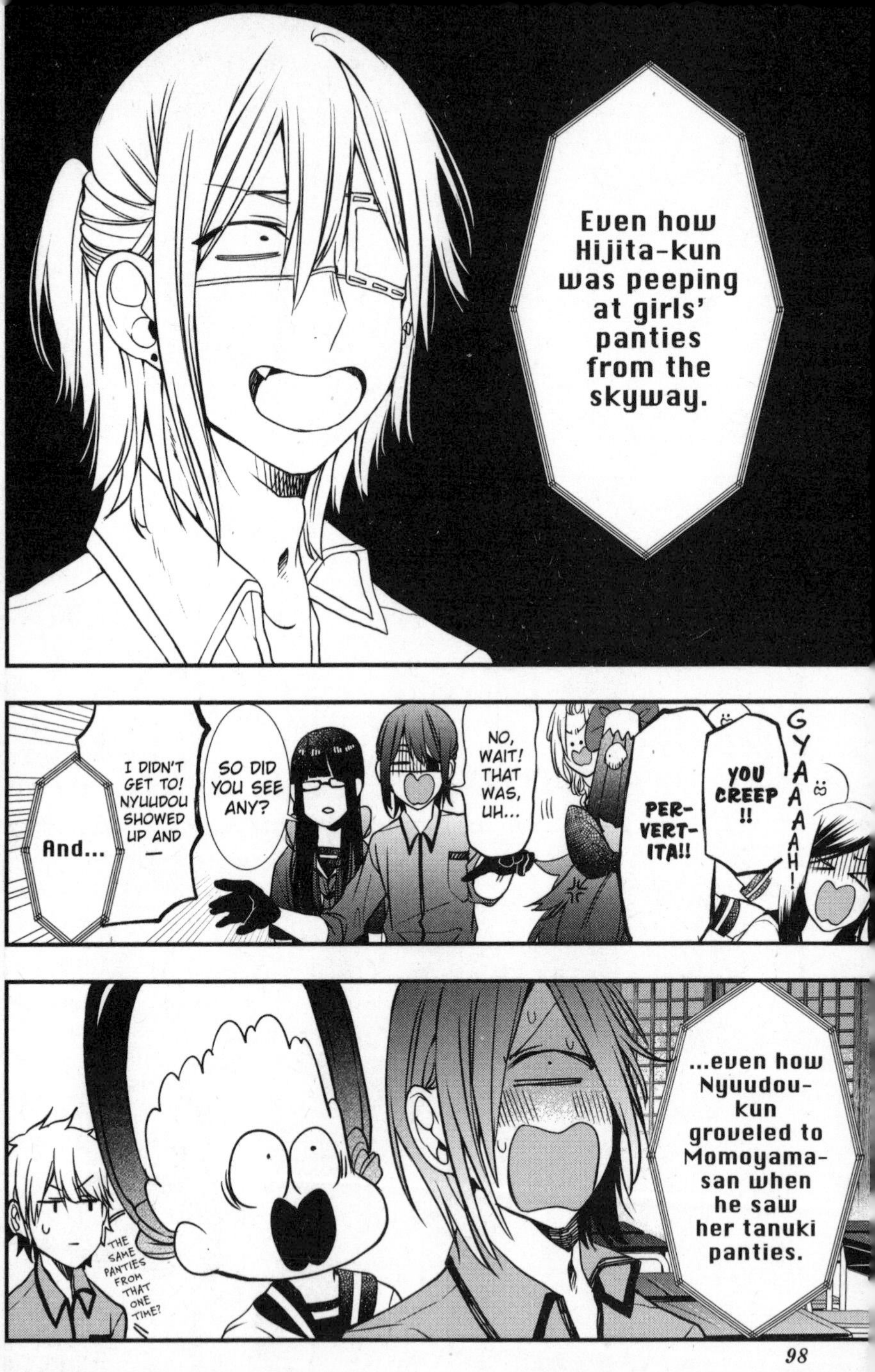
Even how Hijita-kun was peeping at girls' panties from the skyway.
GYAAAAAH!
YOU CREEP!!
PER-VERT-ITA!!
NO, WAIT! THAT WAS, UH...
SO DID YOU SEE ANY?
I DIDN'T GET TO! NYUUDOU SHOWED UP AND—
And...
...even how Nyuudou-kun groveled to Momoyama-san when he saw her tanuki panties.
THE SAME PANTIES FROM THAT ONE TIME?

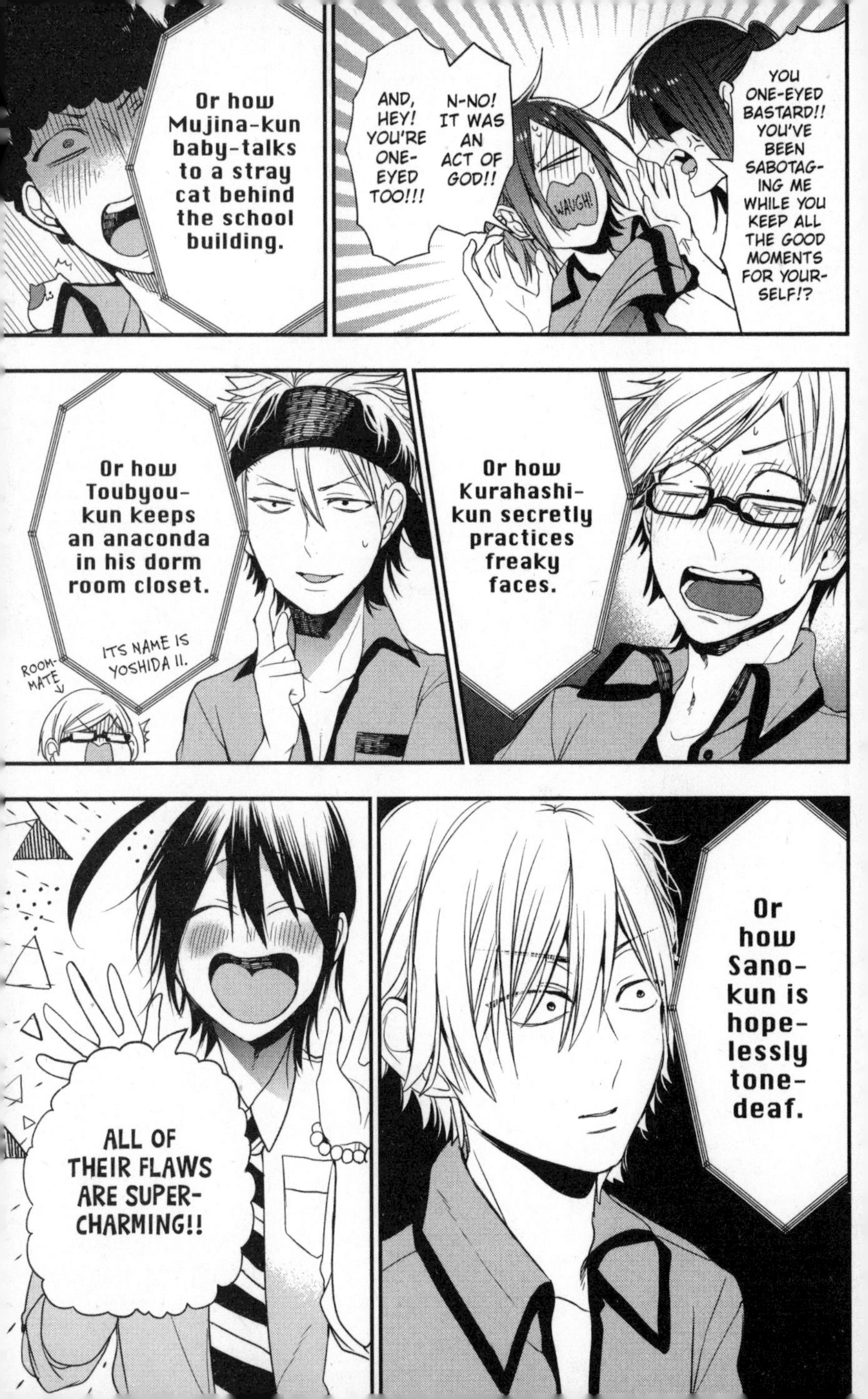
YOU ONE-EYED BASTARD!! YOU'VE BEEN SABOTAGING ME WHILE YOU KEEP ALL THE GOOD MOMENTS FOR YOURSELF!?
WAUGH!
N-NO! IT WAS AN ACT OF GOD!!
AND, HEY! YOU'RE ONE-EYED TOO!!!
Or how Mujina-kun baby-talks to a stray cat behind the school building.
Or how Kurahashi-kun secretly practices freaky faces.
Or how Toubyou-kun keeps an anaconda in his dorm room closet.
ITS NAME IS YOSHIDA II.
ROOM-MATE
Or how Sano-kun is hopelessly tone-deaf.
ALL OF THEIR FLAWS ARE SUPER-CHARMING!!

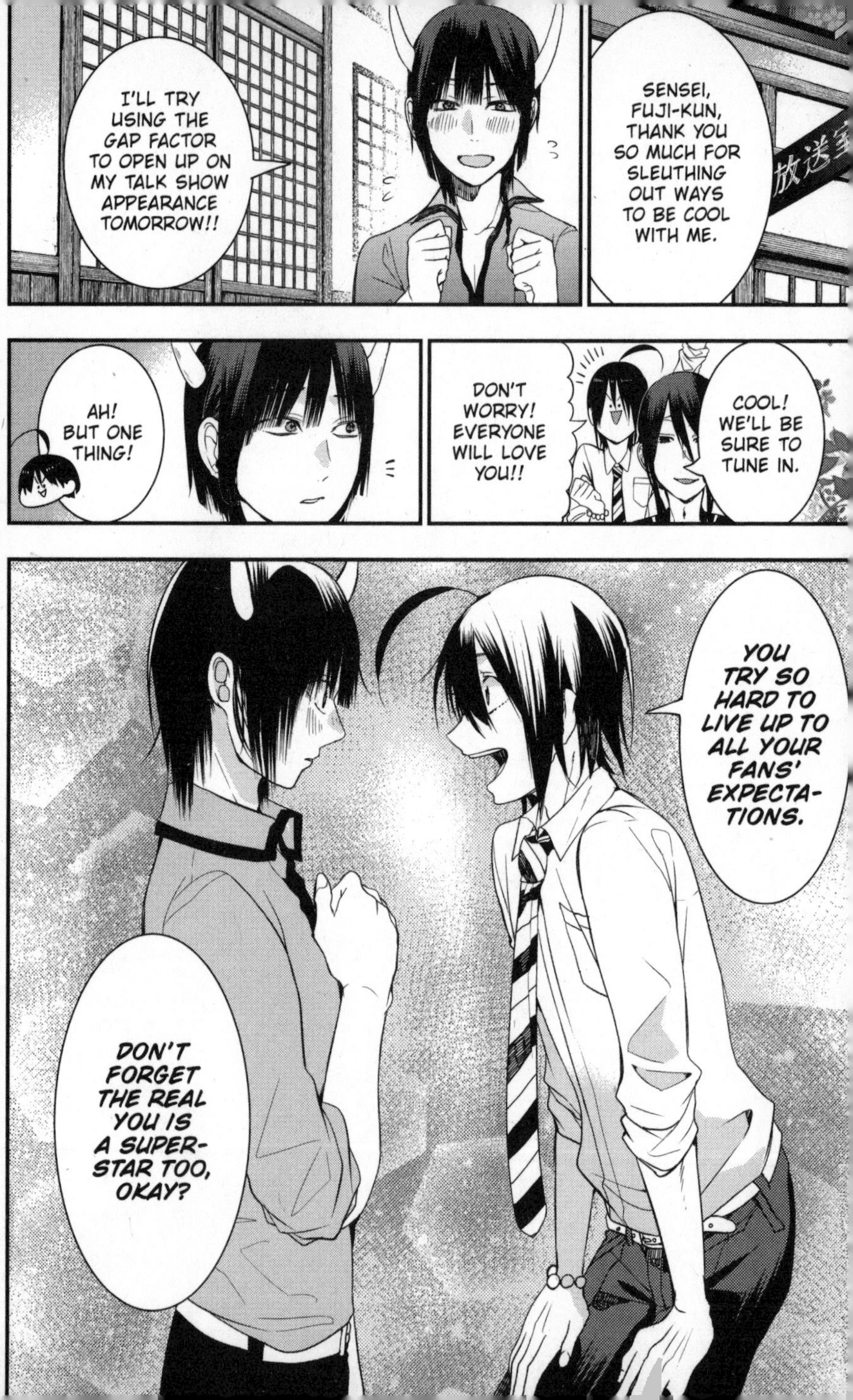
SENSEI, FUJI-KUN, THANK YOU SO MUCH FOR SLEUTHING OUT WAYS TO BE COOL WITH ME.
I'LL TRY USING THE GAP FACTOR TO OPEN UP ON MY TALK SHOW APPEARANCE TOMORROW!!
COOL! WE'LL BE SURE TO TUNE IN.
DON'T WORRY! EVERYONE WILL LOVE YOU!!
AH! BUT ONE THING!
YOU TRY SO HARD TO LIVE UP TO ALL YOUR FANS' EXPECTA-TIONS.
DON'T FORGET THE REAL YOU IS A SUPER-STAR TOO, OKAY?

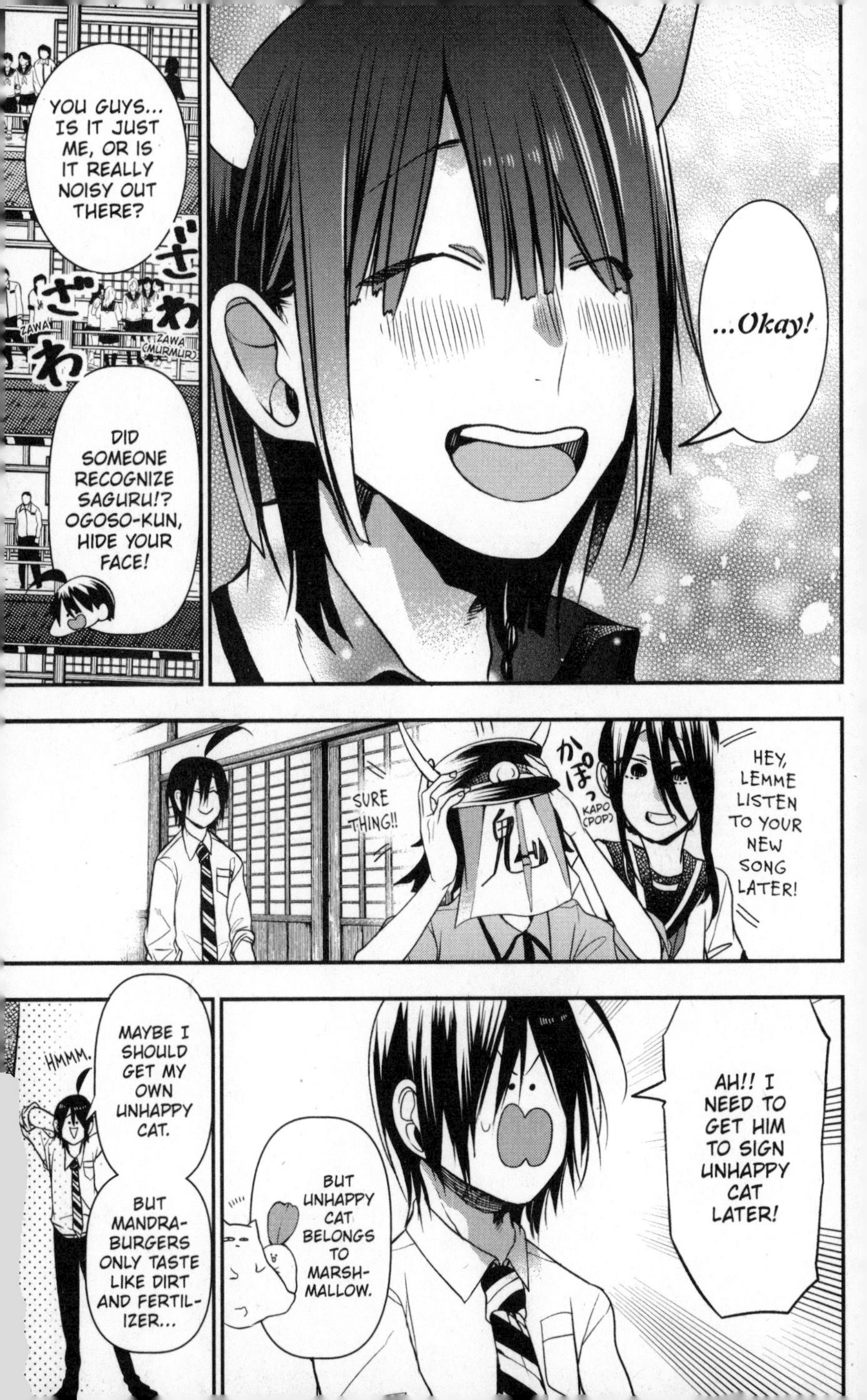
...Okay!
YOU GUYS... IS IT JUST ME, OR IS IT REALLY NOISY OUT THERE?
ざわ ZAWA
ざわ ZAWA (MURMUR)
DID SOMEONE RECOGNIZE SAGURU!? OGOSO-KUN, HIDE YOUR FACE!
HEY, LEMME LISTEN TO YOUR NEW SONG LATER!
かぽっ KAPO (POP)
SURE THING!!
AH!! I NEED TO GET HIM TO SIGN UNHAPPY CAT LATER!
BUT UNHAPPY CAT BELONGS TO MARSHMALLOW.
HMMM.
MAYBE I SHOULD GET MY OWN UNHAPPY CAT.
BUT MANDRA-BURGERS ONLY TASTE LIKE DIRT AND FERTILIZER...

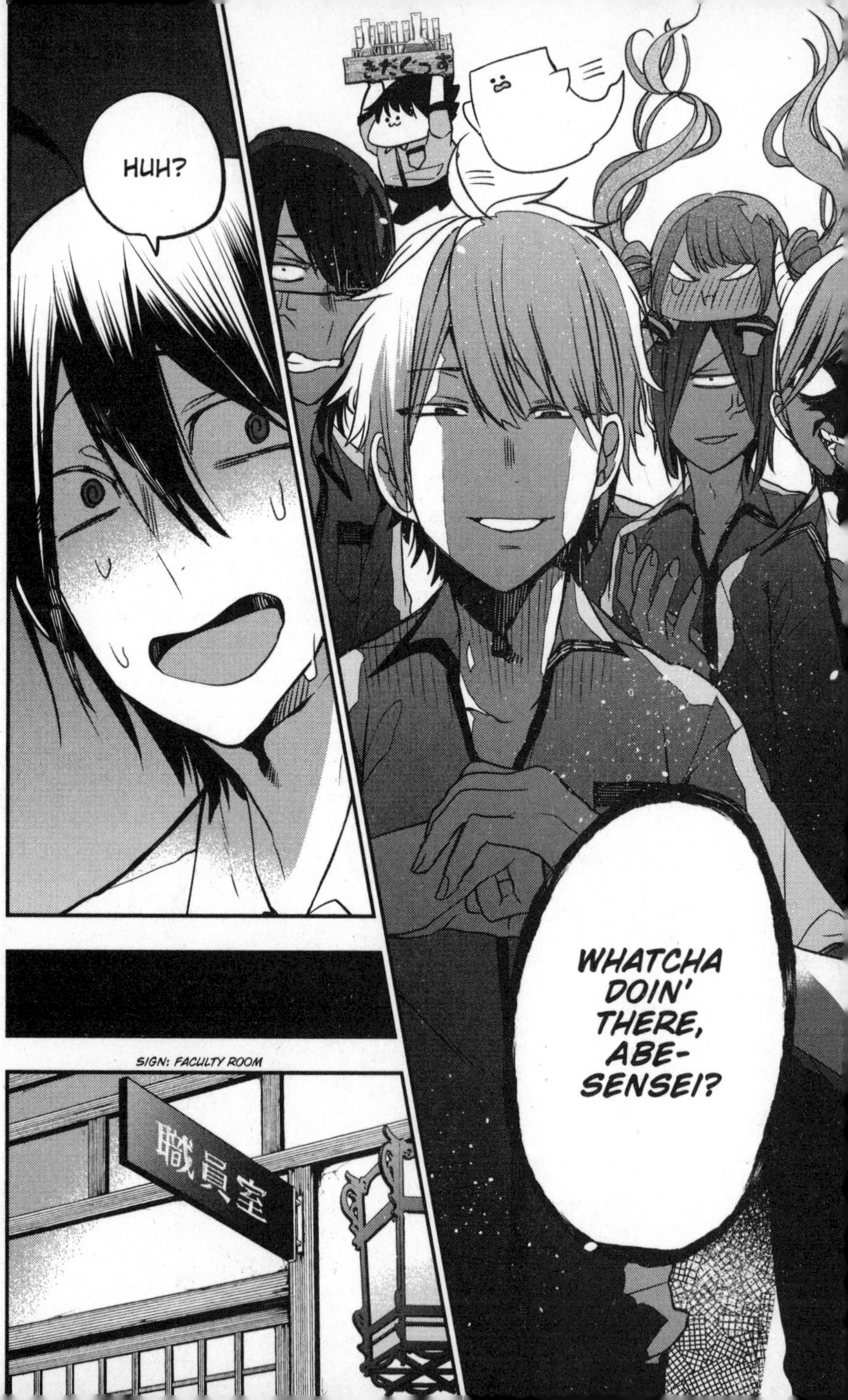
WHATCHA DOIN' THERE, ABE-SENSEI?
HUH?
SIGN: FACULTY ROOM
職員室

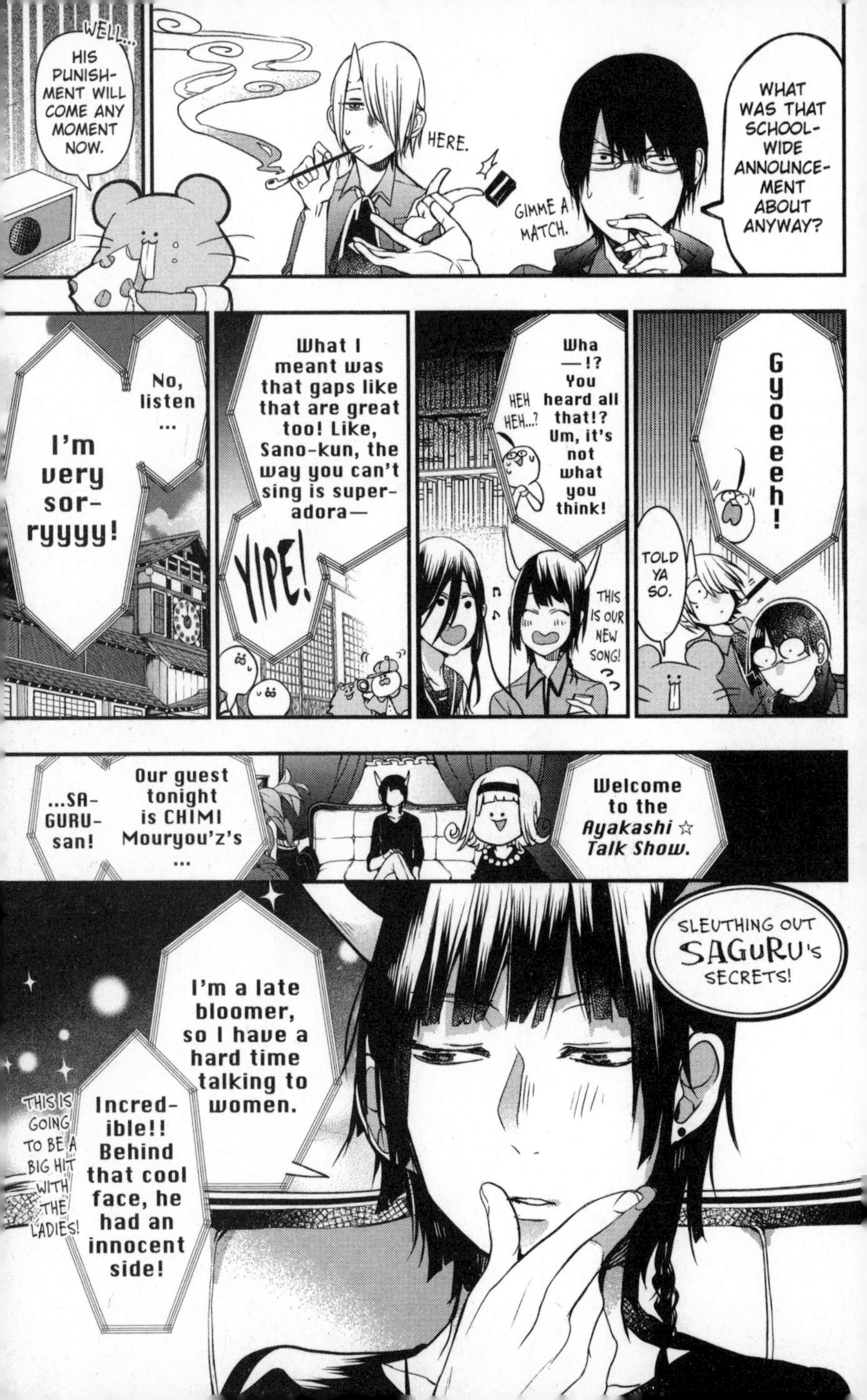

WHAT WAS THAT SCHOOL-WIDE ANNOUNCEMENT ABOUT ANYWAY?
GIMME A MATCH.
HERE.
WELL... HIS PUNISHMENT WILL COME ANY MOMENT NOW.
Gyoeeeh!
TOLD YA SO.
Wha—!? You heard all that!? Um, it's not what you think!
HEH HEH...?
THIS IS OUR NEW SONG!
What I meant was that gaps like that are great too! Like, Sano-kun, the way you can't sing is super-adora—
YIPE!
No, listen...
I'm very sor-ryyyy!
Welcome to the Ayakashi ☆ Talk Show.
Our guest tonight is CHIMI Mouryou'z's...
...SAGURU-san!
SLEUTHING OUT SAGURU's SECRETS!
I'm a late bloomer, so I have a hard time talking to women.
Incredible!! Behind that cool face, he had an innocent side!
THIS IS GOING TO BE A BIG HIT WITH THE LADIES!

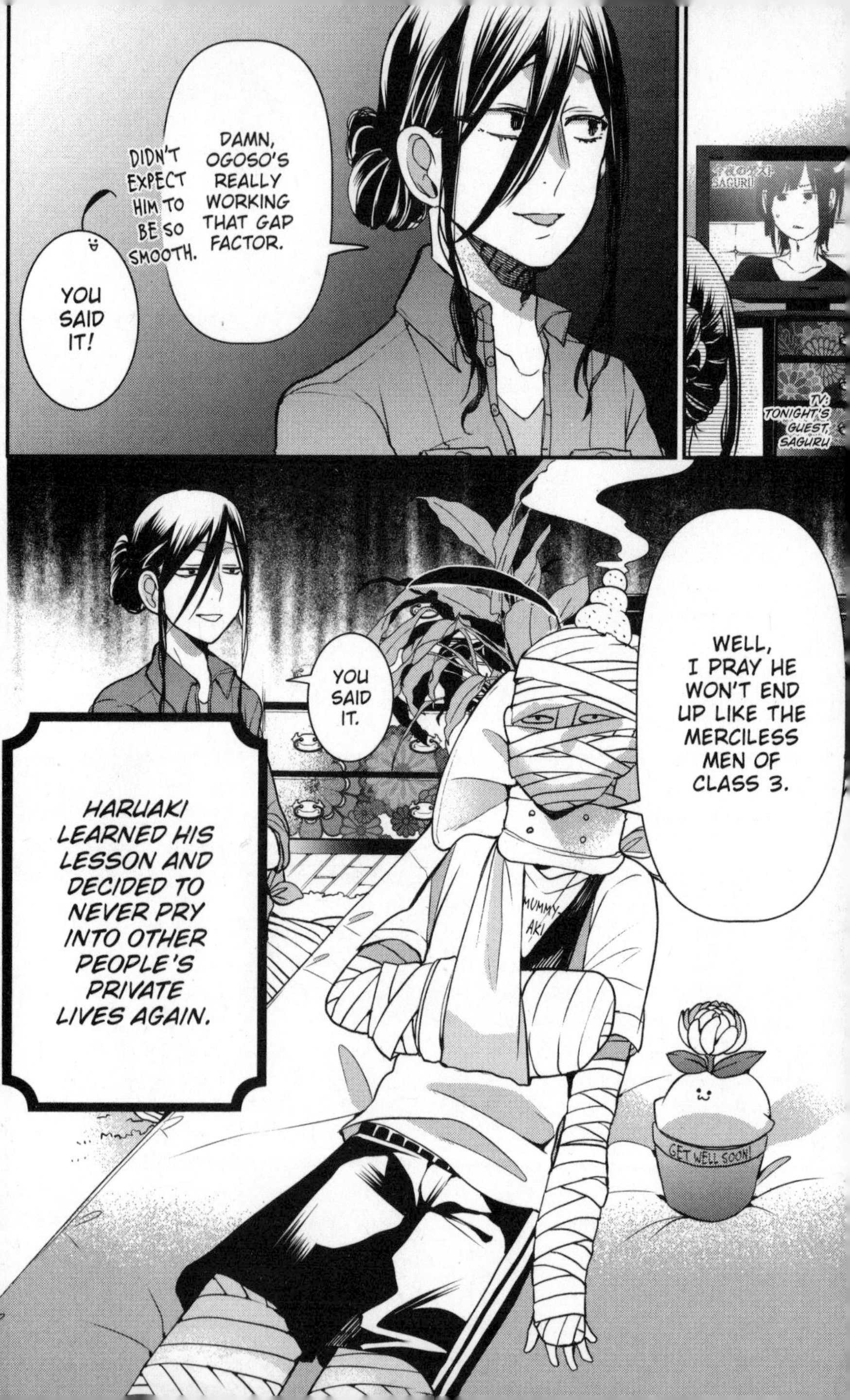
SAGURU
TV: TONIGHT'S GUEST, SAGURU
DAMN, OGOSO'S REALLY WORKING THAT GAP FACTOR.
DIDN'T EXPECT HIM TO BE SO SMOOTH.
YOU SAID IT!
WELL, I PRAY HE WON'T END UP LIKE THE MERCILESS MEN OF CLASS 3.
YOU SAID IT.
MUMMY-AKI
HARUAKI LEARNED HIS LESSON AND DECIDED TO NEVER PRY INTO OTHER PEOPLE'S PRIVATE LIVES AGAIN.
GET WELL SOON!

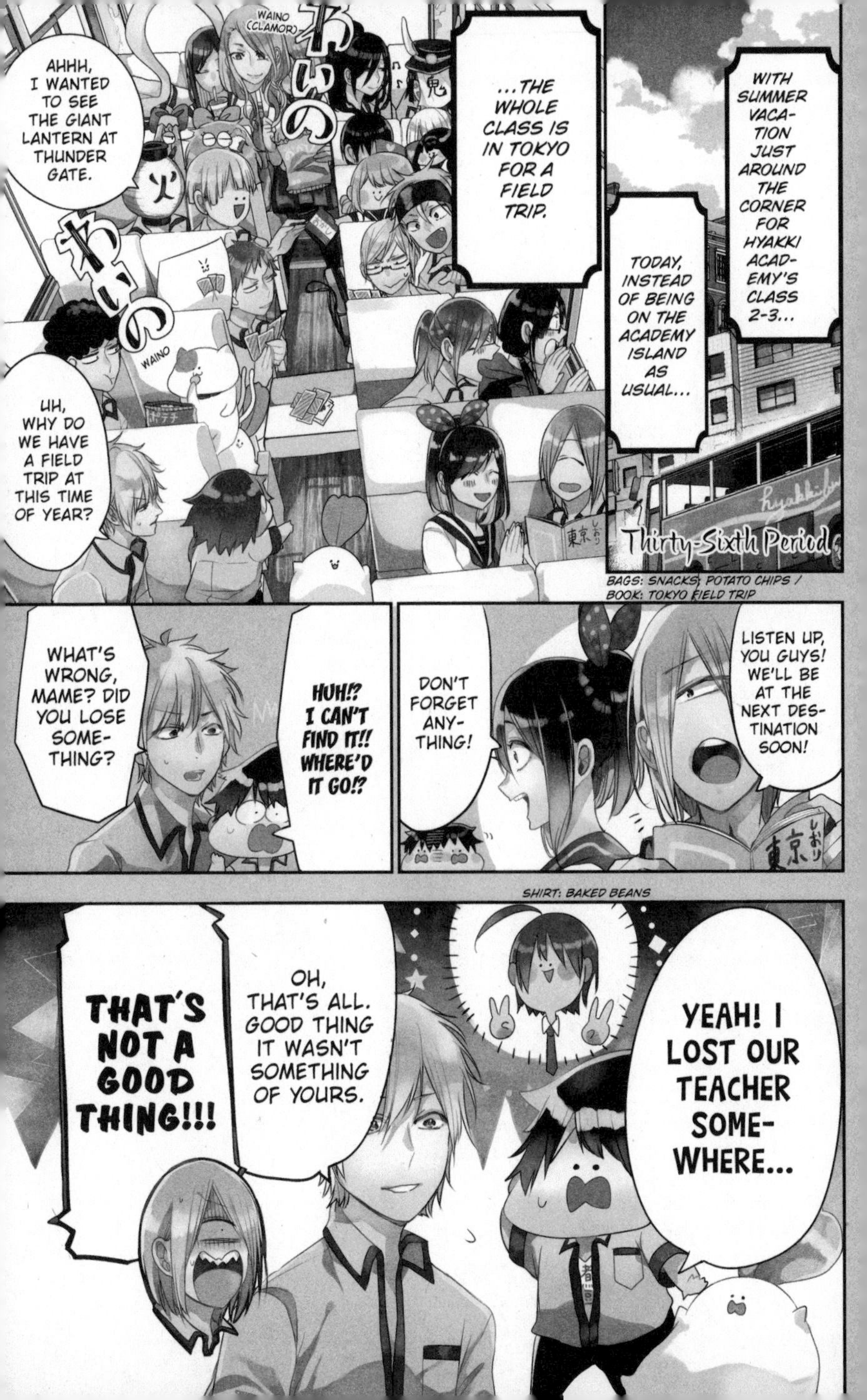
WITH SUMMER VACATION JUST AROUND THE CORNER FOR HYAKKI ACADEMY'S CLASS 2-3...
TODAY, INSTEAD OF BEING ON THE ACADEMY ISLAND AS USUAL...
...THE WHOLE CLASS IS IN TOKYO FOR A FIELD TRIP.
Thirty-Sixth Period
WAINO (CLAMOR)
AHHH, I WANTED TO SEE THE GIANT LANTERN AT THUNDER GATE.
WAINO
UH, WHY DO WE HAVE A FIELD TRIP AT THIS TIME OF YEAR?
BAGS: SNACKS; POTATO CHIPS / BOOK: TOKYO FIELD TRIP
LISTEN UP, YOU GUYS! WE'LL BE AT THE NEXT DESTINATION SOON!
DON'T FORGET ANYTHING!
HUH!? I CAN'T FIND IT!! WHERE'D IT GO!?
WHAT'S WRONG, MAME? DID YOU LOSE SOMETHING?
SHIRT: BAKED BEANS
YEAH! I LOST OUR TEACHER SOMEWHERE...
OH, THAT'S ALL. GOOD THING IT WASN'T SOMETHING OF YOURS.
THAT'S NOT A GOOD THING!!!

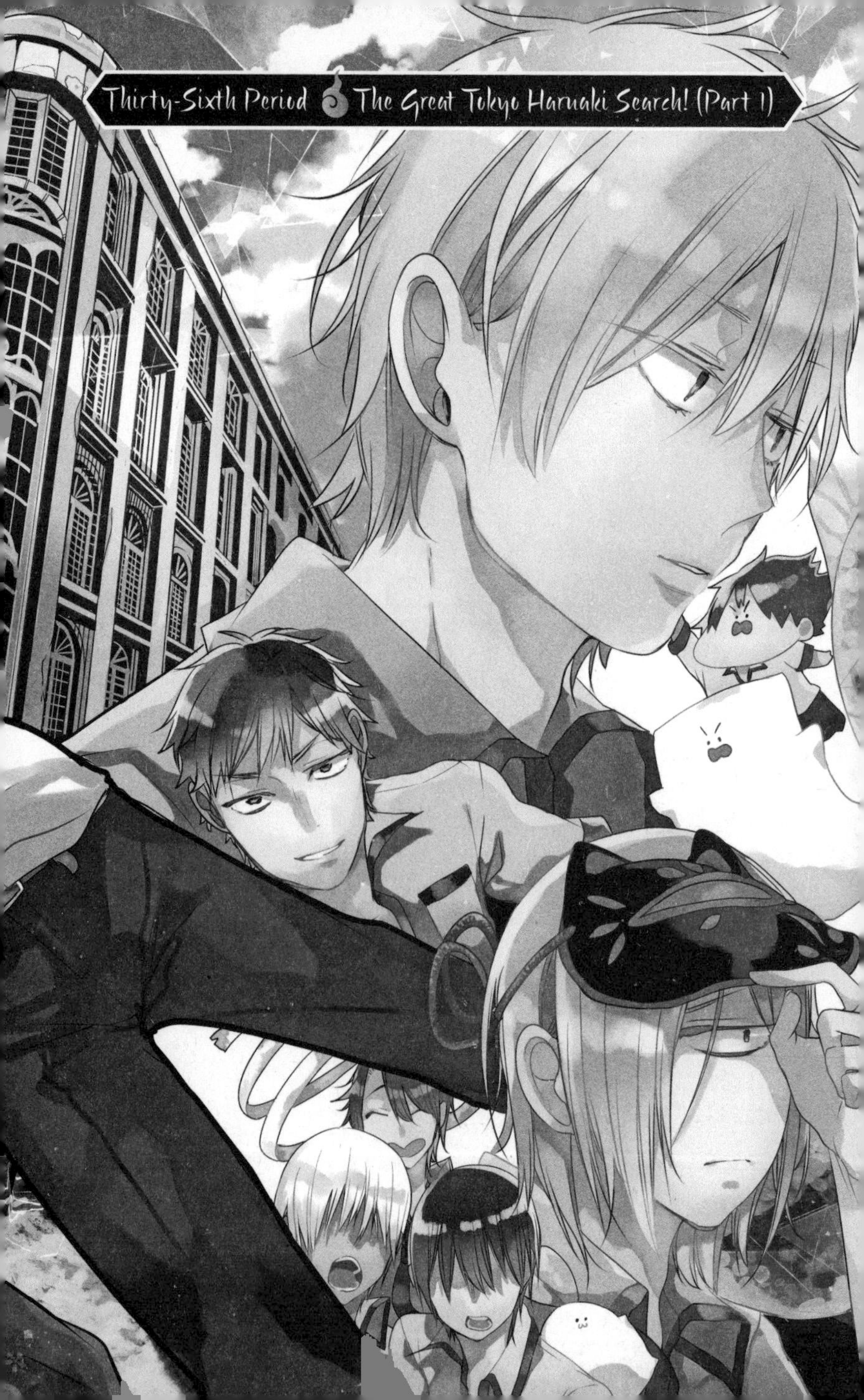
Thirty-Sixth Period The Great Tokyo Harunaki Search! (Part 1)

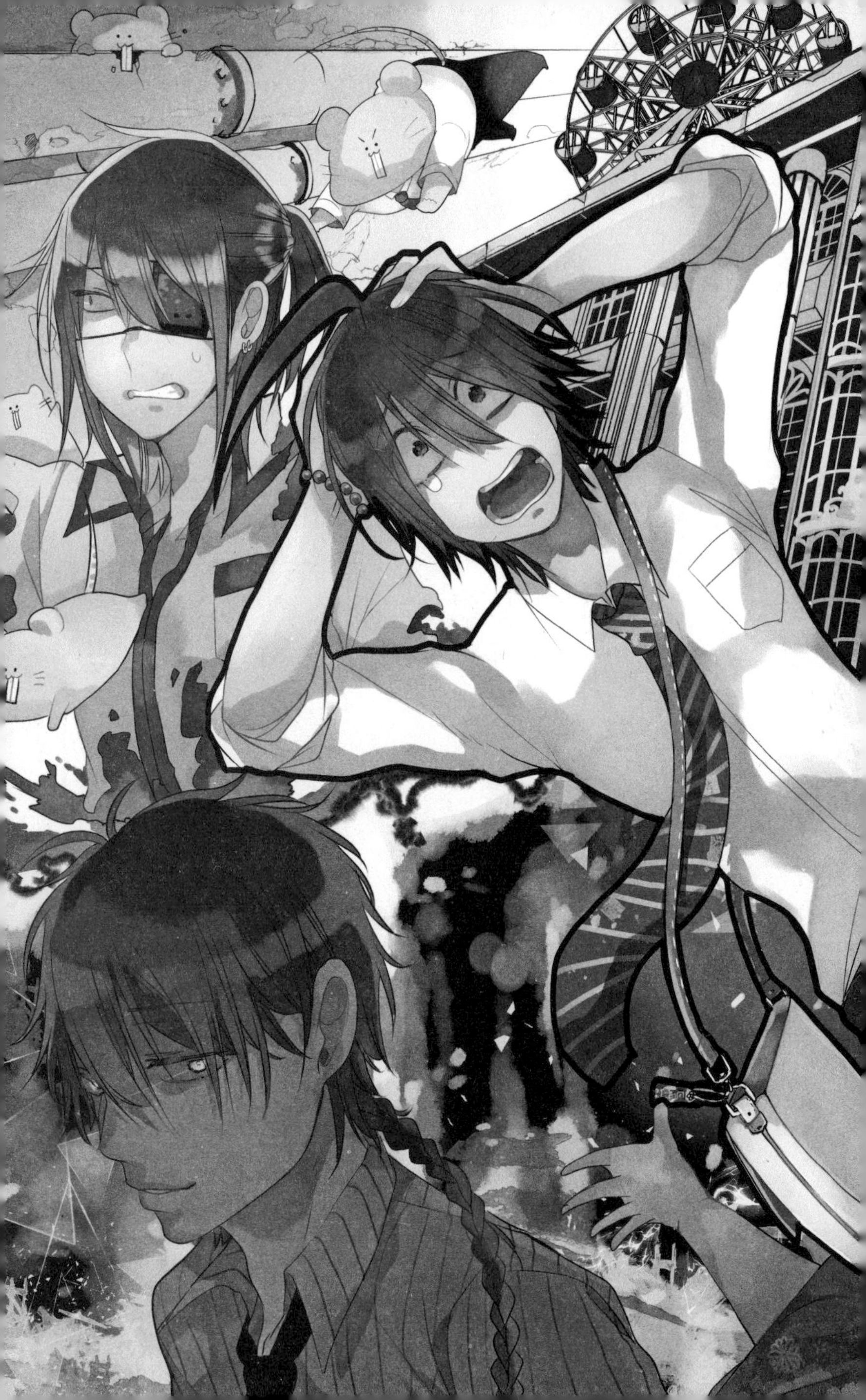

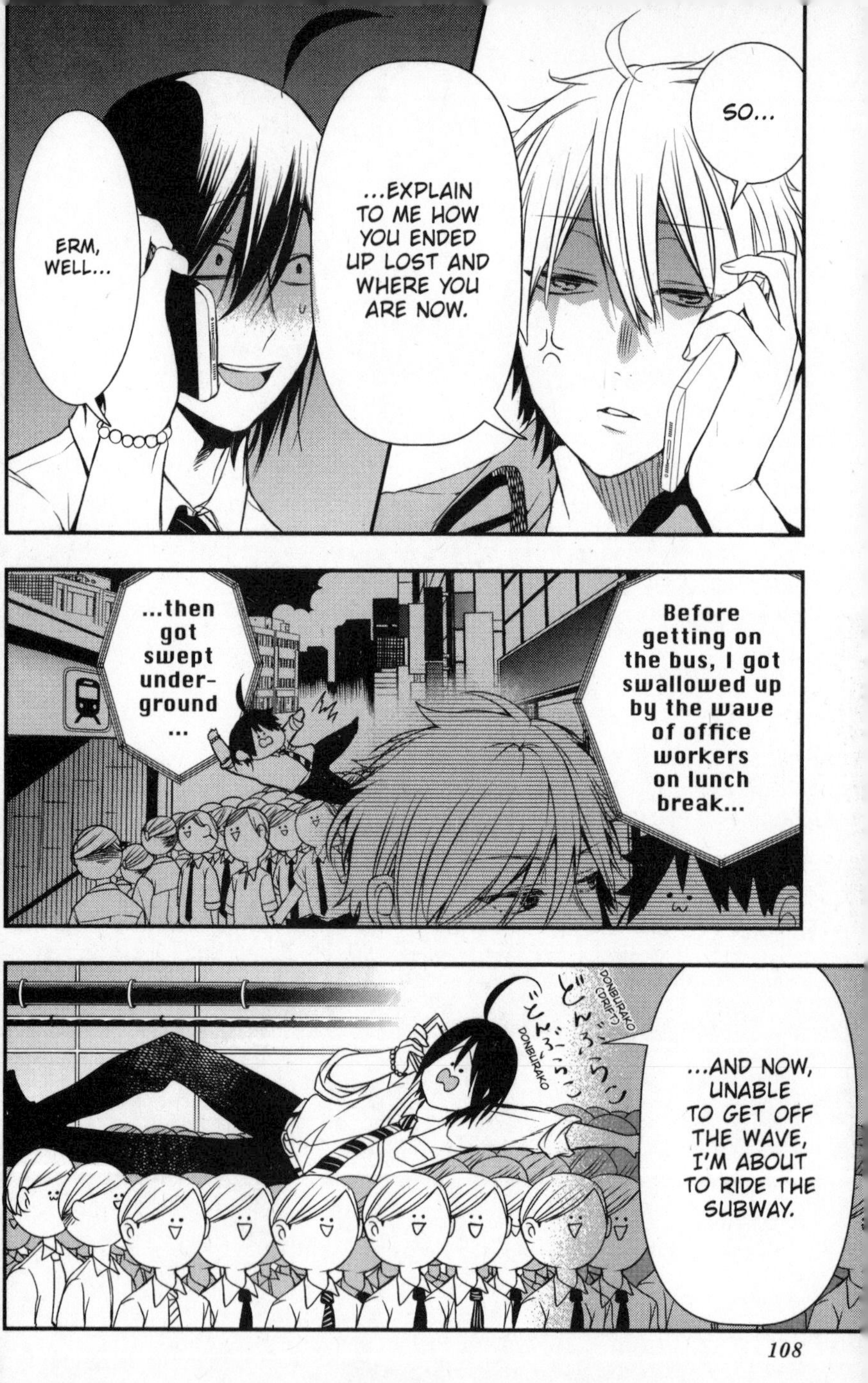
SO...
...EXPLAIN TO ME HOW YOU ENDED UP LOST AND WHERE YOU ARE NOW.
ERM, WELL...
Before getting on the bus, I got swallowed up by the wave of office workers on lunch break...
...then got swept under-ground...
DONBURAKO (DRIFT)
DONBURAKO
...AND NOW, UNABLE TO GET OFF THE WAVE, I'M ABOUT TO RIDE THE SUBWAY.

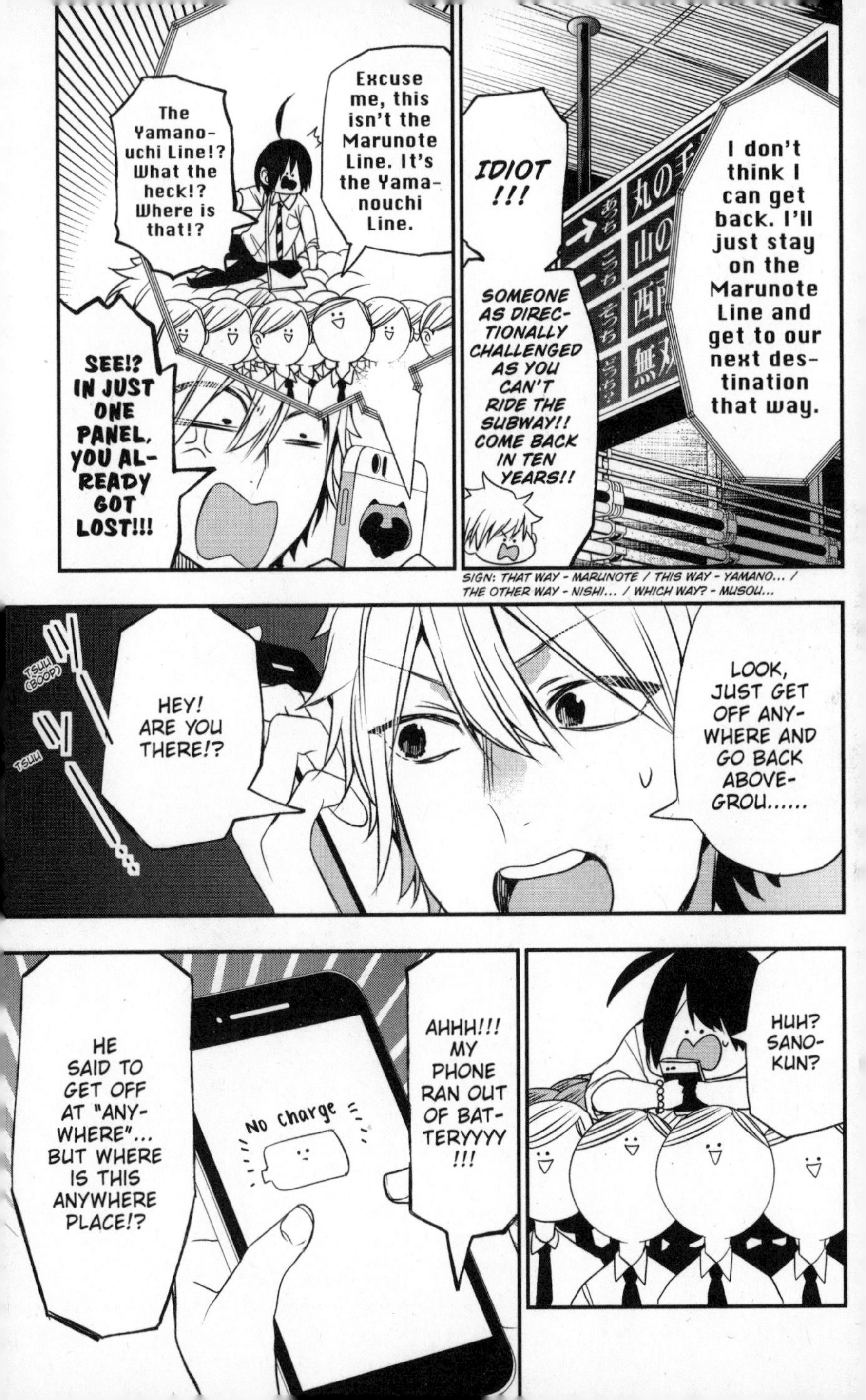
I don't think I can get back. I'll just stay on the Marunote Line and get to our next destination that way.
IDIOT!!!
SOMEONE AS DIRECTIONALLY CHALLENGED AS YOU CAN'T RIDE THE SUBWAY!! COME BACK IN TEN YEARS!!
Excuse me, this isn't the Marunote Line. It's the Yamanouchi Line.
The Yamanouchi Line!? What the heck!? Where is that!?
SEE!? IN JUST ONE PANEL, YOU ALREADY GOT LOST!!!
SIGN: THAT WAY - MARUNOTE / THIS WAY - YAMANO... / THE OTHER WAY - NISHI... / WHICH WAY? - MUSOU...
LOOK, JUST GET OFF ANYWHERE AND GO BACK ABOVEGROU......
HEY! ARE YOU THERE!?
TSUU (BOOP)
TSUU
HUH? SANO-KUN?
AHHH!!! MY PHONE RAN OUT OF BATTERYYYY!!!
No Charge
HE SAID TO GET OFF AT "ANYWHERE"... BUT WHERE IS THIS ANYWHERE PLACE!?

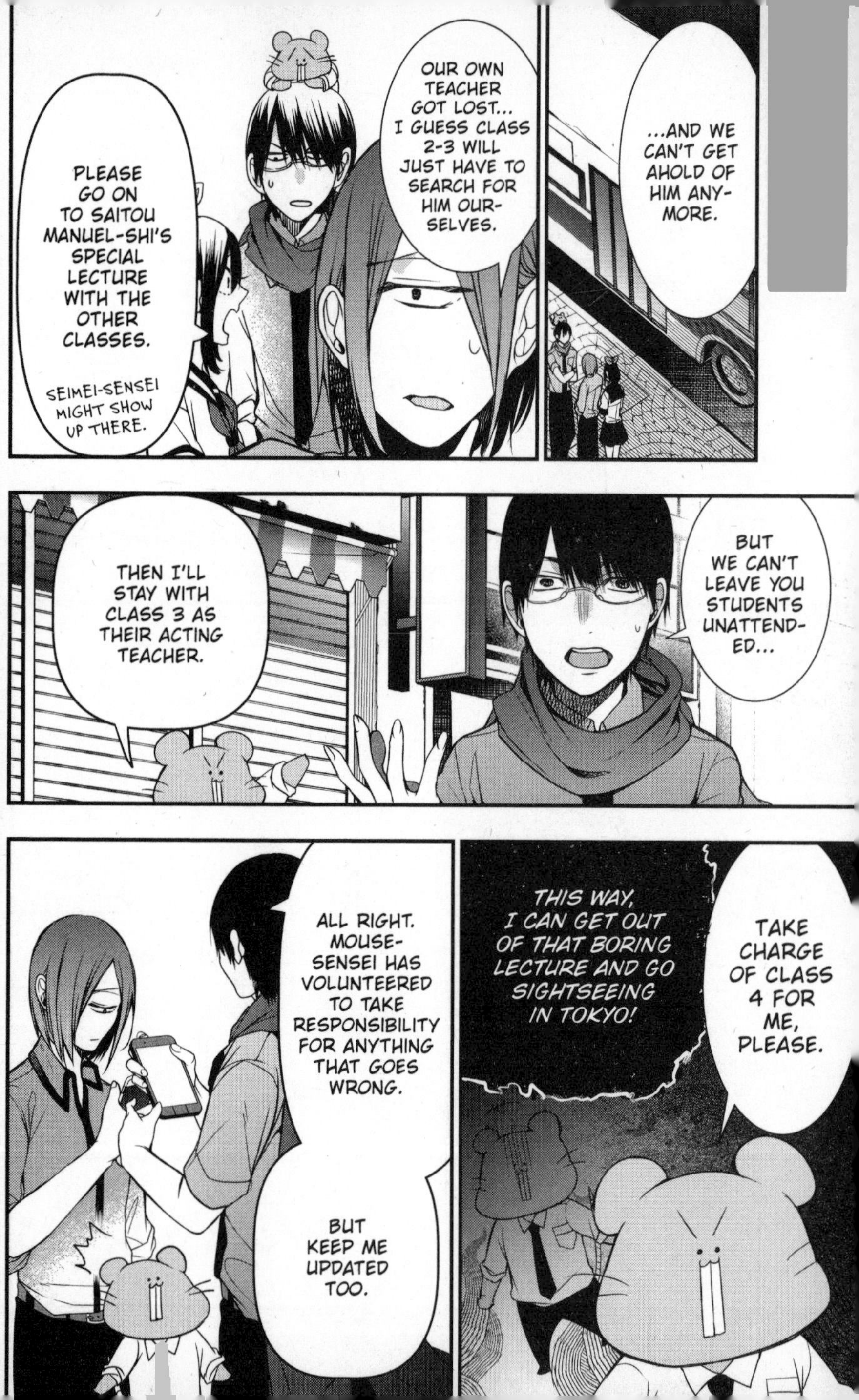
...AND WE CAN'T GET AHOLD OF HIM ANY-MORE.
OUR OWN TEACHER GOT LOST... I GUESS CLASS 2-3 WILL JUST HAVE TO SEARCH FOR HIM OUR-SELVES.
PLEASE GO ON TO SAITOU MANUEL-SHI'S SPECIAL LECTURE WITH THE OTHER CLASSES.
SEIMEI-SENSEI MIGHT SHOW UP THERE.
BUT WE CAN'T LEAVE YOU STUDENTS UNATTEND-ED...
THEN I'LL STAY WITH CLASS 3 AS THEIR ACTING TEACHER.
TAKE CHARGE OF CLASS 4 FOR ME, PLEASE.
THIS WAY, I CAN GET OUT OF THAT BORING LECTURE AND GO SIGHTSEEING IN TOKYO!
ALL RIGHT. MOUSE-SENSEI HAS VOLUNTEERED TO TAKE RESPONSIBILITY FOR ANYTHING THAT GOES WRONG.
BUT KEEP ME UPDATED TOO.

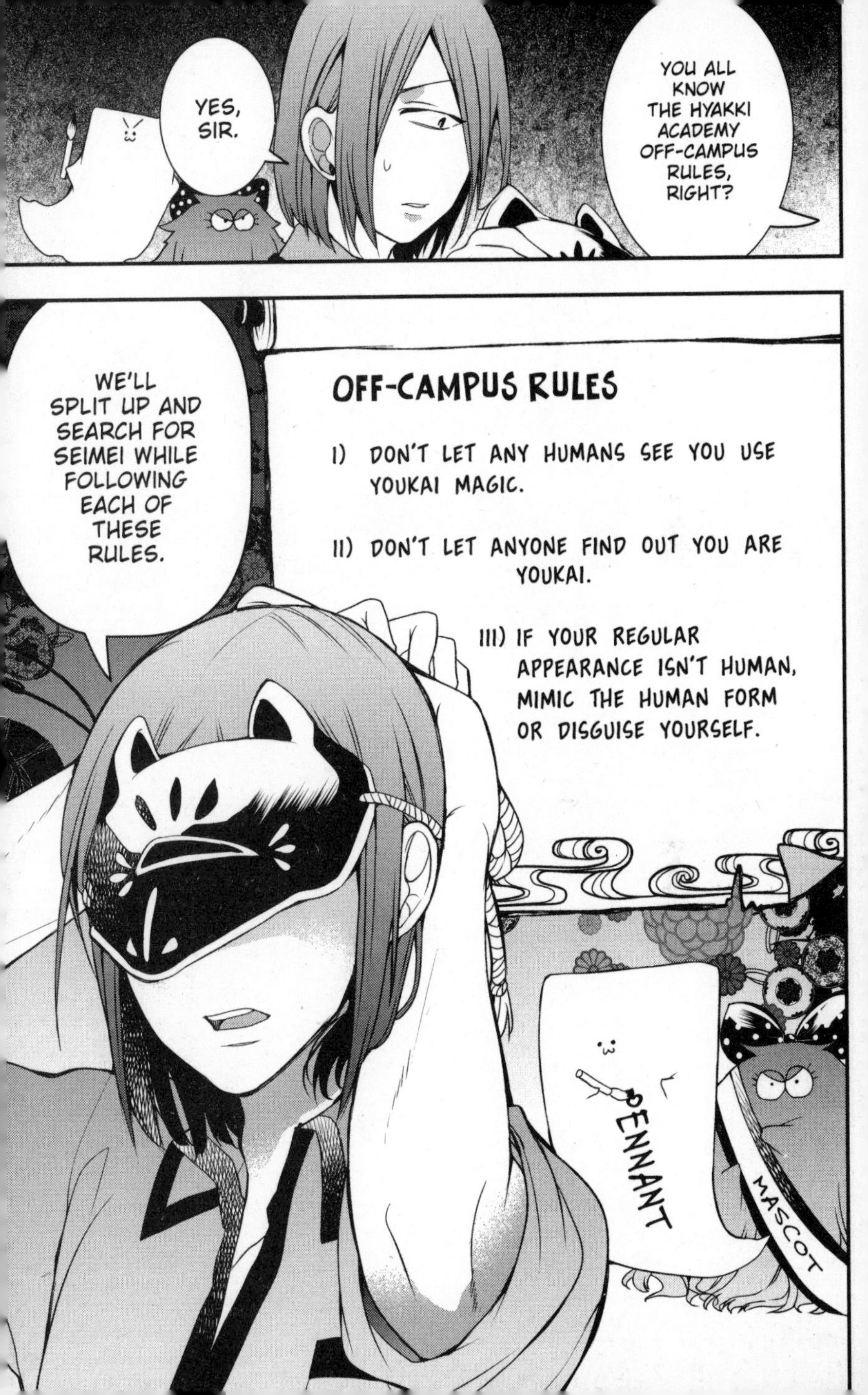
YOU ALL KNOW THE HYAKKI ACADEMY OFF-CAMPUS RULES, RIGHT?
YES, SIR.
OFF-CAMPUS RULES
I) DON'T LET ANY HUMANS SEE YOU USE YOUKAI MAGIC.
II) DON'T LET ANYONE FIND OUT YOU ARE YOUKAI.
III) IF YOUR REGULAR APPEARANCE ISN'T HUMAN, MIMIC THE HUMAN FORM OR DISGUISE YOURSELF.
WE'LL SPLIT UP AND SEARCH FOR SEIMEI WHILE FOLLOWING EACH OF THESE RULES.
PENNANT
MASCOT

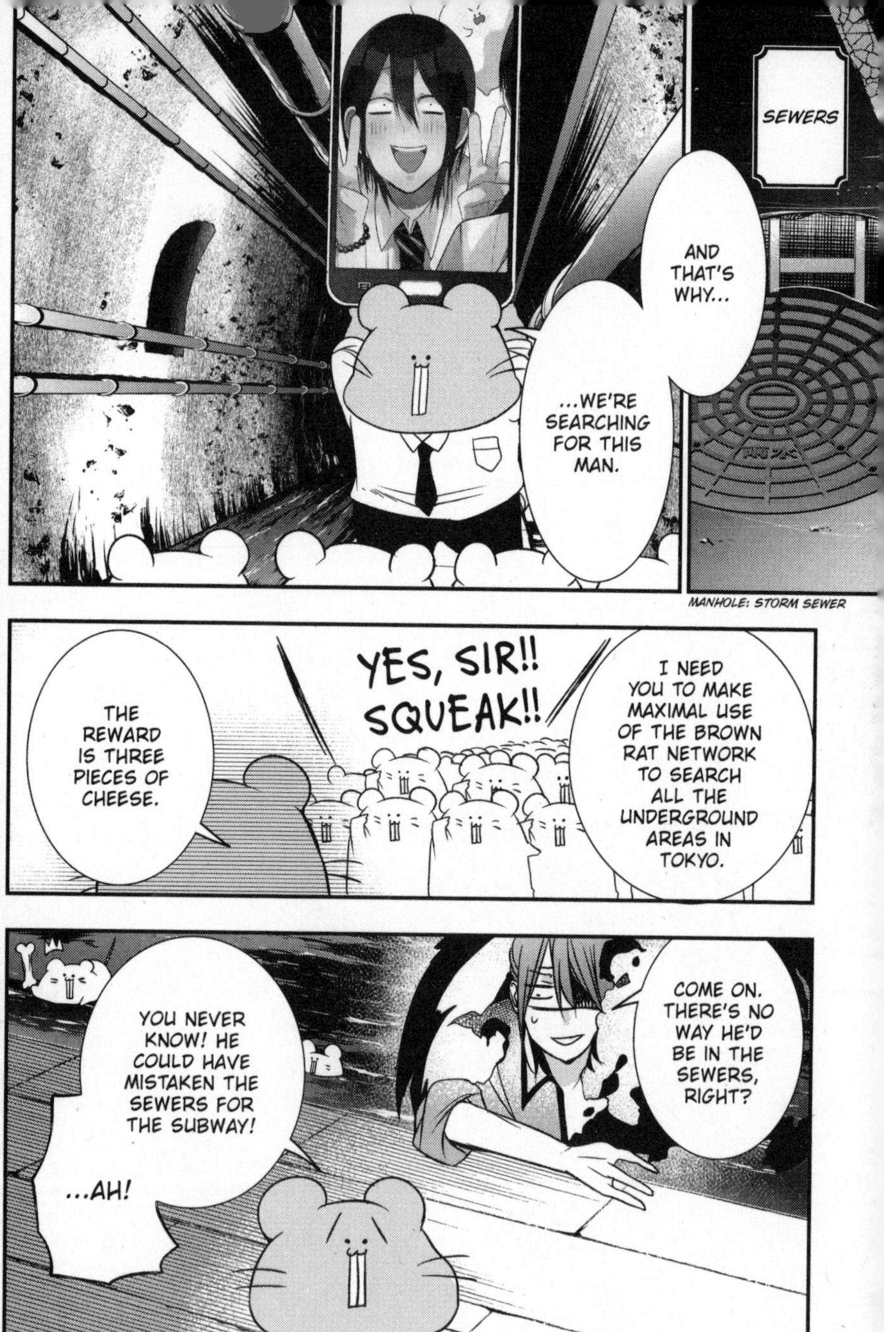
SEWERS
MANHOLE: STORM SEWER
AND THAT'S WHY...
...WE'RE SEARCHING FOR THIS MAN.
I NEED YOU TO MAKE MAXIMAL USE OF THE BROWN RAT NETWORK TO SEARCH ALL THE UNDERGROUND AREAS IN TOKYO.
YES, SIR!! SQUEAK!!
THE REWARD IS THREE PIECES OF CHEESE.
COME ON. THERE'S NO WAY HE'D BE IN THE SEWERS, RIGHT?
YOU NEVER KNOW! HE COULD HAVE MISTAKEN THE SEWERS FOR THE SUBWAY!
...AH!

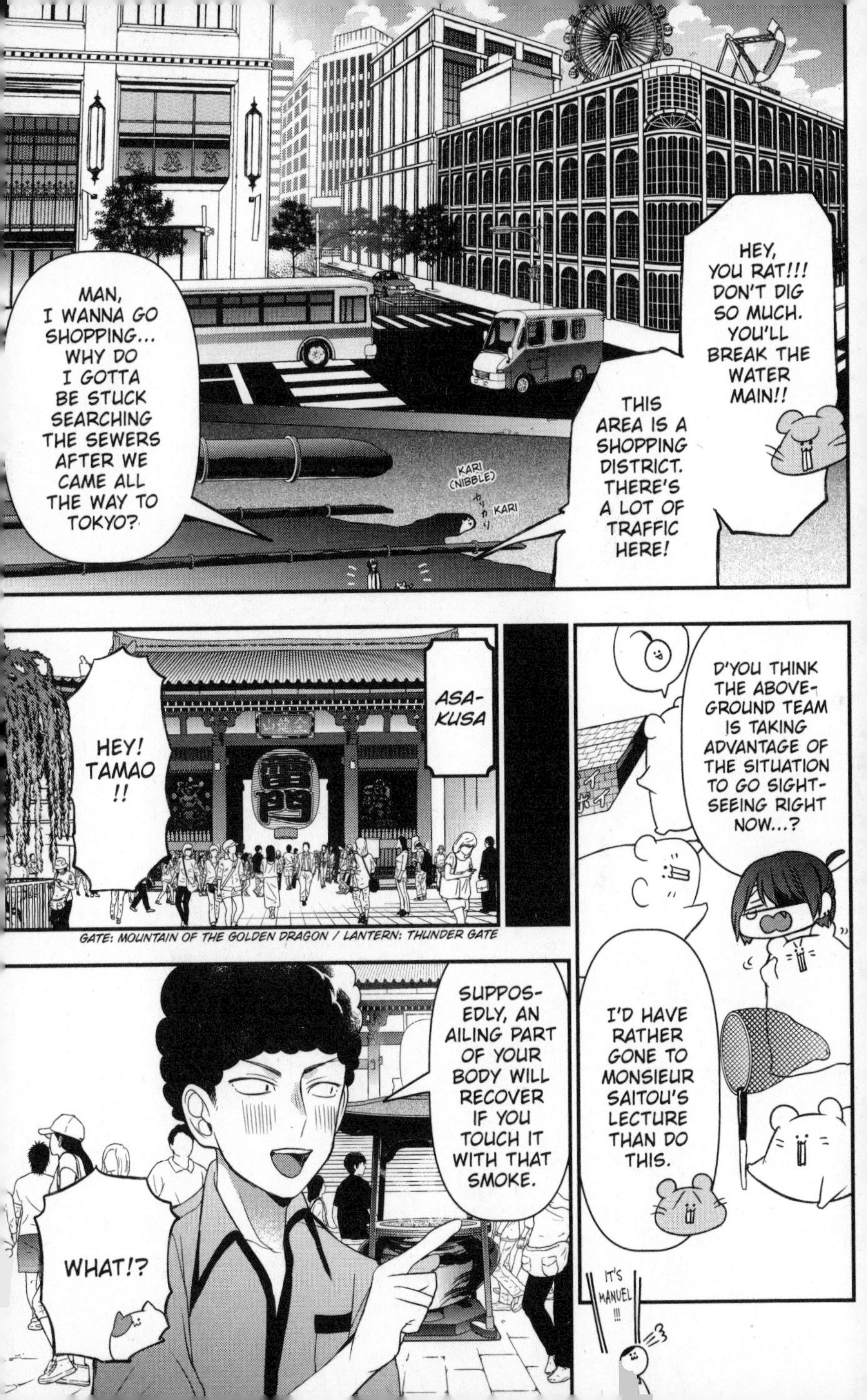
HEY, YOU RAT!!! DON'T DIG SO MUCH. YOU'LL BREAK THE WATER MAIN!!
THIS AREA IS A SHOPPING DISTRICT. THERE'S A LOT OF TRAFFIC HERE!
KARI (NIBBLE)
KARI
MAN, I WANNA GO SHOPPING... WHY DO I GOTTA BE STUCK SEARCHING THE SEWERS AFTER WE CAME ALL THE WAY TO TOKYO?
D'YOU THINK THE ABOVE-GROUND TEAM IS TAKING ADVANTAGE OF THE SITUATION TO GO SIGHT-SEEING RIGHT NOW...?
I'D HAVE RATHER GONE TO MONSIEUR SAITOU'S LECTURE THAN DO THIS.
IT'S MANUEL!!!
ASA-KUSA
HEY! TAMAO!!
GATE: MOUNTAIN OF THE GOLDEN DRAGON / LANTERN: THUNDER GATE
SUPPOS-EDLY, AN AILING PART OF YOUR BODY WILL RECOVER IF YOU TOUCH IT WITH THAT SMOKE.
WHAT!?

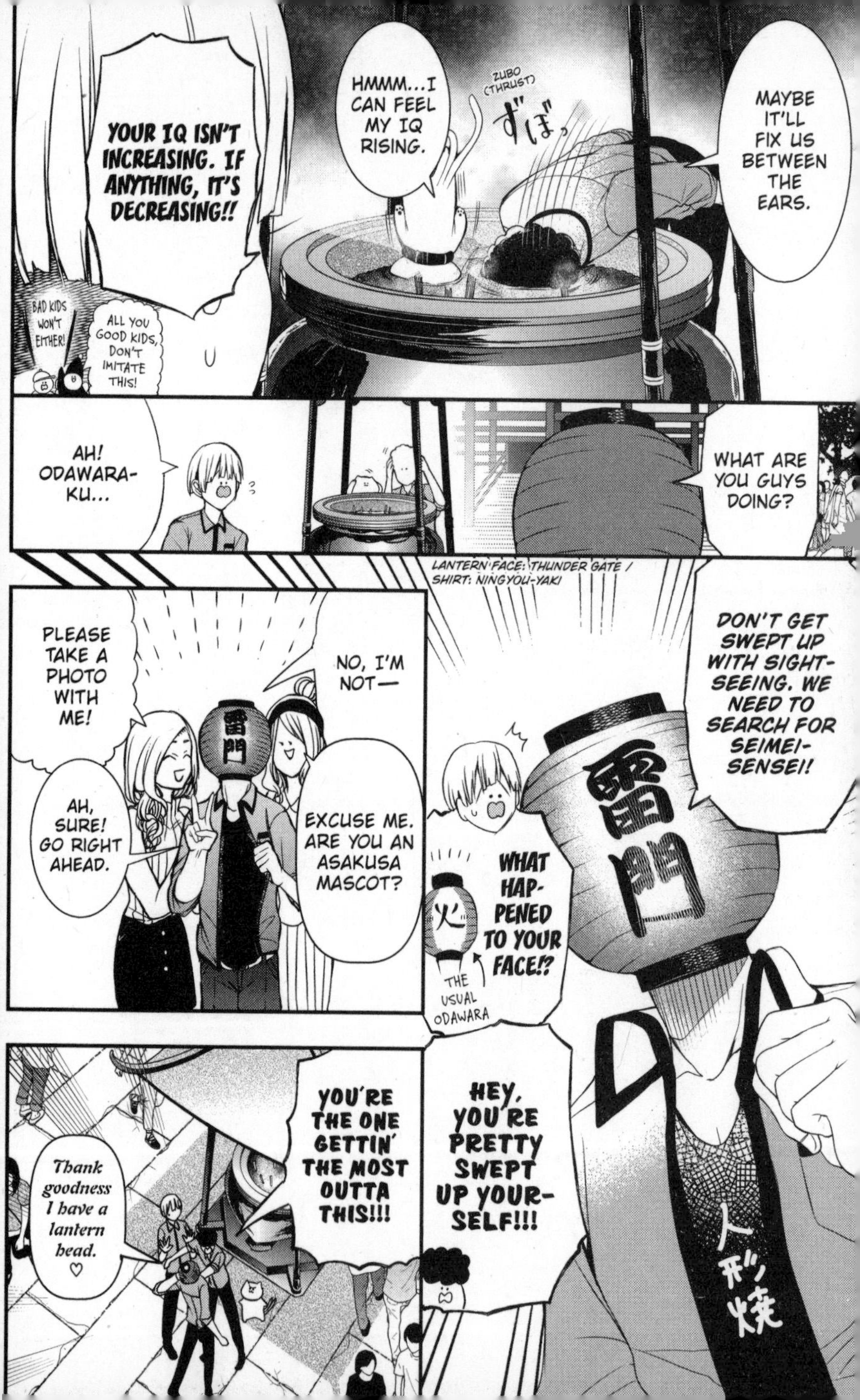
MAYBE IT'LL FIX US BETWEEN THE EARS.
ZUBO (THRUST)
ずぼ
HMMM...I CAN FEEL MY IQ RISING.
YOUR IQ ISN'T INCREASING. IF ANYTHING, IT'S DECREASING!!
ALL YOU GOOD KIDS, DON'T IMITATE THIS!
BAD KIDS WON'T EITHER!
WHAT ARE YOU GUYS DOING?
AH! ODAWARA-KU...
LANTERN FACE: THUNDER GATE / SHIRT: NINGYOU-YAKI
DON'T GET SWEPT UP WITH SIGHT-SEEING. WE NEED TO SEARCH FOR SEIMEI-SENSEI!
WHAT HAP-PENED TO YOUR FACE!?
THE USUAL ODAWARA
NO, I'M NOT—
PLEASE TAKE A PHOTO WITH ME!
EXCUSE ME. ARE YOU AN ASAKUSA MASCOT?
AH, SURE! GO RIGHT AHEAD.
HEY, YOU'RE PRETTY SWEPT UP YOUR-SELF!!!
YOU'RE THE ONE GETTIN' THE MOST OUTTA THIS!!!
Thank goodness I have a lantern head. ♡

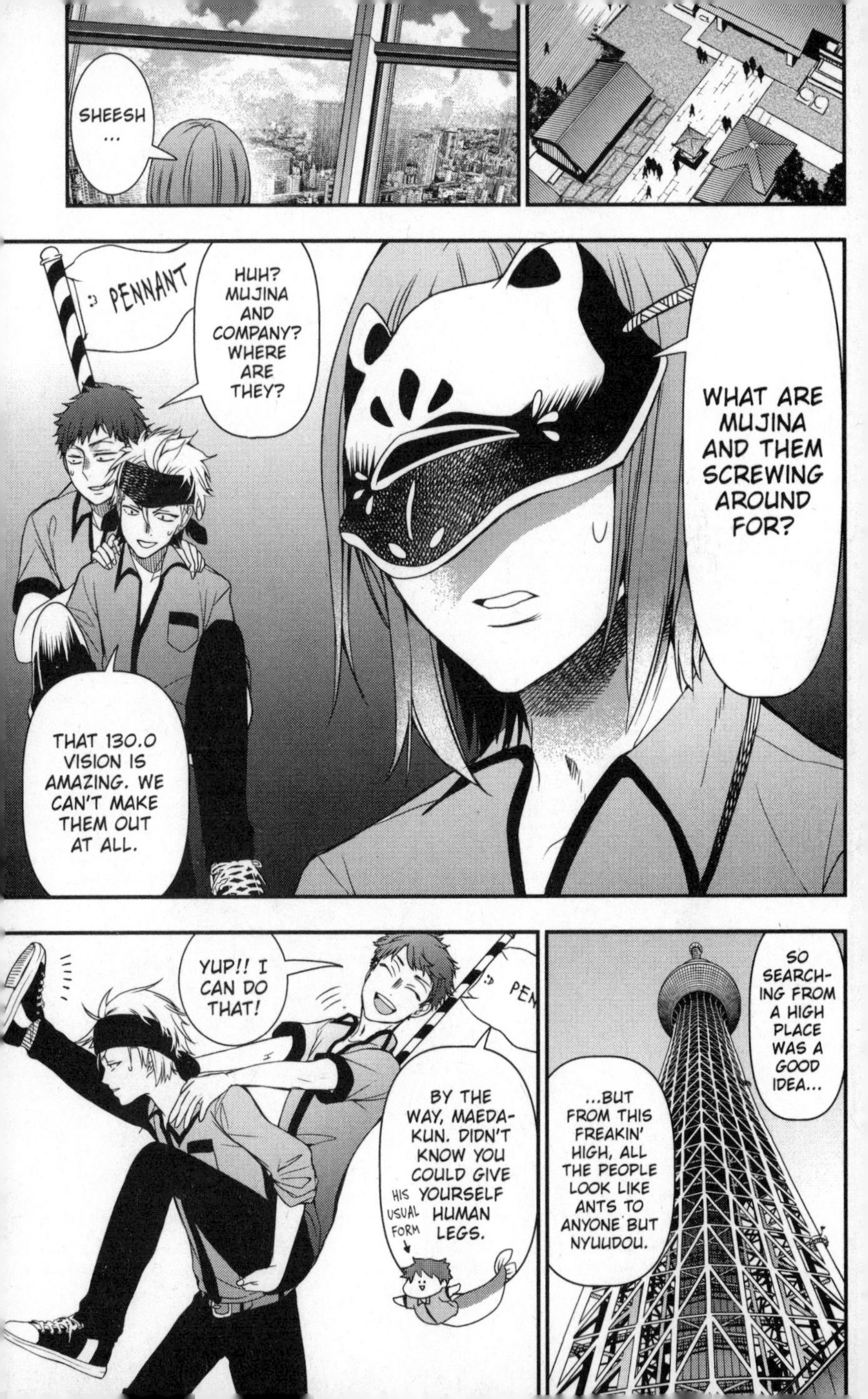
SHEESH ...
WHAT ARE MUJINA AND THEM SCREWING AROUND FOR?
HUH? MUJINA AND COMPANY? WHERE ARE THEY?
PENNANT
THAT 130.0 VISION IS AMAZING. WE CAN'T MAKE THEM OUT AT ALL.
SO SEARCHING FROM A HIGH PLACE WAS A GOOD IDEA...
...BUT FROM THIS FREAKIN' HIGH, ALL THE PEOPLE LOOK LIKE ANTS TO ANYONE BUT NYUUDOU.
YUP!! I CAN DO THAT!
PEN
BY THE WAY, MAEDA-KUN. DIDN'T KNOW YOU COULD GIVE YOURSELF HUMAN LEGS.
HIS USUAL FORM

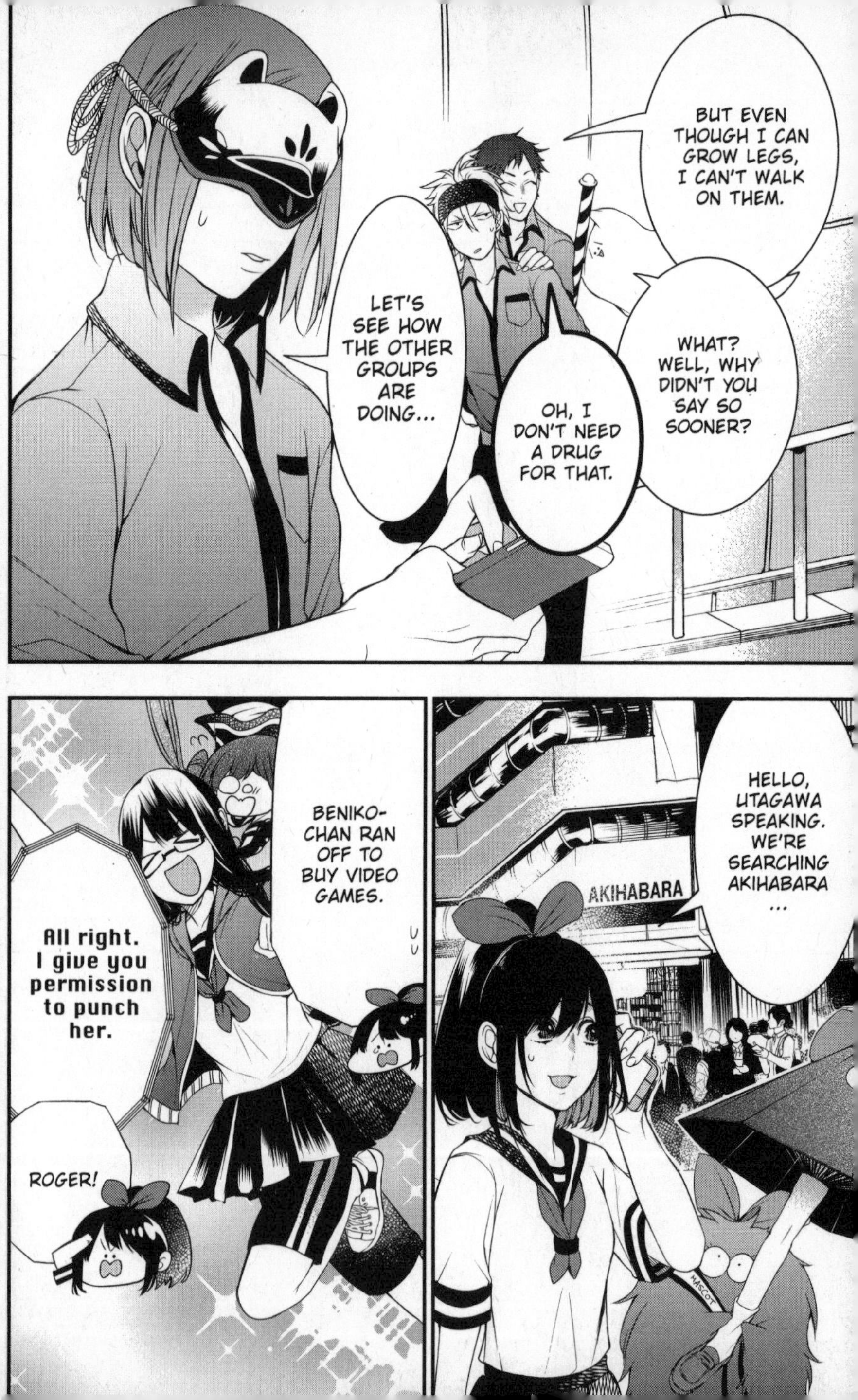
BUT EVEN THOUGH I CAN GROW LEGS, I CAN'T WALK ON THEM.
WHAT? WELL, WHY DIDN'T YOU SAY SO SOONER?
OH, I DON'T NEED A DRUG FOR THAT.
LET'S SEE HOW THE OTHER GROUPS ARE DOING...
HELLO, UTAGAWA SPEAKING. WE'RE SEARCHING AKIHABARA ...
AKIHABARA
MASCOT
BENIKO-CHAN RAN OFF TO BUY VIDEO GAMES.
All right. I give you permission to punch her.
ROGER!

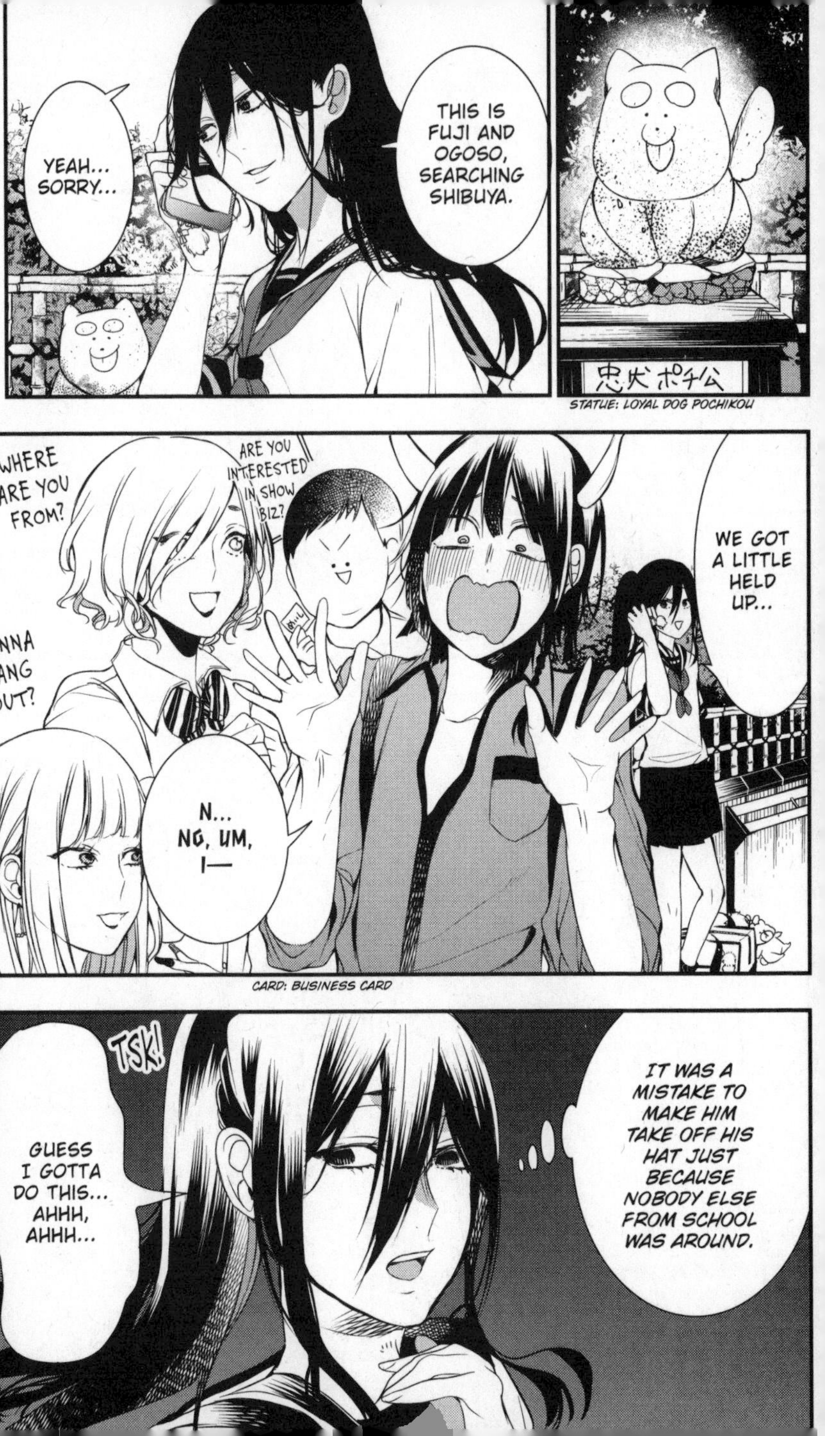
忠犬ポチ公
STATUE: LOYAL DOG POCHIKOU
THIS IS FUJI AND OGOSO, SEARCHING SHIBUYA.
YEAH... SORRY...
WE GOT A LITTLE HELD UP...
ARE YOU INTERESTED IN SHOW BIZ?
WHERE ARE YOU FROM?
WANNA HANG OUT?
N... NO, UM, I—
CARD: BUSINESS CARD
IT WAS A MISTAKE TO MAKE HIM TAKE OFF HIS HAT JUST BECAUSE NOBODY ELSE FROM SCHOOL WAS AROUND.
TSK!
GUESS I GOTTA DO THIS... AHHH, AHHH...

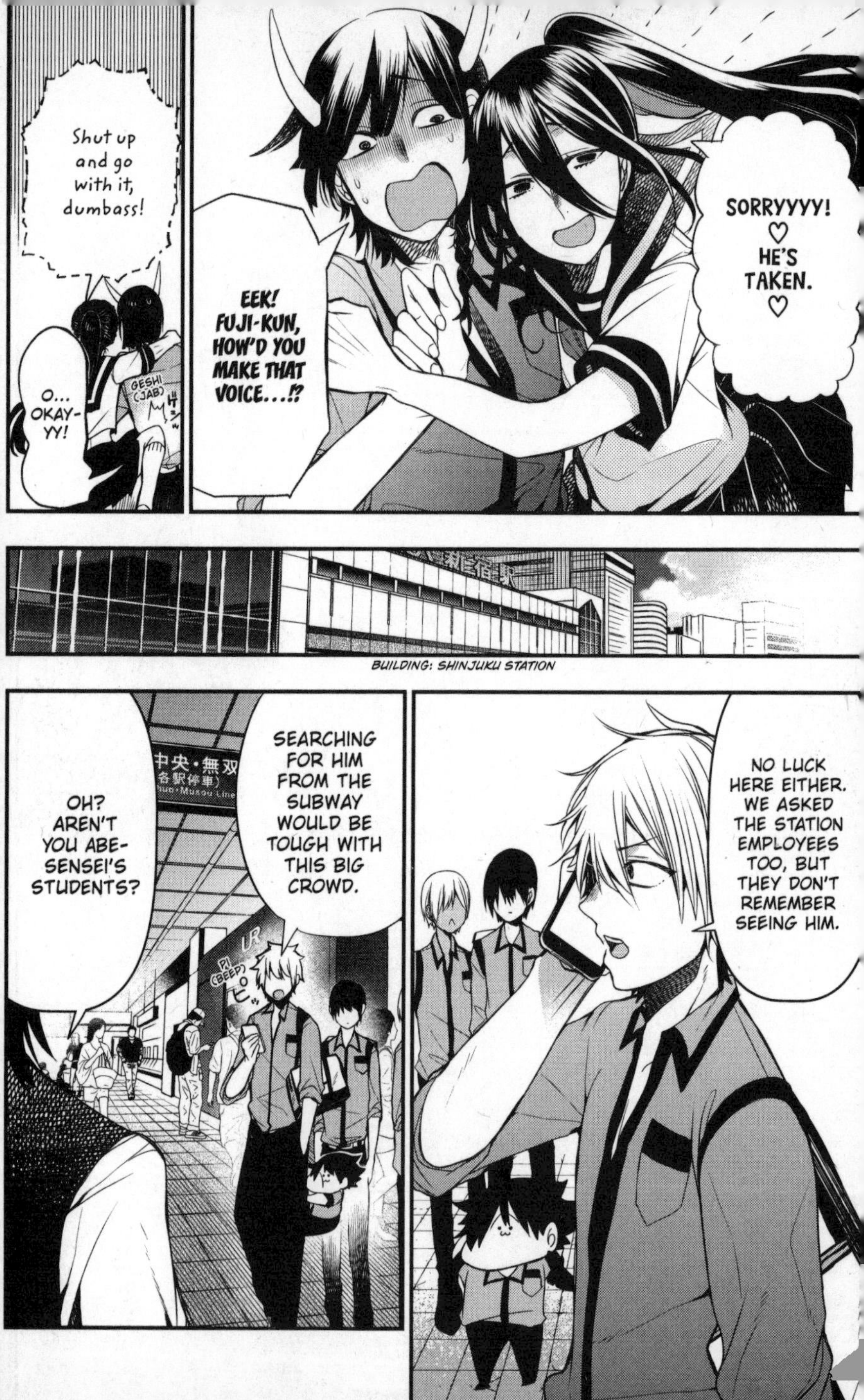
SORRYYYY! ♡ HE'S TAKEN. ♡
EEK! FUJI-KUN, HOW'D YOU MAKE THAT VOICE...!?
Shut up and go with it, dumbass!
GESHI (JAB)
O... OKAY-YY!
BUILDING: SHINJUKU STATION
NO LUCK HERE EITHER. WE ASKED THE STATION EMPLOYEES TOO, BUT THEY DON'T REMEMBER SEEING HIM.
SEARCHING FOR HIM FROM THE SUBWAY WOULD BE TOUGH WITH THIS BIG CROWD.
PI (BEEP)
OH? AREN'T YOU ABE-SENSEI'S STUDENTS?

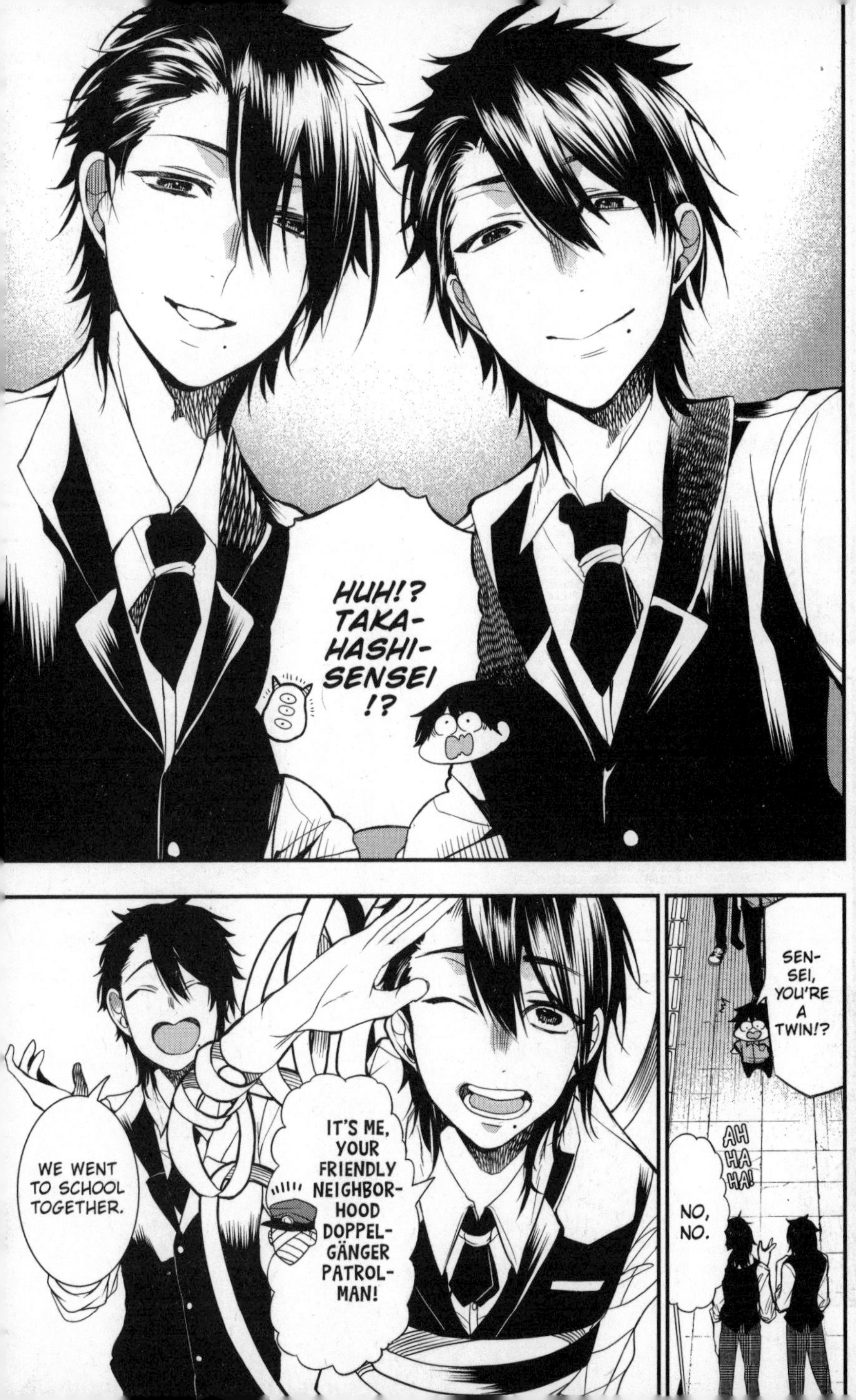
HUH!? TAKA-HASHI-SENSEI!?
SEN-SEI, YOU'RE A TWIN!?
AH HA HA!
NO, NO.
IT'S ME, YOUR FRIENDLY NEIGHBOR-HOOD DOPPEL-GÄNGER PATROL-MAN!
WE WENT TO SCHOOL TOGETHER.

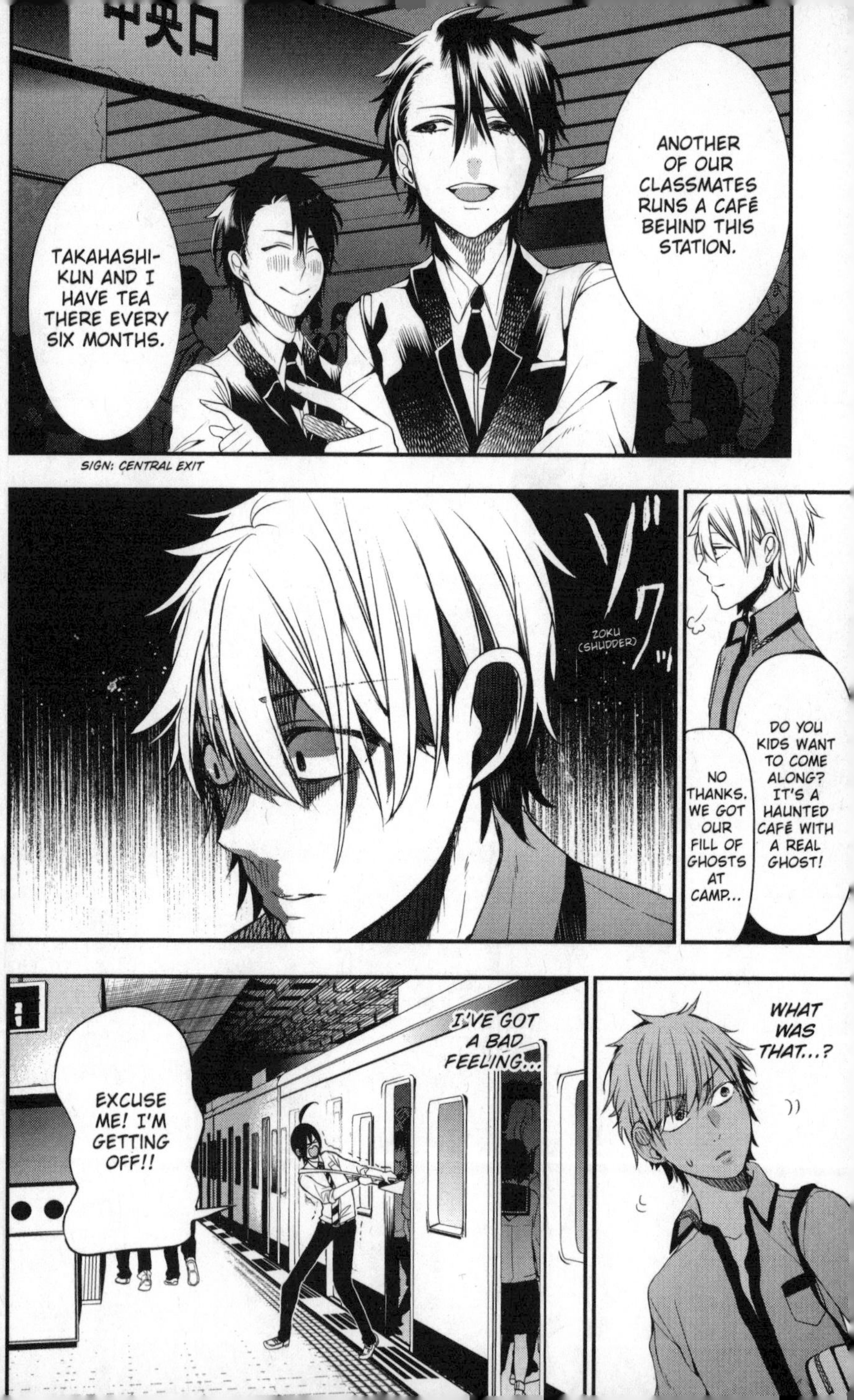
中央口
ANOTHER OF OUR CLASSMATES RUNS A CAFÉ BEHIND THIS STATION.
TAKAHASHI-KUN AND I HAVE TEA THERE EVERY SIX MONTHS.
SIGN: CENTRAL EXIT
DO YOU KIDS WANT TO COME ALONG? IT'S A HAUNTED CAFÉ WITH A REAL GHOST!
NO THANKS. WE GOT OUR FILL OF GHOSTS AT CAMP...
ゾクッ
ZOKU (SHUDDER)
WHAT WAS THAT...?
I'VE GOT A BAD FEELING...
EXCUSE ME! I'M GETTING OFF!!

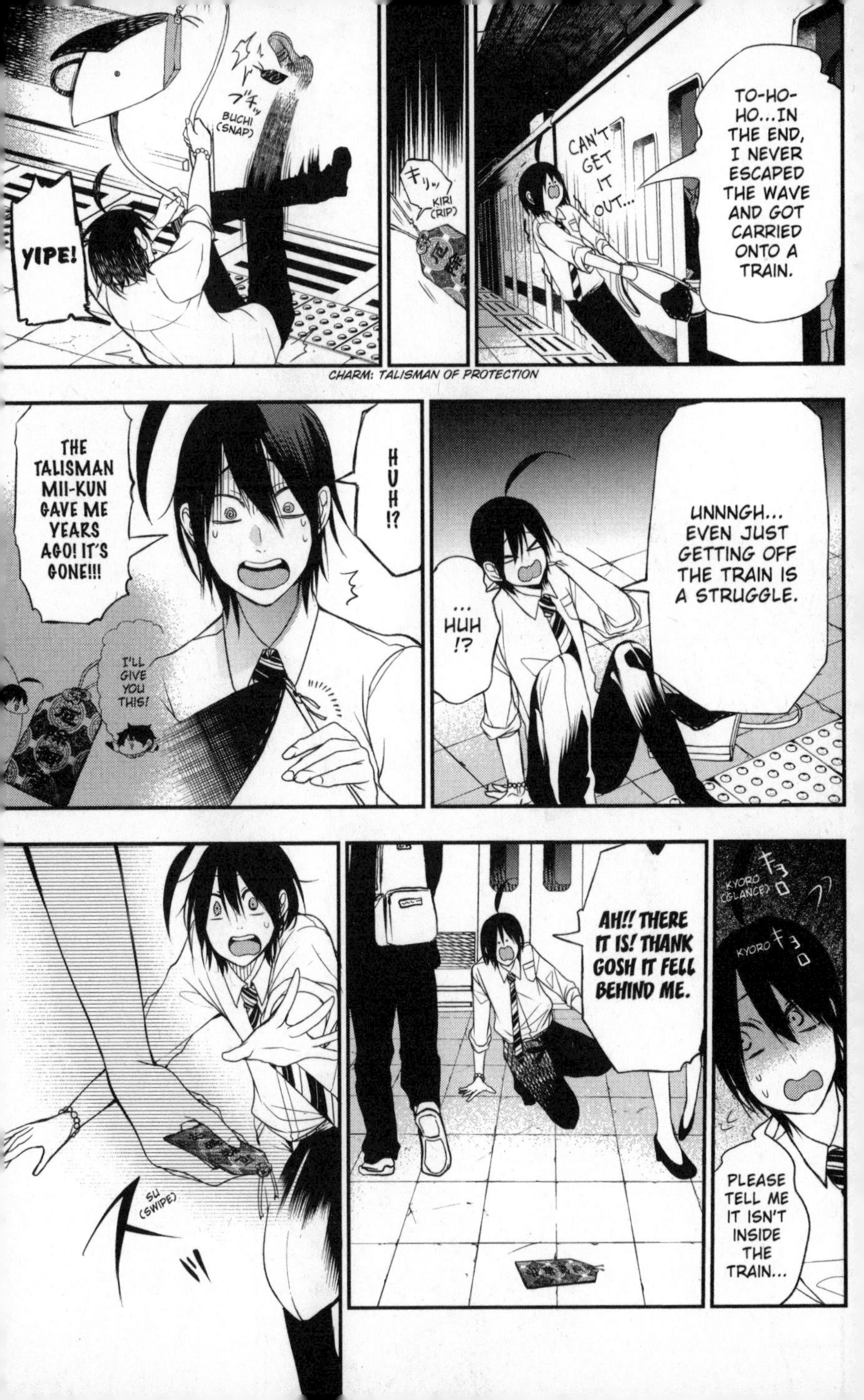
TO-HO-HO...IN THE END, I NEVER ESCAPED THE WAVE AND GOT CARRIED ONTO A TRAIN.
CAN'T GET IT OUT...
KIRI (RIP)
BUCHI (SNAP)
YIPE!
CHARM: TALISMAN OF PROTECTION
UNNNGH... EVEN JUST GETTING OFF THE TRAIN IS A STRUGGLE.
...HUH!?
HUH!?
THE TALISMAN MII-KUN GAVE ME YEARS AGO! IT'S GONE!!!
I'LL GIVE YOU THIS!
KYORO (GLANCE)
KYORO
PLEASE TELL ME IT ISN'T INSIDE THE TRAIN...
AH!! THERE IT IS! THANK GOSH IT FELL BEHIND ME.
SU (SWIPE)

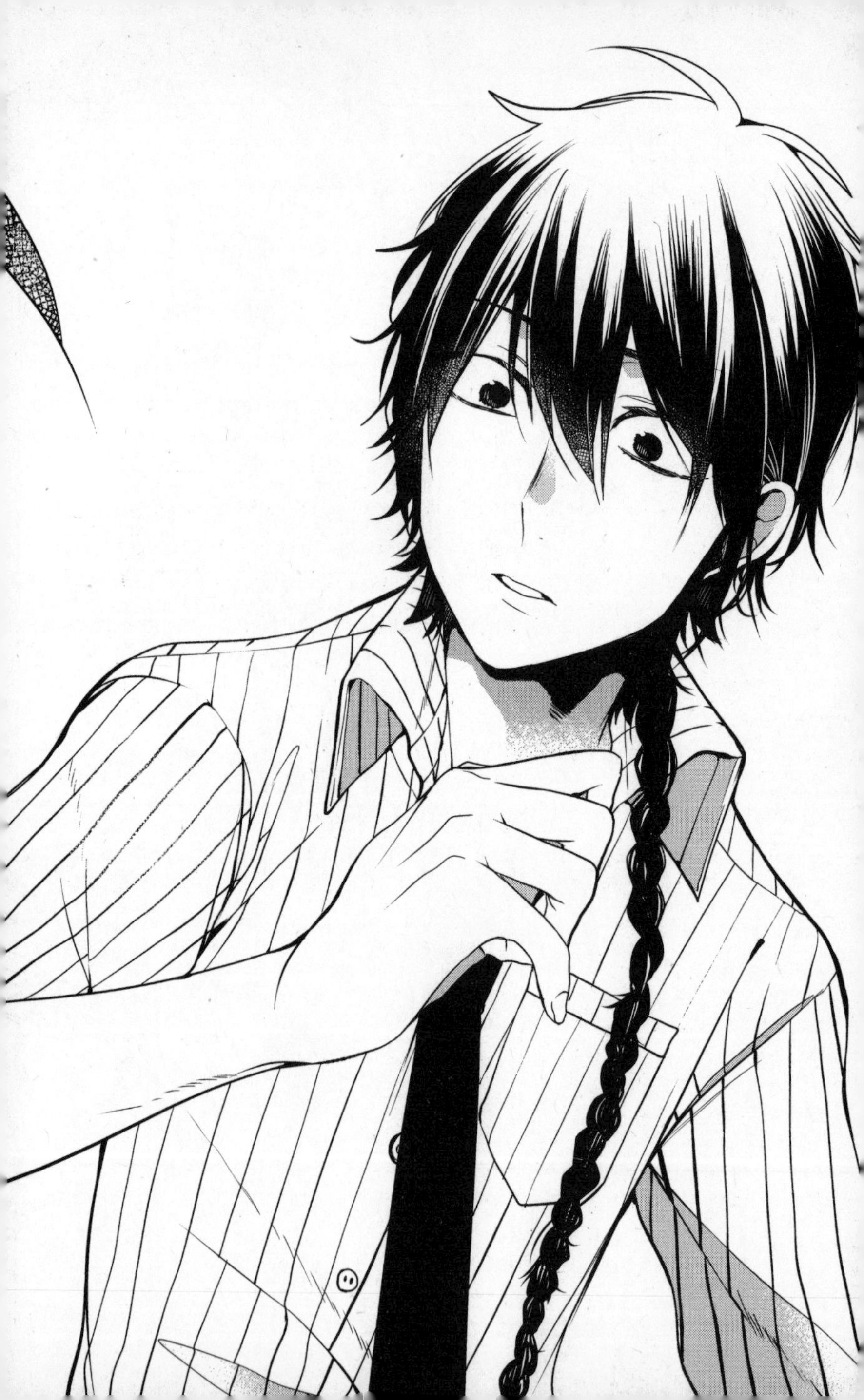

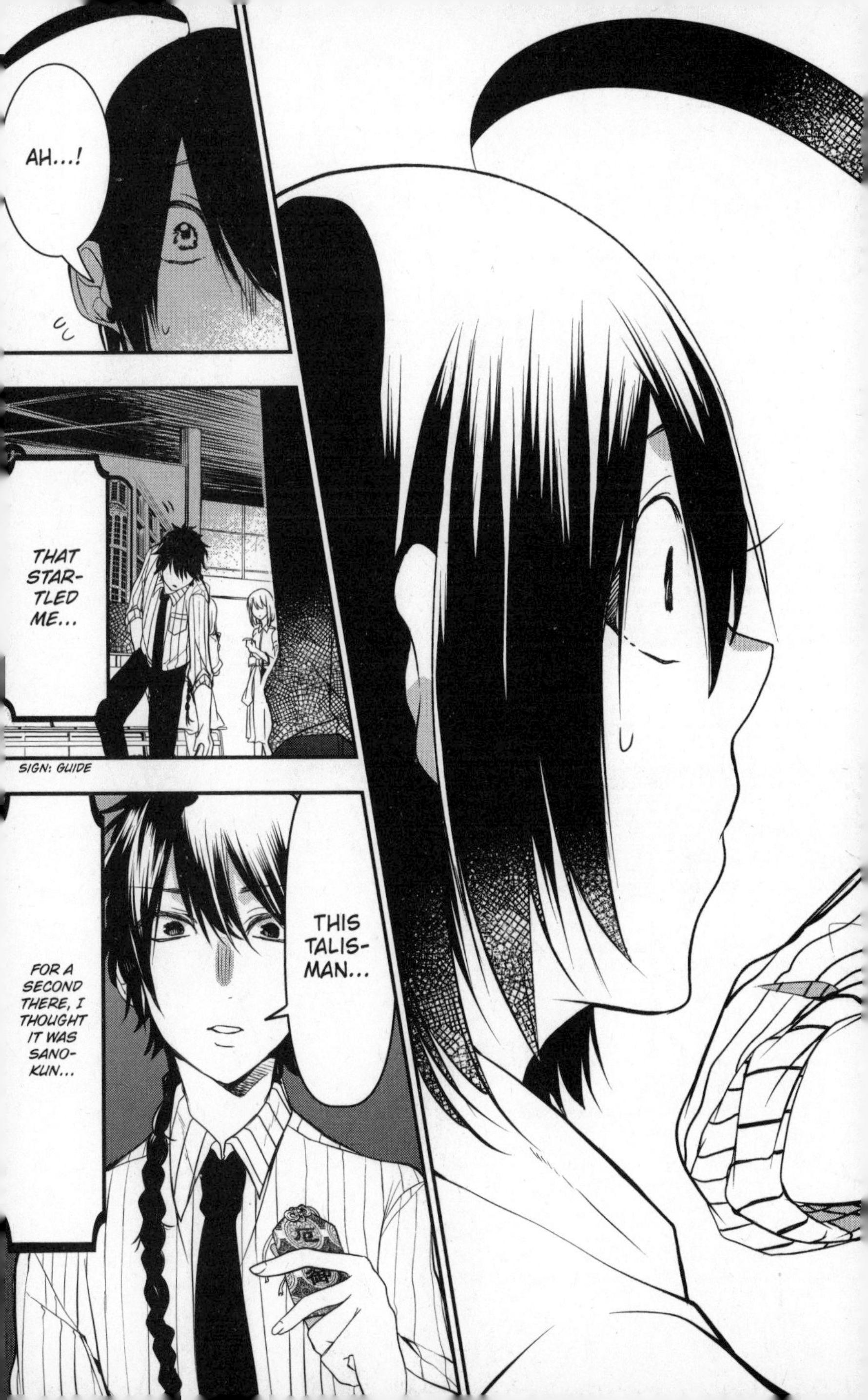
AH...!
THAT STARTLED ME...
SIGN: GUIDE
THIS TALISMAN...
FOR A SECOND THERE, I THOUGHT IT WAS SANO-KUN...

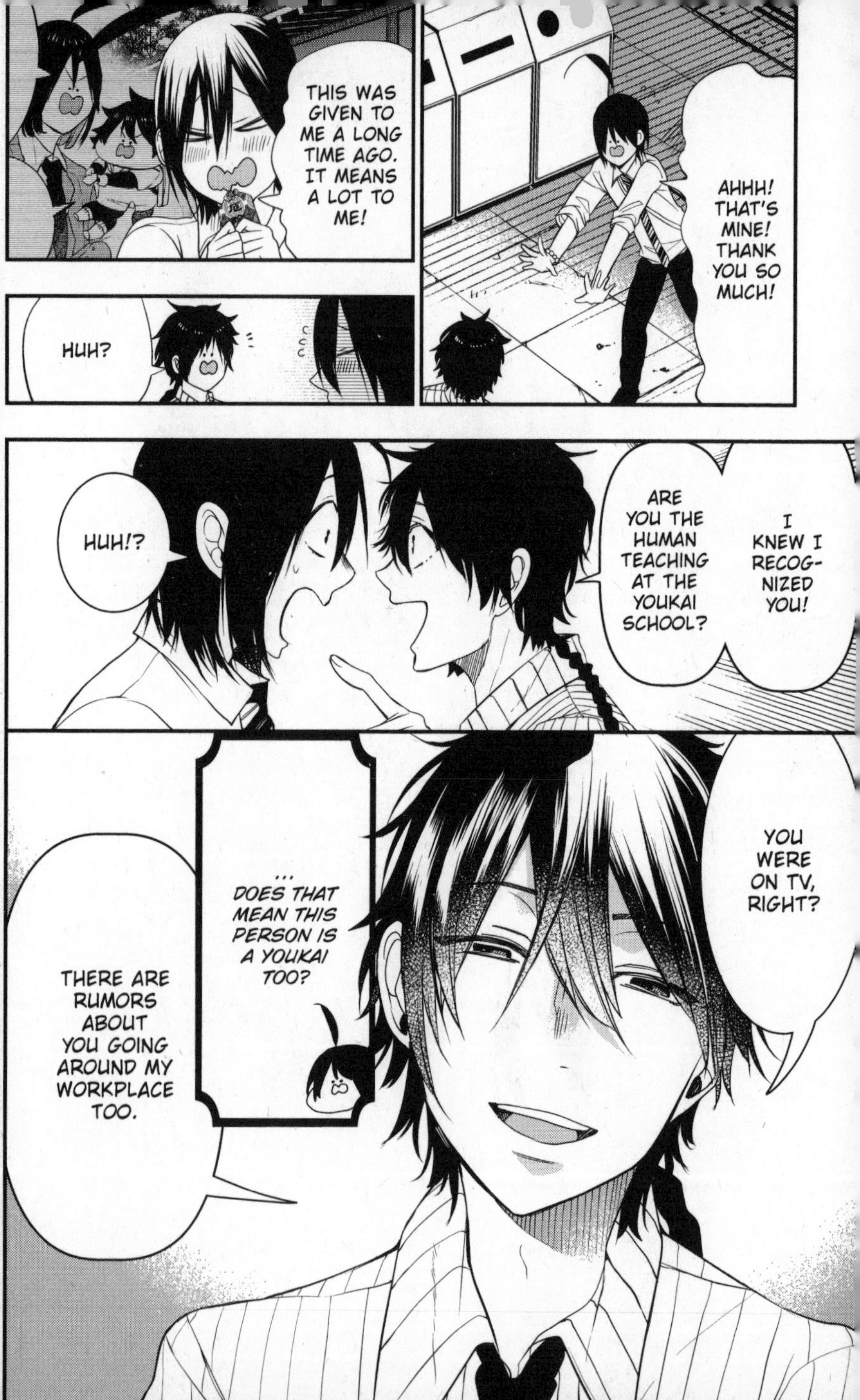
AHHH! THAT'S MINE! THANK YOU SO MUCH!
THIS WAS GIVEN TO ME A LONG TIME AGO. IT MEANS A LOT TO ME!
HUH?
I KNEW I RECOG-NIZED YOU!
ARE YOU THE HUMAN TEACHING AT THE YOUKAI SCHOOL?
HUH!?
YOU WERE ON TV, RIGHT?
...DOES THAT MEAN THIS PERSON IS A YOUKAI TOO?
THERE ARE RUMORS ABOUT YOU GOING AROUND MY WORKPLACE TOO.

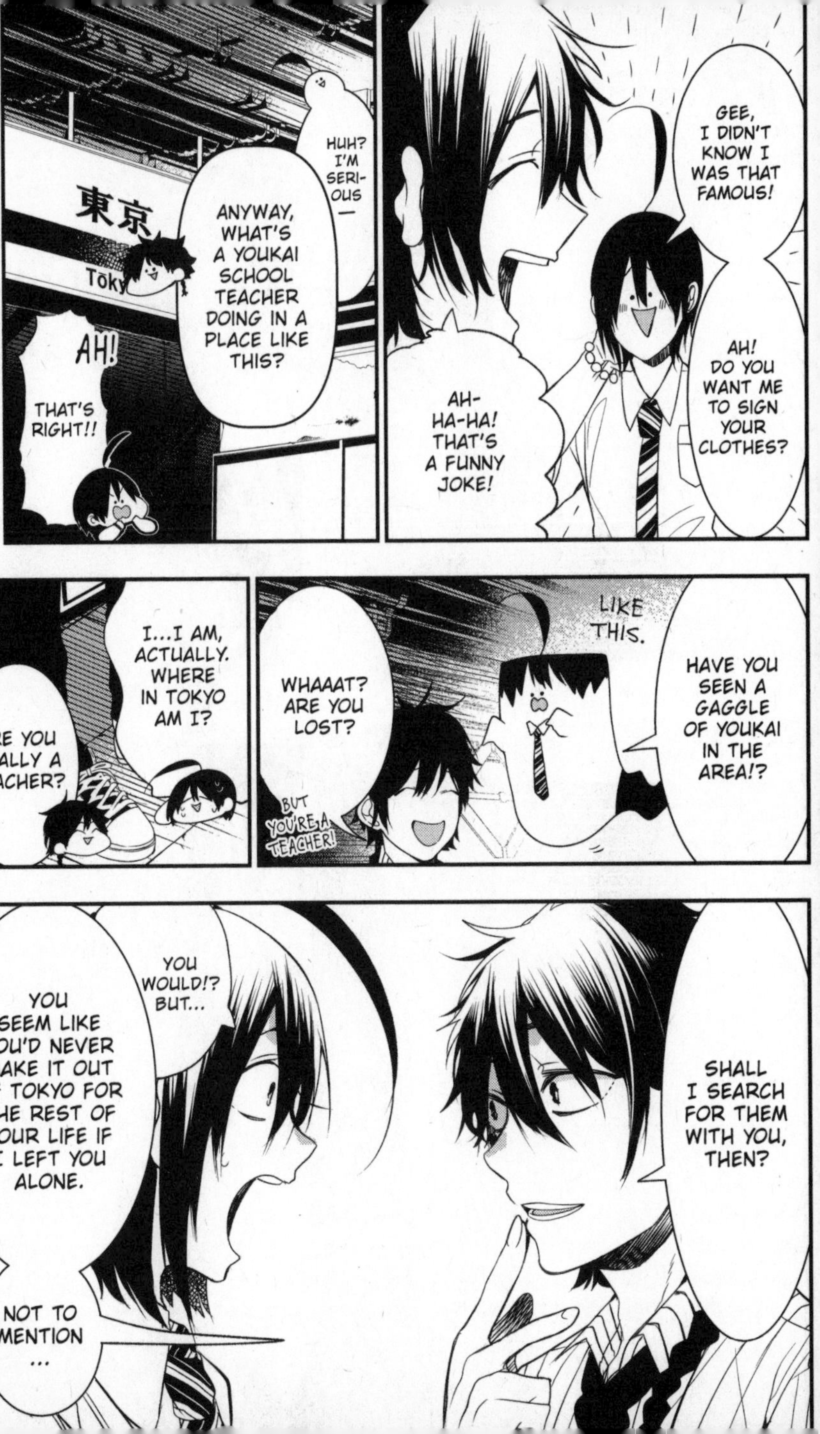
GEE, I DIDN'T KNOW I WAS THAT FAMOUS!
AH! DO YOU WANT ME TO SIGN YOUR CLOTHES?
AH-HA-HA! THAT'S A FUNNY JOKE!
HUH? I'M SERI-OUS—
ANYWAY, WHAT'S A YOUKAI SCHOOL TEACHER DOING IN A PLACE LIKE THIS?
東京
Tōky
AH!
THAT'S RIGHT!!
HAVE YOU SEEN A GAGGLE OF YOUKAI IN THE AREA!?
LIKE THIS.
WHAAAT? ARE YOU LOST?
BUT YOU'RE A TEACHER!
ARE YOU REALLY A TEACHER?
I...I AM, ACTUALLY. WHERE IN TOKYO AM I?
SHALL I SEARCH FOR THEM WITH YOU, THEN?
YOU WOULD!? BUT...
YOU SEEM LIKE YOU'D NEVER MAKE IT OUT OF TOKYO FOR THE REST OF YOUR LIFE IF I LEFT YOU ALONE.
NOT TO MENTION...

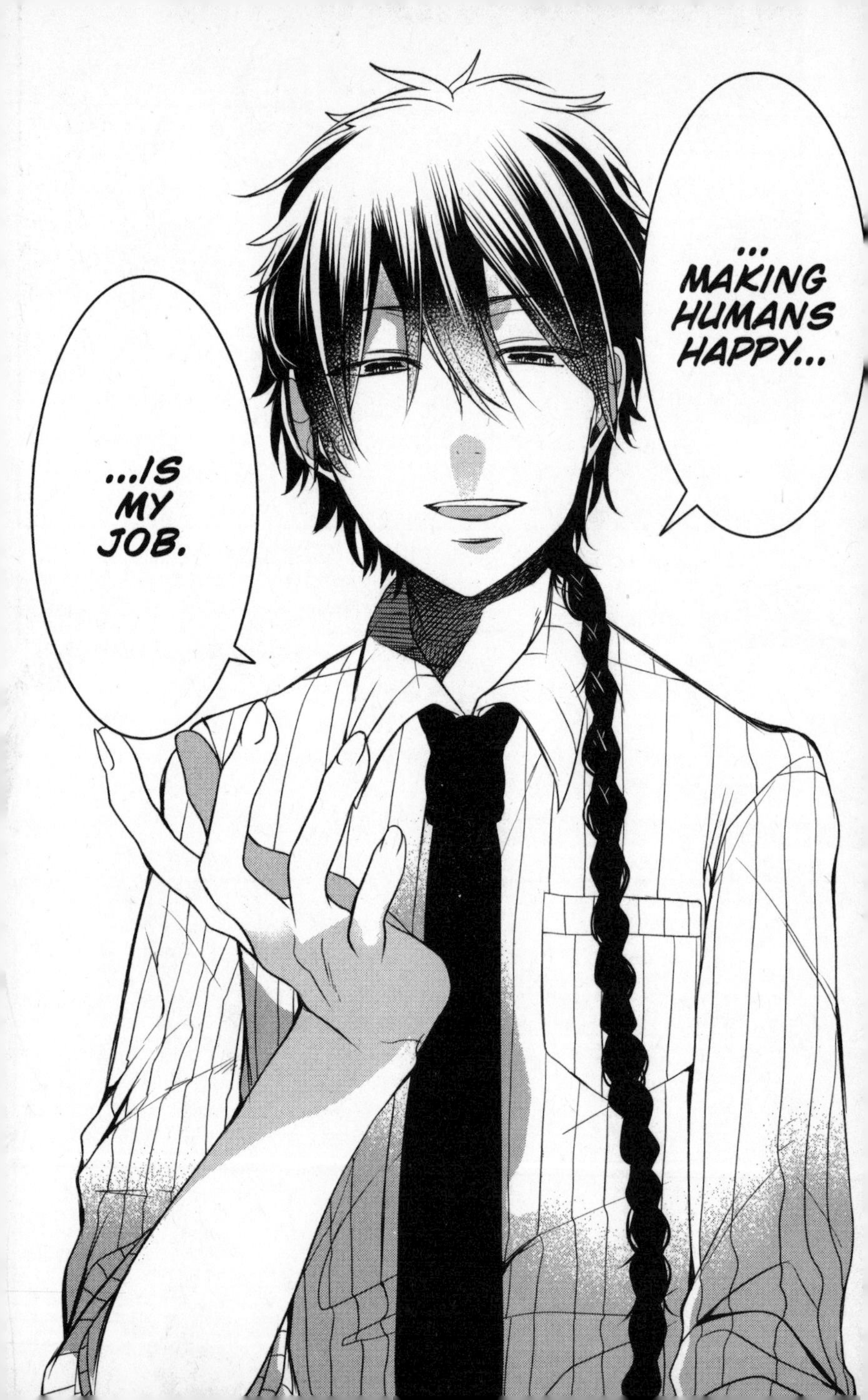
...MAKING HUMANS HAPPY...
...IS MY JOB.

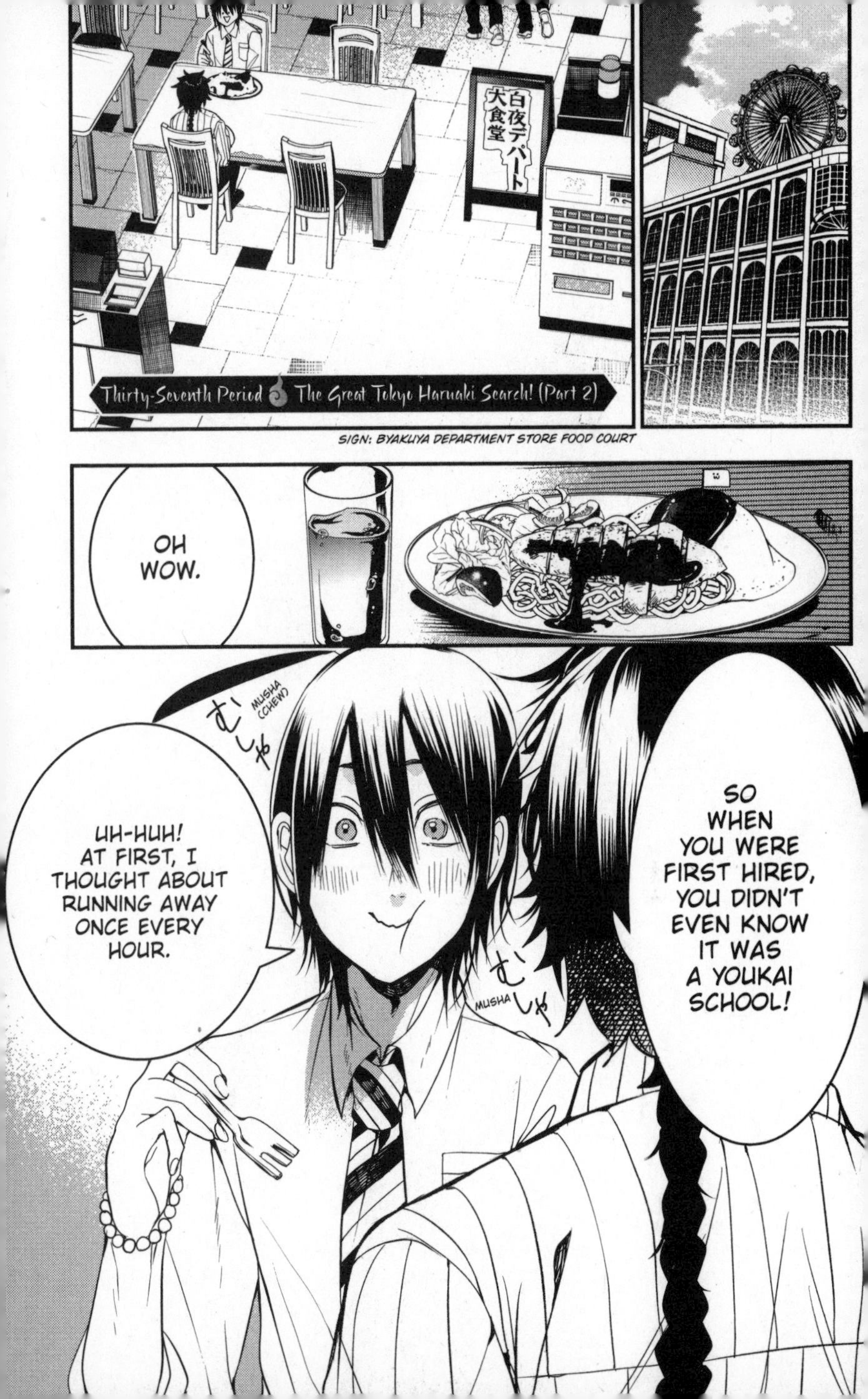
白夜デパート大食堂
Thirty-Seventh Period The Great Tokyo Haruaki Search! (Part 2)
SIGN: BYAKUYA DEPARTMENT STORE FOOD COURT
OH WOW.
SO WHEN YOU WERE FIRST HIRED, YOU DIDN'T EVEN KNOW IT WAS A YOUKAI SCHOOL!
むしゃ MUSHA (CHEW)
UH-HUH! AT FIRST, I THOUGHT ABOUT RUNNING AWAY ONCE EVERY HOUR.
むしゃ MUSHA

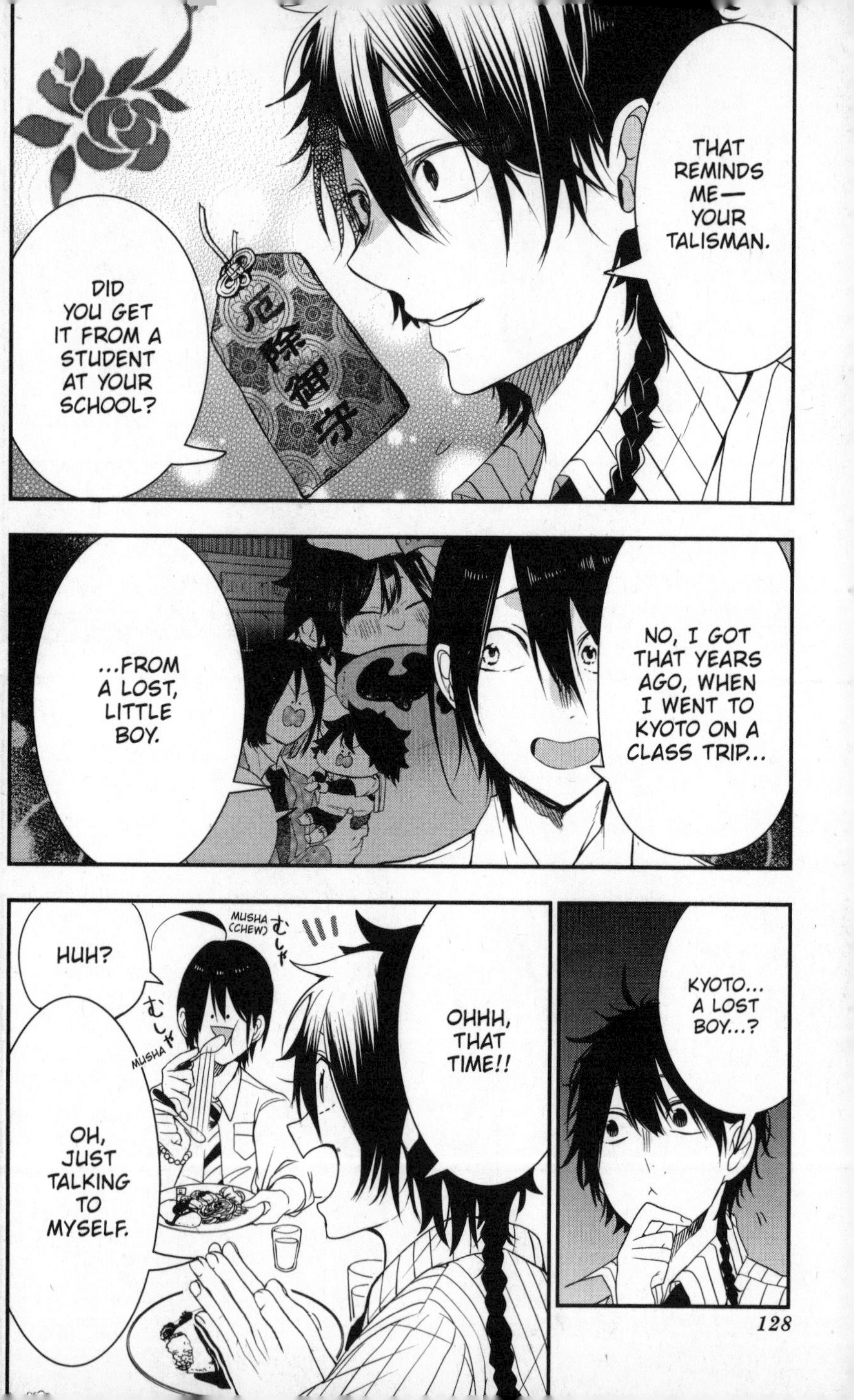
THAT REMINDS ME— YOUR TALISMAN.
厄除御守
DID YOU GET IT FROM A STUDENT AT YOUR SCHOOL?
NO, I GOT THAT YEARS AGO, WHEN I WENT TO KYOTO ON A CLASS TRIP...
...FROM A LOST, LITTLE BOY.
KYOTO... A LOST BOY...?
OHHH, THAT TIME!!
むしゃ MUSHA (CHEW)
HUH?
むしゃ MUSHA
OH, JUST TALKING TO MYSELF.

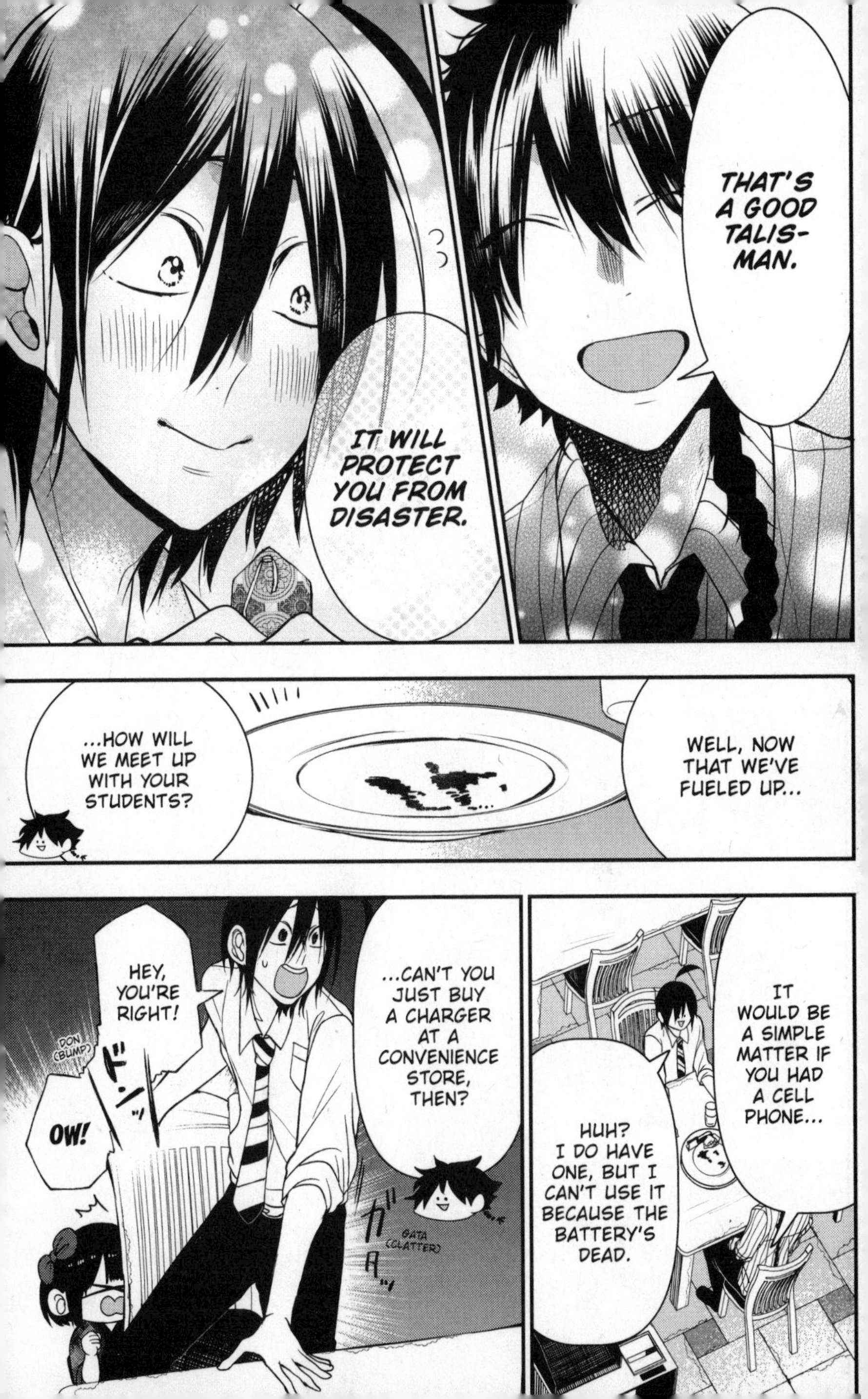
THAT'S A GOOD TALIS-MAN.
IT WILL PROTECT YOU FROM DISASTER.
WELL, NOW THAT WE'VE FUELED UP...
...HOW WILL WE MEET UP WITH YOUR STUDENTS?
IT WOULD BE A SIMPLE MATTER IF YOU HAD A CELL PHONE...
HUH? I DO HAVE ONE, BUT I CAN'T USE IT BECAUSE THE BATTERY'S DEAD.
...CAN'T YOU JUST BUY A CHARGER AT A CONVENIENCE STORE, THEN?
GATA (CLATTER)
HEY, YOU'RE RIGHT!
DON (BUMP)
OW!

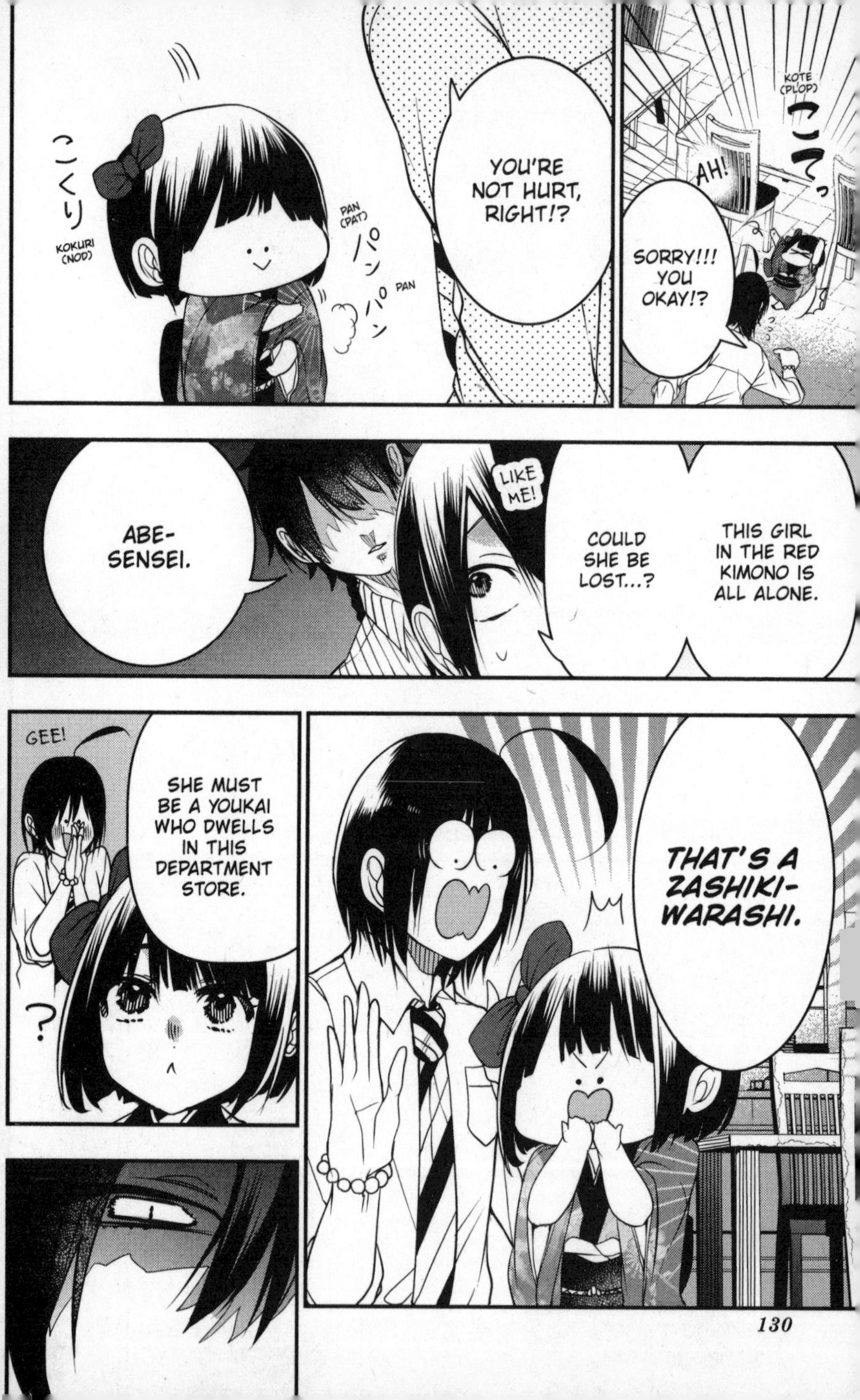
KOTE (PLOP)
こてっ
AH!
SORRY!!! YOU OKAY!?
YOU'RE NOT HURT, RIGHT!?
PAN (PAT) パン
PAN パン
こくり
KOKURI (NOD)
THIS GIRL IN THE RED KIMONO IS ALL ALONE.
COULD SHE BE LOST...?
LIKE ME!
ABE-SENSEI.
THAT'S A ZASHIKI-WARASHI.
SHE MUST BE A YOUKAI WHO DWELLS IN THIS DEPARTMENT STORE.
GEE!
?

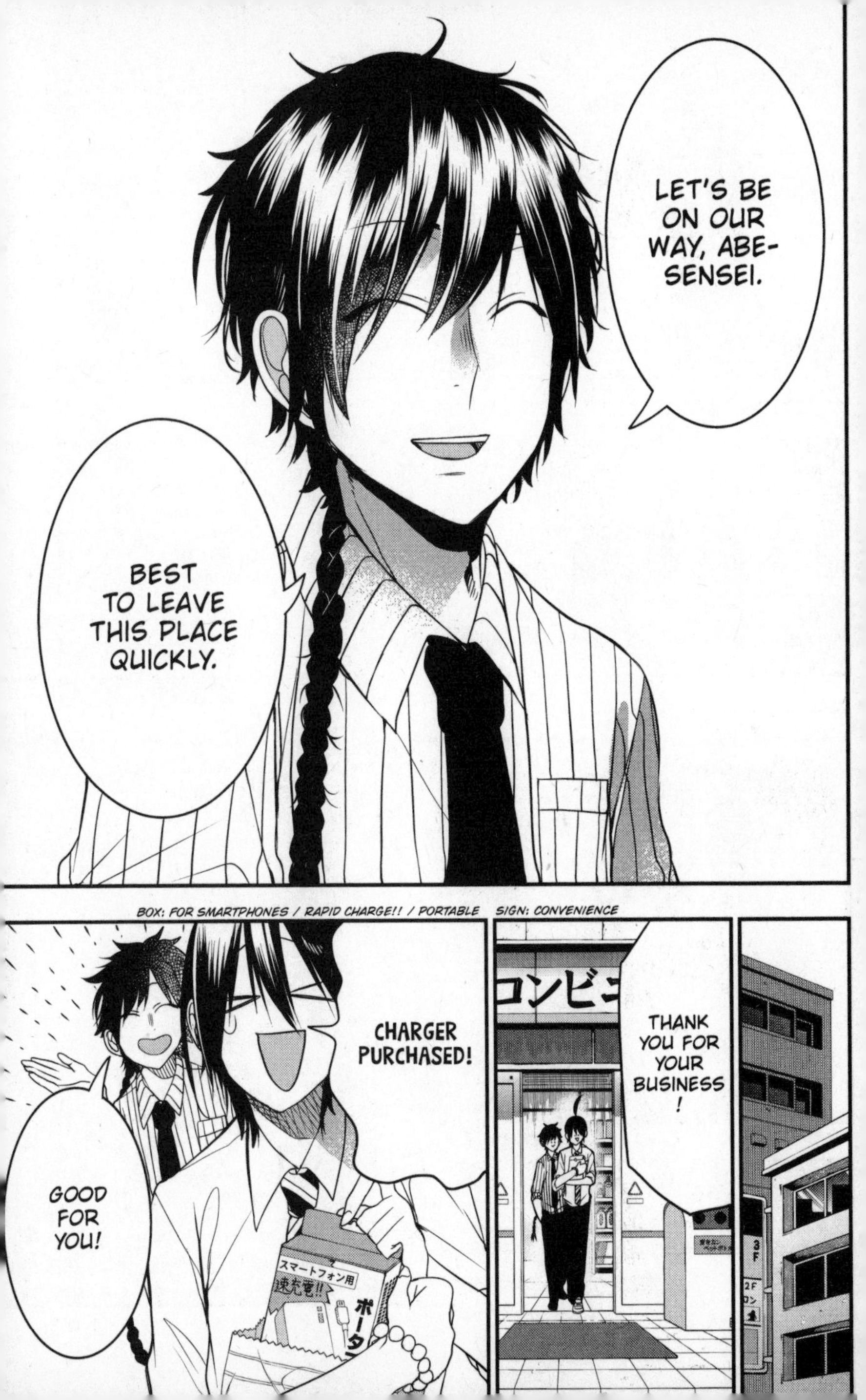
LET'S BE ON OUR WAY, ABE-SENSEI.
BEST TO LEAVE THIS PLACE QUICKLY.
BOX: FOR SMARTPHONES / RAPID CHARGE!! / PORTABLE SIGN: CONVENIENCE
コンビ
THANK YOU FOR YOUR BUSINESS!
CHARGER PURCHASED!
GOOD FOR YOU!
スマートフォン用
速充電!!
ポータ

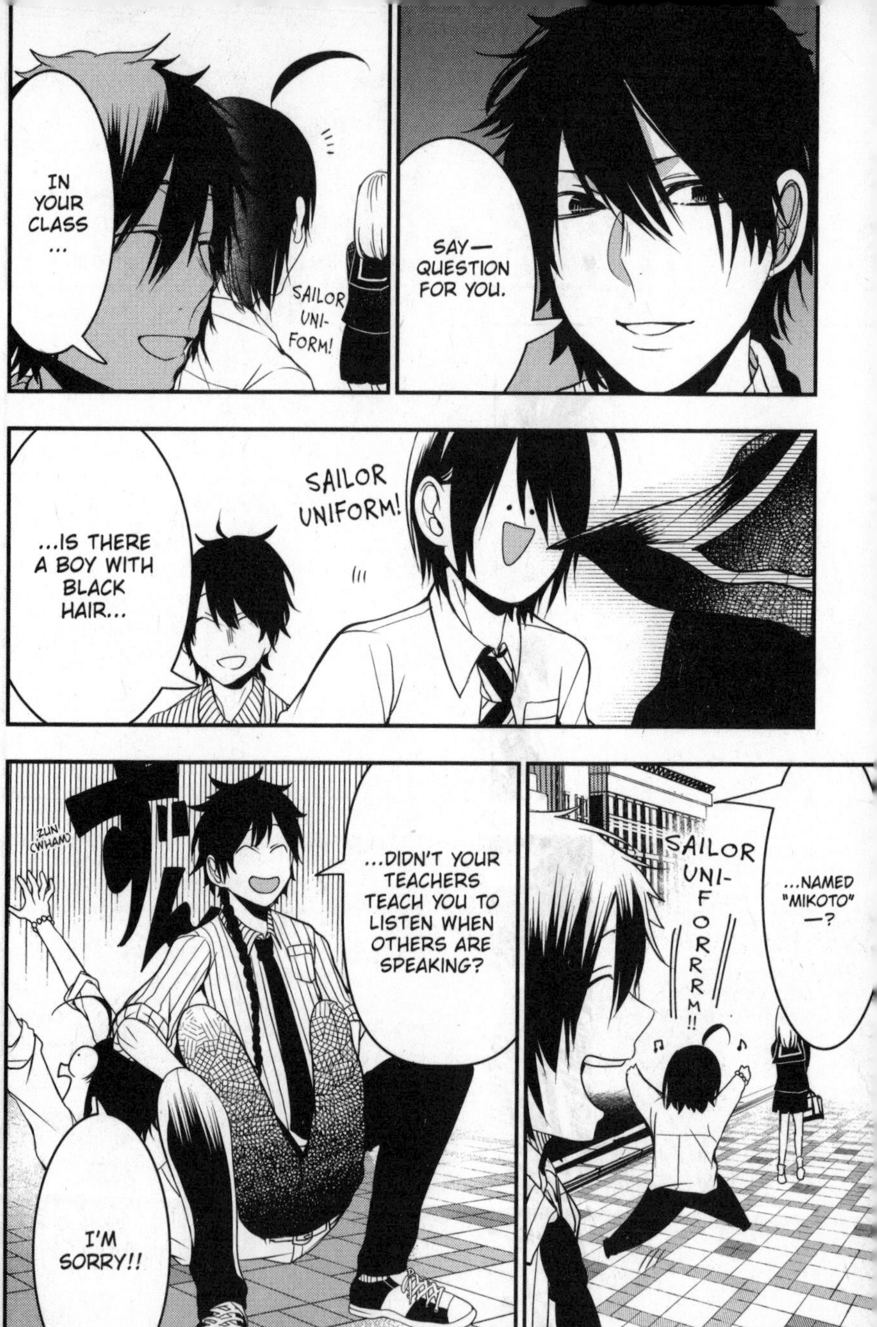
SAY—
QUESTION
FOR YOU.
IN
YOUR
CLASS
...
SAILOR
UNI-
FORM!
SAILOR
UNIFORM!
...IS THERE
A BOY WITH
BLACK
HAIR...
...NAMED
"MIKOTO"
—?
SAILOR
UNI-
FORRRM!!
...DIDN'T YOUR
TEACHERS
TEACH YOU TO
LISTEN WHEN
OTHERS ARE
SPEAKING?
ZUN
(WHAM)
I'M
SORRY!!

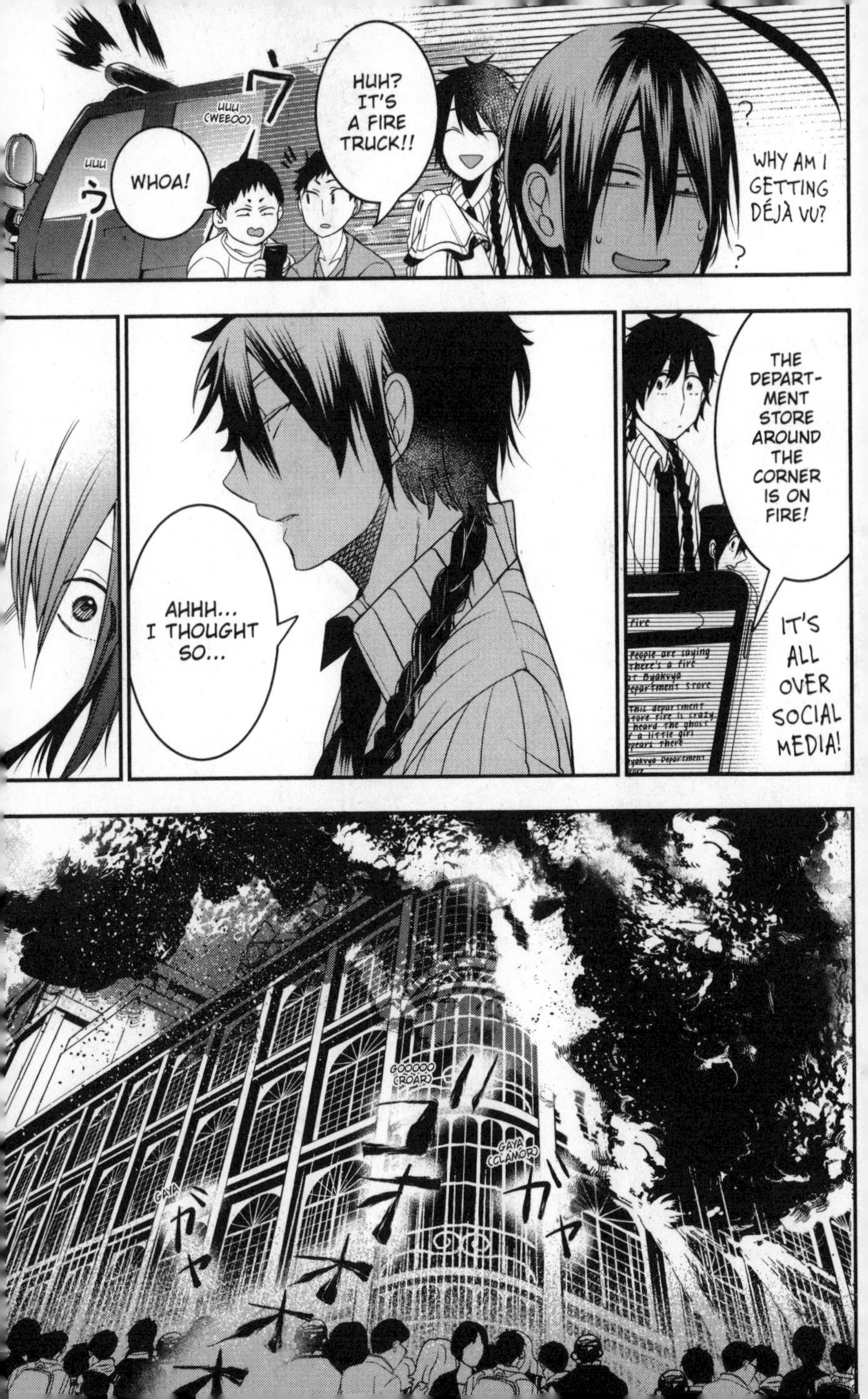
WHY AM I GETTING DÉJÀ VU?
HUH? IT'S A FIRE TRUCK!!
UUU (WEEOO)
WHOA!
UUU
THE DEPARTMENT STORE AROUND THE CORNER IS ON FIRE!
IT'S ALL OVER SOCIAL MEDIA!
AHHH... I THOUGHT SO...
GOOOOO (ROAR)
GAYA (CLAMOR)
GAYA

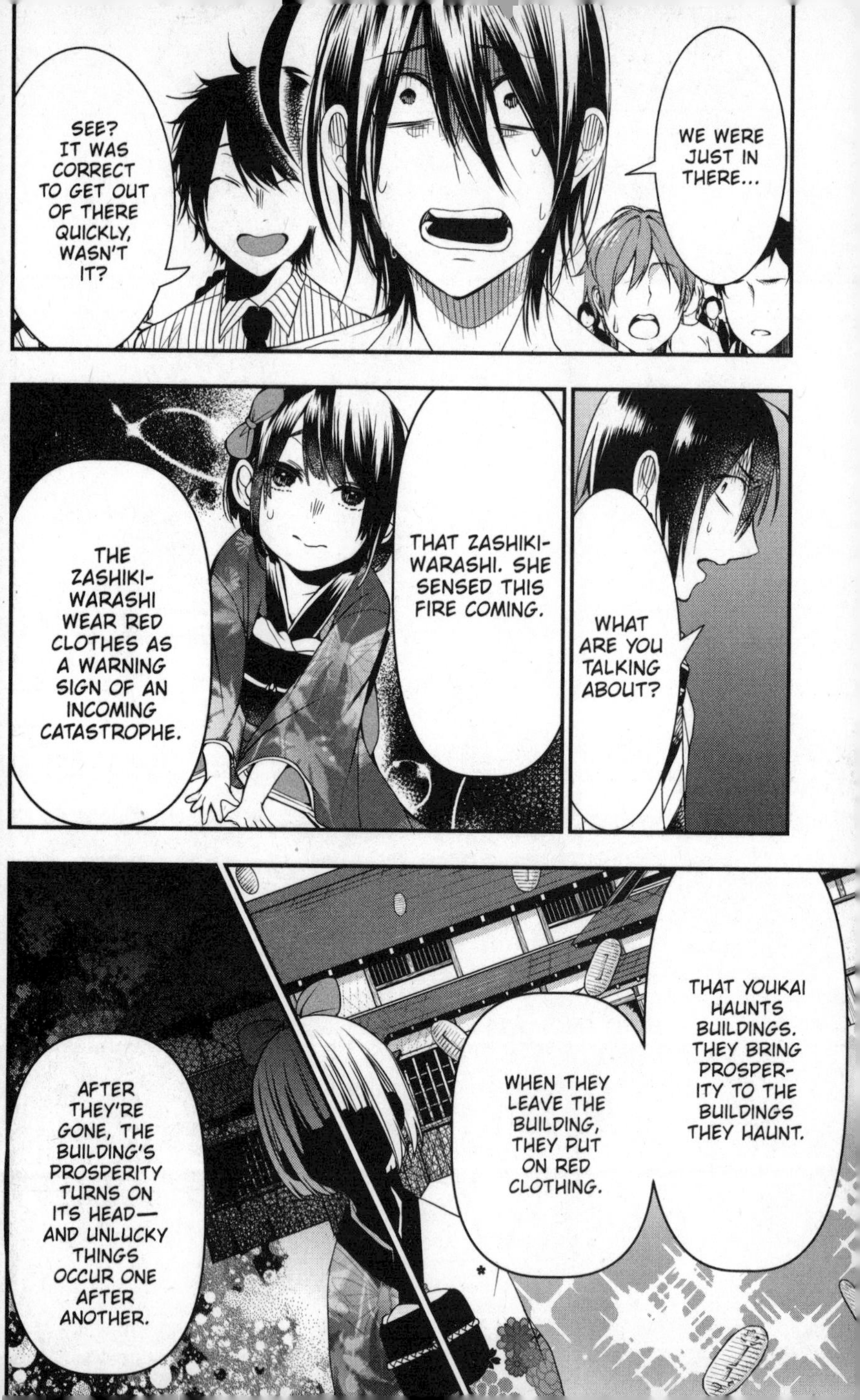
WE WERE JUST IN THERE...
SEE? IT WAS CORRECT TO GET OUT OF THERE QUICKLY, WASN'T IT?
WHAT ARE YOU TALKING ABOUT?
THAT ZASHIKI-WARASHI. SHE SENSED THIS FIRE COMING.
THE ZASHIKI-WARASHI WEAR RED CLOTHES AS A WARNING SIGN OF AN INCOMING CATASTROPHE.
THAT YOUKAI HAUNTS BUILDINGS. THEY BRING PROSPERITY TO THE BUILDINGS THEY HAUNT.
WHEN THEY LEAVE THE BUILDING, THEY PUT ON RED CLOTHING.
AFTER THEY'RE GONE, THE BUILDING'S PROSPERITY TURNS ON ITS HEAD—AND UNLUCKY THINGS OCCUR ONE AFTER ANOTHER.

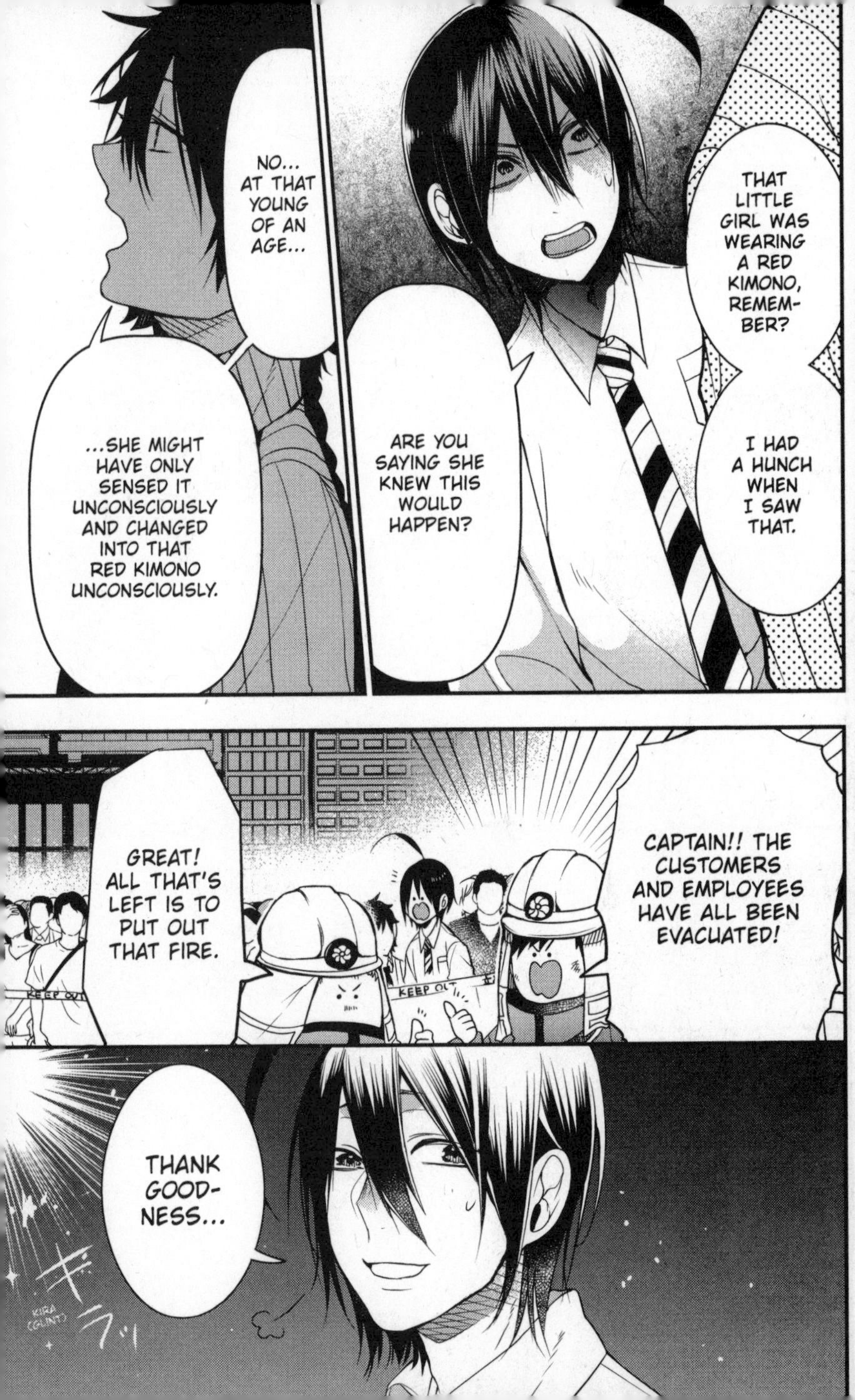
THAT LITTLE GIRL WAS WEARING A RED KIMONO, REMEMBER?
I HAD A HUNCH WHEN I SAW THAT.
ARE YOU SAYING SHE KNEW THIS WOULD HAPPEN?
NO... AT THAT YOUNG OF AN AGE...
...SHE MIGHT HAVE ONLY SENSED IT UNCONSCIOUSLY AND CHANGED INTO THAT RED KIMONO UNCONSCIOUSLY.
CAPTAIN!! THE CUSTOMERS AND EMPLOYEES HAVE ALL BEEN EVACUATED!
KEEP OUT
GREAT! ALL THAT'S LEFT IS TO PUT OUT THAT FIRE.
KEEP OUT
THANK GOOD-NESS...
KIRA (GLINT)

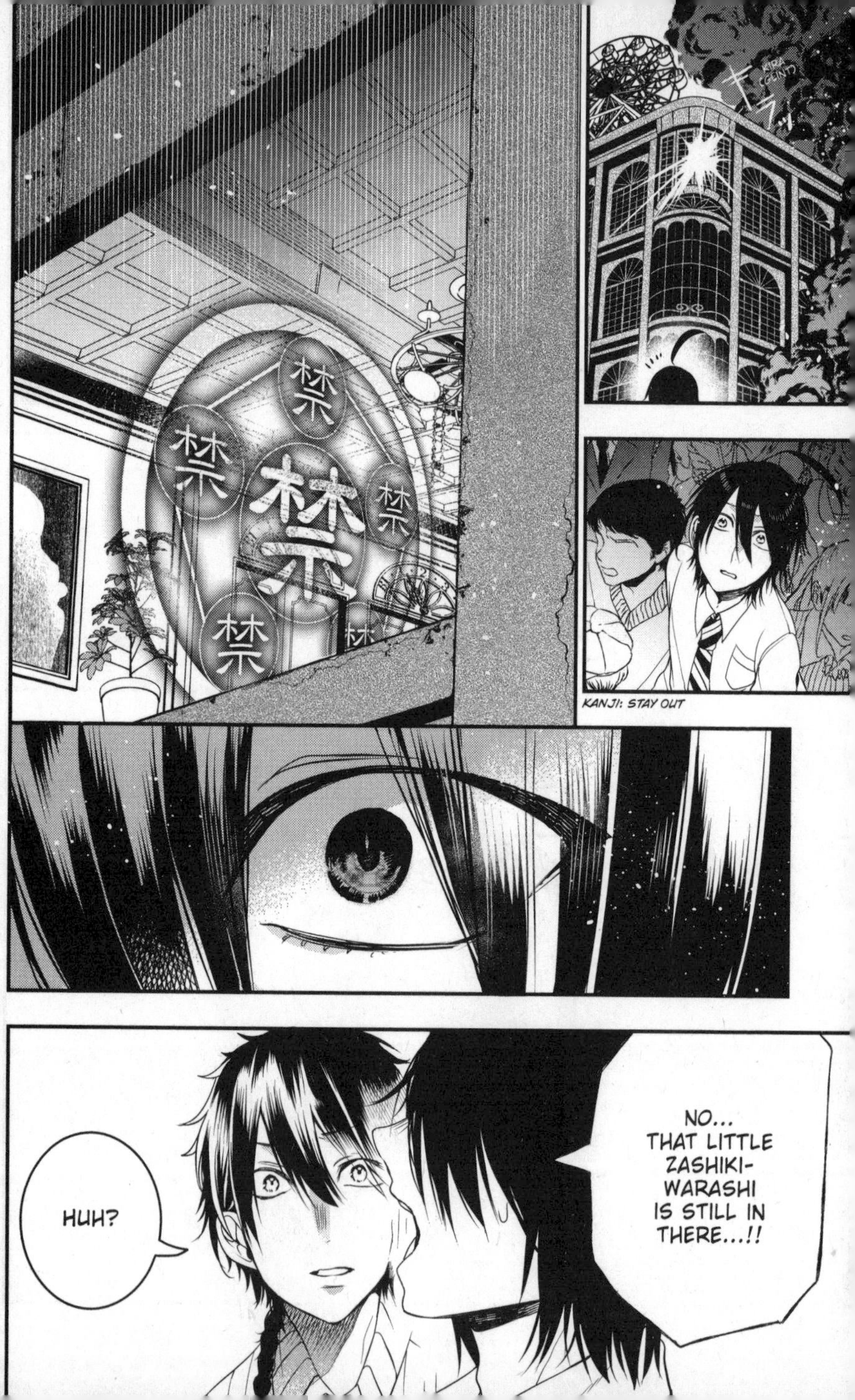
KIRA (GLINT)
KANJI: STAY OUT
NO... THAT LITTLE ZASHIKI-WARASHI IS STILL IN THERE...!!
HUH?

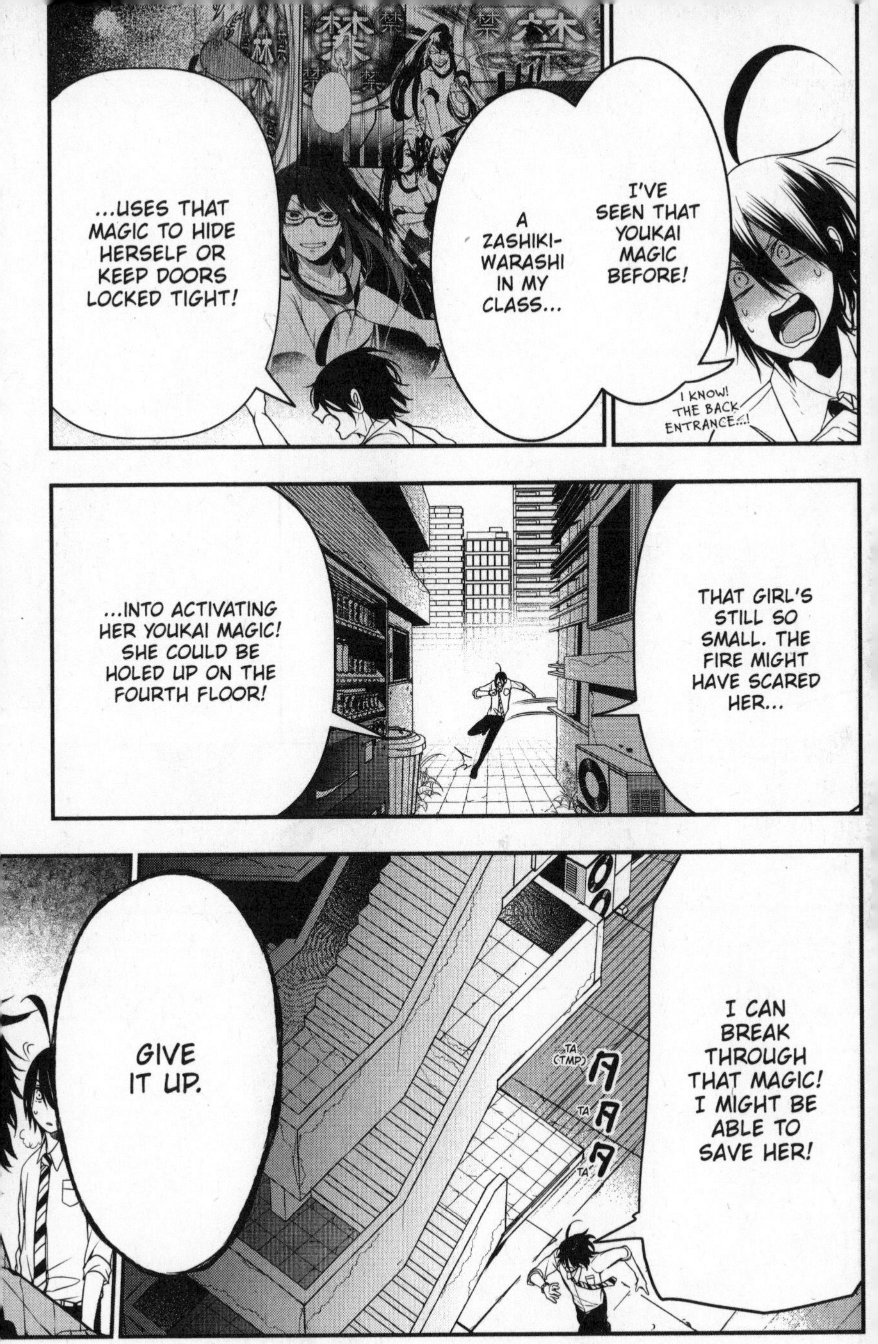
I KNOW! THE BACK ENTRANCE...!
I'VE SEEN THAT YOUKAI MAGIC BEFORE!
A ZASHIKI-WARASHI IN MY CLASS...
...USES THAT MAGIC TO HIDE HERSELF OR KEEP DOORS LOCKED TIGHT!
THAT GIRL'S STILL SO SMALL. THE FIRE MIGHT HAVE SCARED HER...
...INTO ACTIVATING HER YOUKAI MAGIC! SHE COULD BE HOLED UP ON THE FOURTH FLOOR!
I CAN BREAK THROUGH THAT MAGIC! I MIGHT BE ABLE TO SAVE HER!
TA (TMP)
TA
TA
GIVE IT UP.

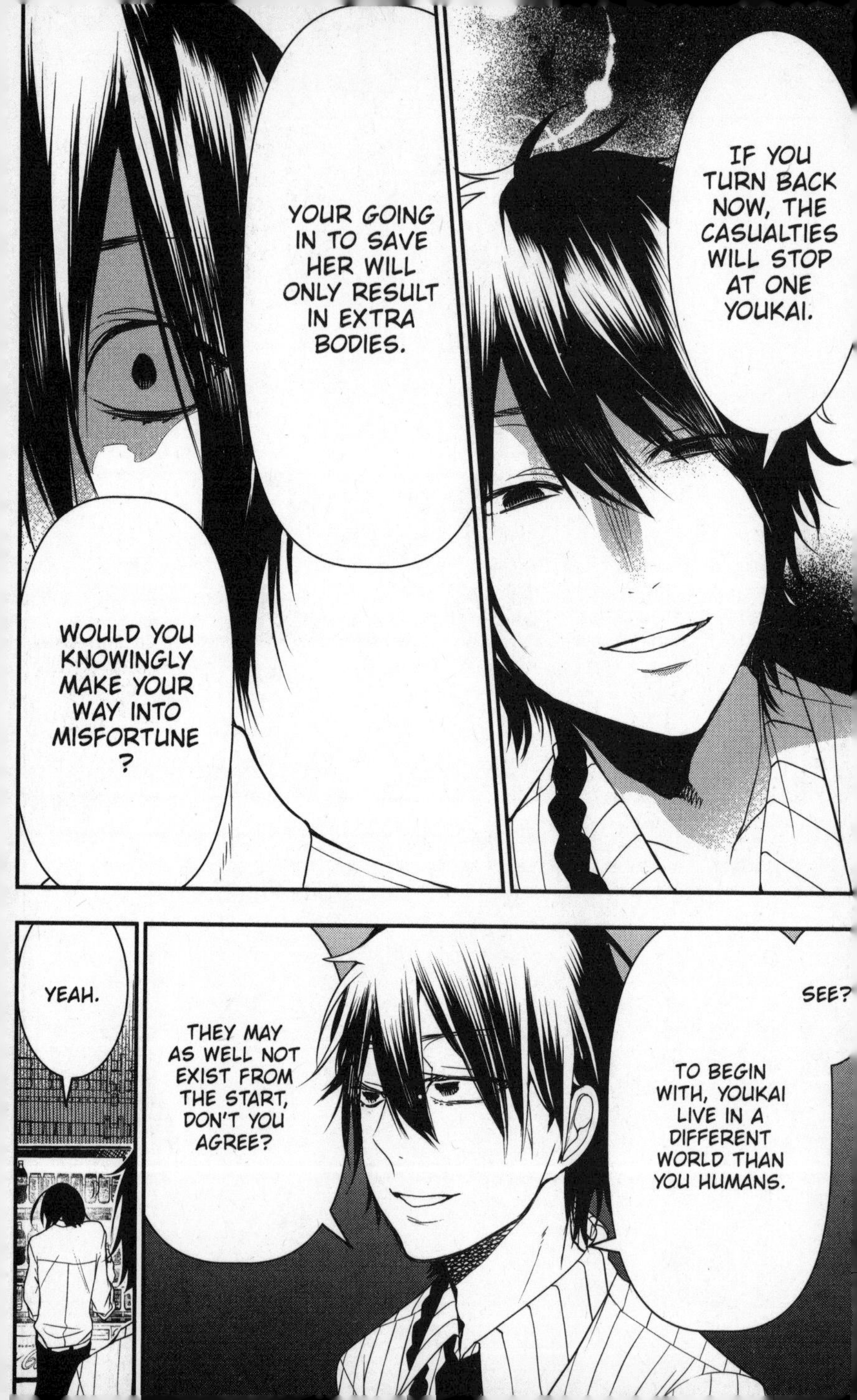
IF YOU TURN BACK NOW, THE CASUALTIES WILL STOP AT ONE YOUKAI.
YOUR GOING IN TO SAVE HER WILL ONLY RESULT IN EXTRA BODIES.
WOULD YOU KNOWINGLY MAKE YOUR WAY INTO MISFORTUNE?
SEE?
TO BEGIN WITH, YOUKAI LIVE IN A DIFFERENT WORLD THAN YOU HUMANS.
THEY MAY AS WELL NOT EXIST FROM THE START, DON'T YOU AGREE?
YEAH.

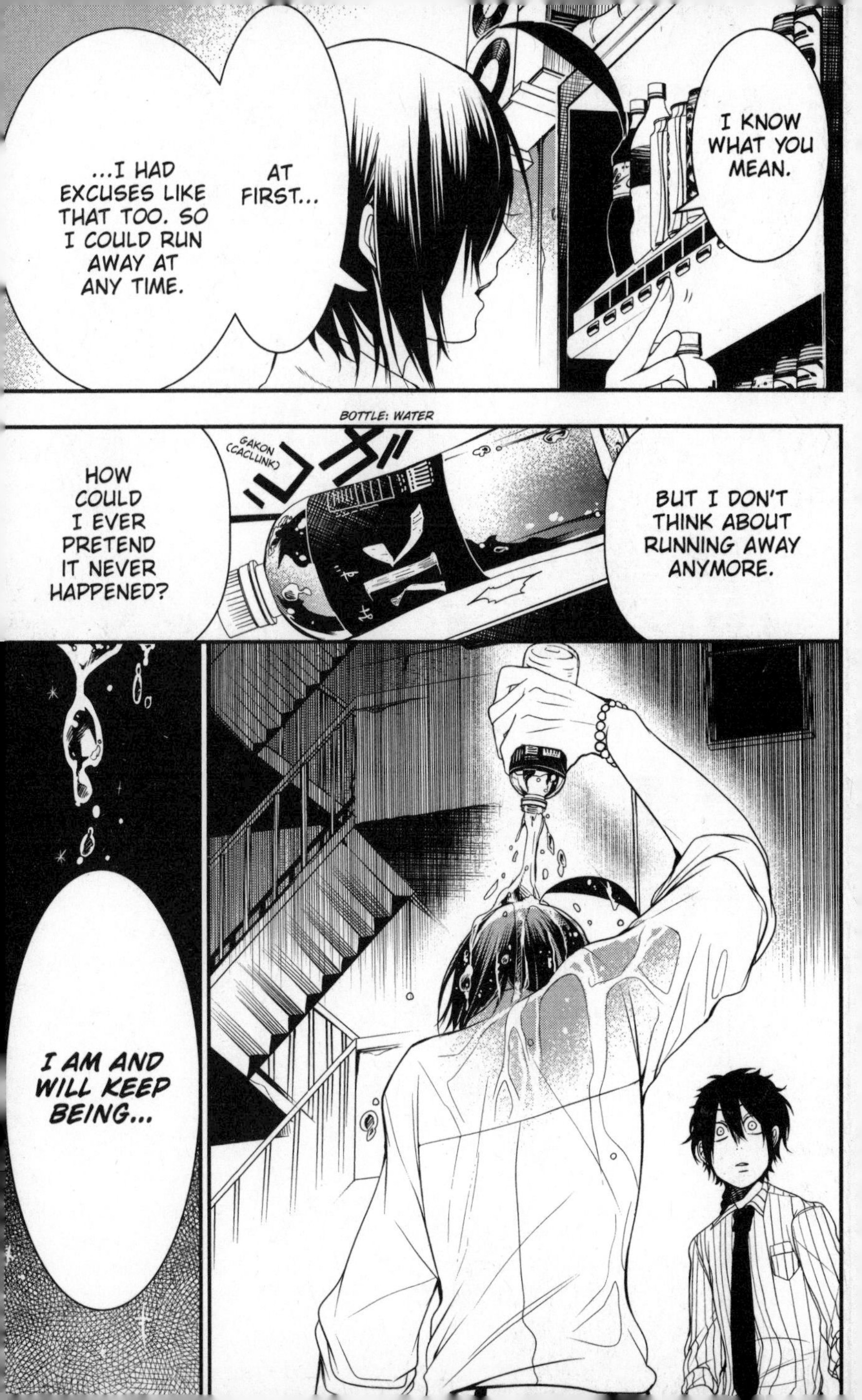
I KNOW WHAT YOU MEAN.
AT FIRST...
...I HAD EXCUSES LIKE THAT TOO. SO I COULD RUN AWAY AT ANY TIME.
BOTTLE: WATER
BUT I DON'T THINK ABOUT RUNNING AWAY ANYMORE.
GAKON (CACLUNK)
HOW COULD I EVER PRETEND IT NEVER HAPPENED?
I AM AND WILL KEEP BEING...

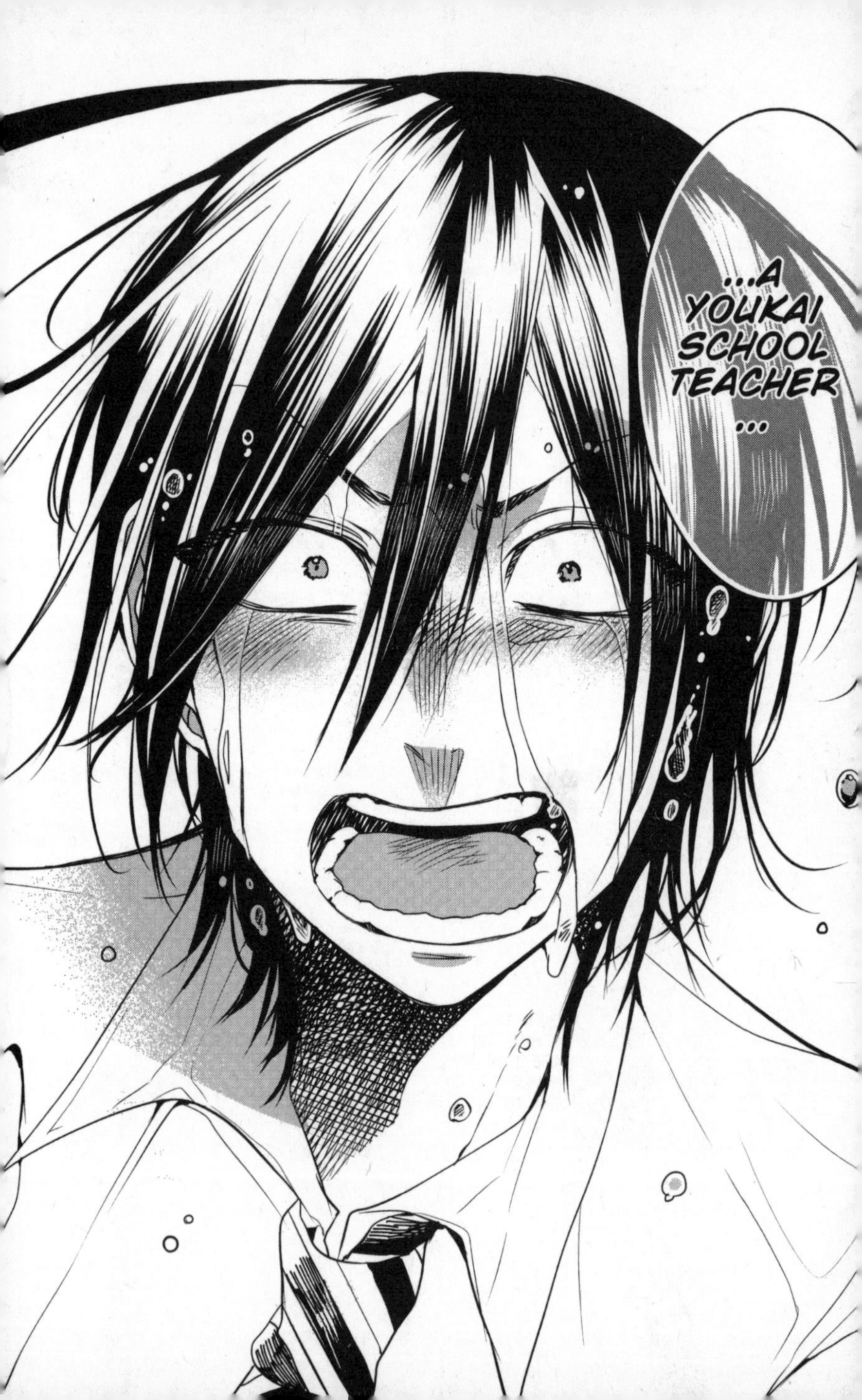
...A YOUKAI SCHOOL TEACHER ...

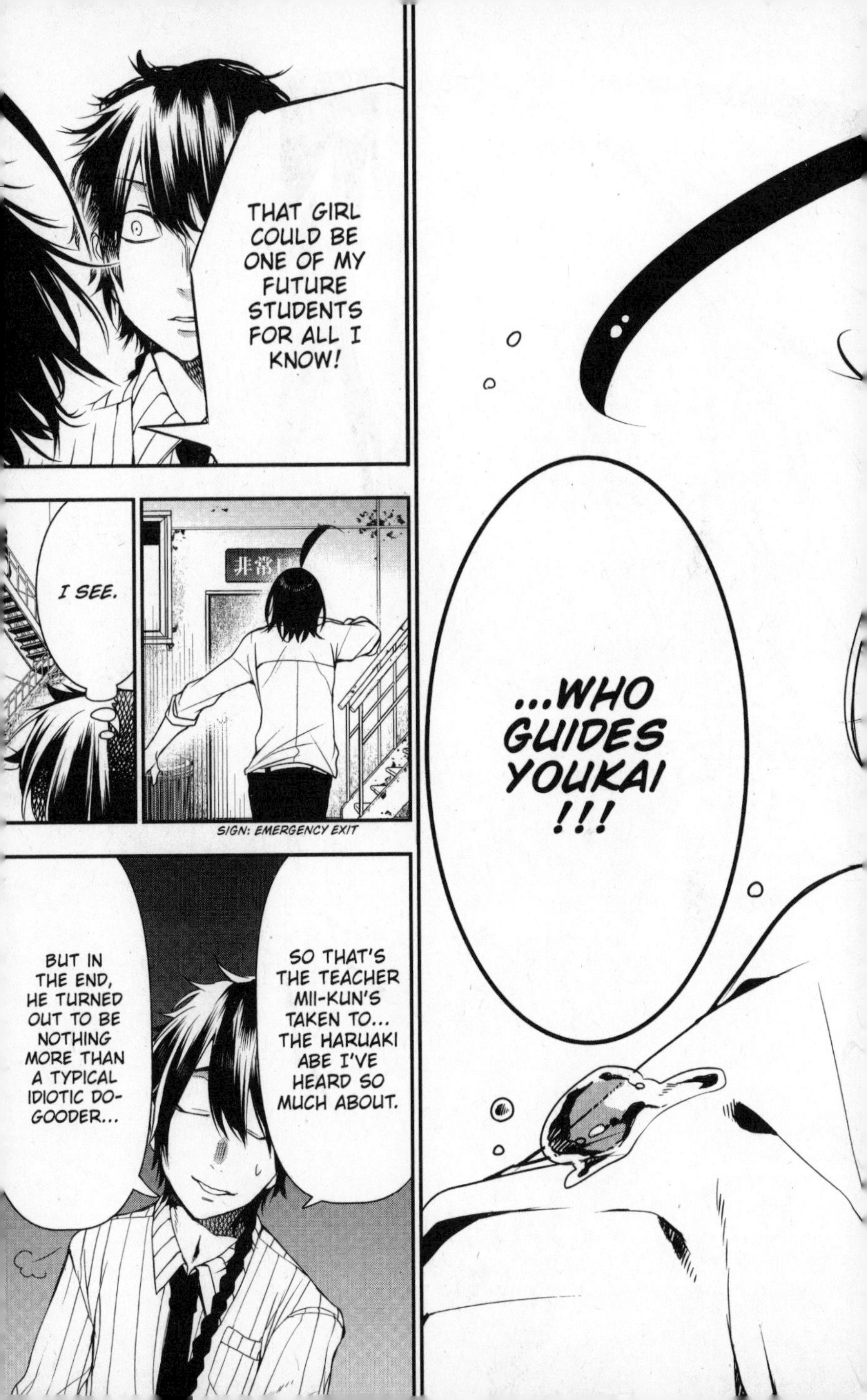
...WHO GUIDES YOUKAI !!!
THAT GIRL COULD BE ONE OF MY FUTURE STUDENTS FOR ALL I KNOW!
非常口
SIGN: EMERGENCY EXIT
I SEE.
SO THAT'S THE TEACHER MII-KUN'S TAKEN TO... THE HARUAKI ABE I'VE HEARD SO MUCH ABOUT.
BUT IN THE END, HE TURNED OUT TO BE NOTHING MORE THAN A TYPICAL IDIOTIC DO-GOODER...

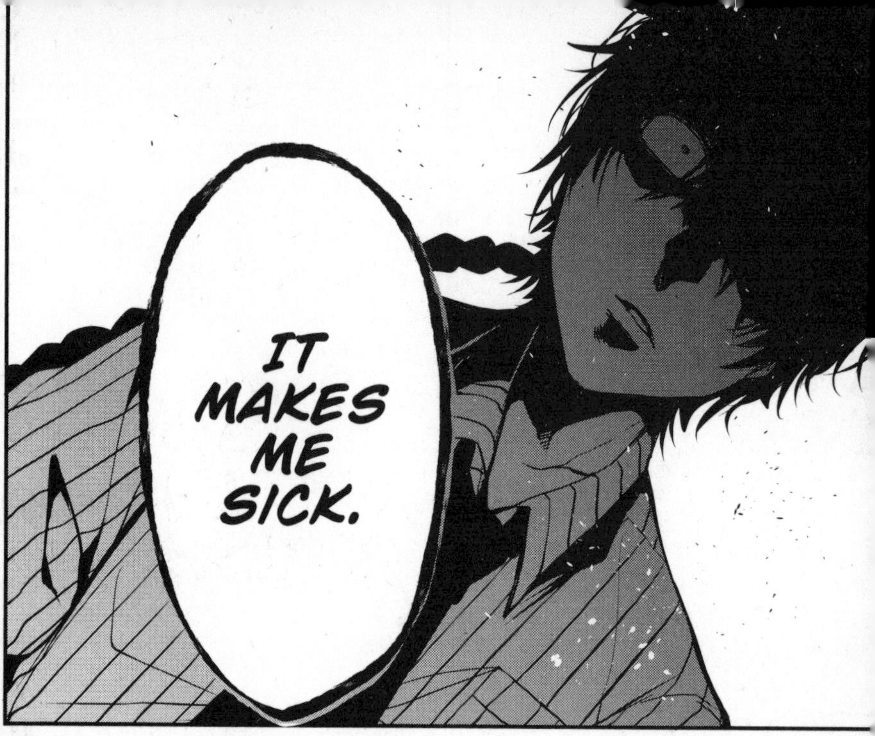
IT MAKES ME SICK.

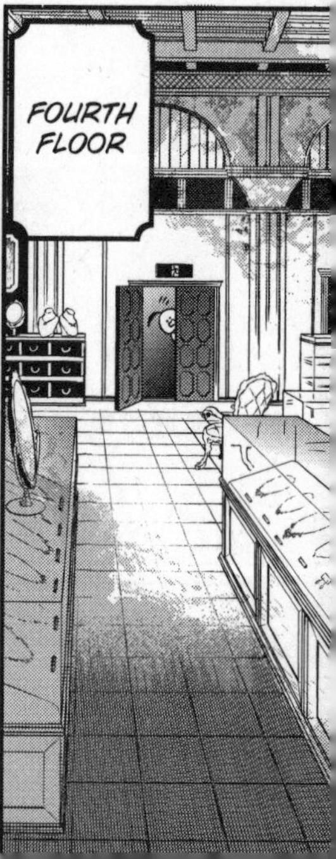
FOURTH FLOOR

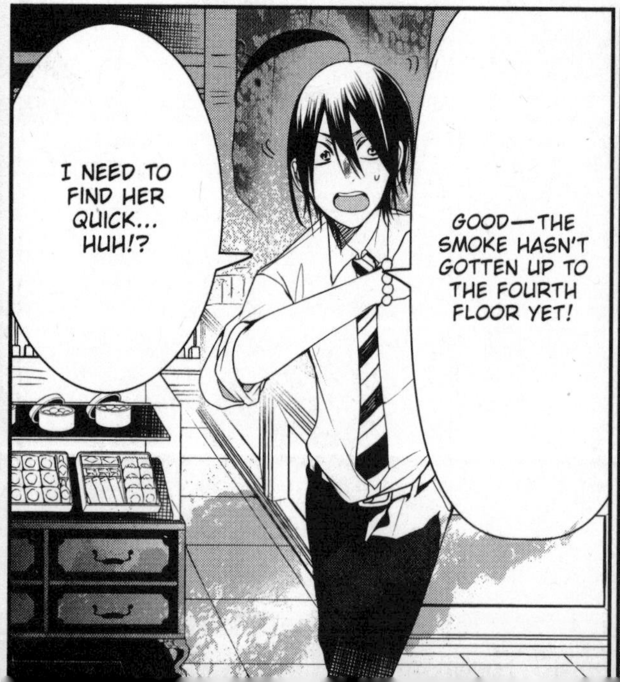
GOOD—THE SMOKE HASN'T GOTTEN UP TO THE FOURTH FLOOR YET!
I NEED TO FIND HER QUICK... HUH!?

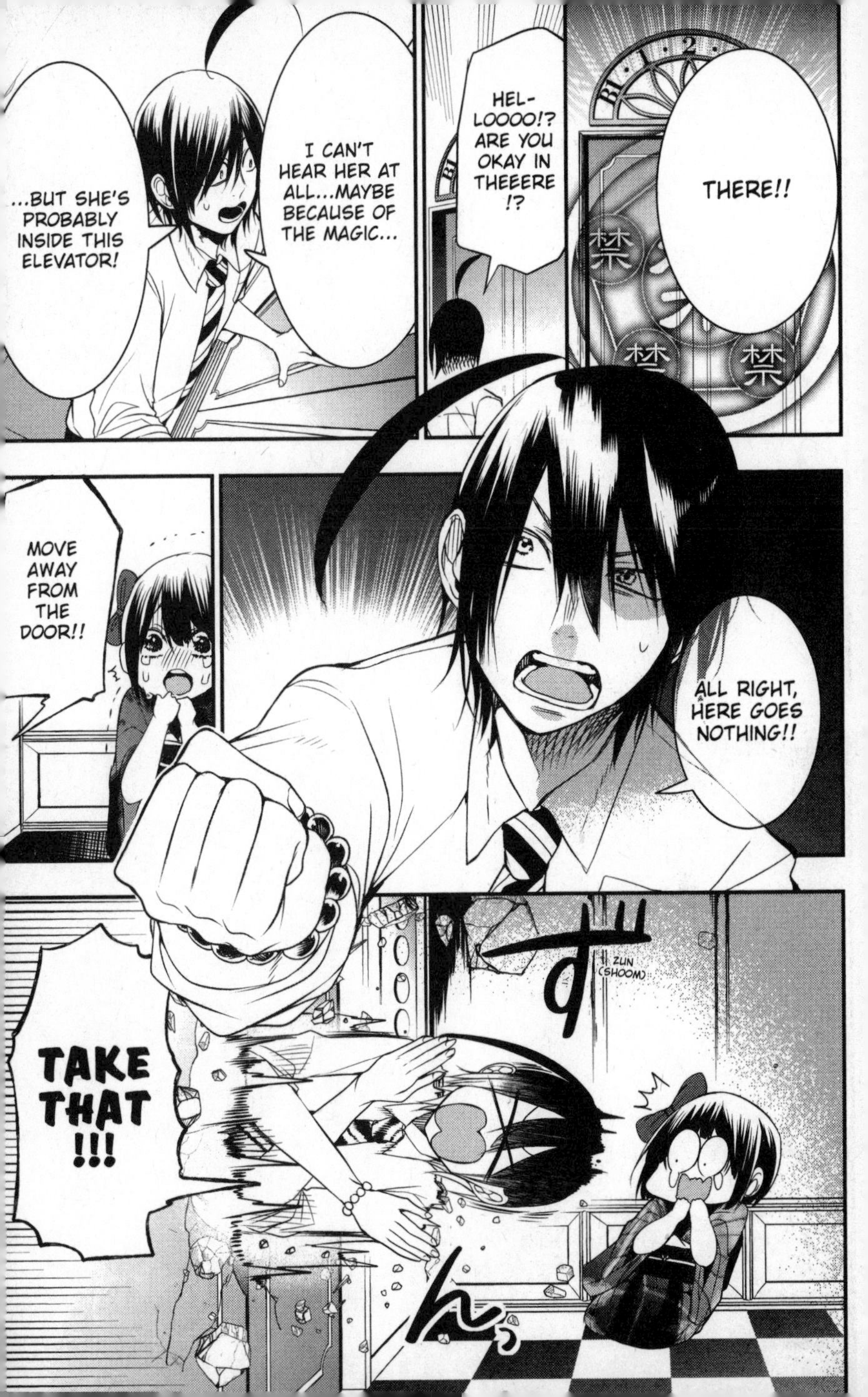
THERE!!
HEL-LOOOO!? ARE YOU OKAY IN THEEERE!?
I CAN'T HEAR HER AT ALL...MAYBE BECAUSE OF THE MAGIC...
...BUT SHE'S PROBABLY INSIDE THIS ELEVATOR!
ALL RIGHT, HERE GOES NOTHING!!
MOVE AWAY FROM THE DOOR!!
ずん
ZUN (SHOOM)
TAKE THAT!!!

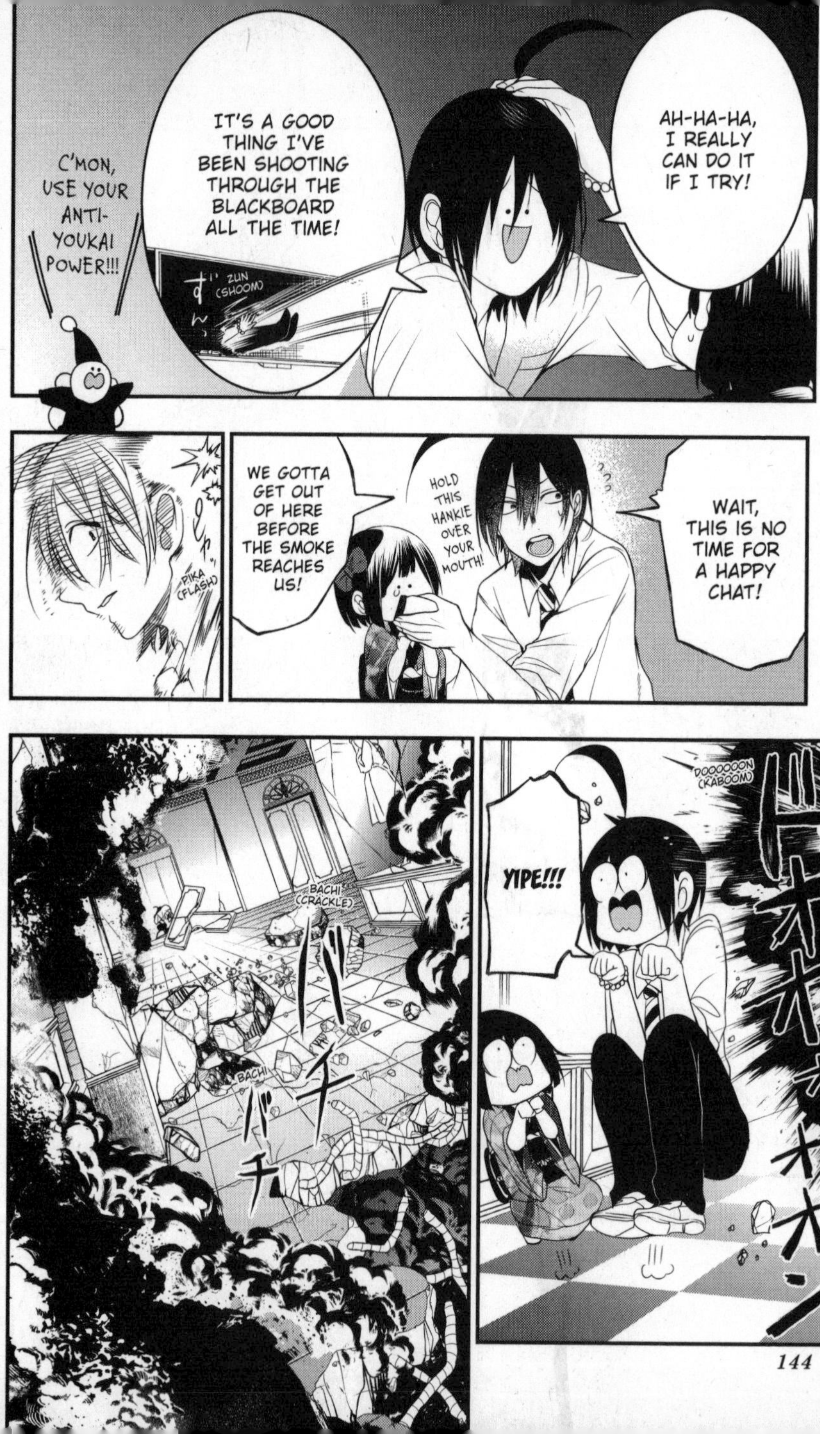
AH-HA-HA, I REALLY CAN DO IT IF I TRY!
IT'S A GOOD THING I'VE BEEN SHOOTING THROUGH THE BLACKBOARD ALL THE TIME!
ZUN (SHOOM)
C'MON, USE YOUR ANTI-YOUKAI POWER!!!
WAIT, THIS IS NO TIME FOR A HAPPY CHAT!
HOLD THIS HANKIE OVER YOUR MOUTH!
WE GOTTA GET OUT OF HERE BEFORE THE SMOKE REACHES US!
PIKA (FLASH)
DOOOOOON (KABOOM)
YIPE!!!
BACHI (CRACKLE)
BACHI

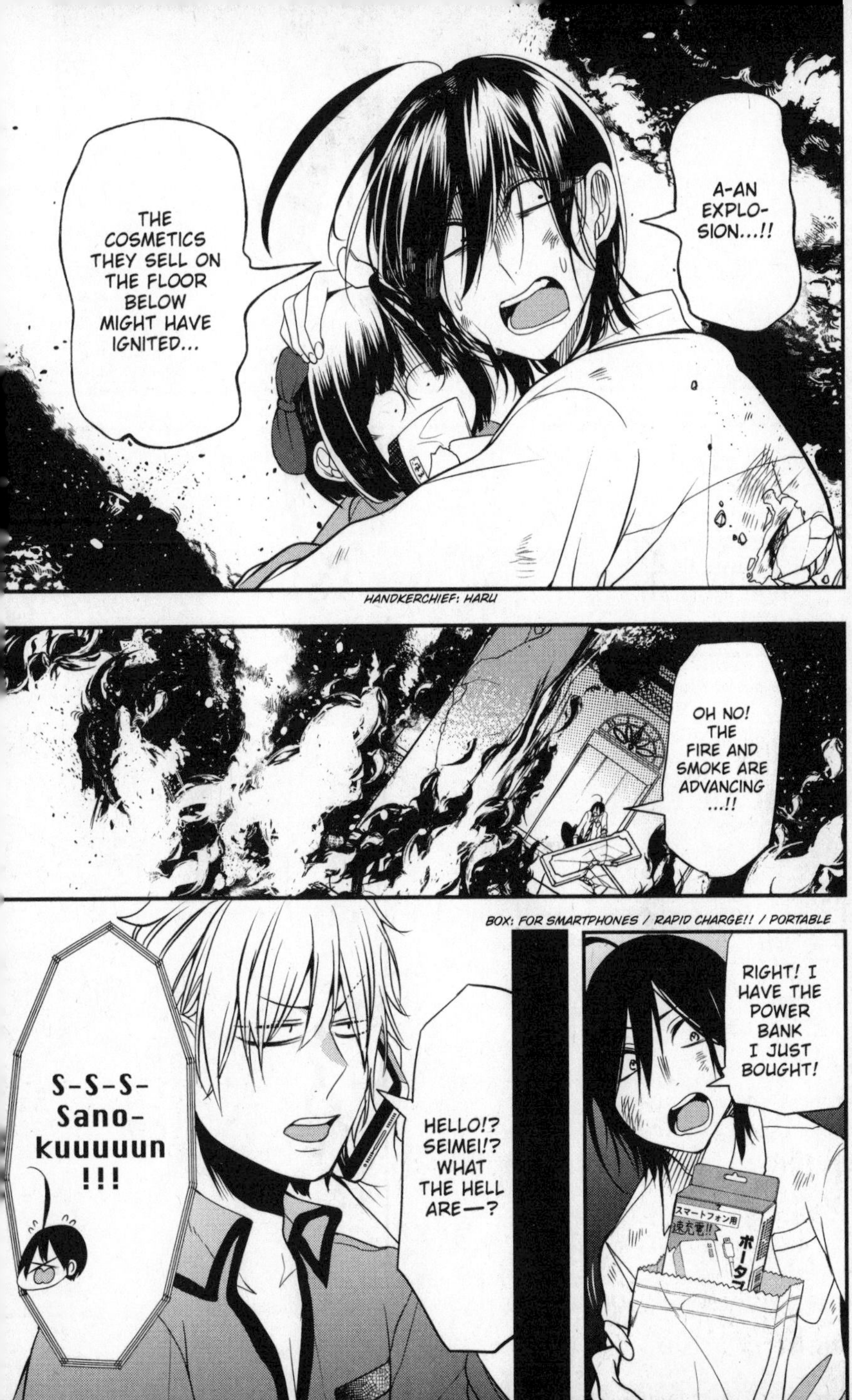
A-AN EXPLOSION...!!
THE COSMETICS THEY SELL ON THE FLOOR BELOW MIGHT HAVE IGNITED...
HANDKERCHIEF: HARU
OH NO! THE FIRE AND SMOKE ARE ADVANCING...!!
BOX: FOR SMARTPHONES / RAPID CHARGE!! / PORTABLE
RIGHT! I HAVE THE POWER BANK I JUST BOUGHT!
スマートフォン用
速充電!!
HELLO!? SEIMEI!? WHAT THE HELL ARE—?
S-S-S-Sano-kuuuuun!!!

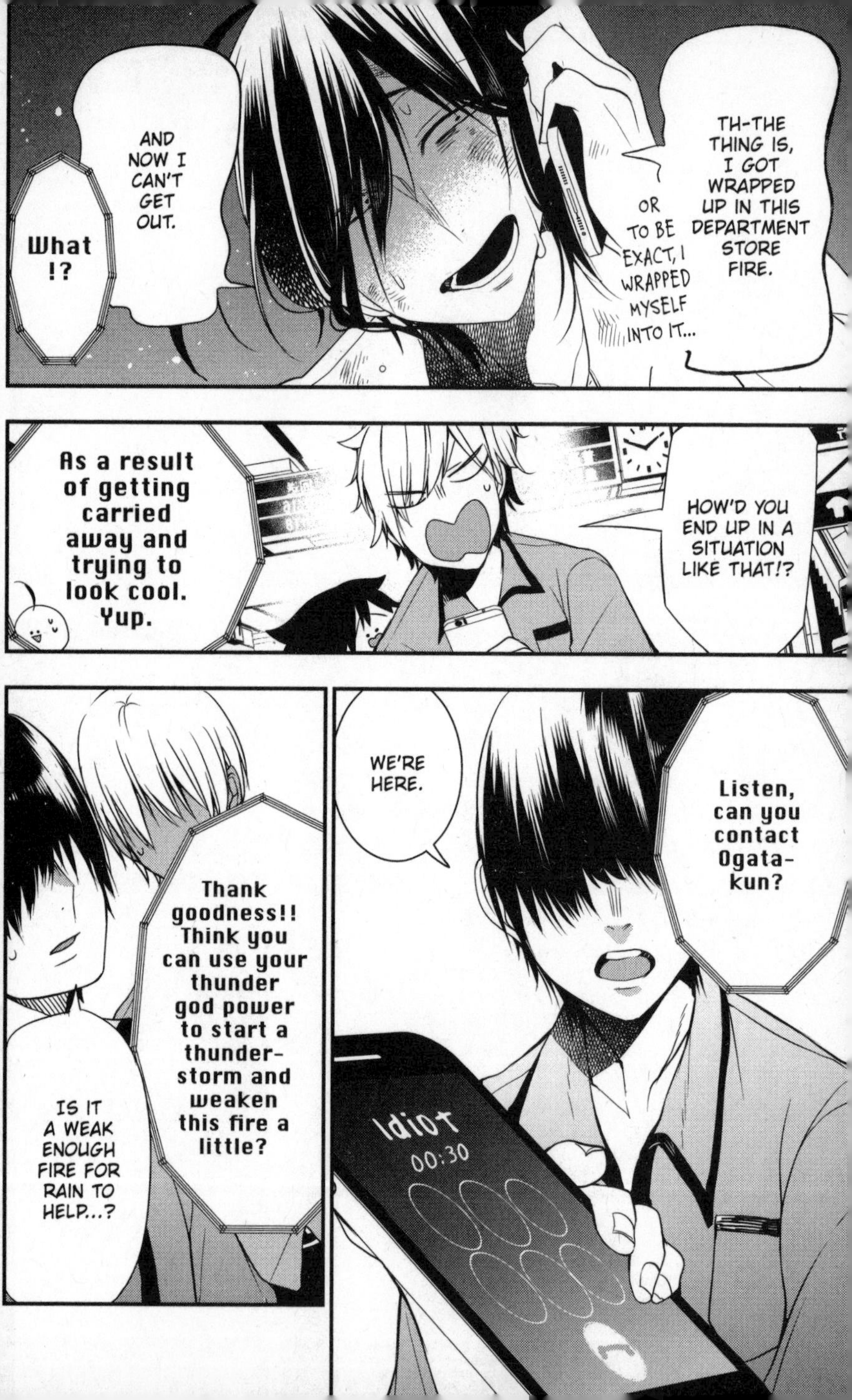
TH-THE THING IS, I GOT WRAPPED UP IN THIS DEPARTMENT STORE FIRE.
OR TO BE EXACT, I WRAPPED MYSELF INTO IT...
AND NOW I CAN'T GET OUT.
What!?
HOW'D YOU END UP IN A SITUATION LIKE THAT!?
As a result of getting carried away and trying to look cool. Yup.
Listen, can you contact Ogata-kun?
WE'RE HERE.
Idiot
00:30
Thank goodness!! Think you can use your thunder god power to start a thunder-storm and weaken this fire a little?
IS IT A WEAK ENOUGH FIRE FOR RAIN TO HELP...?

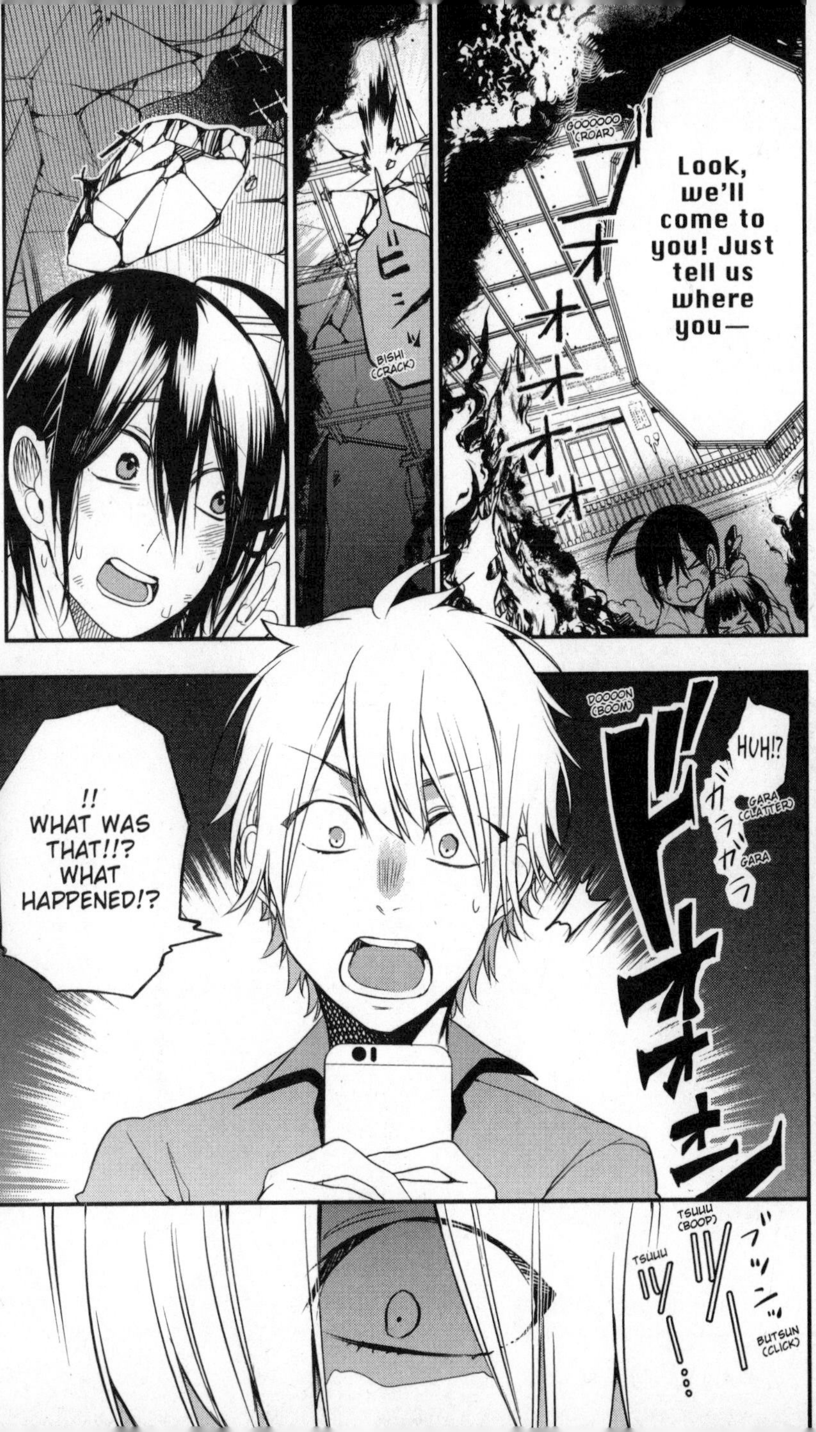
GOOOOOO (ROAR)
Look, we'll come to you! Just tell us where you—
BISHI (CRACK)
DOOOON (BOOM)
HUH!?
GARA (CLATTER)
GARA
!! WHAT WAS THAT!!? WHAT HAPPENED!?
BUTSUN (CLICK)
TSUUU (BOOP)
TSUUU

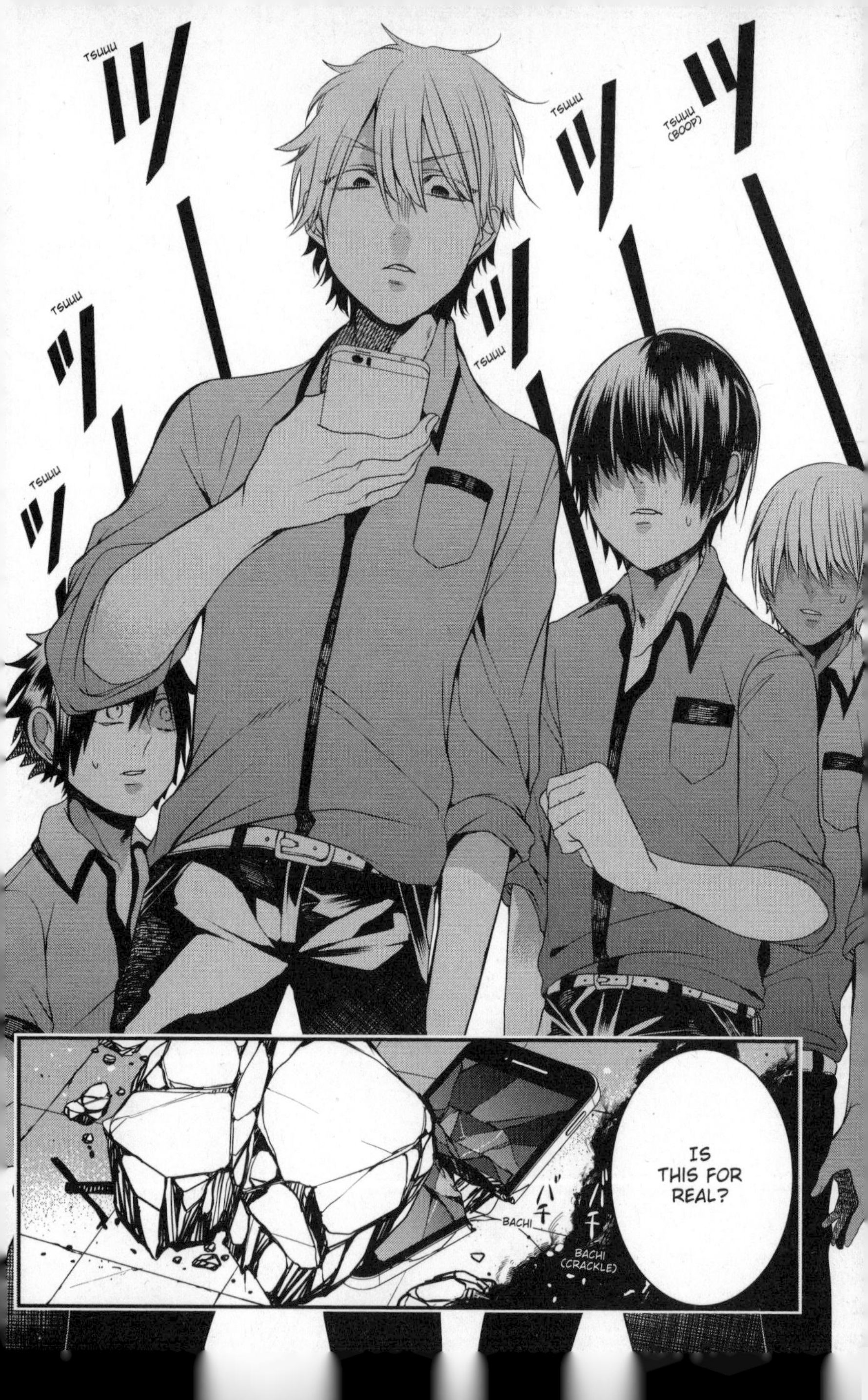
TSUUU (BOOP)
TSUUU
TSUUU
TSUUU
TSUUU
TSUUU
IS THIS FOR REAL?
BACHI (CRACKLE)
BACHI

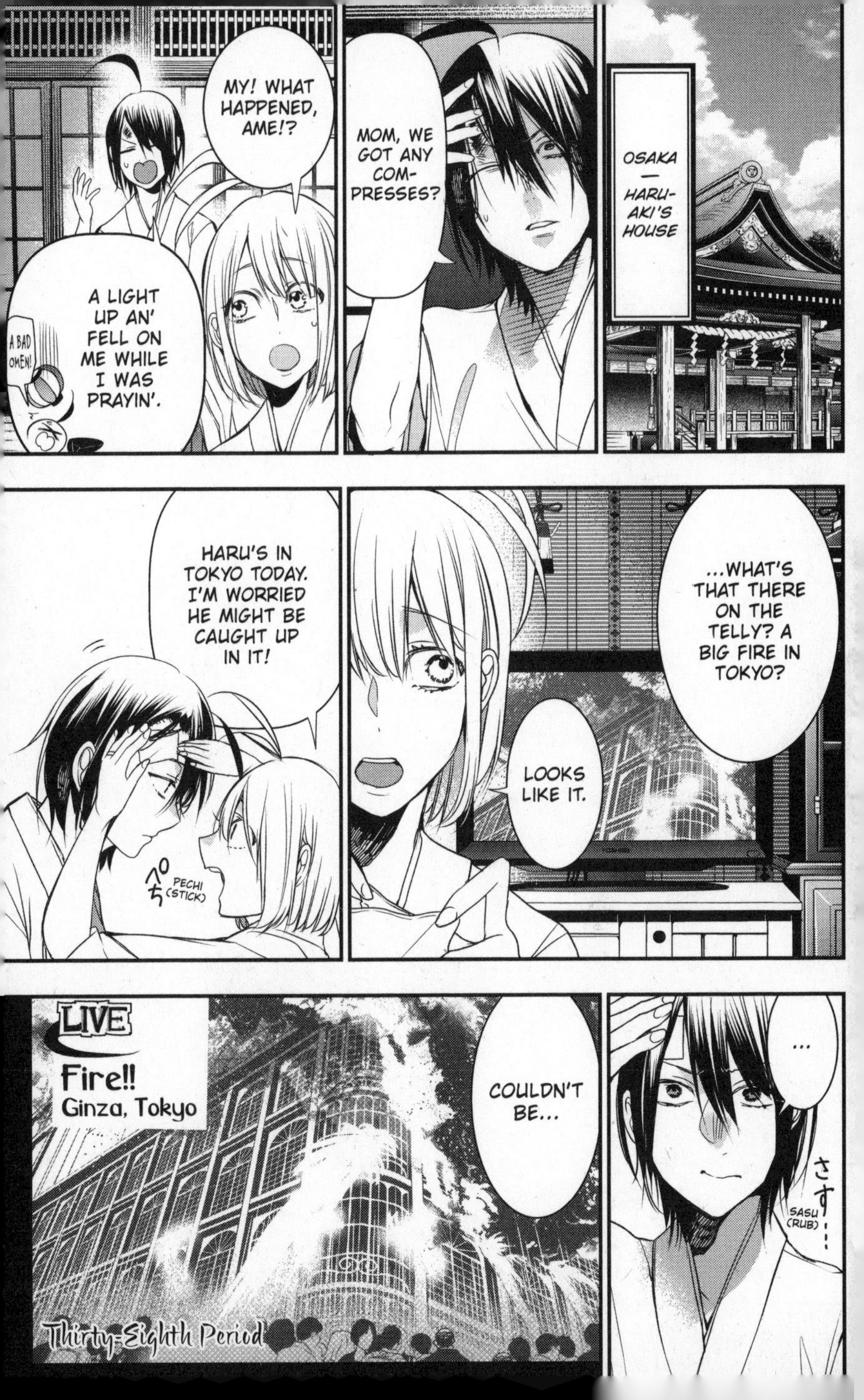
OSAKA — HARUAKI'S HOUSE
MOM, WE GOT ANY COMPRESSES?
MY! WHAT HAPPENED, AME!?
A LIGHT UP AN' FELL ON ME WHILE I WAS PRAYIN'.
A BAD OMEN!
...WHAT'S THAT THERE ON THE TELLY? A BIG FIRE IN TOKYO?
LOOKS LIKE IT.
HARU'S IN TOKYO TODAY. I'M WORRIED HE MIGHT BE CAUGHT UP IN IT!
ぺち
PECHI (STICK)
...
さす...
SASU (RUB)
COULDN'T BE...
LIVE
Fire!!
Ginza, Tokyo
Thirty-Eighth Period

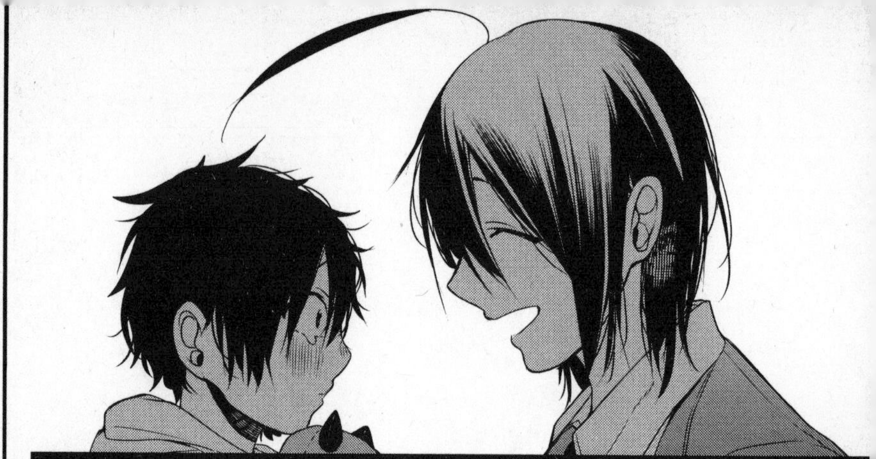

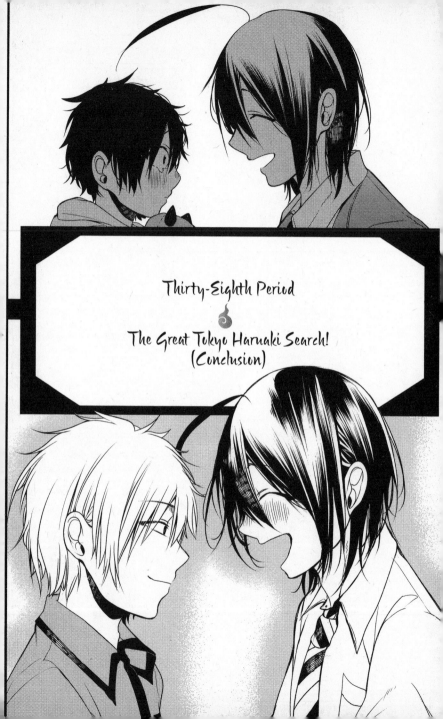

Thirty-Eighth Period

The Great Tokyo Haruaki Search! (Conclusion)

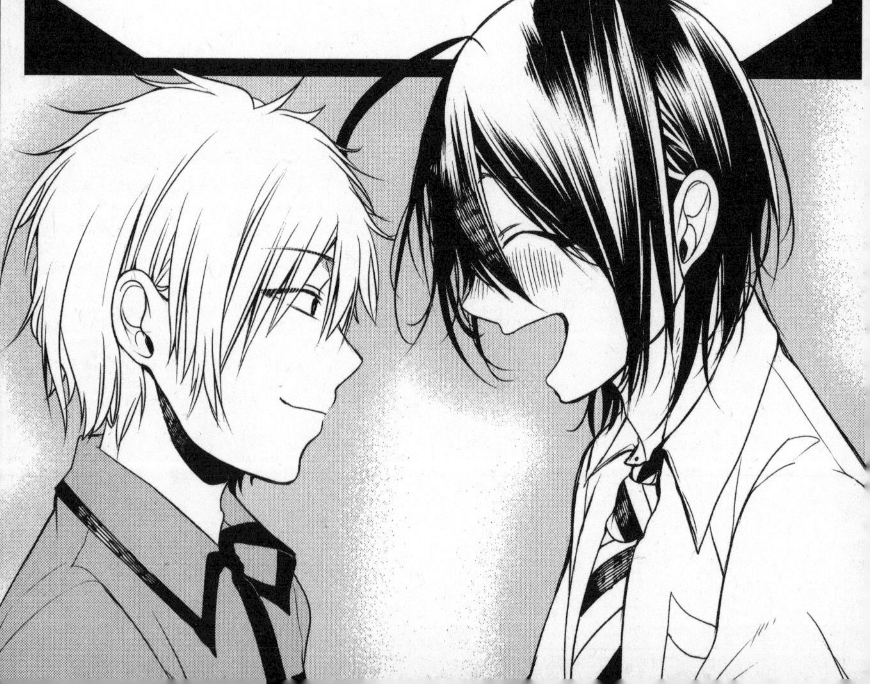

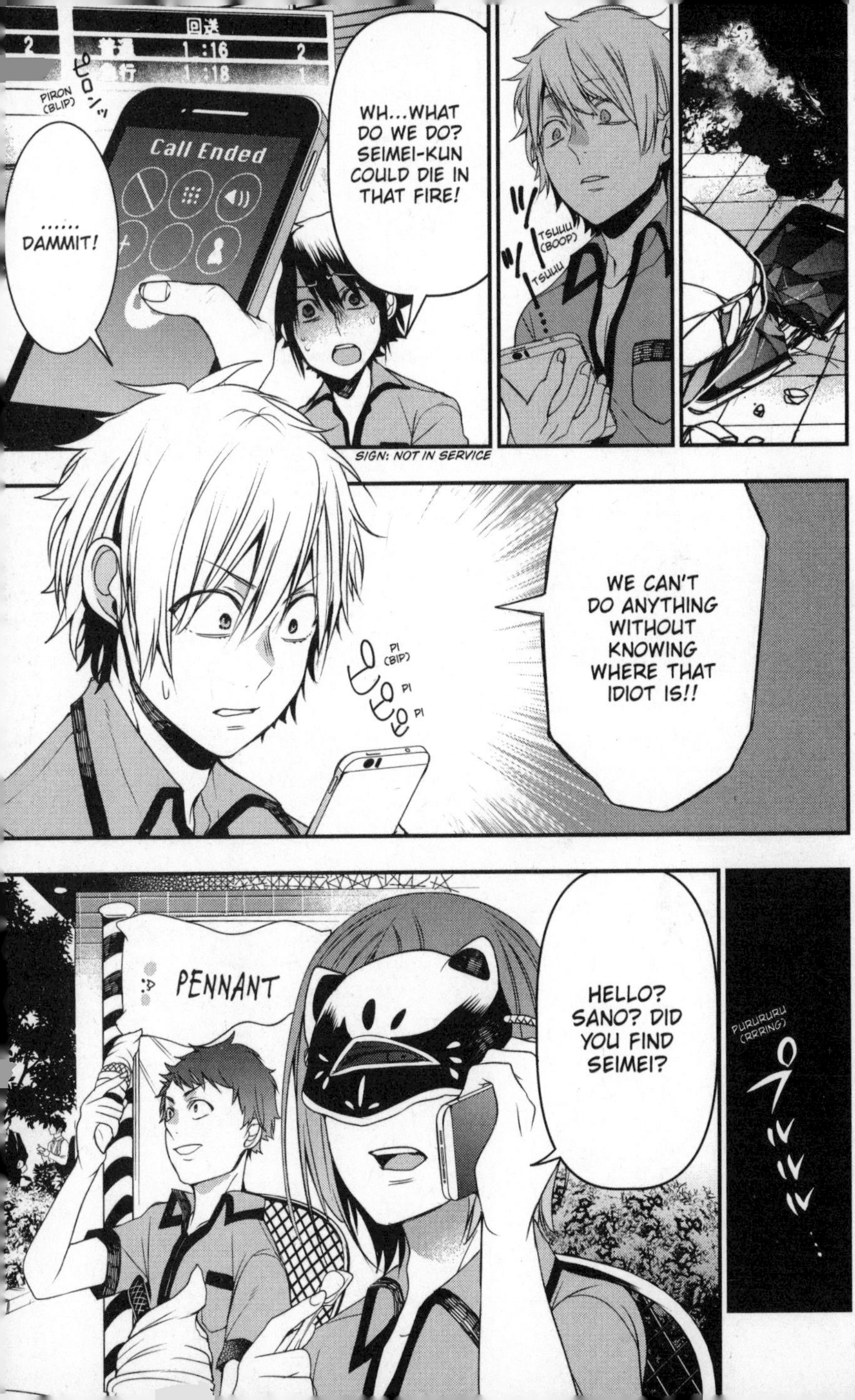
TSUUU (BOOP)
TSUUU
回送
WH...WHAT DO WE DO? SEIMEI-KUN COULD DIE IN THAT FIRE!
ピロンッ
PIRON (BLIP)
Call Ended
...... DAMMIT!
SIGN: NOT IN SERVICE
WE CAN'T DO ANYTHING WITHOUT KNOWING WHERE THAT IDIOT IS!!
PI (BIP)
PI
PI
PURURURU (RRRING)
HELLO? SANO? DID YOU FIND SEIMEI?
PENNANT

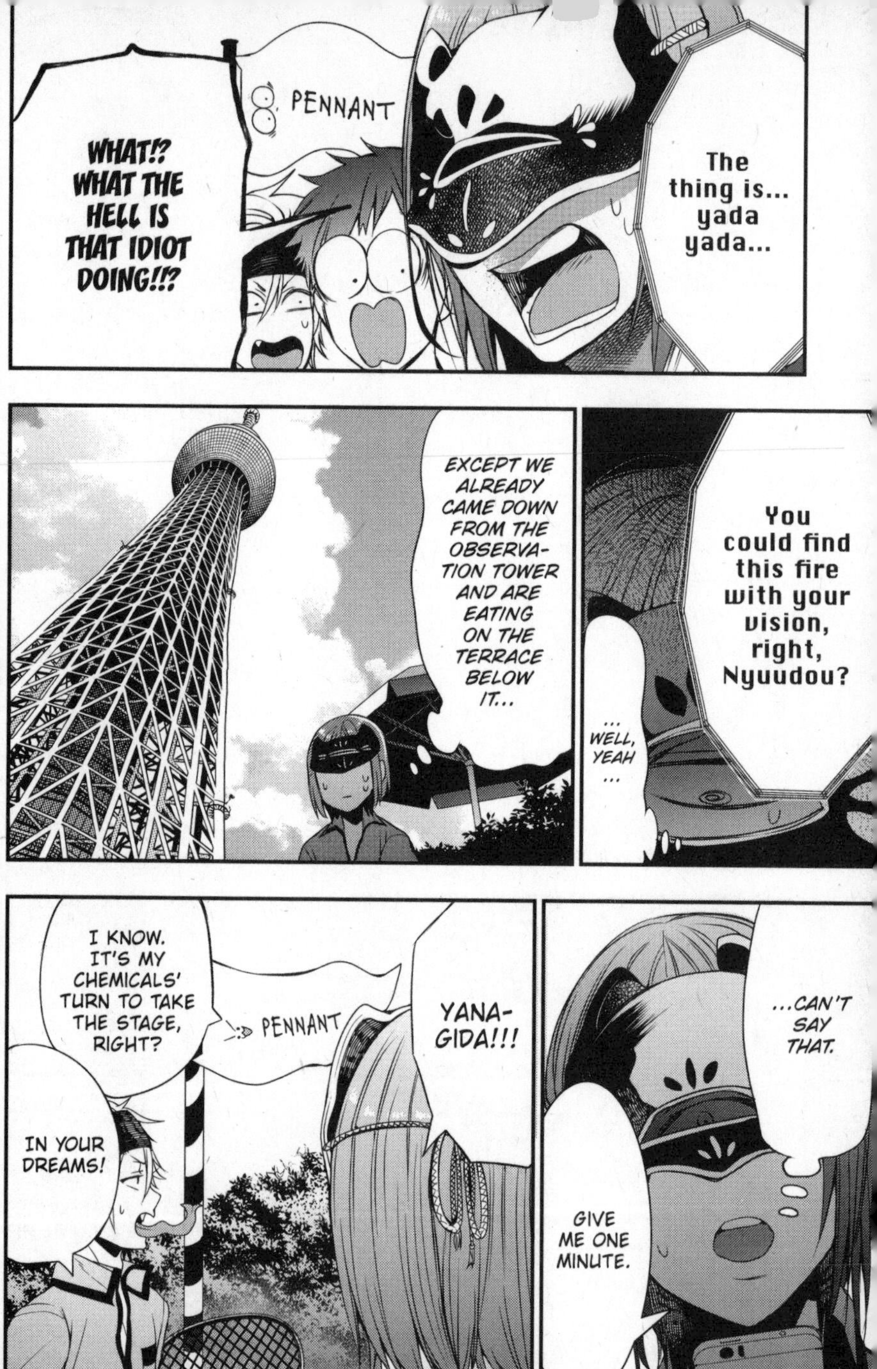
The thing is... yada yada...
PENNANT
WHAT!? WHAT THE HELL IS THAT IDIOT DOING!!?
You could find this fire with your vision, right, Nyuudou?
... WELL, YEAH ...
EXCEPT WE ALREADY CAME DOWN FROM THE OBSERVATION TOWER AND ARE EATING ON THE TERRACE BELOW IT...
...CAN'T SAY THAT.
GIVE ME ONE MINUTE.
YANA-GIDA!!!
I KNOW. IT'S MY CHEMICALS' TURN TO TAKE THE STAGE, RIGHT?
PENNANT
IN YOUR DREAMS!

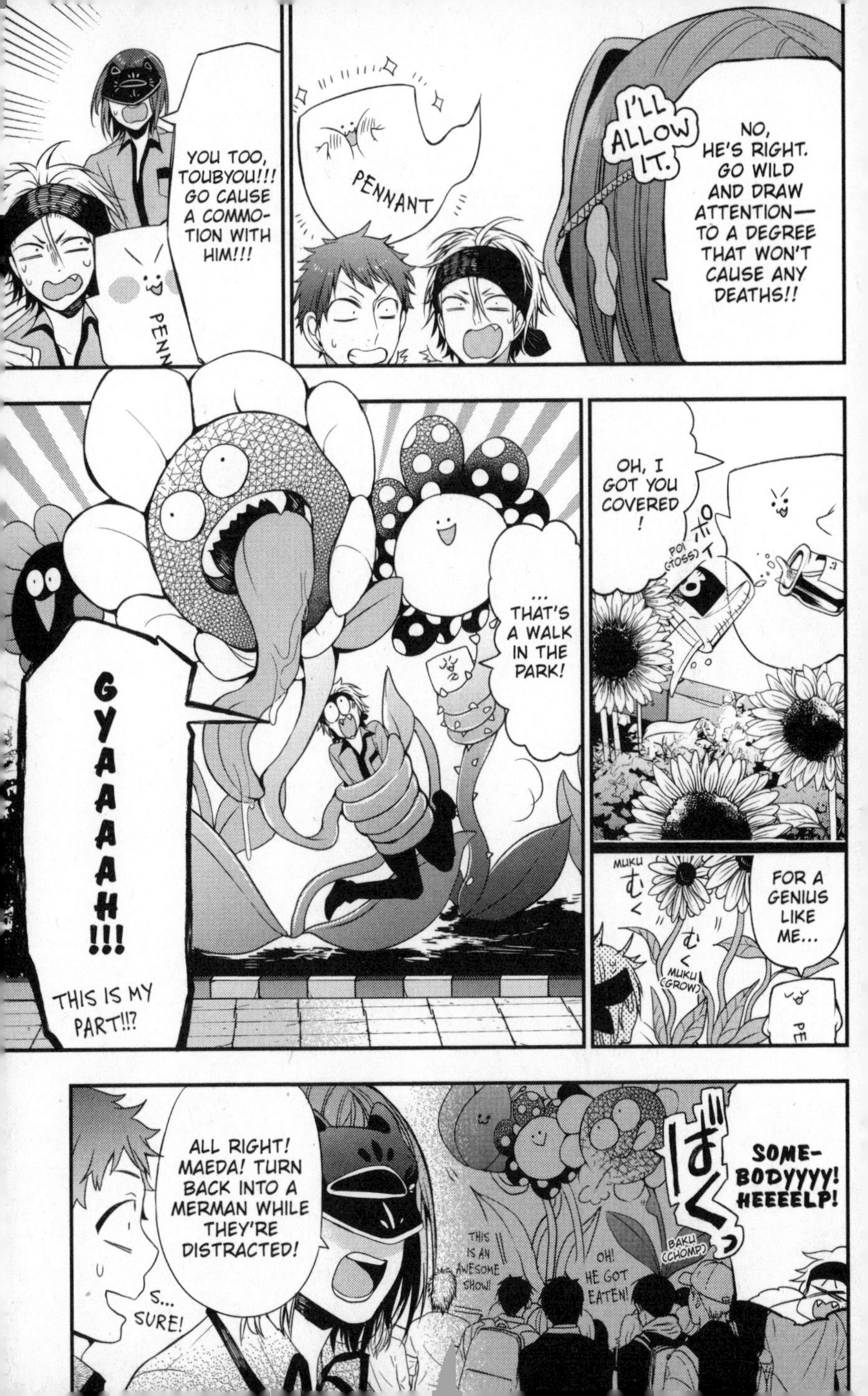
NO, HE'S RIGHT. GO WILD AND DRAW ATTENTION—TO A DEGREE THAT WON'T CAUSE ANY DEATHS!!
I'LL ALLOW IT.
PENNANT
YOU TOO, TOUBYOU!!! GO CAUSE A COMMOTION WITH HIM!!!
PENN
OH, I GOT YOU COVERED!
POI (TOSS)
MUKU
FOR A GENIUS LIKE ME...
MUKU (GROW)
PE
... THAT'S A WALK IN THE PARK!
GYAAAAAH!!!
THIS IS MY PART!!?
SOME-BODYYYY! HEEEELP!
BAKU (CHOMP)
OH! HE GOT EATEN!
THIS IS AN AWESOME SHOW!
ALL RIGHT! MAEDA! TURN BACK INTO A MERMAN WHILE THEY'RE DISTRACTED!
S... SURE!

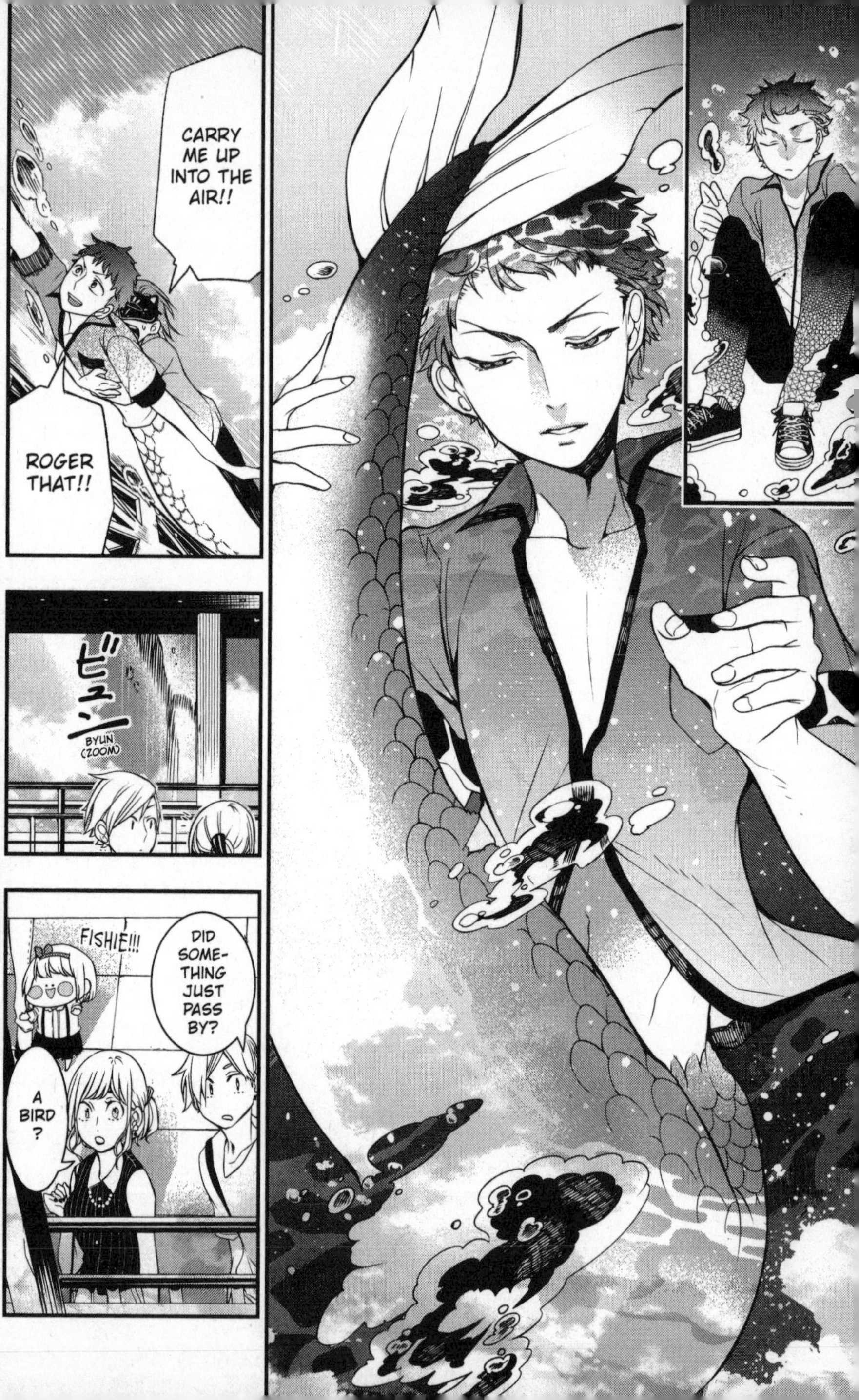
CARRY ME UP INTO THE AIR!!
ROGER THAT!!
ビュン
BYUN (ZOOM)
DID SOME-THING JUST PASS BY?
FISHIE!!!
A BIRD ?

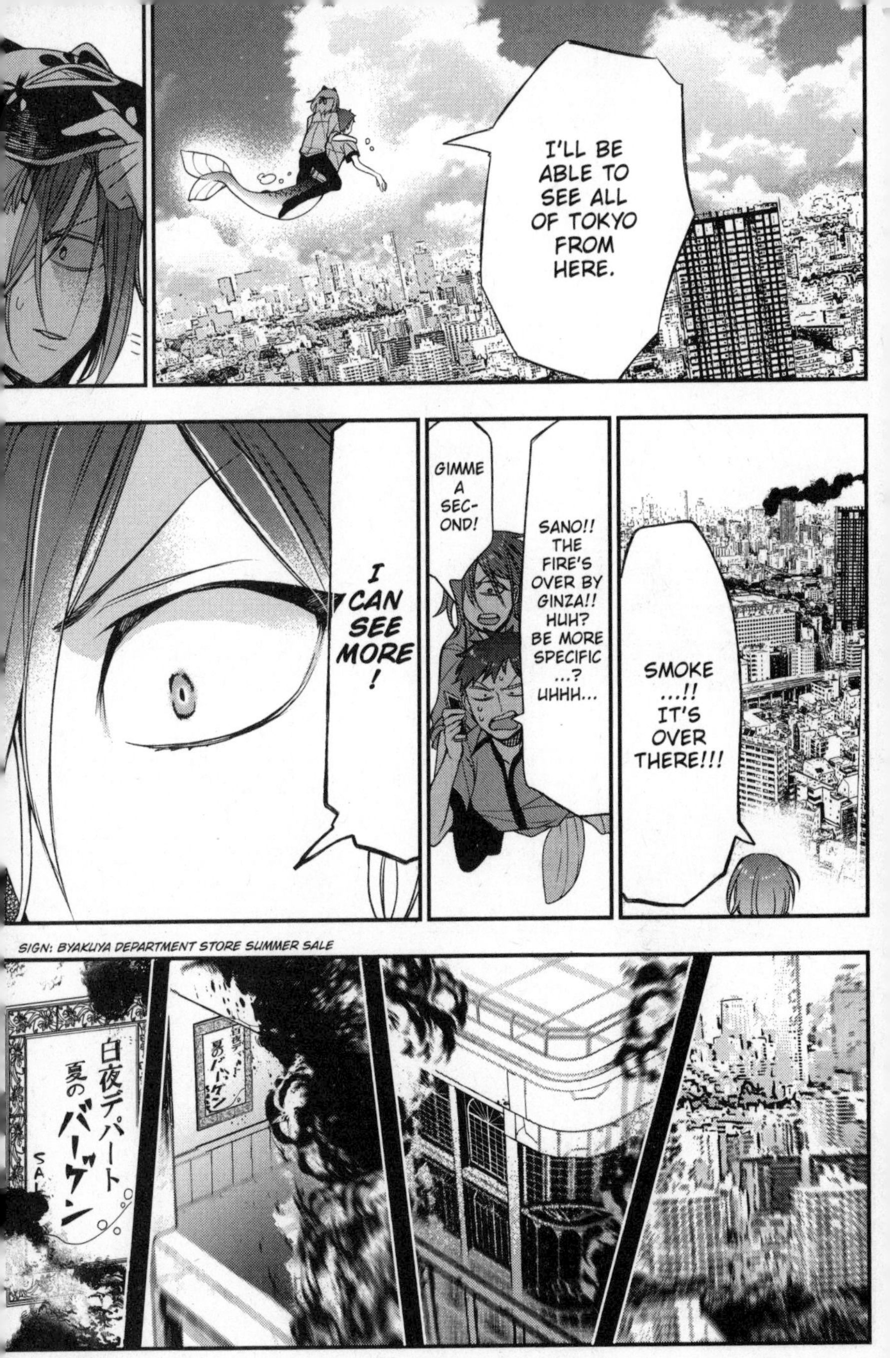

I'LL BE ABLE TO SEE ALL OF TOKYO FROM HERE.
SMOKE ...!! IT'S OVER THERE!!!
SANO!! THE FIRE'S OVER BY GINZA!! HUH? BE MORE SPECIFIC ...? UHHH...
GIMME A SEC-OND!
I CAN SEE MORE!
SIGN: BYAKUYA DEPARTMENT STORE SUMMER SALE
白夜デパート 夏のバーゲン

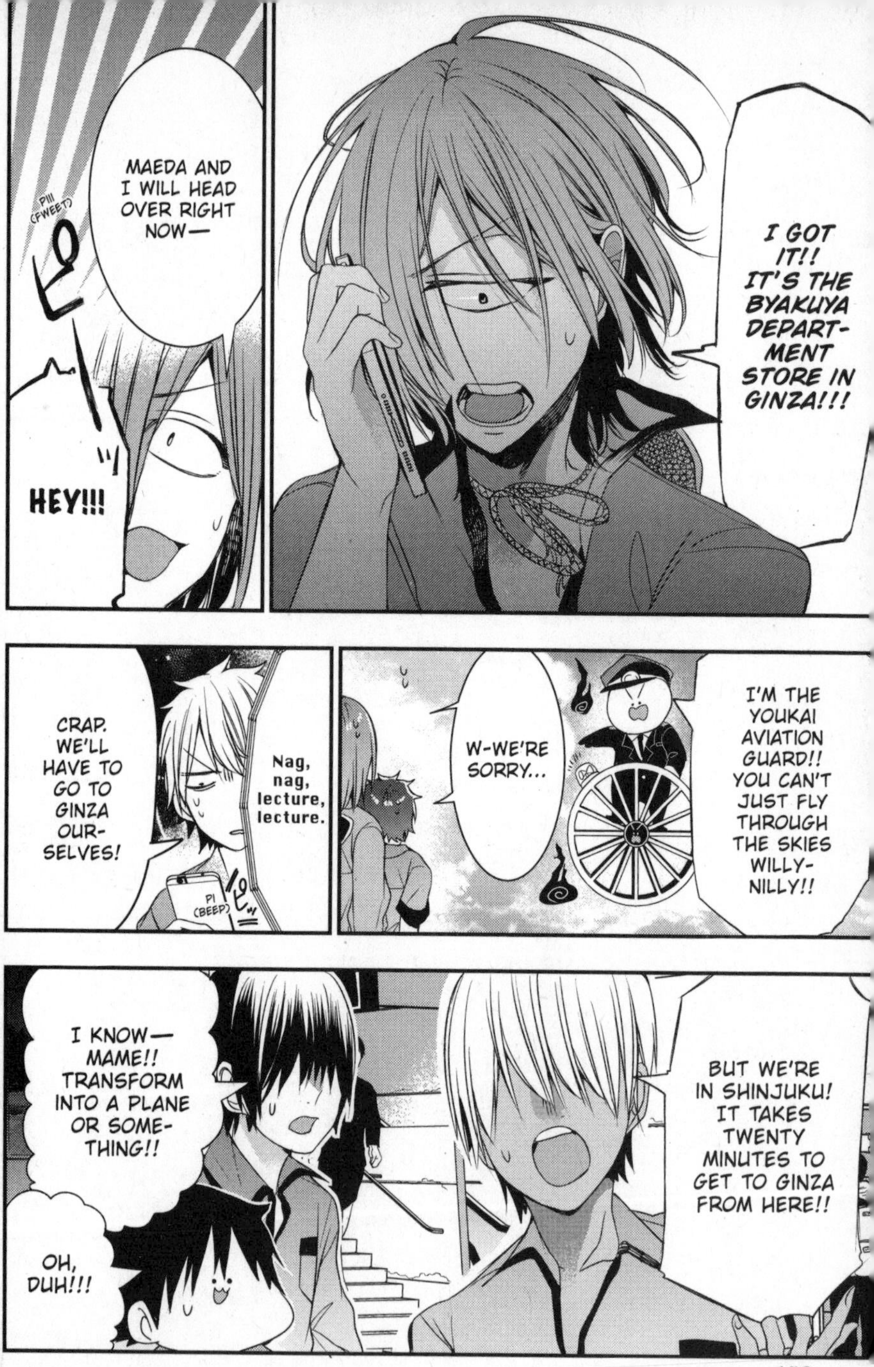
I GOT IT!! IT'S THE BYAKUYA DEPART-MENT STORE IN GINZA!!!
MAEDA AND I WILL HEAD OVER RIGHT NOW—
PIII (FWEET)
HEY!!!
I'M THE YOUKAI AVIATION GUARD!! YOU CAN'T JUST FLY THROUGH THE SKIES WILLY-NILLY!!
W-WE'RE SORRY...
Nag, nag, lecture, lecture.
CRAP. WE'LL HAVE TO GO TO GINZA OUR-SELVES!
PI (BEEP)
BUT WE'RE IN SHINJUKU! IT TAKES TWENTY MINUTES TO GET TO GINZA FROM HERE!!
I KNOW— MAME!! TRANSFORM INTO A PLANE OR SOME-THING!!
OH, DUH!!!

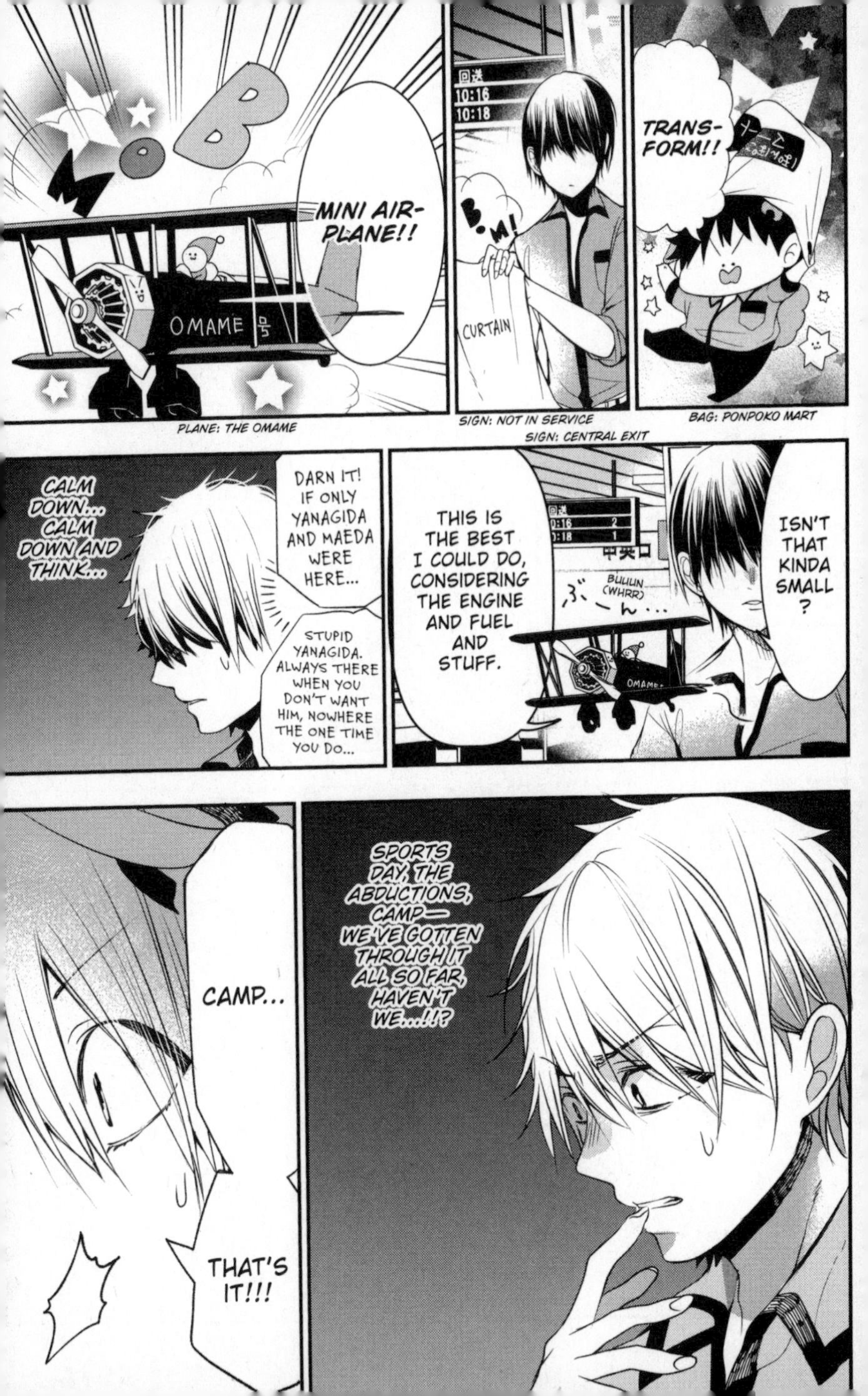
TRANS-FORM!!
BAG: PONPOKO MART
B..M!
CURTAIN
SIGN: NOT IN SERVICE
SIGN: CENTRAL EXIT
MINI AIR-PLANE!!
OMAME
PLANE: THE OMAME
ISN'T THAT KINDA SMALL?
THIS IS THE BEST I COULD DO, CONSIDERING THE ENGINE AND FUEL AND STUFF.
BUUUN (WHRR)
ぶーん…
DARN IT! IF ONLY YANAGIDA AND MAEDA WERE HERE...
STUPID YANAGIDA. ALWAYS THERE WHEN YOU DON'T WANT HIM, NOWHERE THE ONE TIME YOU DO...
CALM DOWN... CALM DOWN AND THINK...
SPORTS DAY, THE ABDUCTIONS, CAMP—WE'VE GOTTEN THROUGH IT ALL SO FAR, HAVEN'T WE...!!?
CAMP...
THAT'S IT!!!

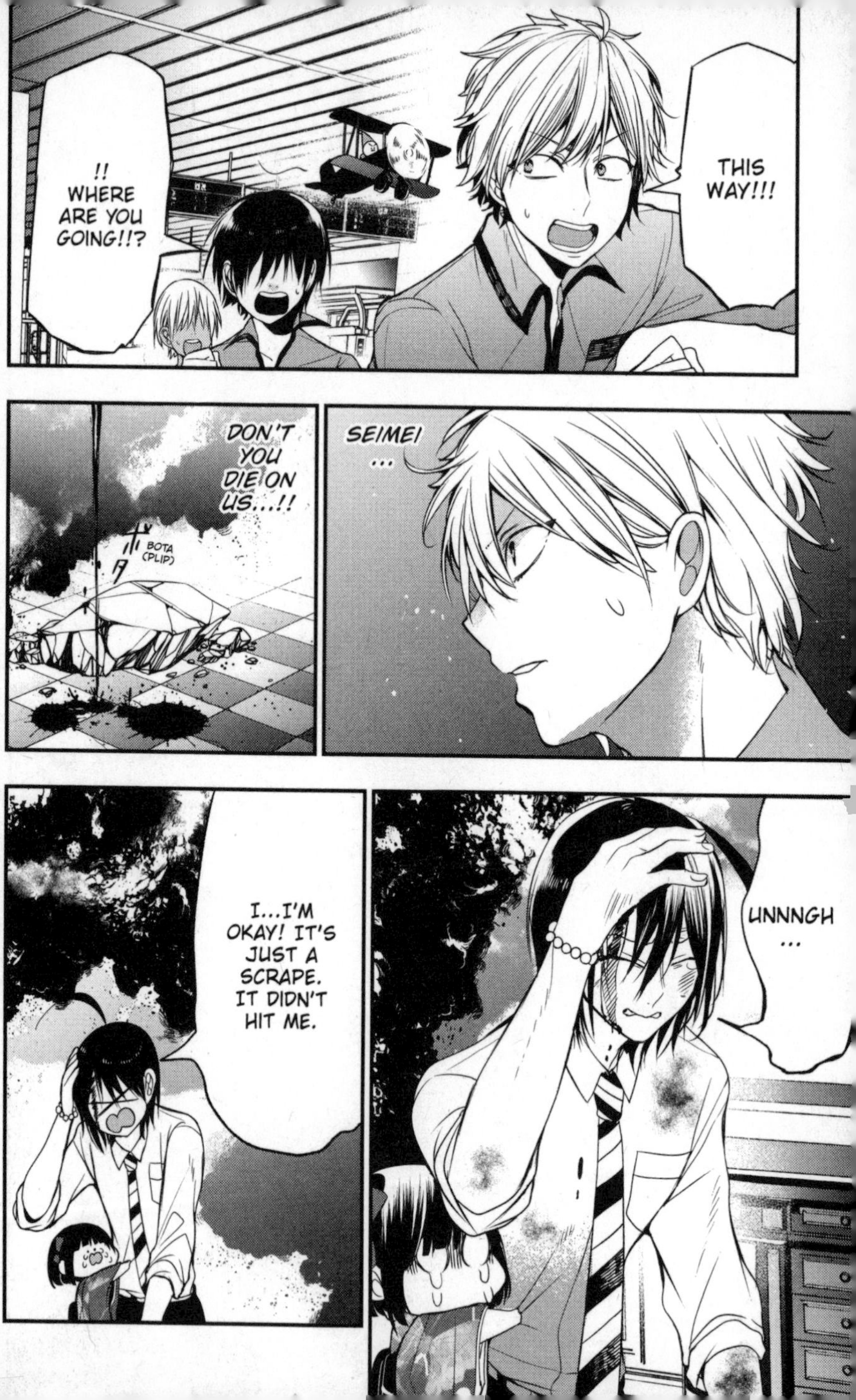
THIS WAY!!!
!! WHERE ARE YOU GOING!!?
SEIMEI ...
DON'T YOU DIE ON US...!!
BOTA (PLIP)
UNNNGH ...
I...I'M OKAY! IT'S JUST A SCRAPE. IT DIDN'T HIT ME.

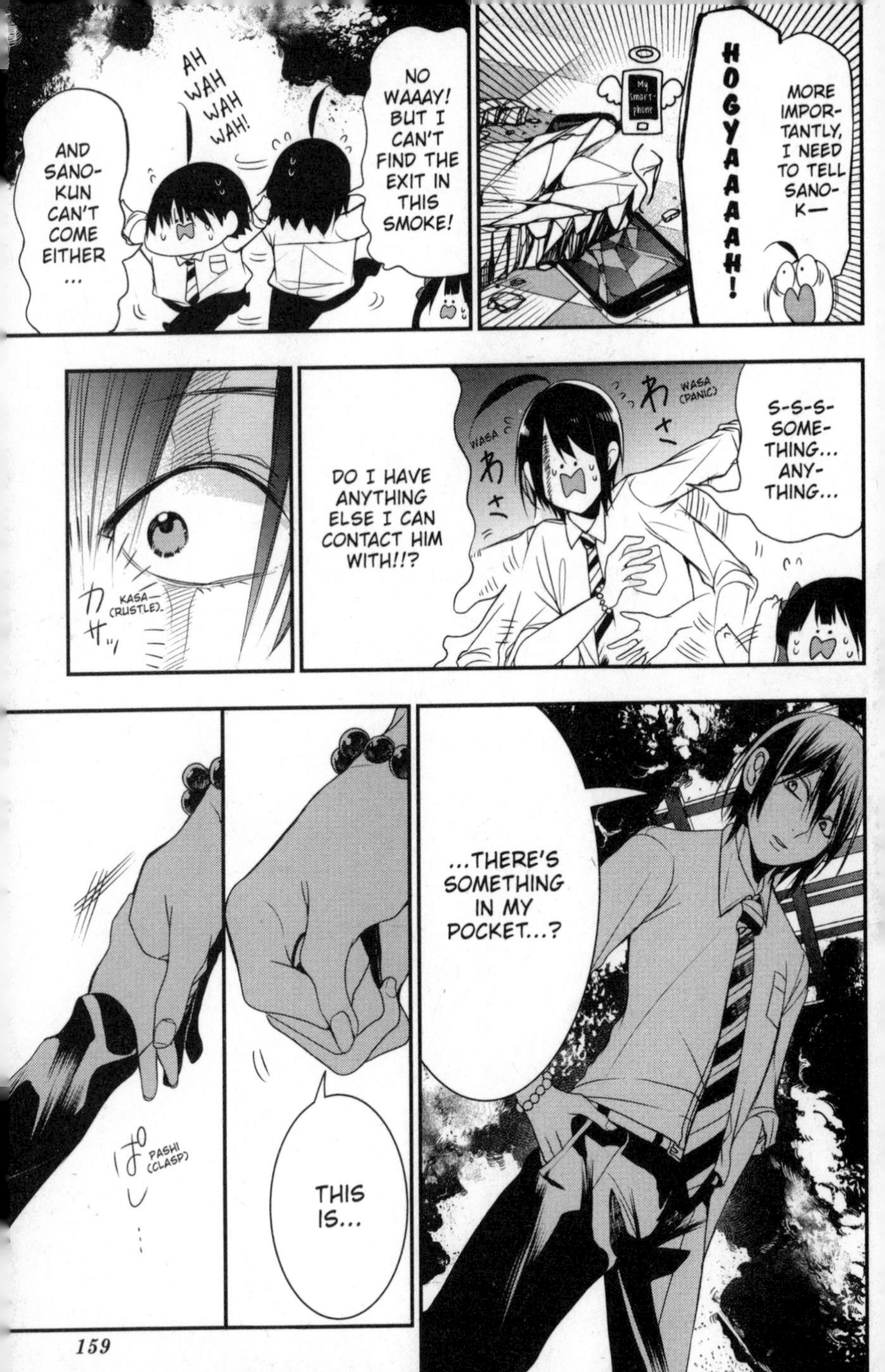
MORE IMPORTANTLY, I NEED TO TELL SANO-K—
HOGYAAAAAH!
My Smart-phone
NO WAAAY! BUT I CAN'T FIND THE EXIT IN THIS SMOKE!
AH WAH WAH WAH!
AND SANO-KUN CAN'T COME EITHER...
S-S-S-SOMETHING... ANYTHING...
WASA (PANIC)
WASA
DO I HAVE ANYTHING ELSE I CAN CONTACT HIM WITH!!?
KASA— (RUSTLE)
...THERE'S SOMETHING IN MY POCKET...?
THIS IS...
PASHI (CLASP)

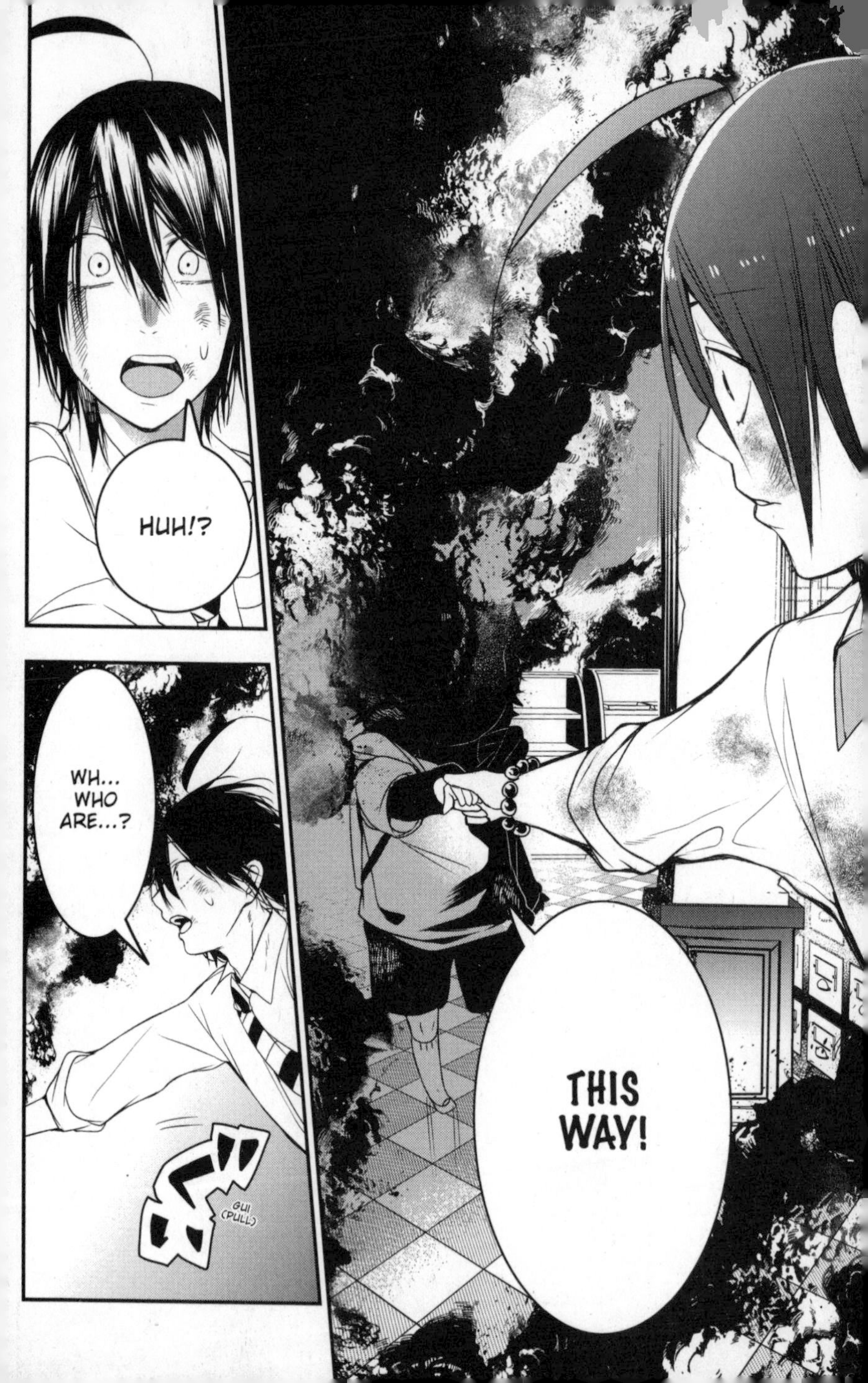
THIS WAY!
HUH!?
WH... WHO ARE...?
GUI (PULL)

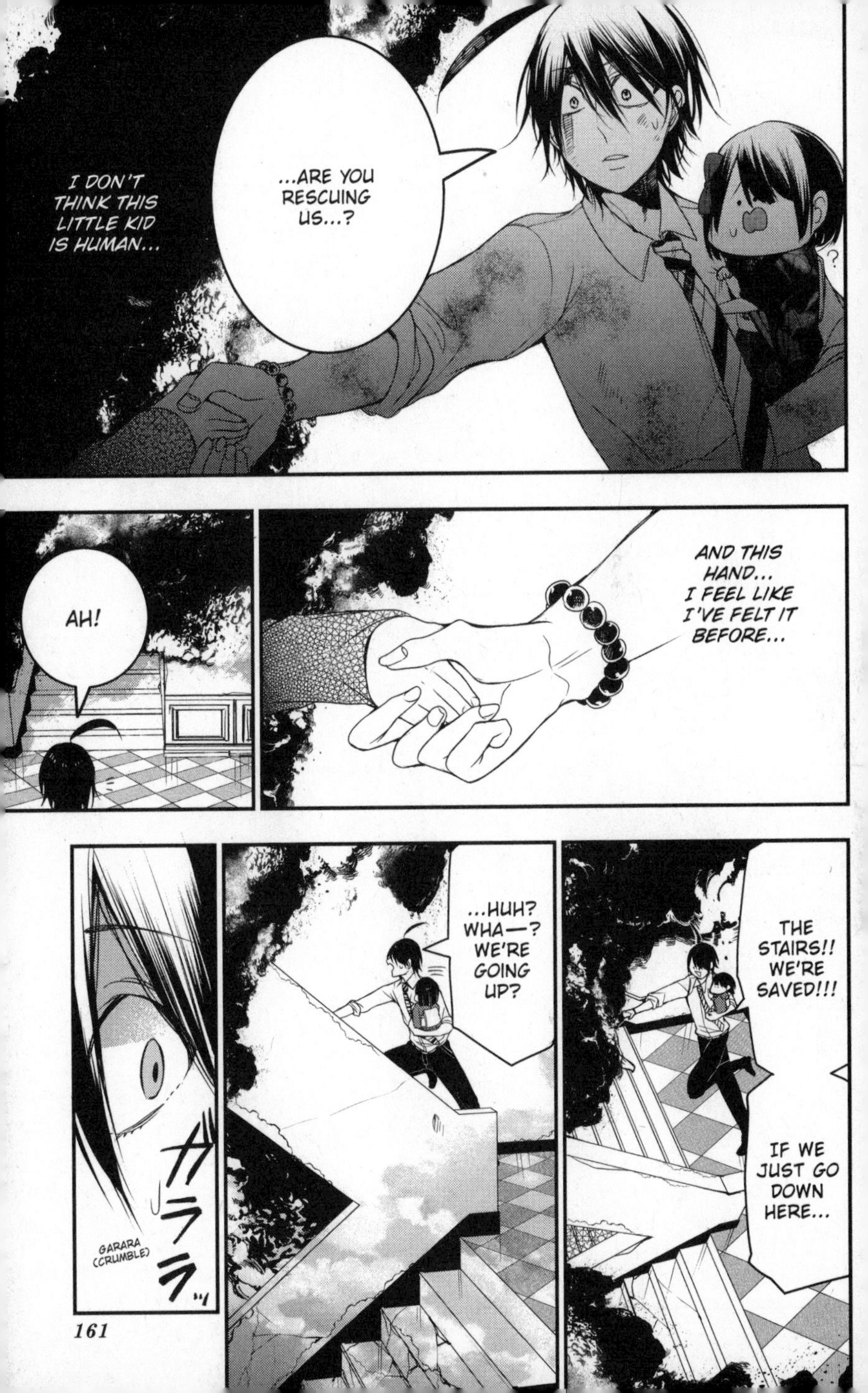
...ARE YOU RESCUING US...?
I DON'T THINK THIS LITTLE KID IS HUMAN...
AND THIS HAND... I FEEL LIKE I'VE FELT IT BEFORE...
AH!
THE STAIRS!! WE'RE SAVED!!!
IF WE JUST GO DOWN HERE...
...HUH? WHA—? WE'RE GOING UP?
GARARA (CRUMBLE)

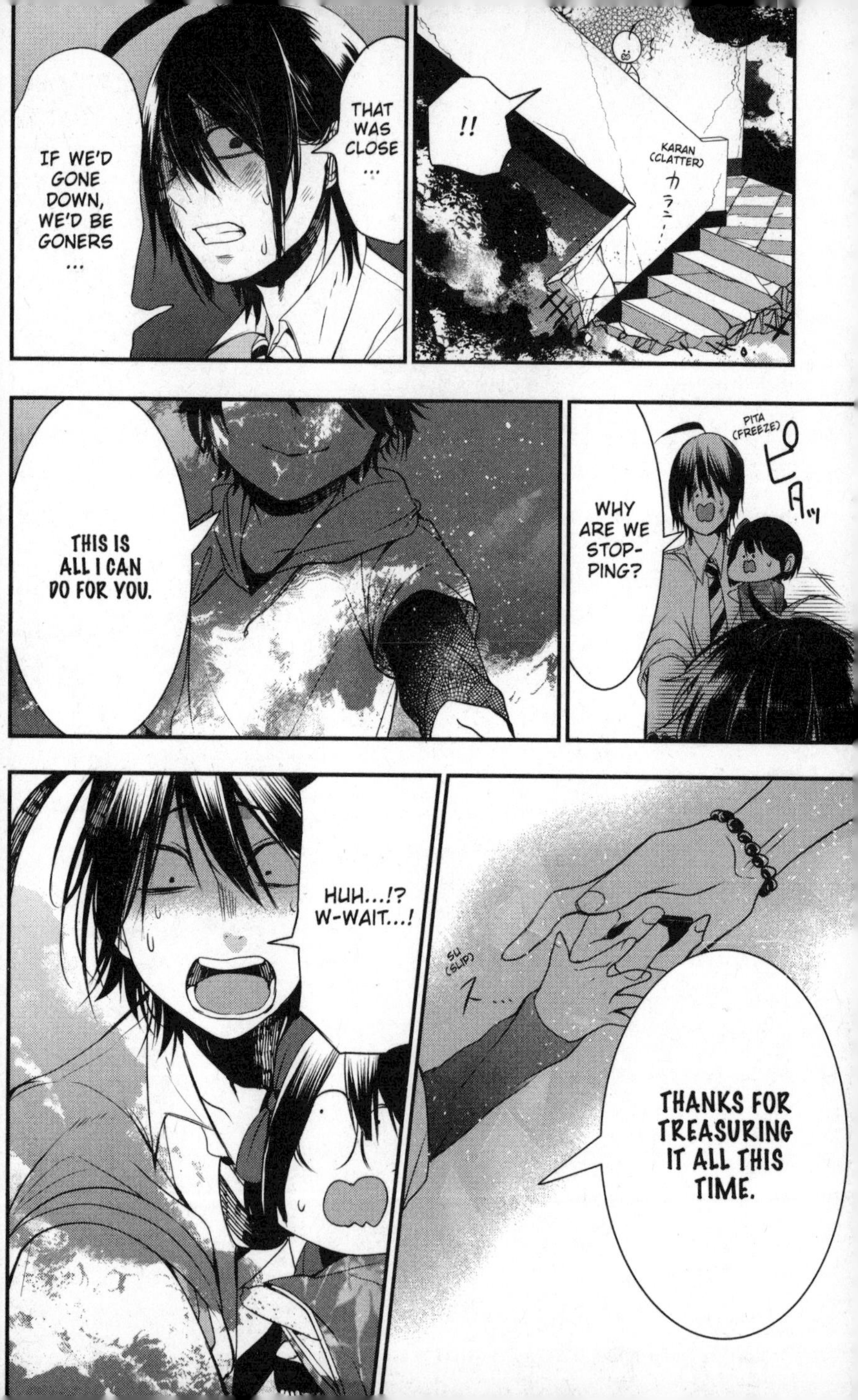
KARAN (CLATTER)
カラ…
!!
THAT WAS CLOSE...
IF WE'D GONE DOWN, WE'D BE GONERS...
PITA (FREEZE)
ピタッ
WHY ARE WE STOP-PING?
THIS IS ALL I CAN DO FOR YOU.
THANKS FOR TREASURING IT ALL THIS TIME.
SU (SLIP)
ス…
HUH...!? W-WAIT...!

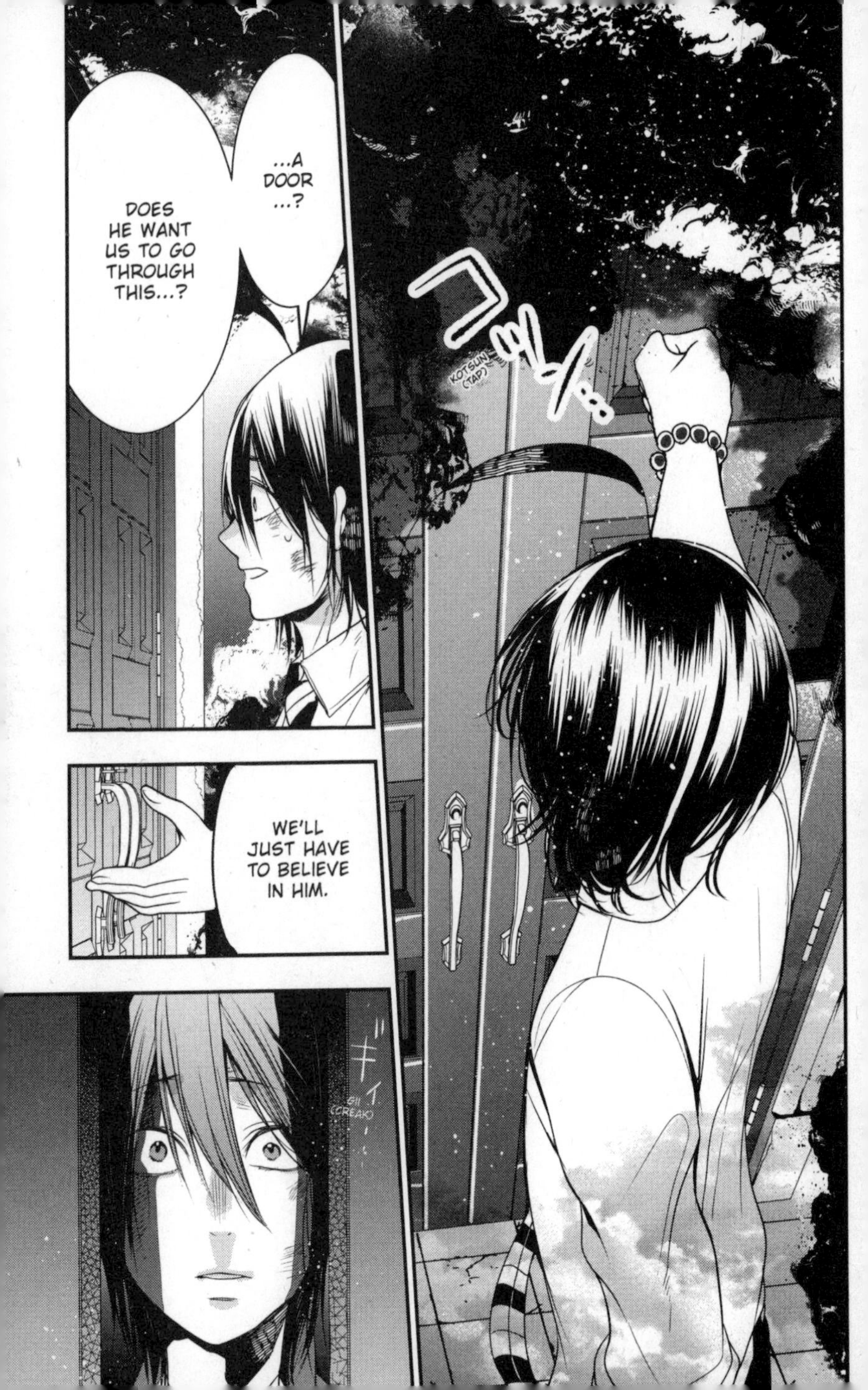
KOTSUN (TAP)
...A DOOR ...?
DOES HE WANT US TO GO THROUGH THIS...?
WE'LL JUST HAVE TO BELIEVE IN HIM.
GII (CREAK)

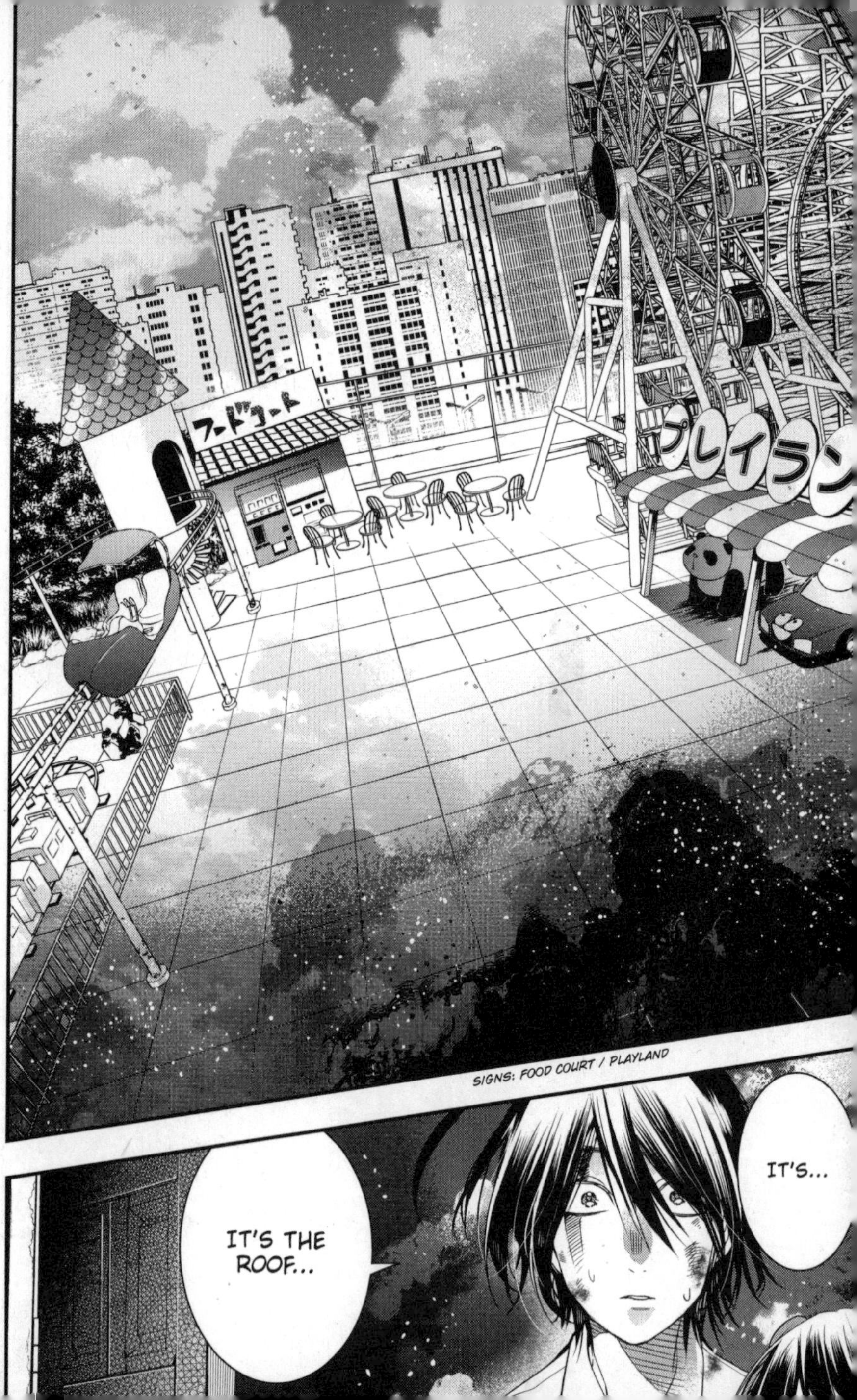
フードコート
SIGNS: FOOD COURT / PLAYLAND
IT'S...
IT'S THE ROOF...

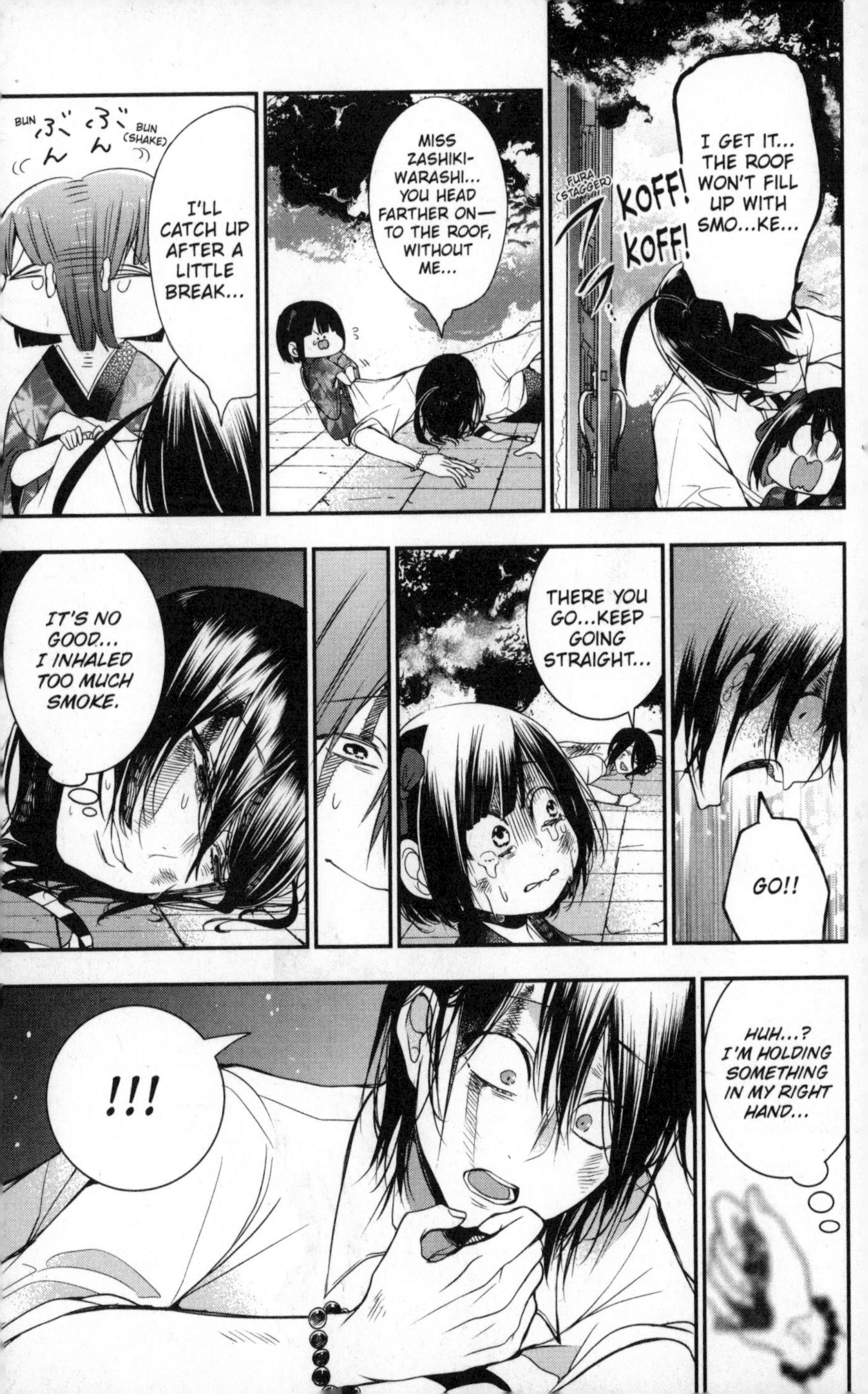
I GET IT... THE ROOF WON'T FILL UP WITH SMO...KE...
KOFF! KOFF!
FURA (STAGGER)
MISS ZASHIKI-WARASHI... YOU HEAD FARTHER ON—TO THE ROOF, WITHOUT ME...
I'LL CATCH UP AFTER A LITTLE BREAK...
BUN ぶん (SHAKE)
BUN ぶん
GO!!
THERE YOU GO...KEEP GOING STRAIGHT...
IT'S NO GOOD... I INHALED TOO MUCH SMOKE.
HUH...? I'M HOLDING SOMETHING IN MY RIGHT HAND...
!!!

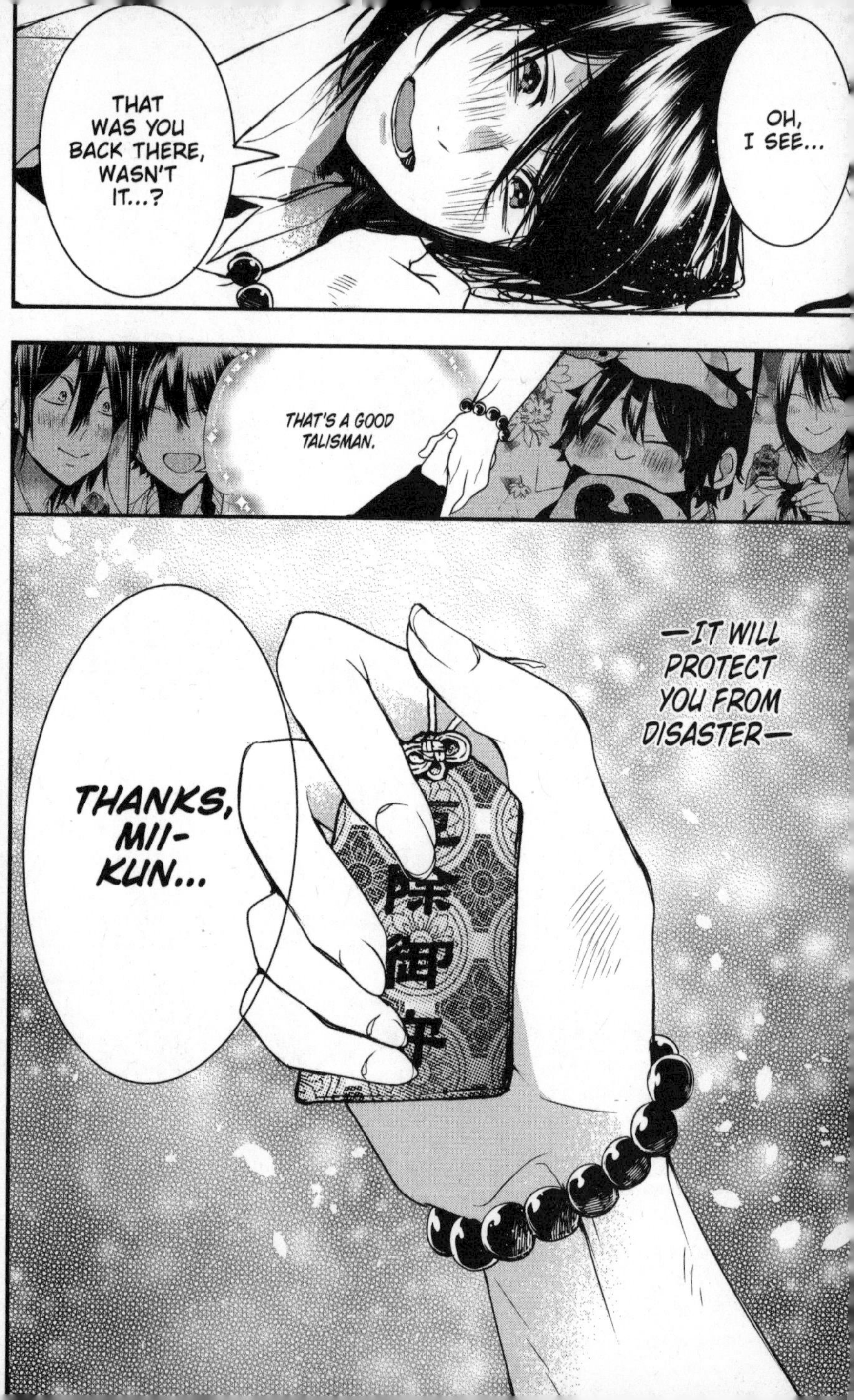
OH, I SEE...
THAT WAS YOU BACK THERE, WASN'T IT...?
THAT'S A GOOD TALISMAN.
—IT WILL PROTECT YOU FROM DISASTER—
THANKS, MII-KUN...

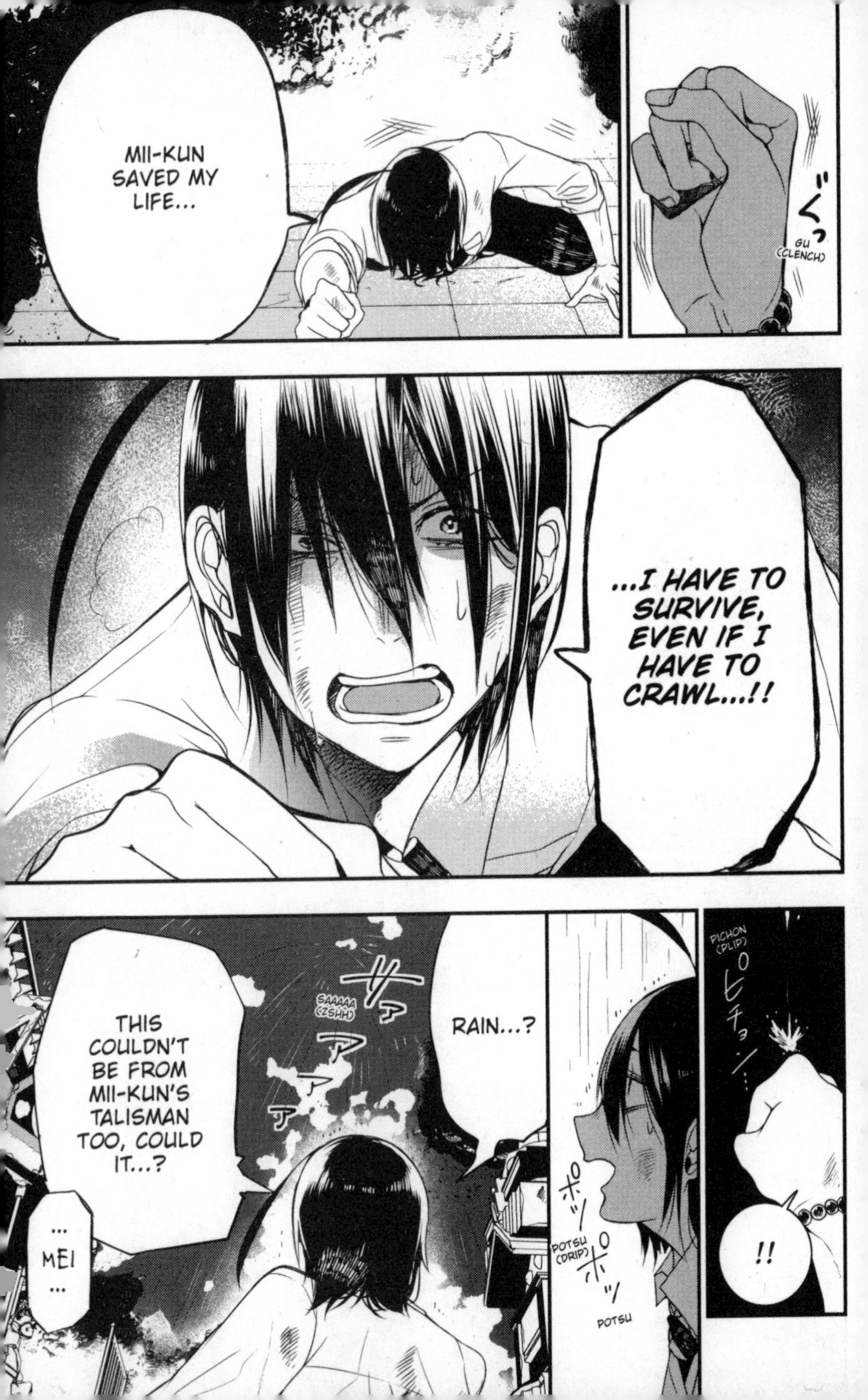
ぐっ
GU (CLENCH)
MII-KUN SAVED MY LIFE...
...I HAVE TO SURVIVE, EVEN IF I HAVE TO CRAWL...!!
ピチョン…
PICHON (PLIP)
!!
ポツ ポツ
POTSU (DRIP)
POTSU
RAIN...?
サァアアア
SAAAAA (ZSHH)
THIS COULDN'T BE FROM MII-KUN'S TALISMAN TOO, COULD IT...?
... MEI ...

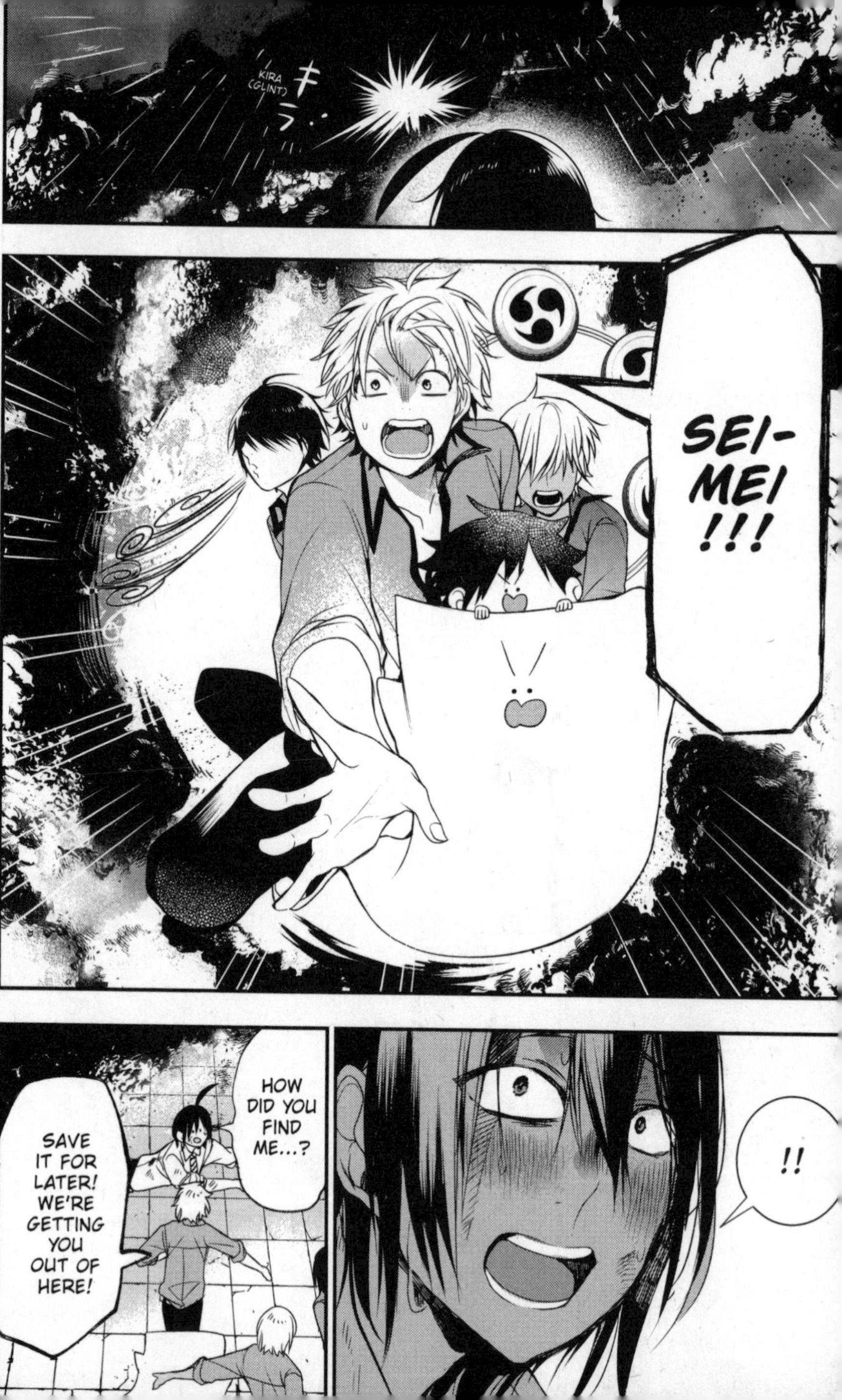
KIRA (GLINT)
SEI-MEI!!!
!!
HOW DID YOU FIND ME...?
SAVE IT FOR LATER! WE'RE GETTING YOU OUT OF HERE!

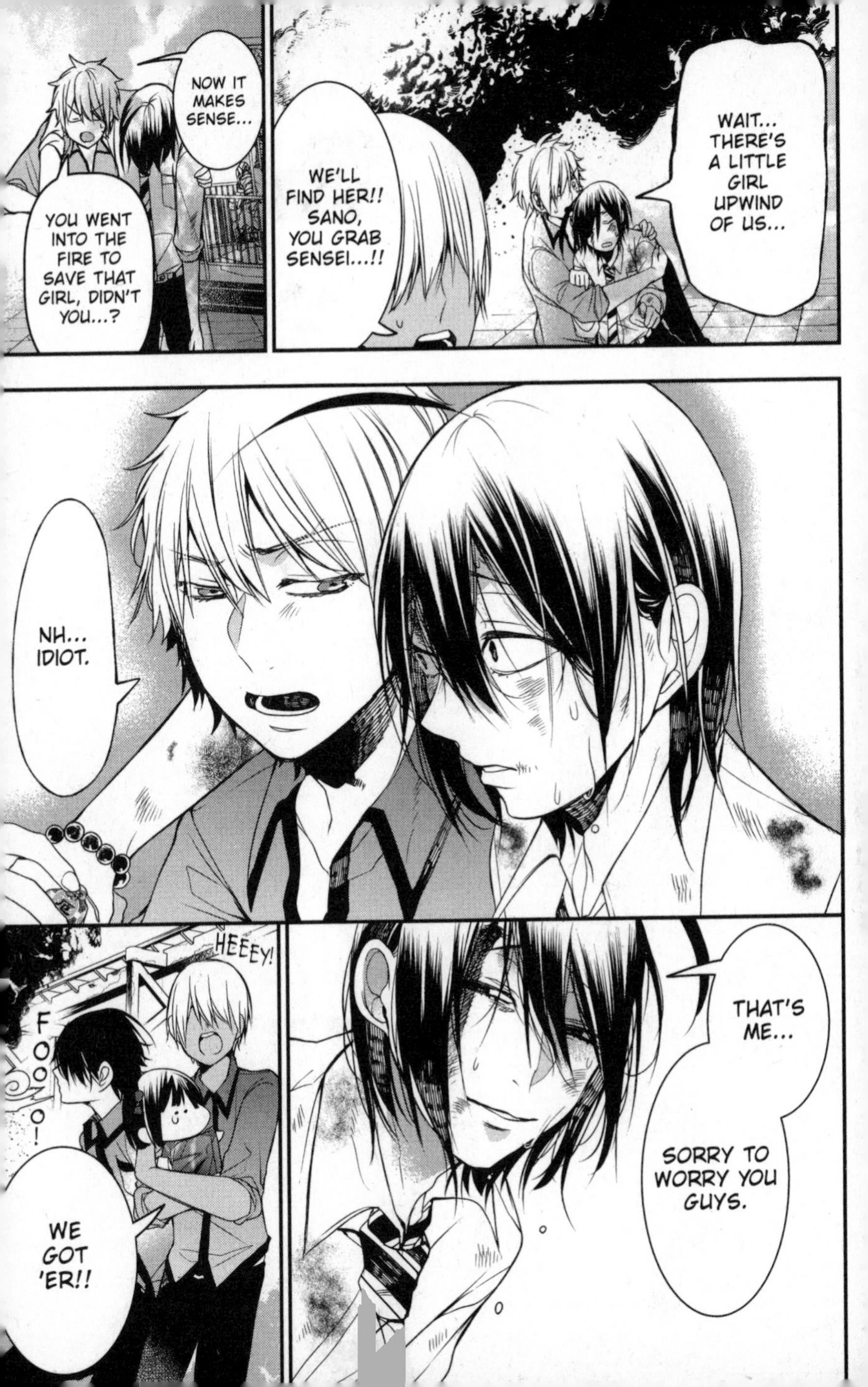
WAIT... THERE'S A LITTLE GIRL UPWIND OF US...
WE'LL FIND HER!! SANO, YOU GRAB SENSEI...!!
NOW IT MAKES SENSE...
YOU WENT INTO THE FIRE TO SAVE THAT GIRL, DIDN'T YOU...?
NH... IDIOT.
THAT'S ME...
SORRY TO WORRY YOU GUYS.
HEEEY!
FOOOO!
WE GOT 'ER!!

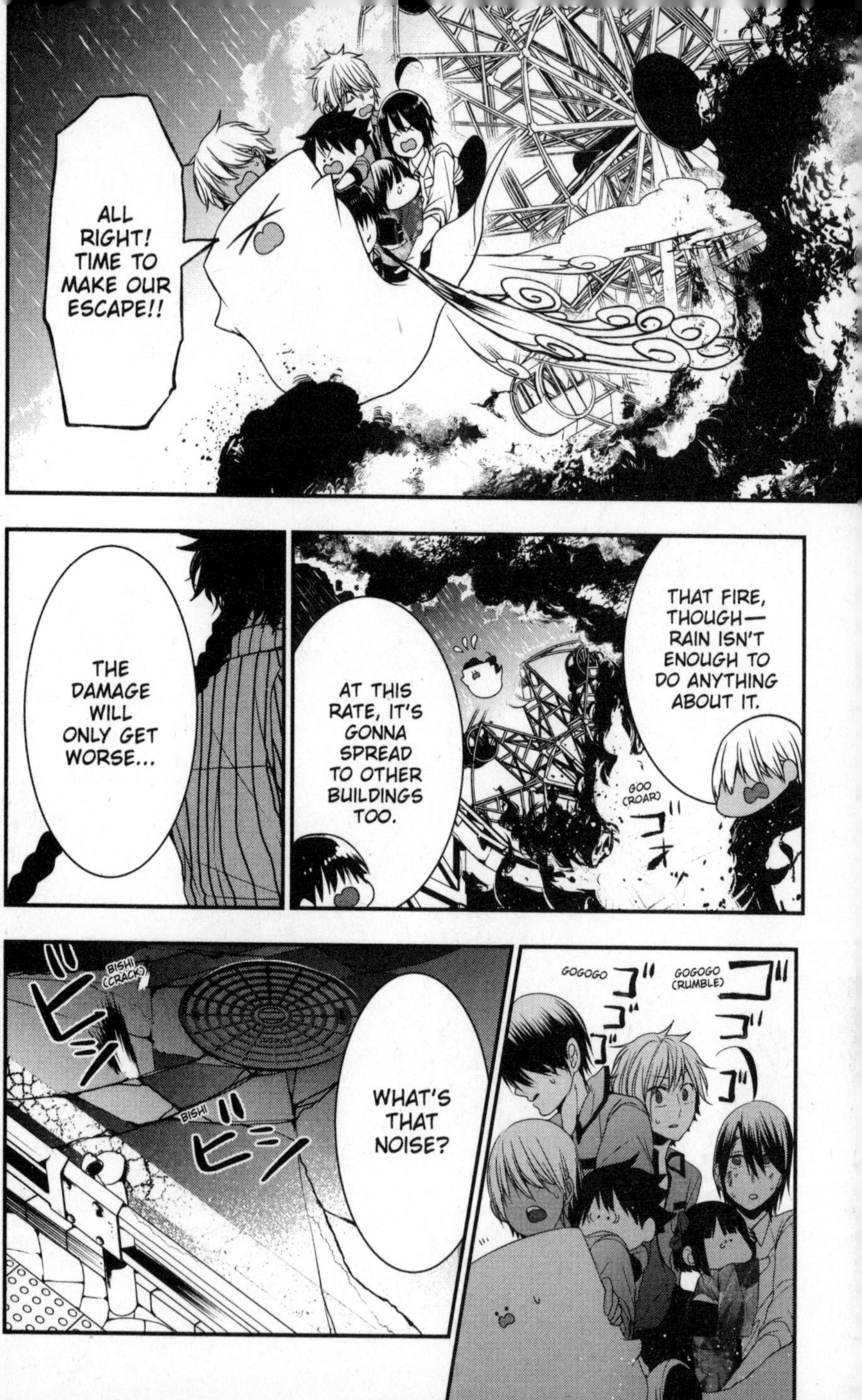

ALL RIGHT! TIME TO MAKE OUR ESCAPE!!
THAT FIRE, THOUGH—RAIN ISN'T ENOUGH TO DO ANYTHING ABOUT IT.
GOO (ROAR)
AT THIS RATE, IT'S GONNA SPREAD TO OTHER BUILDINGS TOO.
THE DAMAGE WILL ONLY GET WORSE...
GOGOGO (RUMBLE)
GOGOGO
WHAT'S THAT NOISE?
BISHI (CRACK)
BISHI

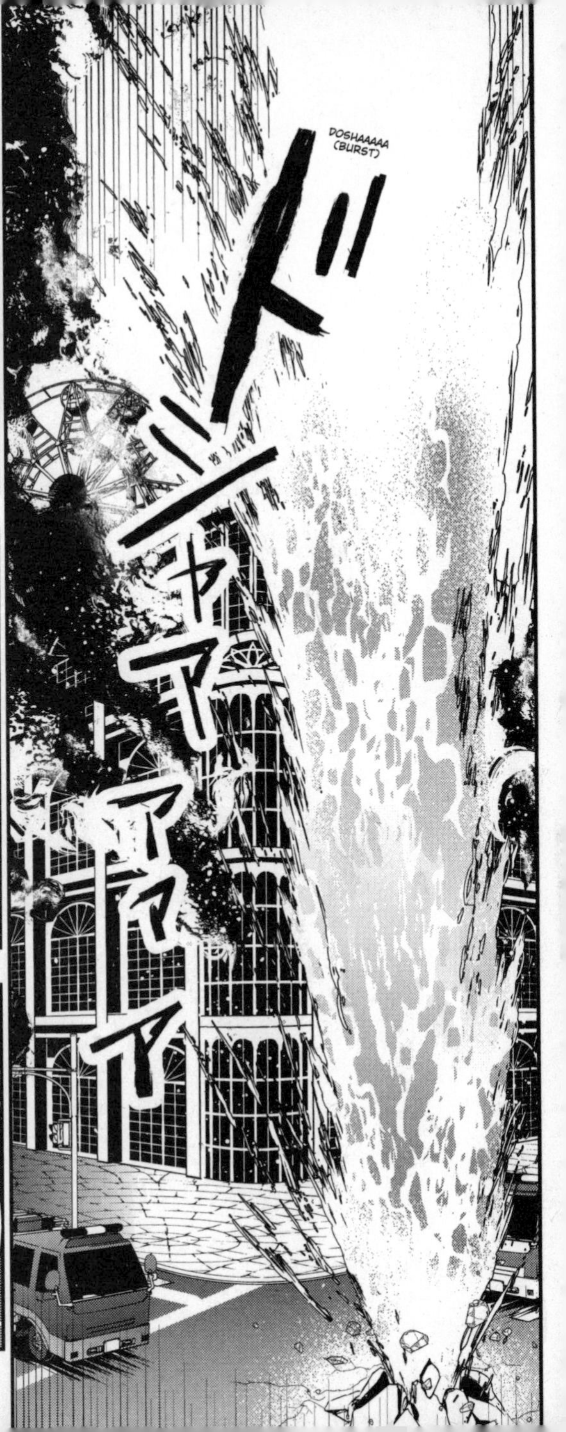
DOSHAAAAA (BURST)

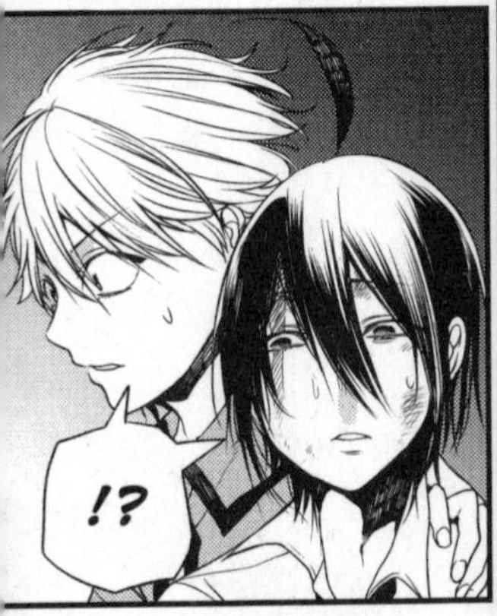
!?

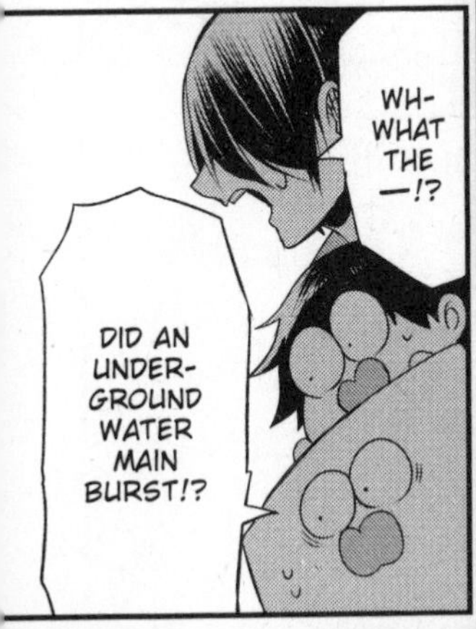
WH- WHAT THE —!?
DID AN UNDER-GROUND WATER MAIN BURST!?

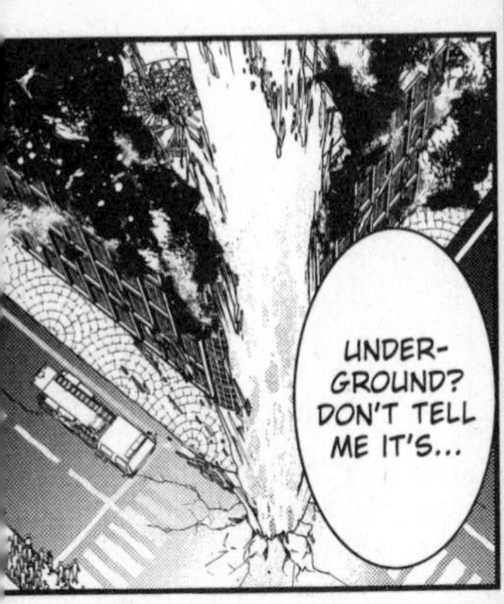
UNDER-GROUND? DON'T TELL ME IT'S...

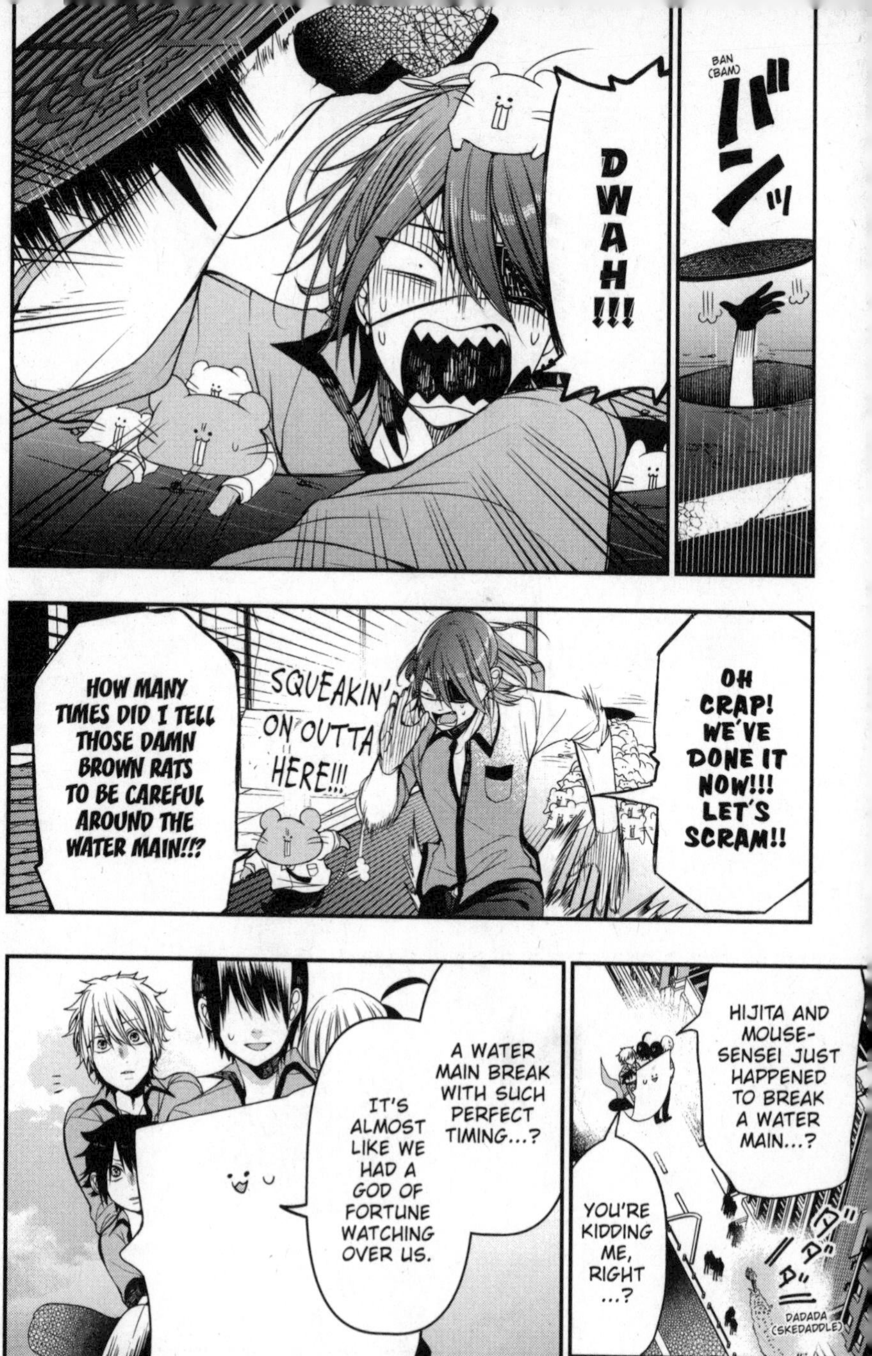
BAN (BAM)
バーンッ
DWAH!!!
OH CRAP! WE'VE DONE IT NOW!!! LET'S SCRAM!!
SQUEAKIN' ON OUTTA HERE!!!
HOW MANY TIMES DID I TELL THOSE DAMN BROWN RATS TO BE CAREFUL AROUND THE WATER MAIN!!?
HIJITA AND MOUSE-SENSEI JUST HAPPENED TO BREAK A WATER MAIN...?
YOU'RE KIDDING ME, RIGHT...?
DADADA (SKEDADDLE)
A WATER MAIN BREAK WITH SUCH PERFECT TIMING...?
IT'S ALMOST LIKE WE HAD A GOD OF FORTUNE WATCHING OVER US.

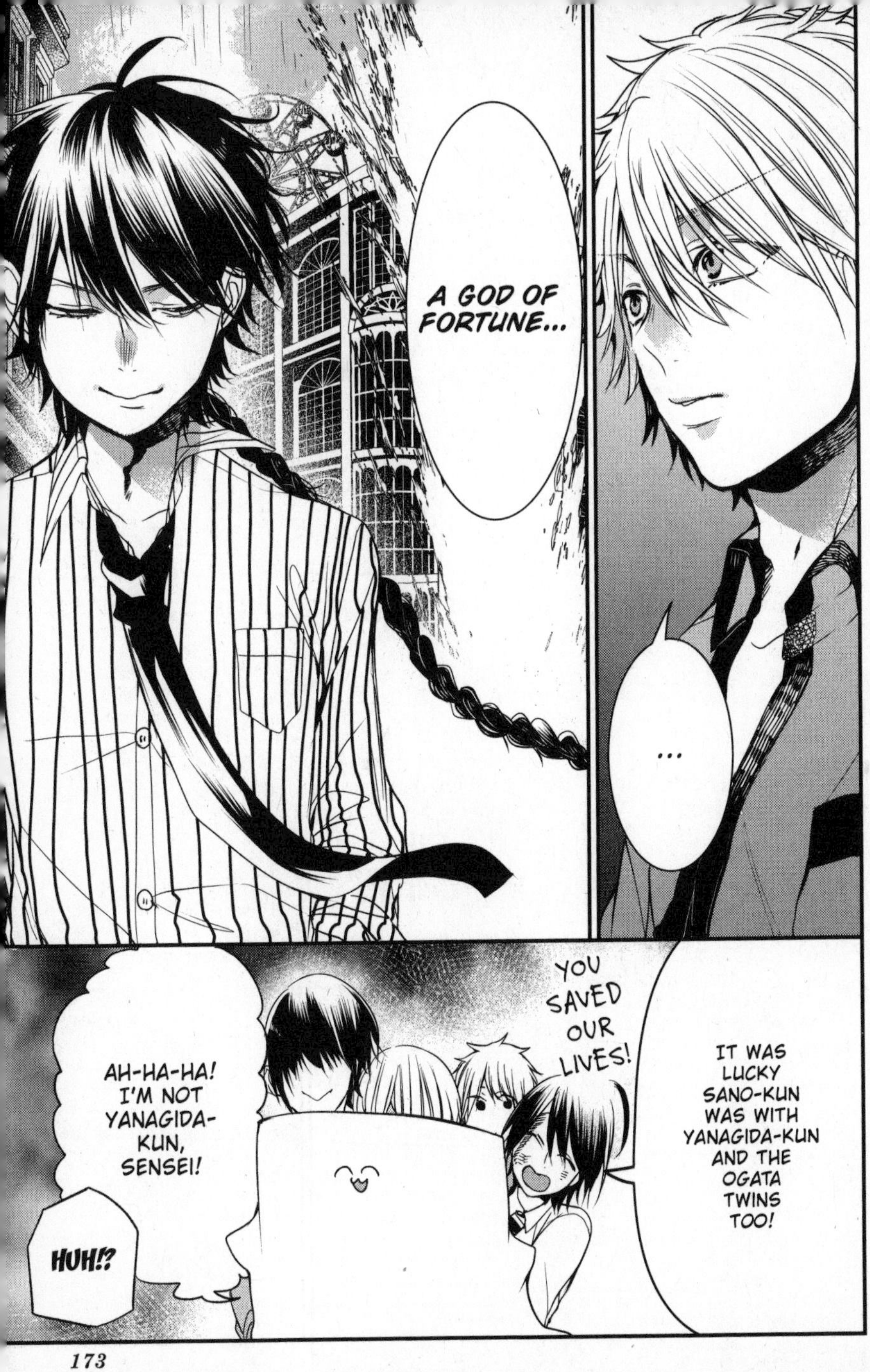
...
A GOD OF FORTUNE...
IT WAS LUCKY SANO-KUN WAS WITH YANAGIDA-KUN AND THE OGATA TWINS TOO!
YOU SAVED OUR LIVES!
AH-HA-HA! I'M NOT YANAGIDA-KUN, SENSEI!
HUH!?

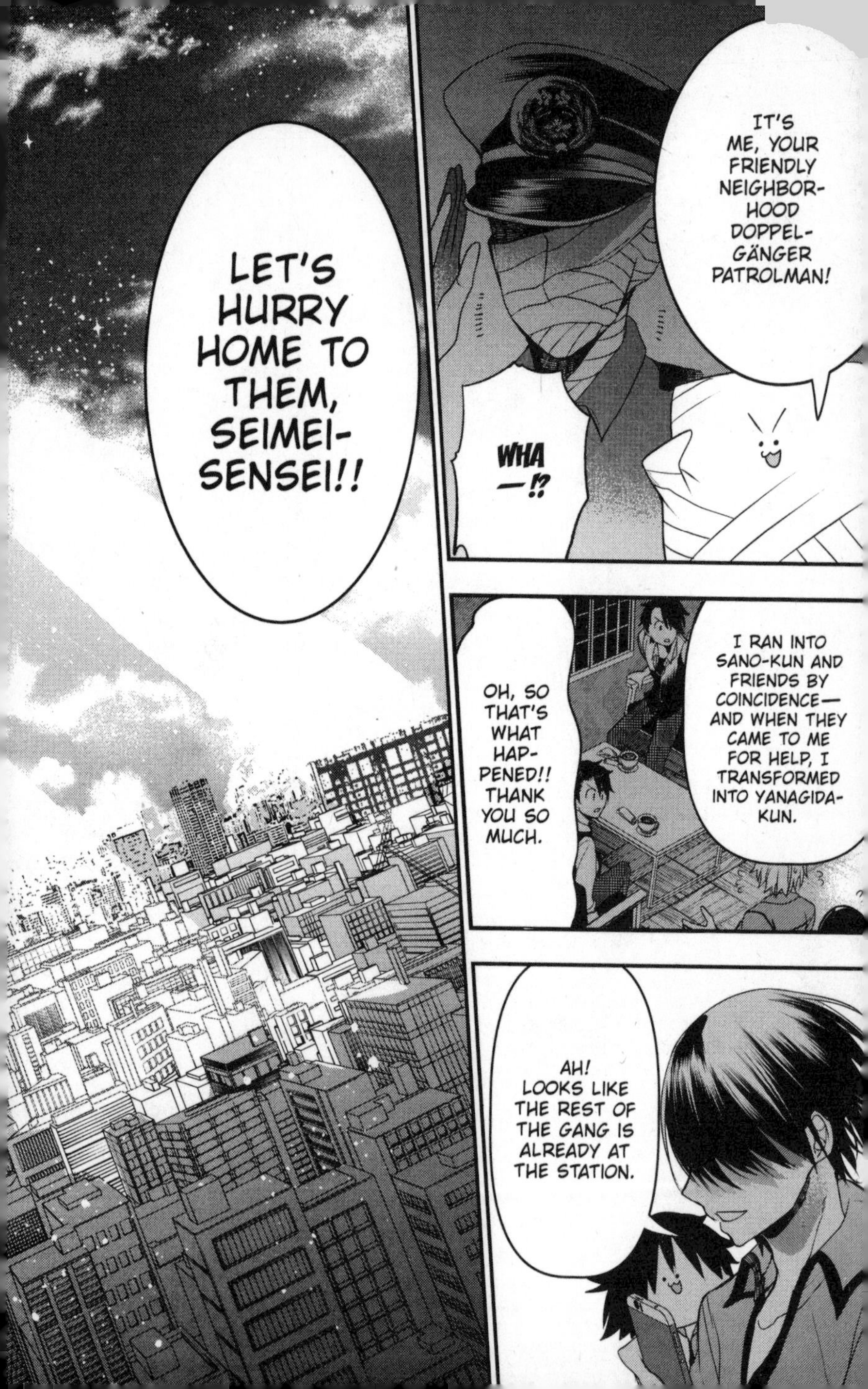
IT'S ME, YOUR FRIENDLY NEIGHBOR-HOOD DOPPEL-GÄNGER PATROLMAN!
WHA—!?
I RAN INTO SANO-KUN AND FRIENDS BY COINCIDENCE—AND WHEN THEY CAME TO ME FOR HELP, I TRANSFORMED INTO YANAGIDA-KUN.
OH, SO THAT'S WHAT HAP-PENED!! THANK YOU SO MUCH.
AH! LOOKS LIKE THE REST OF THE GANG IS ALREADY AT THE STATION.
LET'S HURRY HOME TO THEM, SEIMEI-SENSEI!!

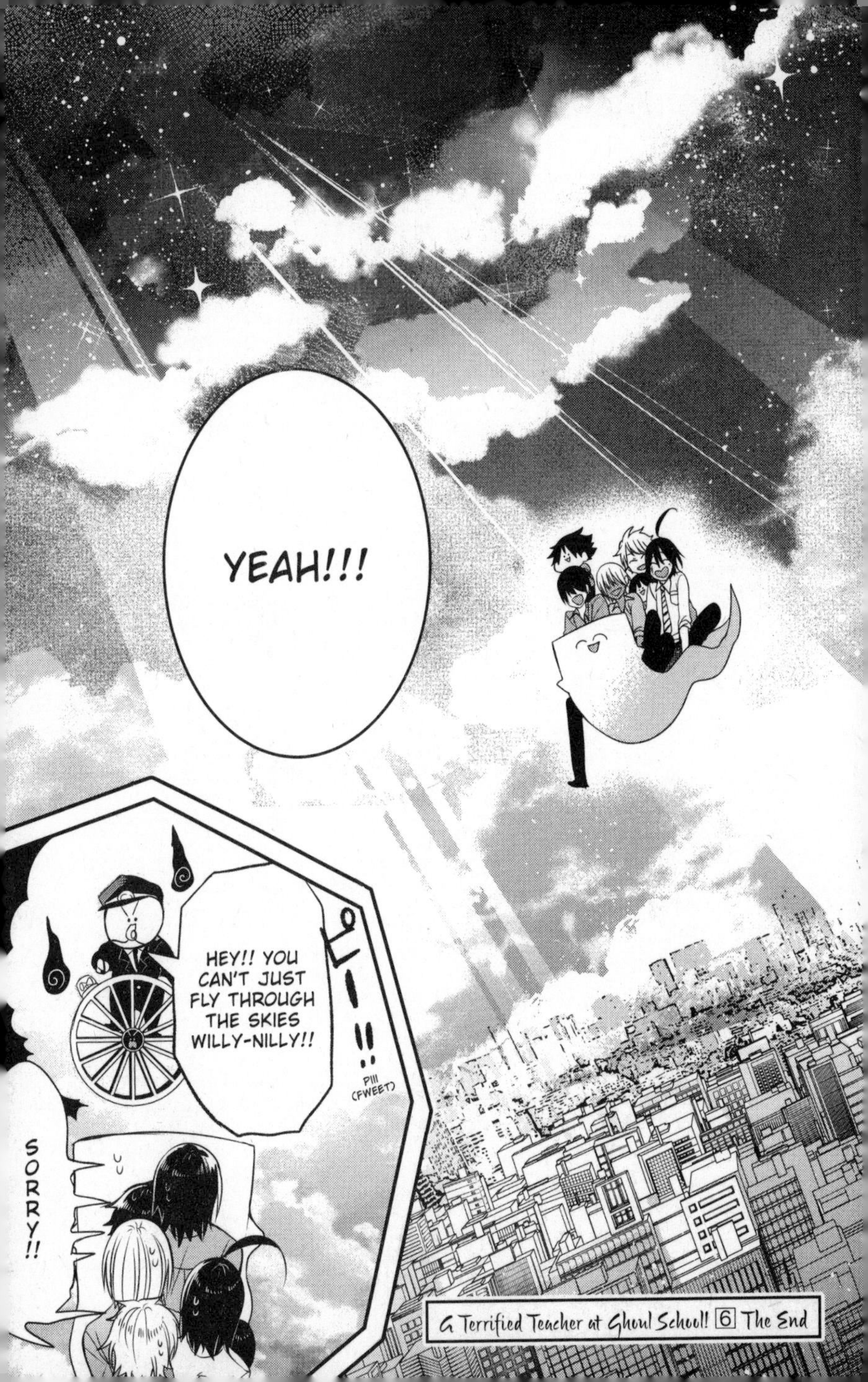
YEAH!!!
HEY!! YOU CAN'T JUST FLY THROUGH THE SKIES WILLY-NILLY!!
PIII (FWEET)
SORRY!!
A Terrified Teacher at Ghoul School! 6 The End

Translation Notes

GENERAL
Thirty centimeters is equal to roughly one foot.

One hundred yen is roughly equal to one US dollar.

INSIDE COVER
The ***kamaitachi*** is a weasel *youkai* with sicklelike claws.

PAGE 3
Shikoku is the smallest of Japan's four main islands.

PAGE 9
Daifuku is a Japanese confection consisting of a sweet filling, usually *azuki* bean paste, wrapped in a glutinous rice cake (*mochi*) shell. ***Mame daifuku*** is mixes whole *azuki* beans or soybeans mixed into the filling.

PAGE 25
The **Naruto Strait**, famous for its whirlpools, is a channel connecting the city of Naruto in Tokushima Prefecture (on Shikoku Island) to Awaji Island.

PAGE 34
In Japan, **names** are usually written in *kanji* (Chinese characters), and Hatanaka-sensei wrote the *kanji* in his given name, Izuna, completely wrong.

PAGE 36
In the **fruit basket game**, players are assigned fruits, and they sit in a circle of chairs. One person without a chair is "it" and must call out the name of a fruit. When their fruit is called, players must leave their seats and find new ones. Whoever is left standing is "it."

PAGE 47
Minamoto no Yoritomo (1147–1199) was the first shogun of the Kamakura shogunate.

PAGE 53
Switching from using someone's family name to their given name can be considered a big step in a relationship. By using Haruaki's given name, Hatanaka-sensei and Miki-sensei are signaling that they have become more than just professional colleagues.

PAGE 57
In Japan, the proprietress of a bar or nightclub is usually addressed as **Mama** or **Mama-san**.

PAGE 64
In Japanese, Haruaki asks, "Who's this *maro*?", with ***maro*** being a term for the historical style of thin eyebrows. *Maro* happens to be spelled the same way as "mallow" in Japanese. Marshmallow then explains that it ended up turning into Marsh*maro*.

PAGE 68
Chimimouryou is a general term for monsters of the mountains (*chimi*) and monsters of the rivers (*mouryou*).

PAGE 84
The ***amanojaku*** (lit. "heavenly evil spirit") is a wicked spirit that provokes humans into giving into their wicked desires.

PAGE 103
Ayakashi is another collective name for *youkai*.

PAGE 109
The subway line names are parodies—their real names are the Marunouchi Line and the Yamanote Line.

PAGE 113
Asakusa is an entertainment district in Tokyo most famous for the Buddhist temple Senso-ji. **Thunder Gate** (Kaminarimon) is a large entrance gate to Senso-ji famously decorated with a giant, red lantern bearing the gate's name and large Raijin and Fujin statues on either side.

PAGE 114
Ningyou-yaki are a popular sweet in Asakusa—they're cakes filled with red bean paste, made in various shapes.

PAGE 116
The **Akihabara** area is considered Tokyo's cultural mecca for video games, anime/manga, and electronics.

PAGE 117
Pochikou is a reference to Hachikou, a famously loyal dog who would go to Shibuya Station to wait for his owner to return from work even years after his owner passed away. Hachikou has a statue outside Shibuya Station.

PAGE 156
Ginza is known as a popular, upscale shopping area in Tokyo. **Shinjuku** is an economic hub and home to the headquarters of many companies.

INSIDE COVER, BACK
Jugemu Jugemu is a Japanese folktale and famous *rakugo* comedy routine about a boy given a ridiculously long name because his parents couldn't decide on one. "Sailor uniform," of course, isn't in the name...

Next Volume

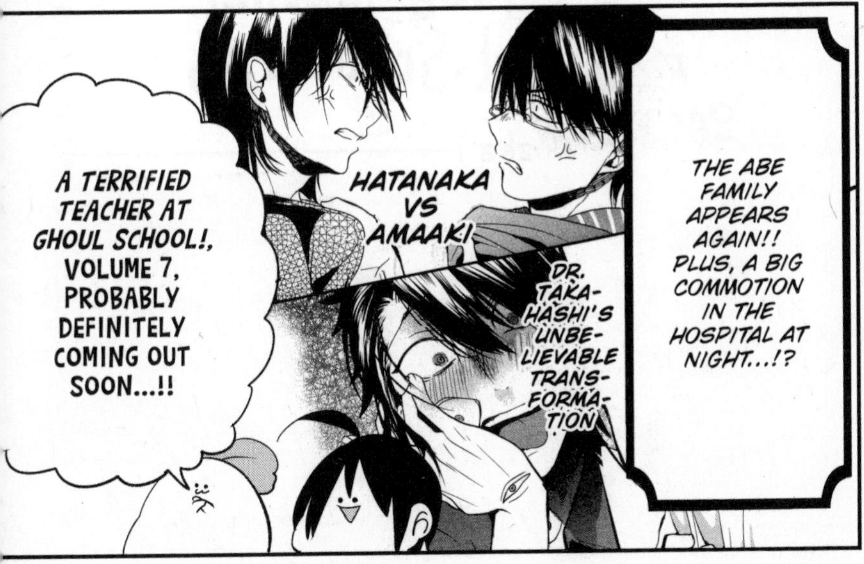
THE ABE FAMILY APPEARS AGAIN!! PLUS, A BIG COMMOTION IN THE HOSPITAL AT NIGHT...!?
HATANAKA VS AMAAKI
DR. TAKAHASHI'S UNBELIEVABLE TRANSFORMATION
A TERRIFIED TEACHER AT GHOUL SCHOOL!, VOLUME 7, PROBABLY DEFINITELY COMING OUT SOON...!!

★ Special Thanks ★

《 My Assistants 》

- Tanaka Unit 2-sama
- Sanihiko-sama
- Aya Izuki-sama
- Sesame Dumplings-sama

《 My Editor 》

- Katou-sama

The editorial department at GFantasy

The designer

All my family, friends, and relatives!

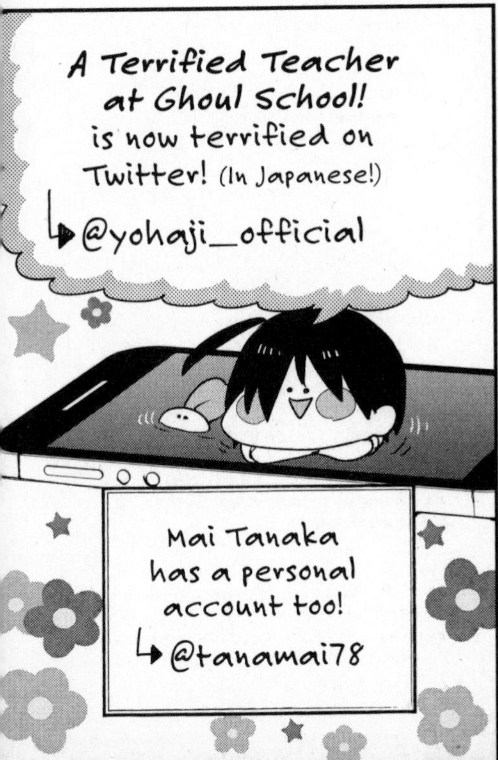
A Terrified Teacher at Ghoul School! is now terrified on Twitter! (In Japanese!)
↳ @yohaji_official
Mai Tanaka has a personal account too!
↳ @tanamai78

A TERRIFIED Teacher

Mai Tan

🔥 **Translation:** AMANDA HALEY
🔥 **Lettering:** LYS BLAKESLEE

This book is a work of fiction. Names, characters, places, and incidents are the product of the author's imagination or are used fictitiously. Any resemblance to actual events, locales, or persons, living or dead, is coincidental.

YOKAI GAKKO NO SENSEI HAJIMEMASHITA! Vol. 6 © 2018 Mai Tanaka/SQUARE ENIX CO., LTD. First published in Japan in 2018 by SQUARE ENIX CO., LTD. English translation rights arranged with SQUARE ENIX CO., LTD. and Yen Press, LLC through Tuttle-Mori Agency, Inc., Tokyo.

English translation © 2019 by SQUARE ENIX CO., LTD.

Yen Press
1290 Avenue of the Americas
New York, NY 10104

Visit us at yenpress.com
facebook.com/yenpress
twitter.com/yenpress
yenpress.tumblr.com
instagram.com/yenpress

First Yen Press Edition: March 2019

Yen Press is an imprint of Yen Press, LLC.
The Yen Press name and logo are trademarks of Yen Press, LLC.

The publisher is not responsible for websites (or their content) that are not owned by the publisher.

Library of Congress Control Number: 2017954141

ISBNs: 978-1-9753-2846-7 (paperback)
978-1-9753-2847-4 (ebook)

10 9 8 7 6 5 4 3 2 1

WOR

Printed in the United States of America